CONSPIRATOR

WITHDRAWN

C. J. CHERRYH

CONSPIRATOR

Foreigner #10

DAW BOOKS, INC.

DONALD A. WOLLHEIM, FOUNDER
375 Hudson Street, New York, NY 10014

ELIZABETH R. WOLLHEIM
SHEILA E. GILBERT
PUBLISHERS
http://www.dawbooks.com

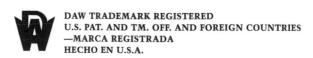

To Jane and to Shejidan—
for keeping me honest.

CONSPIRATOR

1

Spring was coming. Frost still touched the window glass of the Bujavid and whitened the roof tiles of Shejidan at sunrise, but it left daily by mid-morning. This was a sign.

So was the letter, delivered by morning post, discreetly received by staff, and, understood to be important, delivered with Bren Cameron's morning tea.

The little message cylinder hadn't come by the automated systems. It had most certainly traveled the old-fashioned way, by rail, knowing the bent of the sender.

It bore the seal of Lord Tatiseigi of the Atageini of the Padi Valley. It was silver and sea-ivory, with carved lilies.

When opened, its exquisite calligraphy, in green as well as black ink, written on modern vellum, nicely paid courtesies due the paidhi-aiji, the human interpreter for the ruler of three quarters of the planet; the paidhi-aiji, the Lord of the Heavens, etc., etc. . . .

Tatiseigi was being extraordinarily polite, and that, in itself, was an ominous sign, since Bren was currently, and for the last several months, sitting in the old man's city apartment.

Foreboding settled in before his glance skipped past the ornately flowing salutation to the text of the letter.

The paidhi will rejoice to know that repairs here at Tir-namardi have gone extremely well and we have greatly enjoyed this winter sojourn watching the restoration. However, with the legislative session imminent and with business in the capital pressing upon this house, one must regretfully quit these rural pleasures and return to the Bujavid as of the new moon . . .

Two days from now. God!

One most fervently hopes that this will not greatly inconvenience the paidhi-aiji. A separate letter exhorts our staff to assist the paidhi-aiji in whatever arrangements the paidhi-aiji may desire for his comfort and expedition . . .

Expedition, hell! Two days was extreme gall, never mind that he hadn't a leg to stand on . . . nor any place else to go. The man could have phoned. He could well have phoned instead of taking up a whole day of grace using the trains and the whole message process.

One naturally hopes that the difficulties attending the paidhi-aiji's own residence have now been settled . . .

Tatiseigi's current house guest in his country retreat was the aiji-dowager, who absolutely knew everything going on in the capital, including the paidhi's situation. So the old man knew damned well the paidhi-aiji's apartment difficulties were *not* in fact settled in the least, that Tabini-aiji's apartments were not yet repaired, either—which meant Tabini was still residing in the dowager's apartment while the dowager sojourned in Tirnamardi with Lord Tatiseigi.

God, one only imagined whether Tabini might not be in receipt of a similar letter from his grandmother . . . requesting *her* apartment vacated.

He somehow doubted Ilisidi would be that abrupt—or share the roof with her grandson for long. She likely would be off for the distant east, on the other side of the continent, where she had her estate.

He himself might, however, be sitting in the hotel at the foot of the hill in two days. This historic apartment, which he had occupied since Tabini's return to power—and his own return from space—had served him very well through the winter; and, thanks to politics, there had been no delicate way to get him back into his *own* apartment, not as yet. Scions of a Southern clan, the Farai, were camped out in it, and for various reasons Tabini-aiji could not or would not pitch them out and get it back.

He moved himself and his teacup from the sunny morning room to the less sunny, and chillier, office. There he sat down at the desk, laid out a sheet of vellum, and framed a reply which would *not* go by train, or it never would reach Tatiseigi before the lord left for the capital.

To the Lord of the Lilies, Tatiseigi of the Atageini, Master of Tirnamardi, Jewel of the Padi Valley, and its great associations of the townships of . . .

He had the letter for a guide through that maze of relationships, all of which had, in properly formal phrases, to be stated. He refrained from colored ink, even given its availability in the desk supplies.

From the Lord of the Heavens, Bren Cameron of Mospheira, honored to serve the aiji as paidhi-aiji,

Words cannot convey the gratitude of my household to have been housed in such historic and kabiu premises this recent season.

One most earnestly rejoices in the anticipated return of the Lord of the Atageini to his ancestral residence, and further rejoices at the news that the beautiful and historic estate of Tirnamardi again shines as a light to the region.

They'd wait a few years before the hedge out front had grown back. Not to mention the scars on the lawn. The collapse of one historic bedroom into another.

Please convey felicitations also to your distinguished guest. The paidhi-aiji will of course seek his own resources and immediately remove to other premises, hoping to leave this excellent apartment ready for your return. One is sure your staff will rejoice and take great comfort in the presence of their own lord.

That was one letter. He placed it in Tatiseigi's ivory-lily message cylinder, as the reply to the message it had contained, and dropped the cylinder into the outbound mail basket.

Then he wrote another letter, this one to Tabini . . . with less elegant calligraphy, and omitting the formal lines of courtesies: he and the aiji dispensed with those, whcn they wrote in their own hands—a very human-inspired haste and brevity.

Aiji-ma, Lord Tatiseigi has announced his intention to return in two days, in company with the dowager, necessitating my removal to other quarters. One is well aware of the difficulties which surround my former residence and expects no actions in that matter, which might be to disadvantage. One still has the hotel as a recourse, which poses considerable security concern, but if need be, one will ask more assistance with security, to augment staff, and will manage.

In the days before the legislative session, however, this situation does not arrive wholly unforeseen, and this would be an opportune time to visit my estate in Sarini province, barring some directive to the contrary, aiji-ma. One has some preparation yet to do in the month preceeding the legislative session, but the work can travel with me, and the sea air would be pleasant even in this early season. Also one has regional obligations which have long waited on opportunity, not only within the household there, but with the neighboring estate and of course the village.

Accordingly one requests a month's leave to visit Najida, the living which the aiji's generosity has provided me, where I intend to pay courtesies to its staff and its village, and also to pay long-delayed courtesies to the estate of Lord Geigi, which I have these several months promised him to do.

Lord Geigi was lord and administrator not only of the coastal estate of Kajiminda and all of Sarini province, but of all atevi in space, in his capacity as Tabini's viceroy on the space station. And doing a damned fine job of it, up there. But Geigi had left his sister in charge of his estate at Kajiminda, the sister had died, leaving a young and inexperienced nephew in the post, and Geigi understandably wanted a report on affairs there aside from that which the nephew sent him.

In no way will this detract from my attention to legislative and committee matters, but it will at least provide more time to provide for a city residence . . . possibly even taking a house, or establishing in some secure fashion in the hotel . . .

Depressing thought, trekking through the city to reach what would be, were he in his own apartment, a simple trip down in the lift. And a damned great problem to be living and trying to do research in the hotel, where security was a nightmare and spying was rife—all the minor lords being in residence for the session. The Bujavid housed the legislative chambers of the Western Association, the aishidi'tat; it housed the aiji's audience hall, and the national archives. But it also, and year round, housed the most highly-placed lords of the aishidi'tat. A centuries-old hierarchy dictated who resided on what floor, in what historic apartment: the teacup Bren used casually, for instance, was ciabeti artwork, from the Padi Valley's kilns, probably two hundred years old—not to mention the antiquity of the desk, the carpet, and the priceless porcelain on the shelf. Who held what apartment, with what appointment, from what date—all these things meant respect, in proportion to the antiquity of the premises and their connection with or origin from potent clans and associations of clans.

And the aiji's translator, the jumped-up human who had used to occupy the equivalent of a court secretary's post in the garden wing next to the aiji's cook—the human who had risen to share the same floor as the aiji's own apartment, in the depletion of an ancient house which had left it vacant—had now *lost* that lordly apartment to the same coup that had temporarily ousted Tabini from the aijinate.

In the coup, Tabini's own apartment had been shot up, his staff murdered, and Tabini currently endured a sort of exile in his grandmother's apartment, while his own place underwent refurbishment and his staff underwent its own problems of recruitment and security checks.

But the apartment next door to the aiji's proper apartment, the apartment which had briefly been the paidhi's, was now, yes, occupied by the Farai, Southerners, no less, out of the Marid—the very district that had staged the coup and murdered Tabini's staff.

And *why* should Tabini thus favor a Southern clan, by letting them remain there? The Farai were natives of the northern part of the Marid, the Saijin district, specifically Morigi-dar—they were part of a foursome of power in the South, and they claimed high credit for turning coat one more time, opening the doors of the Bujavid and (so they claimed) enabling the aiji to retake the capital—while the rest of the Marid, namely the Tasaigin and the Dojisigin and Dausigin districts of the Marid, currently teetered somewhere between loyalty and renewed rebellion.

If the Farai were telling the truth about a change of loyalty, they were owed some reward for it—and to put a gloss of legitimacy on their seizure of that precious apartment, they claimed inheritance from the Maladesi, the west coast clan that had once owned the apartment in question. It seemed the last living member of that defunct clan had married into the Farai's adjunct clan, the Morigi. Tabini maintained the Maladesi lands had reverted; they claimed inheritance. It was at least a serious claim.

So their seizure of that apartment actually had some justification. Tabini's tossing them out of it might make his own future north apartment wall more secure—having a Southern clan there was a huge security problem . . . but tossing the Farai out of it in favor of the human paidhi, after their very public switch to the aiji's side, would be counted an insult . . . a very strong insult . . . that might damage the Farai's status in the still unstable South. And whether or not the Farai were sincere in their switching allegiances, they *were* challenging the Taisigi clan and seeking to rise in status in the South. Swatting the Farai down might help the Taisigi, who were *not* Tabini's allies in any sense.

So the paidhi had no wish to upset that delicate balance.

And certainly no other clan wanted to be relocated from *their* historic premises, the rights to which went back hundreds of years, to give the paidhi *their* space. They had their rights, the Bujavid had allotted all its upstairs room, and outside of booting out legislative offices in the public floors and starting a new scramble for available apartments below, there was nothing to be done for the paidhi.

All of which boiled down to an uncomfortable situation. They had a clan out of the Marid taking up residence next to Tabini, where it wasn't wanted . . . and for various reasons, it might stay a while. It was quite likely that one of the delays in Tabini getting into his apartment was his security reinforcing, and probably heavily bugging, that wall between him and the Farai.

All of that meant the paidhi was borrowing Lord Tatiseigi's historic apartment—vacant so long as Tatiseigi of the Atageini had been out repairing his own manor, which had been likewise shot up in the coup. The work was nearly finished, the legislature was about to meet—

And the paidhi now had nowhere to go *but* the hotel or the country.

There was, however, a bright spot of coincidence in the current situation . . . should he go to his coastal estate.

His brother Toby had just put out of Jackson, out of the human enclave of Mospheira—Toby fairly well lived on his boat, and plied the waters mostly in the strait between Mospheira and the mainland. He might have to hopscotch a call from here to Mogari-nai and Jackson, but however they got it through, unless Toby was on some specific business, Toby could easily divert over to the mainland, just about as fast as he himself could get to the coast, and they might manage to have that long-delayed visit.

Permission to leave the capital, however, was not certain until Tabini had answered his letter and agreed that he might take that temporary solution and go out to the coast. If Tabini was differently minded, there would be no visit, and he had no idea what he would do: he and his security would have to show up at the hotel tomorrow afternoon with baggage in hand, he supposed . . . but Tabini might think of something he hadn't thought of. There was that possibility, too. So he would call Toby only after he had spoken to Tabini.

He drank the last of the tea, sealed and cylindered the letter to Tabini, then stood up and rang for Madam Saidin, major domo of this extravagant apartment. He gave instructions for both messages to be delivered, the one by courier, within the halls, the other . . .

One of the staff would run the lily cylinder down to the mail center . . . which would fax the content to the post office in the township neighboring Tatiseigi's estate, and have it run up the hill, express, by local truck, to reach the old gentleman . . . while the lily cylinder, itself ancient and precious, came back upstairs to Saidin's keeping, to wait for Tatiseigi's arrival. Proprieties, proprieties, and the motions they went through, to preserve the appearance of the old ways.

Tatiseigi have his own fax? Hell would freeze solid before that modern contraption found a place in Tatiseigi's house. Or here.

"Lord Tatiseigi is coming back, nadi-ji," he told Saidin, in giving her the message.

He looked up to do it. That esteemed lady stood a head taller than he did: skin the color of ink, eyes of molten amber, black hair well-salted with her years—he had no idea how many years. She was, like many of the great houses' highest staff, a member of the Assassins' Guild . . . but she bowed with such graceful sweetness, as she said, "He has sent also to us, nandi. We so regret the short notice."

He would very much miss Saidin. He had stayed here before, never expected to do so again, and fate had surprised him. He laid no bets now, when he departed, whether he would ever be back under her care. "We by no means question it," he said quietly. "My first message felicitates his arrival and the other advises the aiji of the situation. One has requested to take a short vacation in the country."

"The coastal estate at Najida, nandi?" Those golden eyes sparked. "One had intended to suggest that."

So she had thought about his welfare. It was a warm notion, considering their long though intermittent history.

"An excellent notion," he said, "and in that case, I shall count it your good advice. Thank you for the thought, nadi-ji."

"The staff's very earnest wishes, nandi," she said. "We shall miss you."

"Nadi-ji." It was worth a bow, as that worthy lady left on her mission.

Tatiseigi's staff would miss him, that was to say. His own staff, many of them on more or less permanent loan from Tatiseigi or the dowager, or from Tabini himself, were scattered from the space station to the coast, surviving, in the disarrangement of his house . . . so in going to Najida, he simply exchanged one set of observing eyes for another. Spying was just a method of keeping informed about one's allies—in the thinking of the great houses. One knew—and accepted such loans. And his own staff's knowledge of him was consequently disrupted . . . and the persons they reported to—notably Tabini, or the dowager—might be less well informed on his business than, say, at the moment, the Atageini—

Except for one thing. His four bodyguards, his aishid—who knew most everything that went on, and who never left him— they kept information flowing properly, right up the lines of man'chi, of personal attachment, to the aiji himself; and they took care, too, that certain things stayed *outside* Atageini knowledge, or anyone else's, for that matter.

His bodyguard, his caretakers, his advisors—Banichi and Jago were the seniors, Tano and Algini his second-senior, and nobody on earth stood closer to him.

Nobody else had shared as many of his various disasters.

He located them, all of them, in the security station down the main hall—his four best friends, although "friend" was one of those words officially forbidden in the human-atevi inter-face. Sometimes he thought that way. Sometimes he was sane, and considerate of them, and didn't.

This morning he just leaned into the doorway, sighed mas-sively, and said, "A letter has come from Tatiseigi, nadiin-ji."

"We are aware of it, Bren-ji," Banichi said. Little reached the staff that his security didn't learn fast.

"The coast, nadiin-ji," he said. "Granted we get permission from Tabini."

"The only solution," Jago said with a shrug. His lover, Jago— lover: another of those forbidden words, and a word the deeper implications of which would just confuse everyone, including Jago. They'd tried now and again to parse it, and only ended up with Jago concluding "association" was quite sensibly ad-equate to describe them, and that the human sense of involved attachment was very odd.

Tano and Algini didn't say anything, but didn't look overly disturbed about the prospect of a fast move. The aishid was all together again, in a number of senses, and if "love" didn't de-scribe it, it was close enough to it to warm a human heart.

Not enough to make him foolish enough to hug anyone in appreciation, however.

His security team, all of them members of the Assassins' Guild, wore the uniform, the black leather and silver, had the look, had the armament generally in evidence, and traveled with enough gear to outfit a small army: if he moved, they would. They had kept him safe—and his safety having required quite a lot of keeping in the last number of years, he owed them all extravagantly.

He owed them, among other things, a stable household, not a moving target.

He owed them a staff that could support not only his needs in comfort, but theirs. Saidin and her staff had certainly done very well for them—Saidin ran a tight ship; but because she wasn't theirs, she was Tatiseigi's, her attentions were always just a little worrisome. Tatiseigi, that conniving old gentleman had political ambitions that hadn't stopped with getting a niece married to Tabini and a grand-nephew within a heartbeat of the aiji himself. There was that. Tatiseigi *didn't* trust human influence near his grand-nephew: Tatiseigi didn't favor human gadgets, human ideas, or human newfangled inventions, and said grand-nephew had been much too infatuated with humans. And bet that Tatiseigi would want to know every detail of the paidhi-aiji's residence here and all his dealings with Tabini's household.

His going to the coast would cut off that source of information—and put Tatiseigi in immediate reach of Tabini's household. Tatiseigi became Tabini's problem, not his.

"Shall we assume, Bren-ji," Jago said, "and pack?"

"One hardly sees what Tabini can do, else, but agree I should go. Take everything, nadiin-ji: we clearly must go somewhere. My belongings can easily go into storage, in favor of your gear . . ."

"No such thing," Jago said. "All of it will move."

Probably it was wise, after all, not to leave any remnant of his belongings exposed to tampering in storage—or subject to further controversy, should any clerk go nosing about into his bits of gear and his books.

"One assumes," Tano said, "that the aiji will at least advantage himself of the time before the legislature meets . . . to find a solution to the Farai."

"If not, nadiin-ji," Bren said, "one fears we may end up taking a house in the town."

"The paidhi could File on this Southerner," Banichi said,

meaning the head of the Farai clan, and as long as Bren had heard Banichi's humor and his serious suggestions, he wasn't sure if that was dry humor at the moment.

"The paidhi has had cause," Algini added, which made him think Banichi might have just offered a sensible and workable suggestion. Filing Intent: serving legal notice of application to the Assassins' Guild, official Intent to assassinate the person in question—well, he supposed appropriating a lord's apartment would be a legal grievance, if he were an atevi lord with historic standing.

Continuing the insult by continuing to occupy said apartment affected not just his pride, but his staff's honor. There was that.

And for a heartbeat he asked himself if perhaps, just perhaps, that suggestion didn't originate with Banichi—if perhaps it had come from Tabini himself, to whose staff Banichi and Jago still retained some minor ties.

A hint? Relieve me of this troublesome Southerner? The aiji himself had absolute right to remove an obstacle to the association, but politically speaking, had some obligation to prove the Farai were in fact an obstacle. The aiji could decree that they were—but since the aiji had to rule on a Filing, it was somewhat of a case of judge, jury, and executioner . . . an unpopular sort of situation.

The paidhi, however, actually had a legitimate grievance, an exacerbated grievance. The way it worked, in practicality—he could File Intent with the Assassins' Guild, and once the Filing was accepted, it freed his staff to go after the head of that family. The Farai clan would simultaneously counterfile, freeing Assassins in their association to go after *him*. Both sides had legal right, both sides agreed to exempt noninvolved persons from personal harm, and it would all work itself out, probably in his favor, since he'd personally trust his bodyguard to take out the head of the Farai clan with considerable speed and efficiency. It would all be according to law.

Which would end the counterfiling; and a re-Filing would not be viewed with favor in the aiji's court, meaning the Far-ai's wider associations could not then all take after the paidhi's life.

It didn't mean they wouldn't, however, in all practicality. They'd politic left and right with the aiji to allow a Filing, and of course he'd politic with the aiji not to allow it.

And at that point it would all devolve down to who was of more value, the entire southern coast of the aishidi'tat, or the human the aiji had listened to when he'd done some of the more controversial things he had to his credit.

Space travel.

Upsetting the balance of power in the aishidi'tat.

Contact with aliens that could still come down on them . . .

The aiji had been staunchly supportive of his human advi-sor in his return to power; but time—time and politics—could reorder all sorts of priorities.

"The paidhi could File," Jago said with a sigh, "but then we would all be busy for years."

"The paidhi's generosity in withdrawing to the country," Tano said, "if backed by adequate strength, can only trouble the troublemakers."

"Backed by strength," Banichi said. "*And* the aiji. One month. Let the Farai hear that, and take another thought about inconveniencing the paidhi-aiji."

Inconveniencing was one way to put it.

"Do you, nadiin-ji," Bren asked very quietly, "do you think the aiji *does* wish the paidhi to take a moderate course, or am I putting you in danger by my reluctance to File on this clan?"

A small silence. Opaque stares. Yes-no. Maybe. Then Jago, whose stare was generally the most direct, glanced down. No answer.

"See what the *aiji* will do," Algini said, then, "whether he will permit this trip—or not."

Scary enough advice. Tabini *could* decide out of pure pique to throw the Farai out of his apartment, the hell with the South, collectively known as the Marid, which had caused the aiji so much trouble.

That would toss the oil-pot in the fire, for sure.

Or Tabini could use the month to manuever . . . and temporize further with the Marid.

And the paidhi could come back and conspicuously set up in the hotel at the foot of the hill, posing a security nightmare for his staff, inconveniencing all the legislators who did *not* have apartments in the Bujavid, and who relied on that hotel during the upcoming session—

And waiting for the Farai to feel the heat enough to do something overt, either against him, or against Tabini himself. *That* would put Tabini in the right.

He'd personally bet the Farai would do neither, counting on all the paidhi's other enemies to take him out of the way.

And there were certainly sufficient of those. As Jago said, they could become very, very busy, just keeping him alive, if they had to move into exposed circumstances. It was a risk to them, as much as him.

"It is a very uncomfortable position to be in, nadiin-ji," he said. "Likeliest the aiji will give me at least my month, however—whatever we have to do for the session. And in any case, we know we have to pack. We can hardly share the premises with Uncle Tatiseigi."

That produced a little laugh all around.

"Where will the *dowager* lodge?" Tano wondered then, the second good question of the situation: the aiji was lodging in *her* apartment, part of the whole chain of inconvenience. And while it had been mildly titillating to have the aiji-dowager staying under Tatiseigi's roof at Tirnamardi, in that very large estate, it escalated to salacious rumor to consider the dowager sharing the Atageini lord's apartment in the Bujavid, at a very slight remove from her grandson the aiji.

Not that salacious rumor ever displeased the aiji-dowager.

"I suppose she will stay with the aiji and his household," Bren said. That would set the nuclear fuse ticking: give that about a week before the dowager and the aiji were ready to File on each other. "But let us hope we shall be on the coast, safe from all events. For at least the next month."

Nand' Bren was leaving. Cajeiri heard it from Great-grandmother's major domo, Madiri, who had heard it from Cajeiri's father the aiji. Great-uncle Tatiseigi was coming back, Great-grandmother was also coming back, but Great-uncle was pushing nand' Bren out of Great-uncle's apartment, and nand' Bren was going off to live on the coast, which was entirely un-reasonable. And even worse, even worse, Great-uncle was going to be living down the hall.

That was what Cajeiri heard; and being a year short of fortu-nate nine, and already as bored with his existence in the Buja-vid as a young lord could be—his father and mother let him do *nothing* except his studies, and his chosen aishi was up on the station probably forgetting all about him and growing up with-out him—he saw nothing brighter ahead. He had been back to ordinary, boring life in his father's household for three whole *months* since the set-to with Great-grandmother's neighbors in Malguri.

He had so looked forward to spring, and summer, and maybe, *maybe* being able to go visit the wilderness of Taiben, or even go out to Great-uncle's estate at Tirnamardi, where he would mostly have to behave (but Great-grandmother never watched him as closely as his parents, and out there, she would be run-ning his life, so there had been some hope.)

But now—

Now Great-grandmother was going away, and Great-uncle was coming *here* and throwing nand' Bren out.

It was just unfair.

And he had nobody left to talk to. Antaro and Jegari, even,

his two companions from Taiben, who were almost his body-guard, were off enlisting in the Assassins' Guild and training most every day. They did at least show him what they learned that day, or every so-many days, when they were held at the Guild house for overnight. That was where they were today, so he couldn't even tell them the bad news.

If Jegari and Antaro had their Guild status, Cajeiri said to himself, he might set *them* on the nasty Farai and scare them right out of nand' Bren's apartment and solve everything.

But they had no such license, and the Farai had their own Assassins, and besides, his father would find out about it and *that* would stop that.

He should suggest it to Banichi and Jago. *They* could do it. They could scare the Farai all the way back to the Marid, and show them up for the scoundrels they were.

But you had to File Intent to be legal to go after someone. And that took time.

And probably Bren's guard would never listen to him. Even Banichi. Banichi had used to build cars with him, but no longer. He'd had Casimi and Seimaji, that Great-grandmother had set to guard him; but he had not even had them now for days, because they'd both gone back to Great-grandmother. So besides that, he had those two old sticks, Kaidin and Temein, that Great-uncle Tatiseigi had sent to watch over him and spy on his father: and Kaidin and Temein had never been happy at all with him, since they had gotten in trouble for losing him once—

And for the rest of his resources, he just had his father and his mother's guard standing around, and *they* were never under his orders. If he asked them to do something, it was always, "Ask your own guard, young gentleman."

Even worse, mother's sister was visiting for the last three days; *her* two servants were flirting with his father's guards, hanging about the kitchen and being obnoxious. The guards were distracted, being stupid, and nobody even cared what he thought.

There was an advantage, however, to nobody caring what he thought, and to his aunt's maids acting like fools, which was that people grew busy and forgot to pay attention to him. He had not gotten in trouble in at least half a month, which meant that he was not under active restriction at the moment.

So he went down the hall and searched up boring old Kaidin and Temein. They were finishing the day's reports when he found them; and he said:

"Nand' Bren has a book I need for my studies."

A sour look. "We can get it, young lord."

He thought fast. "This is a very old book, and I have to convince nand' Bren I can take care of it. No farther than just down the hall. I need to talk to him. I can go by myself or you can take me there."

"We should ask the aiji's staff," Temein said. He was not the most enterprising of men; and Kaiden thought they should clear the order, too—to Cajeiri's disgust.

"My father's staff by no means cares if I am only in the hall," he said. "Or if you go with me at all or not. But one needs to go *now*, nadiin. I have to meet my tutor before lunch. If you go to asking questions and going through procedures, I shall not get the book read in time, I shall not finish my lessons, my tutor will give a bad report, my father will be upset with me, and I shall be put out with you. Extremely. Come with me. We need to go *now*. It will hardly take a moment."

They muttered to each other. They had only just ordered lunch, were not anxious to leave for a long consultation and getting permission, so the ploy actually worked. He got them out the door, and three doors down, and had them knock on nand' Bren's door—or Uncle Tatiseigi's.

"We need to talk to nand' Bren," Cajeiri said to the maid who answered it, and when Madam Saidin showed up: "Nand' Bren has a book I very much need, Saidin-nadi. May I speak to him?"

"Yes, young gentleman. Come this way," Madam Saidin

said, and, leaving Kaidin and Temein in the foyer, she escorted him to the study, where she knocked softly, and opened the door.

Nand' Bren was writing. He looked up in a little surprise, and stood up to meet him, even if nand' Bren was Lord of the Heavens . . . stood up to just his height, being a human, and just his size, which always made nand' Bren seem more like his own age. Lord Bren was all the colors of a sunny day—pale skin and pale hair and eyes and all. When Cajeiri had been very little, he had wondered if Bren was the only one in all the world like that. When he was older, he had found out Bren's kind came in all sorts of shades; but, even so, very few were Bren's sort . . . and fewer still of any species were as smart as Lord Bren. Lord Bren was his father's trusted advisor, and when Lord Bren talked, his father the aiji listened.

Well, mostly, his father did.

"Nandi," he said to Lord Bren, ever so respectfully—and quietly, aware Temein and Kaidin were just outside, and probably talking and reporting to Saidin, because they *were* actually all from Great-uncle's estate of Tirnamardi. "Please lend me one of Uncle's books. I told Saidin-nadi that I came for one. Are you really going away?"

"Yes," nand' Bren said. "Only for a month, until the legislature meets."

"You mean to go to the coast. Where your boat is."

"Yes," nand' Bren said, just a bit more warily. "Just for a while."

Guilt was useful; and Cajeiri had no hesitation to use it. "You promised when you did ever go on your boat you would take us along."

Nand' Bren looked decidedly uncomfortable. "Not without your father's permission, young lord, one could not possibly—"

"Then one hopes you will ask him, nandi. One ever so wants to go!"

"I shall ask him," nand' Bren said quietly, as if it were an obligation, a very wearying obligation.

That stung. And that made Cajeiri angry.

"Young lord," nand' Bren said, "he will surely say no. But one will make the request."

Nand' Bren still looked tired, and entirely out of sorts. Perhaps it was not himself that nand' Bren was out of sorts with.

"You did promise," Cajeiri said, pushing it, in that thought, "and one is so *bored* with lessons."

"One did promise," Bren agreed with a sigh. "And one regrets to have so little hope of persuading your father, but one fears he will refuse any request. If you recall, young lord, you are intended to become reacquainted with your father and your lady mother, and to learn the court and the legislature—for your own protection and future benefit."

"Great-uncle is entirely unreasonable to send you away!"

"Lord Tatiseigi has been very generous to have lent this apartment at all," Bren said, "and when he comes to the capital, he naturally needs it. Should he take a room in the hotel?"

"But where are you to go when the legislature is in session? Shall you not be here?"

" 'Where are you to go,—*nandi?*' " Nand' Bren corrected his mode of address, since his voice had risen far too sharply and he had just omitted a courtesy to moderate that sharpness.

"Nandi," he amended his question, ducked his head and made his voice and his manner far more quiet and restrained. "But where are you expected to go?"

Nand' Bren smiled sadly, patiently. "Clearly, for the immediate future, to the home I do have, which I am very grateful to have. After that, young lord, perhaps I shall take a town house."

"If *we* could, we would assuredly toss the Farai out of your apartment!"

"One is very sure your father daily entertains the same thought, young lord."

"Then he should do it! He should File on them!"

"One is very sure he would do it, if not for the fragility of the peace, young lord, but in the meantime, my brother happens to be sailing near my estate—I spoke to him a few days ago when he was in port on Mospheira. So my trip to the coast is not all a loss. I shall very probably get to see my brother. I also owe extravagant thanks to my staff in that district, who held out against the rebels, at the risk of their lives. And I owe a debt to Lord Geigi—up on the station: you remember Lord Geigi. His estate is next down the coast."

"One remembers Lord Geigi favorably, yes," he said. Nand' Bren was clearly explaining to him that there were all sorts of social obligations already lined up for him, with no time for taking a boy on his boat, that was what, and he hardly liked to hear the whole list. "One remembers nand' Toby, too. And Barb-daja. *They* would certainly find pleasure in seeing us, and hearing all our adventures."

"Surely they would," Bren said, not unkindly. "And surely the estate staff would be greatly honored by your presence, and so would Lord Geigi's people be glad to receive you, but your father—"

"The paidhi-aiji persuaded all the districts to make peace when they were at each other's throats! Surely you can persuade my parents to let me go to the coast for a month!"

Nand' Bren smiled and shook his head in the human way, and said: "I shall honestly try, young lord. I shall certainly do that." He went and took a book from the shelves, taking a little trouble about it. It was, of course, Great-uncle Tatiseigi's book that nand' Bren lent him.

It was a very handsome little book, very old. Cajeiri appreciated the trouble taken, at least, and folded it to his chest. He bowed respectfully, and nand' Bren bowed.

But when Cajeiri walked out of nand' Bren's office he found himself madder and more frustrated than he had been in a long, long time. He did not even look at Kaidin and Temein on the walk back, nor did he say a word.

When he got safely back to his own room, in his father's borrowed apartment, and was rid of his guard, he flung himself into a chair and flung the book onto the table beside him. It nearly slid off the table. He stopped it.

Then he thought to look at the book. It was the sort of thing his great-uncle would have, the script of a machimi play. But it was one he had never seen or read. It was titled *Blood of Traitors*. The illustration chased into the leather cover, and painted, had swords and castles. And nand' Bren had picked it out, which meant it might be very much better than the volume of court rules and etiquette his tutor was making him memorize.

It was no substitute for sailing on nand' Bren's boat, and none for seeing nand' Toby and Barb-daja.

He had caught a fish on nand' Toby's boat once. It had been venomous, and it had flown all about on his line, making everybody scramble. It was one of his most favorite memories. They had all laughed about it later, himself, and Great-grandmother, mani; and nand' Bren and his associates, even when things were desperate and people had been trying to kill them—even the fish in the sea had had a try at killing them. And that had been the best moment on the whole boat trip.

He so wished he had never told his parents about it.

2

"A very good idea," was Tabini's judgment to Bren regarding his removal to the coast, by no means surprising. A young man, still, a big wide-shouldered man, with the palest stare Bren had ever seen in an ateva—Tabini had ruled the mainland all the years he had served as paidhi. Tabini ruled the atevi world, in effect, though a recent challenge to his authority had racketed from east to west, provoking counter-revolution and skirmishes after.

But Tabini had resurrected himself from rumored death the moment Tabini had been sure he had his assets back in order—notably, when the paidhi and the aiji-dowager and his heir had come back from space alive. Tabini had come back, from what had been a cleverly planned assassination designed to take out first his staff (which had happened) and then isolate and kill Tabini himself (which plainly had not happened.)

In fact, within a few weeks of Tabini's re-emergence from the hills, the capital showed few scars, most of the conspirators were dead, the always troublesome South, the Marid, was quiet, certain few had paid heavily for backing the Kadagidi Lord Murini in his coup, and Tabini had become again what he had always been: ruler of the world's only major continent, owner of half the human-built space station in orbit above them, owner of every functional space shuttle in existence, linking the world to that station; and incidentally owner of a half-built starship, which had been the agreement the ship-humans had made with Tabini in order to get their vitally needed supplies off the planet.

Tabini's space program had put a strain on the economy: that had been the origin of the Troubles, at least in some sense—but the panic and outrage that had attended the departure of the one viable ship and all that investment had abated with the return of said ship from its mission. On new evidence that the ship-humans were actually going to keep their word and honor their agreements, Tabini's stock had risen indeed. Humans on the island enclave of Mospheira had not invaded the mainland: they had in fact cooperated with the ship-humans and with Tabini, and that old fear had proved empty.

It was, in some senses, a new world. Tabini had taken a renewed tight grip on the reins of power, and if there still were minor nuisances, like the Farai still occupying the paidhi's apartment and pretending to be loyalists, it was also true that Tabini was a master of timing. If it was not yet time to pitch the Farai out and stir up the Southern troubles again, the paidhi could only conclude it was definitely not yet time, and the paidhi's best interim course was probably to go visit his brother.

"We shall hope for some solution before the legislative session," Tabini said.

"One thinks of taking a town house, aiji-ma," Bren said, "but staff will deal with that process."

Some legislators did that, at least for the session. Certain town families rented out their premises for the season at a profit. Housing was at that kind of premium in the town. But even if they went to that extreme—it was no permanent solution.

"Give it time, paidhi-ji," Tabini said again, not favoring his proposed solution with a direct answer . . . neither saying the Farai would be out of his apartment in a few weeks, nor saying they wouldn't be.

So a wise and experienced court official simply nodded, thanked the aiji for permission to depart the city and didn't ask another question, even as easy and informal as Tabini had always been with the paidhi-aiji.

But he had promised—once, to take the boy; and a second time, to ask a foredoomed question. "Your son," he began, and got no further before Tabini lifted the fingers of one hand. Stop right there, that meant.

"My son," Tabini said, "just visited your premises."

"He did, aiji-ma. He reminded me I did promise him a boat trip."

"Not recently, surely."

"No, aiji-ma. But your son has an excellent memory."

Tabini sighed. "Indeed. He has lessons. He has duties. He was not to have left the premises. And he asked you to use your good offices with me. Am I right?"

"Entirely, aiji-ma."

"Perhaps we can prevail on the workmen in *our* apartment to make a little more haste," Tabini said, "and solve one problem—but not before my grandmother arrives. No, my son may *not* go to the coast, paidhi-ji. He will stay here to keep his great-grandmother in good humor. Now you have discharged your obligation to him. And *I* relieve you of responsibility for the promise. My son will have to deal with me on that matter. Go, go. We have ordered the red car for your trip; it should be coupled on by now. The paidhi-aiji will have it at his disposal on the return as well, on a day's call. Tell nand' Toby we wish him well."

"Thank you, aiji-ma," he said, and rose, and bowed deeply. The red car, no less. The aiji's own rail car, with all its amenities, and its security. It was no small honor, though one he had almost always enjoyed.

At no time had he mentioned Cajeiri coming to his office, and at no time had he mentioned Toby being near the estate, or intending a visit: but he was not totally astonished that Tabini knew both things.

He simply went to the door, collected Banichi and Jago, and Banichi said,

"The estate has contacted nand' Toby, nandi, and he will be arriving."

"Did he say whether Barb was with him?" he asked. He *hated* to ask. One could always hope she wouldn't be. But Banichi simply lifted a shoulder and said.

"We have never heard she has left."

"Well," he said, which was all there was to say.

Packing had proceeded, even when they had had no permission as yet to quit the city. Tatiseigi being a day short of their doorway, the baggage had been stacked in the hall, the dining room, and the foyer, involving security equipment, armament, ammunition, uniforms for his four bodyguards, and a few meager items of furniture, plus four packing crates with his clothes, his books, and his personal items . . . all this had been the state of things when he had left the apartment to call on Tabini.

Tano and Algini estimated seven rolling carts and some of Tatiseigi's staff to get their baggage down to the train.

"Are we ready to load up, then?" he asked. "The aiji said we should use the red car. That it was being coupled on right now."

That car waited, always ready, always under guard, in the train station below the Bujavid itself; and taking it on took very little time. The train that loaded at the Bujavid station backed up onto that reserved section of track, connected with it and its secure baggage car, and that was that.

"It should be on by the time we get down there," Banichi said, evidently as well-informed from his end of things as the aiji was on the other. "The carts are on their way up. Tano and Algini will see to that."

Things might have gone either way. If Tabini had said no, they would have been on their way to the hotel and most of his goods on their way to storage. As it was, they were on their way to the train station in the Bujavid's basement.

"I should say good-bye to Saidin," he said, and went the few doors to the apartment down the hall to do that personally— knocking at the door that had lately been his, but he no longer felt it was. Madam Saidin answered, perhaps forewarned, via the links the Guild had, and he bowed. She bowed, letting them in, and Banichi and Jago picked up the massive bags they had destined to go with them.

"One is lastingly grateful for the hospitality of this house," he said, and picked up the computer he had left in the foyer; that, and a large briefcase. "One is ever so grateful for your personal kindness, Saidin-nadi, which exceeds all ordinary bounds."

"One has been honored by the paidhi's residence here," she said, with a little second bow, and that was that. He truly felt a little sad once that door shut and he walked away with Banichi and Jago. He would miss the staff. He had staff of his own to look forward to, but he had been resident with these people more than once, and perhaps circumstances would never combine to lodge him in this particular apartment again . . . Tatiseigi's political ambitions had lately become acute, and his age made them urgent. Possibly those same ambitions had made him lend the apartment last year, to solve a problem for Tabini, but with the legislative session coming up, and with Tatiseigi's long-desired familial connection to the aijinate now a reality— in Cajeiri—Tatiseigi now had a motive to bestir himself and actually occupy the seat in the house of lords that he had always been entitled to occupy. The world likely would hear from Tatiseigi this legislative session, and hear from him often . . . not always pleasantly so, one feared. One could see it all coming— and one *so* hoped it observed some sense of restraint.

Jago added the briefcase to her own heavy load as they boarded the lift. The briefcase held several reams of paper notes, correspondence, a little formal stationery and a tightly-capped inkpot, wax, his seal, and his personal message cylinder. He still carried the computer.

And there was one other obligatory stop downstairs, an ad-

visement of his departure and a temporary farewell to his sec-
retarial office, another set of bows and compliments.

And another set of papers which his apologetic office man-
ager said needed his urgent attention.

"I shall see to them," he assured that worthy man. Daisibi
was his name—actually one of Tano's remote relatives. "And
have no hesitation about phoning me. I shall be conducting
business in my office on the estate at least once a day, and the
staff there is entirely my own. Trust them with any message,
and never hesitate if you have a question. I shall be back five
days before the session. Rely on it."

"Have an excellent and restful trip, nandi," Daisibi said,
"and fortune attend throughout."

"Baji-naji," he said cheerfully—that was to say, fate and fortune, the fixed and the random things of the universe. And so
saying, and back in the hallway headed back to the lift, he felt
suddenly a sense of freedom from the Bujavid, even before leaving its halls.

He had a hundred and more staff seeing to things in this office . . . he had them sifting the real crises from the odder elements of his correspondence.

And more to the point, he could *not* be hailed into minor
court crises quite as readily from this moment on.

The Farai were no longer, at the moment, his problem. Uncle
Tatiseigi was not.

And as much as he adored the aiji-dowager, Ilisidi, crisis
would inevitably follow when she was living with an Atageini
lord a few doors down from her own apartment—which was
now and until Tabini's move to his own apartment—under the
management of her grandson Tabini's staff.

Things within the apartment would not be to Ilisidi's liking.
They were bound not to be. The management of her grandson
would become a daily crisis.

Uncle Tatiseigi would voice his own opinions on the boy's
upbringing.

And *he* would be on his boat with his brother, fishing . . . for at least a few hours a day.

He *almost* felt guilty for the thought.

He *almost* felt grateful to the Farai, considering the incoming storm he was about to miss.

Not quite guilty, or grateful, on either account.

The train moved out, slowly and powerfully, and the click of the wheels achieved that modest tempo the train observed while it rolled within the curving tunnels of the Bujavid.

Bren had a drink of more than fruit juice as he settled back against the red velvet seats, beside the velvet-draped window that provided nothing but armor plate to the observation of the outside world: Banichi and Jago still contented themselves with juice, but at least sat down and eased back. Tano and Algini had taken up a comfortable post in the baggage car that accompanied the aiji's personal coach. Bren had offered them the chance to ride with them in greater comfort, but, no, the two insisted on taking that post, despite the recent peace.

"This is no time to let down one's guard, nandi," was Tano's word on the subject, so that was that.

So they made small talk, he and Banichi and Jago, on the prospect for a quiet trip, on the prospect for Lord Tatiseigi's participation in a full legislative session for the first time in twenty-one felicitous years . . . and on the offerings they found in the traveling cold-box, which were very fine, indeed. Those came from the aiji's own cook, with the aiji's seal on them, so they could know they were safe—as if the aiji's own guards hadn't been watching the car until they took possession of it. Even his bodyguard could relax for a few hours.

It was all much more tranquil than other departures in this car. The coast wasn't that far, as train rides went, and the aiji had done them one other kindness—he had lent an engine as well, so the red car was not attached to, say, outbound freight. It was a Special, and their very small train would go directly through the intervening stations with very little pause. They might even make Najida by sundown, and they could contemplate their own staff preparing fine beds under a roof he actually owned for the first time since they had come back from space.

A little snack, a little nap . . . Bren let himself go to the click-clack of the wheels and the luxury of safety, and dreamt. . . .

Dreamt of a steel world and dropping through space-time.

Dreamt of tea and cakes with a massive alien. Cajeiri was in this particular dream, as he had been in actual fact. Prakuyo an Tep loomed quite vivid in Bren's mind, so much so that, in this dream, the language flowed with much less hesitancy than it did in his weekly study of it. He dreamed so vividly that he found himself engaged in a philosophical conversation with that huge gentleman, with Cajeiri, with the aiji-dowager, and with peace and war hanging in the balance.

He promised Prakuyo an Tep that indeed this was the son and grandmother of the great ruler of the atevi planet (a mild exaggeration) and a partner with humans (true, mostly) in their dealings with the cosmos. He had done that, in fact.

Humans having greatly offended the kyo, he had collected the whole stationful of them that had so offended, and delivered them back to the star they shared with atevi.

Humans having so greatly offended the kyo, he had persuaded the kyo that atevi were a very great authority who would make firm policy and guarantee humans' good behavior in future.

Most of all, he had shown the kyo, who had never seen another intelligent species prior to their exiting their own solar system, and who had somehow gotten into space with *no* concept or history of negotiation—one shuddered to think how—that two powerful species could get along with each other *and* with the kyo—a thunderbolt of a concept the paidhi had no illusions would meet universal acceptance among the kyo.

Prakuyo an Tep, over a massive plate of teacakes, miraculously and suddenly resupplied in this dream, vowed to come to the atevi world and document this miracle for his people, a visit which would persuade them to conclude agreements with this powerful atevi ruler and his grandmother and son—agreements which would of course bind all humans—and together they would find a way to deal with the troublesome neighbors on the kyo's *other* perimeter: God knew whether that species had a concept of negotiation, either.

But the paidhi, the official translator, whose job entailed maintenance of the human-atevi interface, and the regulation of mandated human gifts of technology *to* the atevi—according to the treaty which had ended the War of the Landing—had apparently another use in the universe. He was supposed to teach the kyo themselves the techniques of negotiation.

And simultaneously, back on the planet, he had to make sure Tabini's regime was secure and peaceful.

And make sure Tabini's grandmother was in good humor.

And make sure Tabini's son didn't kill himself in some juvenile venture, *and* didn't take so enthusiastically to things human that he ended up creating disaster for his own people on the day he did take over leadership of the aishidi'tat.

He really had hated to say no to the boy, who had harder things to do than most boys. He *had* promised him a boat trip.

And he sat there having tea with the kyo and telling himself he was firmly in charge of all these things. He had lied a lot, lately. He really didn't like being in that position, lying to the boy, lying to the kyo, lying to—

Just about everybody he dealt with, *except* Banichi and Jago, and Tano and Algini. They knew him. They forgave him. They helped him remember what he had told everybody.

And pretty soon now, he was going to have to lie to the atevi legislature and tell them everything was under control . . . when they all knew that there were still plenty of people out there who thought the paidhi *hadn't* done a great job of keeping human technology from disrupting their culture.

This didn't, however, stop atevi from being hell-bent on having wireless phones. Some clans thought his opposing their introduction was a human plot to keep the lordly houses at a disadvantage—because the paidhi's guard had them, and probably Tabini's had them, and nobody else currently could have them. Clearly it was a plot, and Tabini was in the pocket of the humans, who secretly told Tabini what to do . . . they became quite hot about it.

Tea with Prakuyo became the windblown outside of a racing locomotive, with a great Ragi banner atop, and the paidhi sat atop that engine, chilled to the bone by an autumn wind, hoping nobody found his pale skin a particular target.

They were coming into the capital. And the people of Shejidan might or might not be glad to see Tabini return to power . . .

"Bren-ji." Jago's voice. "We have just passed Parodai."

They were approaching the lowlands. In the red car. Carrying all his baggage.

He was appalled, and looked at Banichi and Jago, who had gotten less sleep last night than he had, and who were still wide awake.

Maybe they had napped, alternately. Maybe Tano and Algini were taking the opportunity, safely sealed in the baggage car. He certainly hoped they were.

Had he been wound that tight, that the moment he quitted the capital, he slept the whole day away? He still felt as if he could sleep straight through to the next morning.

But he had now, with Banichi's and Jago's help, to put on his best coat, do up his queue in its best style, and look like the returning lord of his little district.

He owed that, and more, to the people of the district, who had held out against the rebels.

He owed it to the enterprising staff, many of them from the Bujavid—who had fled during the coup and simultaneously spirited away his belongings—which had consequently *not* fallen into the hands of the Farai.

His people had held out on his estate, staying loyal to him when that loyalty could have ultimately cost them their lives.

That it had not come under actual attack had been largely
thanks to the close presence of Geigi's neighboring estate and
the reluctance of *any* outsider to rouse the Edi people of that
district from their long quiet . . . the Edi, long involved in a
sea-based guerilla war with almost everybody, were at peace,
and not even the Marid had found it profitable to add the Edi to
their list of problems. The west coast was remote from the center of the conflict, which had centered around the capital and
the Padi Valley—and it just hadn't been worth it to the rebels
to go after that little center of resistance . . . yet.

He'd gotten home in time. Tabini had launched his counter-
coup in time. The estate had held out long enough. The threat
of war was gone and Najida stood untouched.

And the paidhi-aiji owed them and Geigi's people so very
much.

He had fresh, starched lace at collar and cuffs, had a never-
used ribbon for his queue—the ribbon was the simple satin
white of the paidhi-aiji, not the spangled black of the Lord of
the Heavens, which he very rarely used. He sat down again
carefully, so as not to rumple his beige-and-blue brocade coat,
and let Banichi and Jago put on their own formal uniforms,
Guild black, still, but with silver detail that flashed here and
there. Their queues were immaculately done, their sleek black
hair impeccable—Bren's own tended to escape here and there,
blond wisps that defied confinement.

He opened up his computer for the remainder of the journey.
He'd hoped to work on the way, on matters for the next session. He'd slept, instead, and now there was time only for a few
more notes on the skeleton of an argument he hoped to carry
into various committees. Atevi, accustomed to the various
Guilds exchanging short-range communications, had seen the
advanced distance-spanning communications they had brought
back from the ship, and gotten the notion what could be had.

Worse, humans on Mospheira had adopted the devices

wholesale and set up cell towers, and the continent, thanks to improved communications, knew it.

He had to argue that it wasn't a good idea. He had to persuade an already suspicious legislature, reeling from two successive and bloody purges—one very bloody one when Tabini went into exile, and one somewhat less so when he returned—that he was *not* arguing against their best interests, and that after all the unwelcome human technology he had let land on the continent, he was going to say no to one they wanted. And the paidhi's veto, by treaty law, was supposed to be absolute in that arena. That, too, was under pressure: if he attempted to veto, and if Tabini didn't back him and the legislature went ahead anyway, that override weakened the vital treaty—and did nothing good for the world, either.

He just didn't know what he was going to meet when the legislature met. The last session had seen gunfire in the chambers, blood spilled in the aisle—that memory haunted his worst nights. In the upcoming session, the bloodshed might be figurative, but no less dangerous: undefined new associations trying to form, alliances being made, power-brokering from end to end of the continent, in whole new configurations that had never existed before, never tested themselves against the others.

Everything was undefined with these new representatives coming to the session in Shejidan, people who had come to their posts after the upheaval. The remnant of the old legislature, those canny enough, devious enough, or *stupid* enough not to have had an opinion during the Troubles, were going to meet that tide of "new men" in a month, in the aisles of the hasdrawad and the tashrid. God knew what the flotsam would be on the beaches of those debates, or whether the paidhi's influence could moderate a rush to give Tabini *exactly* what Tabini had always campaigned to have: more and more of the human tech that conferred power, medical advances, comforts, conveniences—and the damned wireless phones.

Too much too fast ran the risk of shipwrecking thousands of

years of atevi culture . . . worse, yet, of running up against that great unknown of social dynamic. Wireless phones in particular made changes in the way people made contact. Easy and informal contact imitated the way humans interacted—humans, who had the word *love* and *friend*; and had alliances outside their kinships. And atevi, who had the word *association*, and who felt the pull of emotions that held clans together—atevi little comprehended the changes it would make if communications started going outside their ordinary channels and if information started flowing between individuals who had no proper power to resolve an issue.

Man'chi was an emotion that to this day the paidhi could neither feel nor grasp, not even in the two nearest and dearest *associates* of his, who sat on the same bench with him. They couldn't feel what he felt; he couldn't feel what passion beat in their hearts; and that was just the way it was . . . all unknown, all fragile, all foreign, all the time . . . but it was what kept the clans together. Banichi and Jago would lay down their lives for him, a concept which, were he to do it for them, would mortally offend their sense of the way the universe had to work, not just the emotional sense—but the basic logic and reason underlying every decision. Such an impulse on his part would be, in their estimation, completely insane.

So when it came to politics, wireless phones and pocket coms, according to Toby, it was *not* just the social perniciousness of instant communication. The cell phone plague now preoccupied humans on the island of Mospheira, a plague making them walk into traffic while in conversation that preempted their awareness of their surroundings; a compulsion that suddenly rendered them incapable of ignoring a phone call in the presence of actual people they should be dealing with. It had gone overnight (from the view of someone two years out of the current) into, Toby said, its own kind of insanity.

Atevi who stood against the establishment of a wireless network argued about clan and Guild prerogatives, but even they little visualized what it would do to the social fabric . . . it was as basic as the decision whether to have a network of highways, or to have a network of rail. The one, with unregulated movement, would have utterly upset the associations that were the very fabric of civilization. Rail managed not to. And upset the mode of communication that preserved clan authority? Make it possible for anybody to call anybody at any time and *without* going through the household? Unthinkable.

The Assassins' Guild had more grasp of the situation than anyone—the Assassins' Guild *and* the Messengers' Guild were both on the paidhi's side in the debate. The Trade Guild and Transport Guild both saw advantages in the proposed technology and wanted it on a limited basis, for themselves. The Academics' Guild stood against, except that they wanted the now-limited computer network to include their research, and libraries.

Greed was not exclusively a human vice . . . and everybody was willing to accept damage for somebody else's venue to benefit their own. Fortunately the Assassins' Guild was a very, very potent Guild, and generally was listened to—out of dread, if nothing else. The paidhi held out hope that, if he could prevail, it would be thanks to the Assassins' Guild this time; and if he didn't—and if this one got past him—

God, the consequent damage could wipe out everything, absolutely every good thing he'd ever tried to accomplish. He could see the aishidi'tat dissolve, right when it was most necessary the world be stable.

At times, since their return from space, he asked himself if he had not already lost control of the flow of technology. He was shocked by the changes. It was as if the floodgates had already opened—as forces for and against the old regime bargained and connived for advantage. Tabini's year-long overthrow, which he had helped end, was in one sense the last gasp of the forces that *opposed* the wholesale import of human technology, but they had bartered, in a sense, with humans, and more significantly—with humans in space. The space station had sent down mobile base stations, landers. Had established communications. Had instructed Mospheira to set up the cell net. Had encouraged Mospheira to provide technology to the atevi resistance, the University doing damned little to prevent it, and the atevi saying no to nothing.

When he'd come back, he'd found himself on Tabini's side, where he had always been, but Tabini had always stood for human contact, more and more human technology. All sorts of proposals were close to opening the floodgates for good and all, importing everything humans had, including the technology in that starship up there, which would change so, so much . . .

It was still the paidhi's job to say no when it was time to say no.

And if he couldn't say no to this one and make it stick, maybe it was time the paidhi left the job.

Maybe a new paidhi could do better. But he didn't know how anybody the University trained could step into the waters now—it had become a rip current, and his own understanding of where they were going had gotten less and less sure.

Maybe the very institution of the paidhi had become outmoded, and humans and atevi actually were far enough along toward unanimity they could find their own way hereafter.

But there were bitter lessons to say that was a dangerous, dangerous assumption ever to make. The paidhi's office existed because humans and atevi had had another lengthy period of accommodation, right after humans had landed on the planet, and good things had flowed from humanity and everybody had just *loved* their new *friends* . . .

Or that was what humans had thought, right before atevi (as humans saw it) went berserk and launched the War of the Landing.

From the atevi point of view, humans had damned near wrecked civilization, and in fact, they nearly had.

So it wasn't safe to start thinking everything could roll along on its own. That, at least once upon a time, had been the point of absolutely terrible danger.

He just didn't have the vision of the future he'd used to have. It was all dark up ahead, and he couldn't see. He'd lost touch with Mospheira: the island of Mospheira, where he'd been born, where he'd grown up, was a place where he was no longer comfortable . . . where the ties he had left were all official ones, political allies . . .

Except Toby and his household.

Household, was it?

He hadn't even been thinking in Mosphei' just now. He'd been thinking in Ragi. That was how it was. He couldn't remember his brother's face when he was apart from him. Toby belonged to a different world, where people came with different features, spoke differently, felt differently, hadn't a clue what went on in his head, and didn't understand why touching another person was just . . . something he didn't do anymore.

Hell.

He was losing his grip, was what. He wasn't looking forward to seeing Toby at the moment. He was outright flinching from the thought.

He'd pitied his predecessor, Wilson, who had just gotten odder and odder. Wilson had quit the post once his aiji, Valasi, had died, and when Valasi's son, Tabini, had been a few weeks in the aijinate. Wilson couldn't deal with the change in regimes, and he'd retired to the university on Mospheira, saying Tabini was a future problem . . .

So one Bren Cameron had taken over the post, young, bright, academic ace, the *only* human, at the time, to master the mathematical intricacies of court Ragi . . . Wilson himself had never been fluent; had never ventured far from his dictionary, and, God, researched every official utterance. . . .

He'd rapidly been better than Wilson. More reckless than Wilson.

Now he had to ask himself which language he was thinking in.

Now he routinely limited his human impulses and curtailed his human instincts, shaping himself into something else . . .

A good talent, up to a point. He didn't know if he'd passed that point. Maybe he'd passed it somewhere in that voyage, when they'd all gone out to get a human station removed from where it had no right to be. . . .

Maybe his usefulness to the world had become something else out there. Maybe he didn't belong on the planet anymore, down in its web of intrigues, plots, and politics. Much as it would hurt—much as it would hurt people he cared about—maybe it might be better if he told Shawn his disconnnect had gotten the better of him, and he wasn't just resigning from representing Mospheira—which he had done, even before he went off to space—he was resigning from functioning on the planet at all.

If he couldn't stop this wireless phone business—God knew, maybe he should go back up to the station and live there, where the view was panoramic and the associations were all knowable and limited.

Represent the aiji to the station-humans. That wasn't a small job.

It wasn't what he emotionally wanted. He'd put down roots here on the mainland. Deep ones. But if he was becoming inconvenient to the very things he was trying to save . . .

Damn. He was losing himself. He was scared, was what.

And in that sense, Tatiseigi's return was extremely inconvenient: he'd wanted uninterrupted time to prepare his arguments and gather data. He almost wished he *didn't* have to deal with Toby. He needed his mind on business: it was a critical issue. He needed to stop this wireless business once for all.

But Toby wouldn't overstay. Neither, for that matter, would Barb.

God.

Barb.

No. No. Not a good thing to go into their visit anticipating trouble. The last meeting had been uncomfortable, to say the least—finding an old and troublesome relationship had now ricocheted to one's divorced brother was, yes, uncomfortable for everybody. But if the paidhi-aiji could negotiate affairs between people bent on killing each other, he surely could find a way to get through a week up close with Barb.

It was the price of seeing Toby.

Which he wasn't sure he wanted to do in this particular week . . .

No. He did. He'd come too far unattached from his own kind. The paidhi might be the better, mentally, for reforging some of those human links, even if they hurt. It was part of what he had been . . . which had been, once upon a time, efficient.

Maybe he just needed to recover his balance. Sharpen the edges, to mix metaphors. Regain a lost dimension of himself. The paidhi-aiji was useful when he *was* human, not when he was embedded so deeply in atevi politics he could no longer be perceived as different from any other clan-centered interest.

Getting that sense of humanness back, getting his thinking process in better order—that might be more useful than research.

Banichi said, "We just passed Nomi Dar, Bren-ji."

Within an hour of the coast. "We might have sandwiches," he decided. Staff at the estate knew when they were to arrive—they'd have consulted the train station. And he knew nothing would dissuade staff from having a meal ready, no matter the hour; but nothing would dissuade staff, either, from the formalities of meeting, and that might require a little fortification.

So he had one of the small sandwiches—small, by atevi standards—and gave half to Banichi. He had a cup of fresh-made tea, and with carbohydrates hitting his system, even mustered a sense of anticipation for Toby's visit. The air seemed to smell differently—or weigh differently—as they came down toward the coast.

The sea—changed things. Healed things. He began to feel it.

And when the train finally slowed to a stop and they had reached the station, he was properly kitted out and ready. He carried his own computer: Banichi and Jago stood near the door awaiting the signal from Tano and Algini that they had found things proper outside.

Then and only then did Banichi throw back the lever and shove the door open, and a pleasant cool breeze met them—a breeze and a cheer from the station platform, where very many familiar faces waited.

His staff. His people. Familiar faces . . . chief among them, Ramaso, his major domo—silver-haired, entirely now, around the face: that was a shock. Ramaso was a cousin of Narani's, that excellent man, his major domo from up on station; and looked very like him, now that the hair had changed.

There was Saidaro, who almost single-handedly had saved his boat from destruction; there was Husaro, and Anakara . . . there was a whole crowd.

"Nandi," Ramaso said, with a deep bow and a beaming face. "One understands there is baggage: we brought the truck as well as the bus. The boys will take care of the baggage. You and your bodyguard should come in the bus."

"One doubts being able to persuade my aishid, nadi-ji, but they will quite happily let the young lads do the loading."

"Indeed," Banichi said, at his shoulder, and Jago relayed that information to Tano and Algini—the baggage car had opened up, and some of the group was tending in that direction: a glance showed Tano outside on the platform, and doubtless talking to Jago.

It suddenly all felt better. Ramaso, and Saidaro, Husaro and others, some lifelong domestics, some clerical staff who had retired from office service during the Troubles, and who had come here to Najida to live out their retirement in service to the estate—mostly attending the needs of the adjacent village, teaching the children, handling forms and applications and helping out in general. The names came back to him, the faces moderately changed, in some cases the hair newly salted with white . . . all of them wearing their finest, and positively beaming. They bowed. He bowed. They crowded about—as much as atevi ever would crowd and jostle.

"Have you heard from my brother yet, nadi-ji?" Bren asked Ramaso, and that worthy smiled and nodded.

"His boat was tying up at dock as we left to meet the train, nandi. Staff will see him and the lady up to the house. He will be settled in the south room. Will that suit?"

"One is extremely gratified," he said, and meant it. He bowed again, and they all bowed, and Ramaso showed him and Banichi and Jago toward the platform steps, and the waiting bus. As he had thought, Tano and Algini, not leaving his baggage even to this devoted crew, marshaled junior staff to carry baggage down to the truck, which waited behind the bus.

Najida Estate, the bus said on the side, with a bright, rope-encircled picture of a peaceful blue bay and a small ship right below the name.

The truck was a little less decorated: its side panel said just, Najida, which was the village: a market truck, well-maintained, perfectly adequate for their baggage. Bren saw that matter going well, and climbed up and took his seat on the bus just behind the driver, with Banichi and Jago just behind him, and Ramaso and Saidaro just opposite, as other staff piled on in noisy commotion, all those who weren't seeing to the baggage-loading.

The dedicated train would go back the way it had come, with no passengers—possibly with a car or two of freight for Shejidan, if the stationmaster so decided—back to Tabini, to wait the aiji's pleasure. So they were here, peacefully settled, in rural solitude until that train made the return trip to pick them up . . . closer than the airport; and much more leisurely a passage.

The grassy road, greening in spring, showed recent mowing; and the dust of fairly frequent use—mostly the village and the estate going back and forth for supplies, very little in the way of passenger traffic. They passed thickets into which caiki dived for cover . . . nice to think that his land sheltered the little creatures: bobkins, Mospheirans called them, quick, gray little diggers that undermined planted gardens, common on the Island as well as the mainland . . . food for larger hunters, which were scarce here, so the caiki thrived. A small herd of gigiin grazed on the hillside above the village, fat and prosperous and complaisant, not seeming alarmed by their presence. Nobody hunted them in this season. The hunt was permitted only for seven days a year.

Najida mostly fished the bay for its living, hunted very little. It sold a part of its take for farm goods and supplied its village as its village supplied it, mostly by green-gardens; and during the summer the village kids probably hunted bobkins out of the village gardens, making some items out of the hides.

It was typical seaside rural life, keeping a schedule that didn't have committee meetings looming, and didn't greatly worry about the capital, in the best times. The village gardens would still lie asleep for the winter, areas nearest the houses probably being turned now for the first time, but the vines still were protected under neat straw rows, down in the fenced fields, the orchard trunks wrapped with straw rope in the old way. Bren gazed out the bus window, taking it in, always fascinated by the attention to detail, using so many materials that never passed through a mercantile chain—just made off the land, out of waste straw from neighboring grain fields.

His mother's house on Mospheira had never had a garden: they'd been city-dwellers, though Toby had once made a try at a garden when he'd lived on the North Shore, and probably harvested three tomatoes and a few carrots after his summer of trying. Next year, at least, the garden had gone back to flowers.

And Jill—Toby's wife, then—and the kids—they'd laughed about it when he asked how it had gone.

Pity that Jill hadn't stuck it out. He hadn't had time to ask Toby the details of that breakup. He knew there was too much of his own fault in it, his fault that he hadn't been home to take care of their mother, his fault that Toby'd done it all . . . done too much of it. Way too much, but that had been Toby's choice, in his own opinion.

And Jill had taken the kids and left.

No more little house on the north coast. No more family. Toby had sold the house, bought a bigger boat . . .

And God help him, Toby had immediately taken up with Barb . . . with his brother's old near-fiancée . . . if you asked Barb about their relationship. He'd been trying his best to shed Barb. Barb had immediately flung herself into one bad marriage, then gotten out of that and straightway moved in on *their* mother, taken care of her in her last illness . . .

And who had shown up regularly at that same bedside, if not the ever-dutiful if not the favorite son? Toby. Toby, who'd worked all his life for the kind of recognition their mother lavished on her absent son the paidhi-aiji . . . and never, to his knowledge, got a shred of thanks.

Barb had lost no time. Moved right in on Toby while Toby was visiting their mother in the hospital. Mum had died, Jill had left Toby, and—oh, yes—there was Barb, as fast as decency possibly allowed, moving right onto Toby's boat . . . just helping out.

Well, Toby could use a hand on the boat, that was sure. It was safer sailing, with two of them: hand Barb that.

So he could worry less about Toby, knowing he had somebody with him, in bad weather and the lonely stretches of water where he persisted in sailing . . . sometimes on covert business for the Mospheiran government.

Just so Barb stayed with him. That was all he asked. He forgave her everything, if she'd stay with Toby, so Toby had somebody.

The bus passed the village, took the curve, and his own land spread out across the windows, the sinking sun just touching the bay in the distance, spreading gold across the water. The red tile roofs and limestone walls of Najida estate showed from the height, a mazy collection of courtyards traditional in the west coast provinces; and at the bottom of its landscaped terraces, two yachts rode with sails furled, one at anchor—his own *Jeishan—Northwind*—that he hadn't seen in more than three years, riding at anchor; and, tied up to the estate's little wooden pier, Toby's slightly larger *Brighter Days*, that he'd last seen when Toby had let his party off ashore on the mainland, well north of here.

It was a cheerful sight. Banichi and Jago had noted it, he was sure, and he suddenly realized he hadn't said a word to them since they'd left the train.

"Toby's boat," he said.

"Yes," Banichi said, the obvious, and Jago: "It shows no activity."

Meaning Toby and Barb must surely be up at the house by now, which was where their bus and the trailing truck were going—directly so, now that they made the turn from the main road to the estate drive, a modest little track lined by old weathered evergreens, the sort of seaside scrub that, aged as it was, never grew much larger than he stood tall, all twisted shapes and dark spikes in the waning light.

Lamps glowed at the portico, a warm, welcoming light for them at the edge of twilight, showing the flagstone porch—his own porch, a place he'd rarely been, but been often enough to love in every detail.

The bus pulled to a stop. Banichi and Jago got up in the last moment of braking, got to the door as it opened, and were first on the ground. He followed, down the atevi-scale steps, and onto the stone drive, up the walk, as Ramaso and the staff poured off the bus behind him and other staff came out of the open doors to welcome him. The house staff bowed. He bowed, and when he lifted his head there was Toby in the open doorway, with Barb behind him.

"Toby," he said, and was halfway embarrassed by old habit, the impulse to open his arms, as Toby did—and there was Toby oncoming, and nothing to do: Toby embraced him; he, with no choice, embraced Toby, a little distressed. Toby slapped him on the back and, hell, he did the same with Toby, stood him back and had a look at him, grinning. "Missed you," Toby said.

"*Missed* me! Hell! *Worried* about you, damn it, when you dropped out of contact after you dropped us off."

"*You* worried! *You* were the one getting shot at!"

"I was safe enough," he said, with a nod over his shoulder toward Banichi and Jago. "*They* make me keep my head down." The reserve he cultivated was deserting him. Staff had seen it before. Hell, he said to himself, there was no teaching Toby differently. He had stood back enough to look at Toby. Toby's face was getting sun-lines that showed plainly in the lamplight: his wasn't. Toby lived in the sun and the weather. He rarely saw the out of doors and took care of his skin with lotions. Time passed. Things changed. They both grew older. Further apart. But now was now. "Missed you," he said.

"Mutual," Toby said. And despite everything, all the water under that bridge—it was probably still true.

He truly hoped Barb wouldn't move in for her turn, but she did: a public hug that had more warmth in it than the one he returned.

A woman, his brother's lover, and in public: it was far more of a scandal to the staff than the human habit of embracing brothers, but there it was, and he treated it as natural, if only for the benefit of his watching staff and bodyguard. More to the point, he *felt* Jago's gaze on his back in that moment, and set Barb firmly back at arms' length, seeing the faint traces of weather on her face as well. "You're looking good," he said. "The sea agrees with you."

"You never change," she said.

That meant several things, and he knew which. His perfunctory smile had an edge—just like the statement.

"Nice to know." He let Barb go and said, to Ramaso, "Thank you, nadi, and thank the staff, for your welcome to my Mospheiran household, and to me."

"Indeed, nadi." The worthy gentleman bowed. "The kitchen has a supper ready, at the lord's pleasure, rooms are ready, and water is hot."

Supper, or rest, or a hot bath. Every possibility.

But cooks could hardly be disrespected. And the truck had pulled around to the garden gate, where Tano and Algini were busy supervising the offloading of baggage and belongings. "One will visit the room, wash, and enjoy a leisurely supper, nadi-ji," he said quietly to Ramaso, and to Toby and Barb: "Wash up and dinner, forthwith. I'll see you at table."

"Right," Toby said.

The south room, Ramaso had said, which was actually a small suite, but with only one bedroom. The staff had lodged his family before. And someone had found a way to ask, apparently, about bedrooms—that, or staff had been unable to dislodge Barb from Toby's arm.

The brother of the paidhi-aiji and the paidhi-aiji's former lover, together under the paidhi's roof. Atevi did readily comprehend political realignments. And knew how to accept them without comment.

"Tano and Algini have gone the back way, nandi," Banichi said as they reached the door of his room—*his* room, indisputably his, and when he opened the door . . .

He knew that carpet. He knew that vase on the peculiarly carved table. That bed. That coverlet.

They were from his apartment in the Bujavid. He had known that staff had rescued significant items of his furnishings and gotten them out by train. And there they were, his bedroom, reconstituted just as it had been. He was quite amazed.

They didn't enter alone. Domestic staff arrived to take his traveling coat, and to supervise the arrival of his personal luggage, followed by more staff, who set things in the hall of his two-room suite. Banichi and Jago directed matters while Bren changed his shirt and coat—or changed it with the help of two of the staff who deftly assisted him with the lace cuffs and the collar: staff he knew, staff who'd been his for years: Koharu and Supani, who'd grown at least half a hand while he'd been gone and, gangly young men that they both were, grinned like fools and kept bowing, delighted as they could be. He felt—

Comfortable, finally. Truly home, truly safe. Even his bodyguard let these people come and go in confidence, and let this staff arrange his wardrobe in the rooms allotted to them. Banichi and Jago, Tano and Algini officially shared quarters just down the hall—though Jago would likely not sleep there.

And with the arrival of the various cases, it was a massive unpacking . . . an absolute fire brigade of clothing going from cases to closets, hand to hand, a steadily increasing staff all cheerful and quick about their jobs, and not a step out of order. They were excellent at their jobs, as fine a staff as any house could have; and Bren couldn't but catch their mood. A man could *work* in this environment; a man could concentrate on his job in absolute confidence that everything was taken care of, impeccably managed, all in order. He'd be fed like a prince, he'd be dressed and taken care of, nobody would ever mess with his papers and his computer—he could rely on that. He could look out the windows and watch the sun set with no worries beyond the research he had to do.

And maybe he *would* have ample time for the boat, and a little fishing, and a visit with his brother—he put the thought of Barb completely aside—before Toby headed back out to sea.

Oh, it was a *good* set of circumstances that had brought him back. He'd held it off for months as both a promised reward and a necessary burden—and now that he was here—it was going to work. He could reward himself with a little time and it wasn't going to put him off his duties at all. He could rest. His bodyguard could sleep decent hours and lean back and relax in real security, remote from the political angst that went with living in the Bujavid—and in the borrowed apartment and with the staff of a politically interested and very conservative lord.

And what was more, they could enjoy dinner with absolute confidence a borrowed chef on one of the Bujavid's frequent dinner engagements wasn't going to make a lethal mistake and poison the visiting human. This was Suba in charge of the kitchen. Suba absolutely understood what humans could and couldn't eat: he was not the finest cook on the planet—but he cooked excellent regional dishes. And that was one more stage of relaxation . . . which Mospheira itself couldn't afford him nowadays: too many crazy people there, too many agendas, too much controversy. Here, after a hellish year, he heaved a deep sigh as Supani made a final tweak at his collar and Koharu straightened the lace cuffs from the sleeves, and was just well content with himself and current company.

Even Barb's presence under the same roof—if Toby wanted her, if she did good for Toby, that was all fine. He'd be pleasant. She could be. They could have some family time, do a little fishing—settle some personal business he didn't exactly look forward to, but Toby probably wanted to say some things to him about the missed years, and clear the air, and he was obliged at least to listen and apologize. That needed doing . . . if Toby wanted to do it.

Banichi and Jago turned up ready for formal duty in their best black leather, gleaming with polished silver rings and fastenings—and they'd stand by while he ate and socialized, come hell or high water, since it was an official estate dinner, while Tano and Algini, on room duty and not obliged to formal dress, had their supper with staff, put their feet up, and watched the house servants unpack everything they were allowed to touch.

No arguing with the Guild's sense of propriety, however. He headed out with Banichi and Jago, not, as it would be in the Bujavid, through the main hall of his quarters, out the foyer, and so on into the halls, but directly down the warm, wood-paneled hall of the main building . . . this wasn't a building he shared with other lords, or even guests, ordinarily. Unlike the arrangement in other places he lived, this *was* his house, and when he went out his bedroom door he was immediately in the larger house, and when he walked down to the dining room, it was the dining room for himself and everybody who wasn't staff.

He loved this hallway. It had something quite rare in atevi architecture, a technique perhaps borrowed, centuries ago, from Mospheirans. The wing ended in a stained-glass window, a huge affair: staff had lit the outside lanterns, which only hinted at its colors. He looked forward to morning, when its smoldering reds and blues and golds would bloom into pastels and light, a rare representation of an actual object—atevi art was given to patterns completely overwhelming any hint of a person or a tree or a landscape. This was indisputably a tree, with branches more natural than patterned, and he loved the piece. He'd almost, of all things, forgotten it; and the little he could see of it was precious to him, the final touch on his homecoming. He loved this whole place—small, as lordly houses went, cozy. He found himself completely at peace as he entered the dining room, smelled the savory aromas wafting in from the service hall, and met three familiar faces—serving staff he and Banichi and Jago had known and trusted for years.

"Nadiin-ji," he said warmly. "So very good to see you."

"Nandi." Bows. Equally warm greetings. "Will a before-dinner drink be in order?"

He named it, an old favorite, perfectly safe.

And saw those three calm expressions change to shock,

as Toby entered—with Barb clinging to his arm and with her blonde curly head pressed against his shoulder. Laughing.

His face must have registered almost the same shock as his servants. Toby stopped, taking the cue. Barb left Toby and came and hooked her arm into *his,* tugging at him as he stood fast.

"Bren. This place is so *marvelous.*"

"Thank you," he said, and disengaged his arm enough to bow slightly, to Toby, then, in complete disengagement, to her. He said, then, soberly: "Customs are different here. People don't touch. Forgive me."

"Well, but we're family," Toby said, trying to cover it all.

"So are my staff," Bren said shortly. It was an unhappy moment. He saw resentment in his brother, beyond just a natural embarrassment . . . old, old issue, the matter of atevi culture, which, the more he had taken it on, had separated him further and further from Toby . . . and their mother. And *that* was the sore point. "Sorry, Toby. Sit down. What will you drink? No beer, I'm afraid. We have vodka and some import wine. Vodka and shebai is good. I recommend it." He was talking too much, too urgently. He was on the verge of embarrassing his staff as well as himself, doing their job instead of translating. And he resented the situation Barb had put him in. "Take the shebai."

"Sure," Toby said. "Barb?"

"White wine."

He turned and translated for the staff. "Nand' Toby will enjoy shebai. Barb-daja will have the pale wine, nadiin-ji. Forgive them." He saw, in the tail of his eye, Barb reattaching herself to Toby, and he didn't know what to do about it.

Neither did his staff, who would have seated them.

"Toby. Barb. Take those endmost seats, if you please. Toby. *Please.*"

"I think he means no touching," Toby said to Barb, attempting humor. Barb actually blushed vivid pink, and shot him a look.

Jago shot a look back, Bren caught that from the tail of his eye as he turned to sit down, and as he took his seat at the head of the table, Banichi simply walked to Toby's end of the dining room, in the ample space the reduced table size allowed, and stood there, looming over the couple while a very embarrassed servant moved to seat first Toby, who had started to seat Barb himself. It was a thoroughly bollixed set of social signals . . . and dammit, Toby had guested here. Toby knew better.

"Toby always sits first," Bren said in Mosphei', to Barb. He didn't add that Toby, as his brother, outranked Barb—and that the staff's opinion of Barb's social standing was surely sinking faster by the minute. He could imagine the talk in the kitchen . . . questions as to whether Toby had brought an entertainer—and a stupid one, at that—to a formal dinner under his brother's very proper roof.

It was a social disaster and he was furious at Barb: Toby clearly knew better; and Barb was not that unread—but no, Barb decided she could push the whole atevi social system, here, under his roof, to assert herself—which Toby might or might not read the same way; and there was no way on earth he was going to convince Toby what her game really was. There was no way he could bring it up at the dinner table, for damned sure.

There was one way to defuse it gracefully: diplomacy, the art of saying what one didn't believe, in order to swing the behavior toward what one wanted: guidance, more than lying. So he needed to have had a special talk with them. He clearly needed to have a talk with them, but not now, with personal embarrassment in the mix. It was likely Banichi and Jago would have that talk—by now, he was sure they *intended* to have it in Mosphei' the minute they had the chance; and logically they *would* have had it immediately with Toby's personal guard, if Toby had arrived with one . . . which, of course, he hadn't—unless one counted Barb. It was the sort of social glitch-up and attitude that had led to the War of the Landing. Humans were sure atevi would adapt to their very friendly way with just enough encouragement. Atevi—who didn't even have a word for friendship—assumed humans, who seemed so intelligent, would eventually learn civilized manners. Atevi assumed since they owned the planet, humans were in *their* house, while humans considered that they could just naturally get atevi to relax the rules, since their motives were the best . . . or for mutual profit.

"Drinks will arrive momentarily," Bren said quietly. "I do owe you both a profound apology for not mentioning certain things beforehand. This is a formal occasion. It's my fault."

"You've been here too long," Toby said, and it came out like a retort.

"I live here," Bren said, just a trifle unwisely: he knew that once he'd said it, and added, the truth: "I won't likely live on Mospheira again. So yes, I've changed." That, for Barb, just a trifle pointedly, and for Toby, with gentler intent: "I've done things a certain way so long I'm afraid I've lost part of my function as a translator, because I truly should have translated the situation. An atevi house is never informal—but tonight is official. Barb, forgive me, you have to keep a respectful distance from each other except in the bedroom. If someone does something for you in your quarters, bow your head just slightly and say mayei-ta. About the seating: Toby takes precedence because he's my relative and this is my house; gender has no part at all in the etiquette."

"You mean we just shocked them," Barb said.

"Profoundly," Bren said mercilessly. "The same as if they'd surprised you in bed." He actually succeeded in shocking her—not in what he said; but where he said it. And the drinks were arriving. He smiled at Barb with edged politesse, and wiped the hardness off his face in a nod to his staff. "Mayei-tami, nadiin-ji. Sa heigieta so witai so kantai."

Which was to say, "Thank you, esteemed people. Your service is timely and very considerate."

"Mayei-ta," Barb said with a little nod, on getting her drink. "Mayei-ta," Toby muttered, "nadiin-ji."

"A amei, nandi." This from the young server, who did *not* accord Barb a notice, except to use the dual-plus-one, to make the number fortunate, and who paid a second, parting bow to Bren, a unity of one. He left via the serving door, and Jago turned smartly and tracked the young person straight out of the dining room, probably to deliver a certain explanation to the staff . . .

What, that the lord's brother-of-the-same-house was attempting to civilize the human he had brought under the lord's roof? That Toby was likely equally embarrassed, put on the spot by the lady, and was trying not to make an issue of it?

Probably not. Jago was *not* a diplomat. The talk probably ran something like: "Bren-nandi tolerates this woman because his brother and this woman recently risked their lives in the aiji's service. The lord will deal with his brother, who will, one hopes, deal forcefully with this woman."

Certainly Jago was back in just about that amount of time, and took up her position on the other side of the serving door, stiffly formal.

"Good," Toby had said, meanwhile, regarding the drink, and Barb had agreed.

"How is the aiji's household?" Toby asked. "Is that all right to ask?"

"Perfectly in order," Bren said in some relief, and relaxed a little, with a sip of his drink. "Everyone is in good health. Nand' Cajeiri is back with his father and mother, the relatives have mostly gone back to the country—*I* have nowhere to live, since I've been using Lord Tatiseigi's apartment while he was patching up the damage to his estate, and he's on his way back to the capital."

"Well, *I'd* think you'd be a priority," Barb said. "I don't know why you're shunted out to the coast."

"I'm a very high priority," he said equably, "but it's his apartment. The aiji himself is still living in his grandmother's apartment, since his residence was shot up; and mine just happens to be full of Southerners at the moment. It's tangled. A defunct clan, the Maladesi, owned both this estate and the Bujavid apartment, both of which came to me; but they have remote relatives, the Farai, who claim to have opened the upper doors to the aiji on his return—someone did, for certain—never mind that Tabini was actually coming up from the basement; but the doors did open to a small force that was coming up the hill. It's the thought that counts, so to say, and therefore there's a debt. The Farai had taken over my apartment, in my absence, and they're still in there, politely failing to hear any polite suggestion they move out."

"And the *aiji* can't move them?" Toby said. "I'd think he could at least offer them a trade. Or you some other apartment."

"Well, that's easier said than done. Apartments in the Bujavid can't be had: it's on a hill, there's no convenient way to build on, though some have suggested doing away with legislative offices as a possibility— The point is, there's not only no place to put me, there's no room for half a dozen other clans that had rather have that honor—some of them really deserving it. There's a certain natural resentment among the conservatives that *I* stand as high as I do, so that's a touchy point that publicity just doesn't help. *And* the Farai are Southern, which is its own problem."

"Aren't they the batch that just rebelled?"

"Related to them. Neighboring district. Their opening the doors to the aiji was a clear double cross of Southern interests, but since Murini's Southern allies suffered a rash of assassinations, and since clans have changed leadership, the whole political geography down there has shifted—somewhat. Understand: Tabini-aiji is Ragi atevi. North central district. The South is Marid atevi, different dialect, different manners, four different ethnic groups, and historically independent. They were dragged kicking and screaming into the aishidi'tat by Tabini's grandfather; they've rebelled three times, generally been on the other side of every issue the aiji supports, but they are economically important to the continent—major fishing industry, southern shipping routes: fishing is important."

"Nonseasonal." Toby knew that: certain foods could only be eaten in certain seasons, but most fishes had no season, and were an important mainstay in the diet—one of the few foods that could be legitimately preserved.

"Nonseasonal, and essential. If it weren't for the fishing industry, the seasonal economy would be difficult, to say the least. So the aishidi'tat needs the South, the Marid. Needs all that association, as it needs the western coast. All very important. And by promoting the Farai in importance—however inconvenient to *me*—the aiji can make important inroads into the Southern political mindset. You always handle the South with tongs, because, however annoying the Marid leadership has been to the aishidi'tat, the people *are* loyal to their own aijiin. The Farai are Senjin Marid, as opposed to the Tasaigin Marid and the Dojisigin Marid. They're northernmost of the four Southern Associations, and they appear to have switched sides."

"Four Associations," Toby said. "Isn't that an infelicity?"

"Extremely," Bren said. "In all senses. It's unstable as hell. Double crosses abound in that relationship. One clan or the other is always playing for power—lately mostly the Tasaigi, which swallowed up the fifth Association, the islands, which has no living clan, and has the most territory. The Tasaigi argue that one strong aiji in *their* Association, dominating the other clans, makes a felicitous arrangement. The Senji, the Dojisigi, the Dausigi—all have their own opinions, but the Tasaigi usually lead. Except lately. Since the Tasaigi's puppet Murini fell from power, the Farai of the Senji district seem to be bidding to control the South."

"The ones in your apartment."

"Exactly. The Tasaigin Marid has produced three serious conspiracies to take power . . . all failing. If Tabini-aiji should actually give Farai that apartment permanently—that nice little honor of residing *in* the halls of power— Well, the theory is that the Farai, and thus the Senjin Marid, might become a Southern power that can actually be dealt with, which would calm down the South. I personally don't think it's going to work. But in one sense, my apartment could end up being a small sacrifice to a general peace—until the Farai revert to Southern politics as usual; or until someone in the South takes out a Contract on them. Which could happen next week, as the wind blows. What's a current security nightmare is the fact that my old apartment shares a small section of wall with Tabini's proper apartment. So that's being fixed—in case the Farai presence there becomes permanent. Who knows? It could. At least they didn't make a claim on this estate. I'd be *very* upset if that happened."

"It's very beautiful," Barb said.

"Palatial," Toby said. "I can only imagine what your place in the Bujavid must have looked like."

A little laugh. An easier feeling. "Well, Najida's a little smaller, actually. And the rooms here all let out into a hall that I *also* own, which always feels odd to me. I think this whole house would fit inside the aiji's apartment in the Bujavid." He saw a little tilt of Banichi's head, Banichi being in position to have a view down the serving hall, and read that as a signal. "Staff's preparing to serve the first course. And with apologies, let me give you a fast primer on formal dinners: no business, no politics, nothing but the lightest, most pleasant conversation during the dinner itself, nothing heavy until we retire for after-dinner drinks. We keep it light, keep it happy, take modest bites, at a modest tempo, and don't try to signal staff for drink: you'll embarrass them. They'll be on an empty glass in a heartbeat. A simple open hand at the edge of the plate will signal them you want a second helping of a dish: be careful, or you *will* get one; and if you see them give me a flat palm for a signal, that means they're running out of a particular course and want to advance the service, so don't ask for seconds then, or they'll be scrambling back there to try to produce an extra, probably one of their own meals. There'll be an opening course, a mid-course, a meat presentation, and a dessert, different wine with each, so expect that. And somewhere during the meat presentation the cook will look in, we'll invite him in, praise the dish—it's going to be spectacular, I'm sure—and thank him and the staff. There's going to be much more food than you can possibly afford seconds of, if you want my advice. And then we'll thank the staff again, and get up and go to the parlor for drinks and politics, if you like."

They took that advisement in good humor, at least. It forecast at least a patch on things.

Barb, however, was on her own agenda since she'd arrived at the front door. He'd known her long enough to spot that.

And being Barb, she didn't think her agenda through all the way to the real end, just the immediate result she fantasized having. She wanted to make him uncomfortable: she wanted him to acknowledge he'd been utterly wrong to drop her. The fact it could have international repercussions was so far off her horizon it was in another universe. The possibility of setting him and Toby permanently at odds, well, that just wouldn't happen, in her thinking, because she controlled everything and that wasn't the way she planned.

That was how she'd ended up marrying the dullest man on Mospheira, to get back at him, and had an emotional crisis when it turned out he wished her well and walked off; it was how she'd spent years of her life taking care of his and Toby's mother, once she got her divorce—because she was just essential to their family, wasn't she?

In point of fact, if he hadn't had to run the gauntlet of Barb's emotions to get to his mother's bedside, maybe he'd have found a way over to the island more often—

No, that was a lie. Circumstances a lot more potent than Barb's angst had made him unavailable and finally sent him off the planet and into a two-year absence. So that hadn't been

Barb's fault, wasn't his, wasn't Toby's fault, either, but it had done for Toby's marriage, all the same.

And where did Barb go after Toby's divorce—hell, *before* the divorce? Barb had been at their mother's place. So had Toby. They'd both been at the hospital all day. Toby's wife Jill had taken the kids and bailed.

He didn't want to think about that, not the whole few days Toby and Barb might be here. He'd be damned sure there wasn't another scene. He had to talk to Toby, was what. There was no use talking to Barb. That was precisely what she wanted.

He was precisely what she wanted, because he'd been too distracted to give a damn when she'd left him. There was the lasting trouble.

He put on his best diplomatic smile while staff served the first course, eggs floating in sauce; and didn't let himself think too far down the course of events. They'd get out on the boat, they'd do some fishing. There was no real reason to have a deep heart-to-heart with Toby on the matters of atevi manners, Barb, or the particular reasons he hadn't been there when their mother needed him. Fact was, Barb was going to do what Barb intended to do, and there was no way to warn a man off a personal relationship and stay on good terms with him. They could put a patch on it and smile at each other; fishing would keep them all busy, wear them out, and they could do some beachside fish-roasting and keep the issues between him and Toby and him and Barb off the agenda entirely until it was time for the formal farewell dinner.

They could get through that, too. With luck, they never would have to discuss the reasons for their problems at all.

3

Great-uncle Tatiseigi was coming back to the Bujavid, and that was by no means good, in Cajeiri's estimation.

But Great-grandmother was coming with him, and that *was* welcome news. Great-grandmother understood him better than his parents did, and better still, Great-grandmother could make his father listen, being *Father's* grandmother, and powerful in her own right.

Things were definitely looking up, almost making up for his losing nand' Bren—who hadn't been able to talk to him before he left, not really. Great-grandmother's major domo, Madiri, was hurrying about, berating tardy staff. Cajeiri's own door guards, Temien and Kaidin—his wardens, in his own estimation—who were on loan from Uncle, were in their best uniforms; his mother and father were dressing for the aiji-dowager's arrival—it being her apartment they all were living in.

And very possibly—Cajeiri thought—they might soon be in the same case as nand' Bren, having to move out to let *mani* have her apartment back, the same as nand' Bren had had to move out to let Uncle Tatiseigi have his. They might have to move out to the hunting lodge out at Taiben, which was where his own personal staff, Antaro and Jegari, had come from.

And that would be attractive: Taiben lodge was bigger, and he would have much more room; and there was the woods; and there was riding mecheiti and running about with Antaro and

Jegari, who would be absolutely afire to show him things . . . that would be good.

Maybe his tutor would stay in the capital. That would be even better.

But he had ever so much rather be left here in Shejidan, in the Bujavid, and live in mani's apartment, and be with her, the way he'd grown up—well, several years of his growing up, but the best years, the years that really, truly mattered: his time in the country, his little sojourn at mani's estate of Malguri, his stays with Uncle Tatiseigi when mani was in charge of him . . . not to mention his two years in space, with just mani and nand' Bren . . . and his human companions, Gene, Artur, and Irene and all—those had been the good times, the very best times. Everything had gone absolutely his way for two wonderful years—

And then they'd come home to a mess in the capital, and in the Bujavid, and his parents had demanded to have him back and would not let him have access to nand' Bren or Banichi anymore. His father being the aiji, his father got what he wanted, and got him back, just as simply as that, and put him under one and the other tutor and told everybody in his whole association except Jegari and Antaro to get entirely away from him and leave him solely with his parents.

Which was why nand' Bren had to avoid talking to him, even if he lived almost next door.

And why mani had gone away to Tirnamardi with Uncle, leaving her own apartment and her comforts and her staff behind.

It was why there was absolutely no chance at all his father was going to send up to the ship-aijiin and request Gene and Artur to come down to visit him. The space shuttles were flying again, and Gene and Artur didn't mass much, compared to all the loads of food and electronics they were flying up there to the station. But no. He didn't even get messages from Gene and Artur, just one, when he wrote to tell them he was safe, and about all his adventures. Gene and Artur and Irene had each written him a letter admiring his adventures and asking questions, and he had written back, but there had been no answers since then; and he knew his letters were either never sent, or their answers had never gotten to him; and Gene and Artur and Irene would take his silence as hopeless, and give up trying . . . forever.

He was a prisoner, was what. A prisoner. He'd tunneled out when his father's enemies had tried to keep him. But there was no lock on his door in his father's residence—just guards, just his tutor, just ten thousand eyes that were going to report it if he stepped sideways.

And then where would he go if he did get out? He could hardly get aboard the shuttle in secret, and they would only send him back when they caught him. If he went anywhere in the whole wide world, they would send him back to his father.

He treasured those three letters, as his most precious things in the whole world.

So . . . with mani-ma in residence . . . maybe he would have no better luck with letters, though he would certainly tell her he suspected connivance against him! But one of two fairly good things could happen with mani: mani-ma could settle in to stay with them and perhaps coddle him a *little* . . . or his father and mother could take a vacation at Taiben, and even if they took him away with them, he would have that. Neither was too bad.

So, foreseeing the need for a good appearance, he became a model of good behavior. He dressed, with Jegari's help, in his finest, with lace at cuffs and collar. Jegari braided his queue and tied on the red-and-black ribbons of the aiji's house, and he waited, pacing, until Jegari and his sister Antaro had gotten each other into their best—very little lace, since they were Taibeni, foresters, but very fine leather coats and immaculate brown twill for the rest: mani could not possibly find fault with them.

"I want to talk to mani before she goes into the dining room, nadiin-ji," Cajeiri said. "We need to put her in a good mood toward us."

"Yes," Antaro said, and, "Yes," Jegari said. So they left the room, not escaping the attendance of his assigned grown-up bodyguard—and headed down the hall toward the drawing room.

He saw Cenedi, silver-haired Cenedi, mani's bodyguard and chief of staff, resplendent in his formal uniform; and immediately next to him he saw mani herself, small, erect, and absolutely impeccable, walking with her cane, tap, tap, tap, toward the dining room.

He lengthened his stride to intercept mani and Cenedi, and met them with a little bow, exactly proper.

"Mani-ma! Welcome! One is very glad!"

"Well, well." The aiji-dowager—Ilisidi was her name—rested both hands on the formidable cane and looked him up and down, making him wonder if somehow his collar was askew or he had gotten a spot on his coat. His heart beat high. No. He was sure he had no fault. Mani looked at everybody that way, dissecting them as she went. "We see some improvement."

Another bow. "One is gratified, mani-ma. One has studied ever so hard."

And a reciprocal scrutiny. "My great-grandson is availing himself of my library."

"Indeed, mani-ma. I am reading, especially the machimi."

"Well, well, an improvement there, as well."

"You will teach me now! You know so much more than the tutors!"

"Flattery, flattery."

"Truth, mani!"

"Well, but we will not be at hand to tutor you, Great-grandson. We are here only for the night, then back to Malguri."

His heart sank. Malguri was mani's own district, clear across the continent, a mountain fortress. He had been there.

And it was an alternative—if he could go there. There were mecheiti to ride. Rocks to climb. "I could come there, mani. Take me with you! I learn far less with the tutor than with you and Cenedi!"

Did she soften, ever so little? She hesitated a few heartbeats: he saw it in her eyes. Then: "Impossible. You are here to become acquainted with your father. You are here to learn the arts of governance."

"But I have!" He lapsed into the children's language, realized it, and amended himself, in proper Ragi. "Mani, one has improved entirely." He saw his grand chances slipping away from him and snatched after something more reasonable. "A few weeks, mani. One would wish to visit you in Malguri for only a few weeks, and then go back to lessons. Surely you could persuade my father."

"No," mani said regretfully. "No, boy. We have had our time, in two years on the ship. Now you have to learn from your father."

"Then stay here, please! This is a big apartment!"

"Not big enough," Ilisidi said. "Not large enough for your father's staff and mine, not large enough to keep us from arguments, and your father has enough to do in the upcoming legislature."

"And he will be busy, and have no time for me!"

"Language, boy."

"He will be busy, mani, and I shall be obliged to stay to my tutor. Even nand' Bren has gone away to his estate. I shall have no supervision and you know I should have!"

"Your great-uncle will be here."

That was the grimmest prospect of all, but he kept that behind his teeth and simply bowed acknowledgment of the fact. "But one will miss your society, mani. One could learn so much . . . of manners, and protocols, and history . . ."

"Well, well, but not at Malguri, I regret to say, where I must be, and you must be here, boy, you simply must. Come, let us go to dinner; and then we will say our good-byes tonight. Weather is moving in from the west, and we shall be leaving before dawn tomorrow, at an hour much before a young boy will find it convenient, quite certainly."

"One will get up to say good-bye, all the same."

"Oh, by no means," Great-grandmother said, and tapped the cane on the floor, rap-tap, a punctuation to the conversation, as she started walking again, and so did Cenedi, and he was obliged to keep pace. "You will get your proper sleep and apply yourself profitably to your lessons. We shall be taking off before first light. We know, we know your situation. You must bear it."

"Mani." He was utterly downcast, but he had mani's sympathy, and that was an asset never to waste. If he could not get one thing he wanted, he could try for another, and he had his choice: permission for a television in his room, which his father would probably forbid, or mani's backing in the business of the letters to the space station—which was as important to him. "Mani, to my letters—which I wrote to the station—there has been no answer; and one almost suspects these letters are being held, which would be a reasonable consequence, mani, if one had not applied oneself to one's studies, which one has done, very zealously! So if you could possibly, possibly ask my father about communications to the space station, and find out if Gene has even received my letter or if possibly—possibly there is some security question from the ship-aijiin, or maybe Gene has said something improper, or I have— It is so important, is it not, mani-ma, for me to understand these proprieties and maintain contact with my associates up above, and not to lose this advantage of association, when I am aiji? One cannot be offending these individuals. It would hardly be politic to offend them due to some foolish misperception!"

Tap went the cane, sharply. "Rascal." She saw right through him. Clear as glass.

"Yes, mani. But—"

"Your argument is rational."

A little hope. A little lessening of Great-grandmother's frown. "One earnestly hopes to be rational, mani."

"We shall think on it."

"Yes, mani." It was not the agreement he hoped for. He got pleasantness: he got warmth: but he did not get yes.

Still, with Great-grandmother, one did not sulk. One definitely did not sulk, nor allow an expression of discontent. Never let an opponent see into your thoughts, mani would say. And: *What* is that expression, boy?

Mani was more than hard to argue with. "Think on it" was as much as he was going to get if he kept after her for reasons, and mani would not be persuaded to stay. He would have Great-uncle down the hall, arguing with his father and trying to instruct the guards Great-uncle had set over him, and, worse, asking them when he breathed in and when he breathed out. He was not happy with the evening thus far.

But mani had taught him how to release his face from his unhappiness. One could be as angry as it was possible to be, and completely relax the face, even smile . . . he knew how to add that little touch, without giving away anything. He could do it with his father and his mother. But he did not try it with Great-grandmother, foreseeing a thwack to the ear—she was only as tall as he was, but she could manage it, being able, he had once thought, to read his mind. Not the case, of course: that was for the human dramas nand' Bren had lent him; but read his *actions*, oh, indeed she did that, better than anyone.

So they walked in to dinner together, and he kept his self-control. He was gracious to mani, to his mother, and to his father. He tested his self-control—and the situation—by saying, conversationally, "One had very much hoped that mani would take up residence again. There is surely room enough." He darkly suspected that his father might have discouraged Great-grandmother from staying. He knew that propriety would be strained to the limits *and* his father would have been held up to blame had Great-grandmother taken up residency down the hall, with Uncle Tatiseigi . . . so he said it the polite way, and was unrewarded. His father said:

"She wished otherwise, did you not, esteemed grandmother?"

"We have affairs to tend in the East," mani said.

"But I might go there!" he said, his control slipping just for a moment. He added, mildly, "If my father and honored mother could spare me from lessons only for a month or so." *Surely* his parents' apartment, promised to be ready before now, would be ready by then . . . and mani could come back with him to She-jidan and everything would be better.

"One regrets to disappoint," his father said without a shred of remorse, and said, directly to Great-grandmother: "He has frustrated three tutors and driven one into retirement."

"Honored father," Cajeiri protested. "You said yourself—"

"That the man was a fool? An excellent numbers man. A fool. But despise the numbers as you may, my enlightened and too modern son, you still need to know them."

"Why?" mani shot at him, at *him*, not his father, and he answered, meekly,

"Because 'counters have political power and superstitious people are very excitable, mani, so one should *know* the numbers of a situation to know what superstitious people will believe."

His father laughed. "There, grandmother, you have produced a cynic."

"Next year," Cajeiri said, doggedly being what Great-grandmother would call *pert*, "I shall be a more fortunate number in age . . ." He was infelicitous eight, divisible by unfortunate four, each bisected by unhappy two. "And then perhaps people will hear me seriously."

"You have been fortunate," his father said, "to be alive, young gentleman."

"Fortunate to sit at this table," his mother said. "Wheedling is not becoming anywhere."

"Forgive me, honored mother. It was excessive." Decidedly, it had been. He had gone much too far. He sighed, hating his own impulsiveness, and helped himself to more sauce for the meat course, fighting to cool the temper that had roused up. Great-grandmother assured him he had inherited that temper from Great-grandfather, and his grandfather, and his father. "Find *my* inheritance in you!" she had repeatedly instructed him. "Mountain air is chill. It stimulates the *wit*, young man. *Choler* only ruins one's digestion."

It was good advice. He had been in Great-grandmother's mountains. He had been in the snow. He understood. And like nand' Bren's rock, paper, scissors—he had seen how wit beat choler, every time.

So he reined in his anger, ate his dinner, and while mani and his mother and father chatted about the weather, the hunting, the repairs to the apartment—he thought.

He thought about nand' Bren having to leave.

He thought about Uncle Tatiseigi being right down the hall and having his guards right outside his door, and Uncle Tatiseigi calling on his father every time he did a thing out of the routine.

He thought about all these things, and the whole situation was what mani called—intolerable.

Nand' Bren had promised to take him on his boat when things settled down and people stopped shooting at each other, and it had been quiet for months, had it not?

His parents were convinced he was a fool, untrustworthy even if he should go to Taiben, where Antaro's and Jegari's parents and the lord of the Taibeni (who was a relation) would take extraordinary care of him. He saved that hope for absolute last.

He had asked to have his own staff and his own apartment, even if it let out into theirs, but he knew what modifications they were making to his parents' old domicile, and there was *no* provision for him in that place having anything but a foyer, a closet of a study, and a small bedroom of his own, not even his own bath—they said another bath was impossible without tapping into the lines next door, which were in Bren's proper apartment, which was being occupied by the Farai, and *no* one lately offended the Farai, not even for Lord Bren's sake. And it was a security risk. They were building a monitoring station against that wall, which he was not supposed to say.

But it was all just disgusting.

Still, he kept a pleasant face, and had his dinner, and said a proper good-bye to mani, and a good night to his father and his mother, leaving the adults to their brandy. He gathered up Antaro and Jegari and the two guards who were Uncle Tatiseigi's and went back to his quarters.

He said, to the guards, "You should have your supper now. Go. I shall have an early night. You might have some brandy, too."

"Nandi," they said, and went off, unsuspecting and cheerful in the suggestion. They were not nearly as bright as his father's guards.

Antaro and Jegari followed him inside and looked worried. They *were* as bright as anybody could ask.

And he walked over to his closet and took out his rougher clothes, and laid them on the bed. He knew the handsigns the Guild used. He used several of them to say, "downstairs," and "all of us," and "going."

"Where?" Antaro signed back, in some distress.

"Nand' Bren," was a sign they had, the same that Bren's own guard used.

"Your parents," came back at him.

He gave them that tranquil, pleasant look he had practiced so hard. And laid his fist over his heart, which was to say, "Carry out orders."

They didn't say a thing. They went to their nook and into their separate rooms and brought back changes of clothing. They weren't Guild. They had no weapons, nor anything like the communications the Guild had. They just quietly packed things in a single duffle, and meanwhile Cajeiri opened his savings-box, emptied that, found a few mangled ribbons of the Ajuri colors, his mother's clan, and the green of the Taibeni, and, yes, finally, a somewhat dog-eared train schedule book he had gotten from his father's office.

He opened that and found that, yes, a train did leave the Bujavid station in the night: it went down to the freight depot, probably to pick up supplies, which was exactly the thing. Cook would be cleaning up in the kitchen, and the major domo would be engaged with mani—Cook was hers, more than his parents', and that conversation would take a little time. The whole house would be focused on mani, because most everyone was hers, except his father's and his mother's staff, and those few would be paying attention to his father and mother, because everyone else would be waiting on mani and making sure she had all she wanted.

Mani probably would socialize late—for her—turn in, and catch several hours' sound sleep before she got up to go to the airport.

Perfect.

4

Brandy, in the sitting room, with the comfortable wood fire, the rustic stone hearth . . . beneath ancient beams. The furniture looked a little out of place, being ornate and carved and far from rustic in its needlepoint seats and backs. The carpet was straight from the Bujavid: it gave the place, to Bren's eye, a sort of a piratical air, the furnishings all having been smuggled off to the coast during the city riots and none of the furniture quite matching.

But, formal or not, they were comforting, like old friends, every stick of the furnishings, the priceless porcelain vases on their pedestals. Bren was delighted with everything the staff had done, and expressed as much to the staff who served there. "One is astonished," he said. "One knew you had extraordinary daring to make off with the dining room carpet, nadiin, but however did you get the furniture here?"

"In a truck, nandi," was the answer. "In several trucks. We pretended to loot it, we hid it in Matruso's cousin's house, and we took it by back roads."

"Extraordinary," was all he could find to say. "One is extremely grateful, nadiin-ji. Say so to all the staff—and to Matruso's cousin!"

"Shall we serve, nandi?"

"To be sure," he said. Banichi and Jago were still with him, standing, and didn't meet his eyes, which indicated they weren't looking for a signal to sit down, and didn't in the least want one.

Barb and Toby were also standing, on best behavior—finally.
"Sit down, sit down, Barb, Toby. We're all informal here, after
dinner. Any chair you like."

They were all outsized chairs for a human frame—Toby's
feet reached the floor, Barb's didn't, so she crossed her ankles
and swung them a moment, feeling over the carved wood with
pink-lacquered fingernails.

"Very fancy," Barb said.

"This," Bren said, slowly taking his own favored chair, "is
the spoils of my Bujavid apartment. My staff risked their necks
getting it away—or God knows what would have happened
to it. Carted off to the South, likeliest. They shot up the aiji's
apartments, killed poor old Eidi, broke things—you have to understand, it's like breaking things in a museum. These things
are national treasures. The finest of the finest."

"They don't have museums, do they?" Toby asked. Most
every city on Mospheira did have.

"Not as such," he said, "but people do tour historic places,
and the great houses do rotate pieces downstairs, into the public areas, during their own tour season. Anybody can go to the
Bujavid, on the lower levels; anybody can apply to visit the library and the collections. Anyone with scholarly interest can
apply to have certain articles moved into a viewing room. You
just don't fire off guns in a place like that. It shocked everyone;
it created great public resentment, once that fact got out. It
was one thing that Murini's lot shot people; it was another that
his fools ripped up pieces of the past. You can't imagine the
furor."

"Well, I'd think people were more valuable," Barb said.

"People are valuable to their clan. The past is valuable to
everybody. Losing that—is losing part of the collective. Part
of the social fabric. It ripped. But restorers and copyists are at
work. That's one thing that's taken so long. The aiji's carpet
that was ruined—the fools set a fire, for God's sake—that's
going to take years to restore. In the meanwhile there will be

a copy. The restored piece will probably go down to a formal room in the lower Bujavid."

"The repairs will be part of its history, I suppose," Toby said.

He was pleased. Sometimes Toby did get things. "Very much so. Exactly."

The brandy came, sizable doses, delivered by staff on a silver tray.

"Quite the life," Toby said, and shifted an uneasy glance toward Banichi and Jago, who hadn't moved, not an inch. Toby didn't say anything. But the thought was plain . . . Can't they sit?

"A good life," Bren said, ignoring the issue. He had no apology for the staff's formality, no protest about anything staff wanted to do. They were on edge, in foreign presence, touchy about his dignity, which they saw as offended. But he was very content at the moment, with a smoky brandy, a warm fire, and his brother at hand. He did relax.

"You have to wear that all the time?"

"The vest?" He did. He'd shed the dinner coat, and sat quite informally in this family setting, though staff had offered to bring him an evening jacket. Putting one on would be a struggle with the lace, and he'd opted not to bother. "This, I assure you, is informal."

"The shirt," Toby said. "The whole outfit. I have a spare sweater, pair of pants that would fit you."

He shook his head, gave a little laugh. "I really couldn't. The staff is on their best behavior. Guests, you know. They would be a little hurt if I didn't look the way they like."

"Well, I suppose we look a little shabby," Toby said.

"I could find you a shirt and coat," he said. "Boots, now, boots are always at a premium."

Toby laughed uneasily and laid a hand on his middle. "I wouldn't look that good in a cutaway, I'm afraid."

"I'd like to try what the women wear," Barb said.

That was a poser. "None in my wardrobe, I'm afraid."

"Oh, but there's staff," Barb said.

"I can't quite," Bren said. "And it wouldn't fit you." He couldn't envision going to one of the servants and asking to borrow *her* wardrobe—not to mention the issues of rank and guest status and Barb's already shaky standing with staff. "Best not ask. Next time, next time you visit, I'll send you both a package, country court regalia, the whole thing."

"Not me, in the lace," Toby said. "I'd have that in the soup." And then he added: "You used to wear casuals here."

"A long time ago. Different occasion." Silence hung in the air a moment.

"A few years," Toby said. "Not that long ago."

"It's different," he said. "It's just different now."

"You're Lord Bren, now. Is that more than being the paidhi?"

"A bit more."

"When are you going to visit Mospheira?"

"It's what I said. It's not likely I will," he said into a deeper and deeper silence. "Not that I wouldn't enjoy certain places. Certain people. But it's just different."

And the silence just lay there a moment. "You can't say 'enjoy old friends,' can you?"

"Toby," Barb said, a caution.

Which said, didn't it, that he'd been the subject of at least one unhappy conversation?

"I'm kind of out of the habit," he said. "And no, not the way I think of 'friends.' Nobody on the island's in that category any longer. Shawn Tyers, maybe. But he's busy being President. Sonja Podesta. Sandra Johnson. Who's gone on to have a life." He'd named two women and he saw Barb frown. "I have friends up on the station. Jase, for one. Jase is a *good* friend. But—" That was headed down its own dark alley. He stopped, before it got to its destination, which was that it wasn't easy to keep friendships polished when he was more likely to get back to the station sooner than Jase would get a chance to visit the planet. And that wasn't going to be any time soon. "On the continent I have my associates," he said. "My *aishi*."

Toby didn't look happy with that statement, but *damned* if Toby was going to sit there in front of Banichi and Jago, who did understand Mosphei', and tell him that atevi sentiments were in some measure deficient for a human.

"Trust me," Bren said, pointedly, "that I'm extremely content in my household. I'm not alone. I'm never alone, not for an hour out of the day. And I do ask you both to understand that, in all possible ways."

Again the small silence.

"*I* brought you a present," Toby exclaimed suddenly, getting up, shattering the dark mood entirely. "I have it in our room."

"Let Banichi go with you," Bren said gently, and with a little restoration of humor. "*You* don't run about alone, either. You come here with no bodyguard, unless Barb wants to take that post . . . you can't just run up and down the halls as if you were my staff. You're a guest. You need an escort. You don't open your own doors. It's my social obligation."

Toby looked at him as if he were sure he was being gigged, but he stayed quite sober.

"I'm serious. It's just good manners. Mine, not yours, but be patient."

"So who's going to escort . . . Barb?" Toby asked, and slid a glance toward Jago, the only woman in his personal guard—Jago, who had as soon consign Barb to the bay.

"Exactly," Bren said, and in Ragi: "Banichi-ji, please see Toby to his room. He forgot an item."

"Nandi," Banichi said gravely, and went to the hall door and opened it for Toby.

Which left him, and Barb, and Jago standing by the door.

"So," Barb said in the ensuing silence, "you *are* happy, Bren."

"Very," he said. "You?"

"Very," she said, and slid in the chair and stood up, walking over to the fire, which played nicely on her fair curls. She bent down and put a stick of wood in. "I love fires. Not something you do on board."

He sat where he was. "Not likely. You live aboard the boat, year round?"

She nodded, and looked back at him, and walked back toward her chair.

Or toward him. She rested a hip on the outsized arm of his chair. He didn't make his arm convenient to her. She laid a hand on his shoulder.

"She wouldn't object, would she?"

"She may, and I *do*. Move off, Barb."

"Bren, I'm your sister-in-law. Well, sort of."

"*Marry* him, then." He wished he hadn't said that. He couldn't get up without shoving Barb off the arm and he could all but feel Jago's eyes burning a hole in Barb. "It's not funny, Barb."

"I just don't see why—"

He put his hand on her to shove her off the chair arm, just as the door opened and Toby walked in.

And stopped.

Barb got up sedately. Cool as ice. In that moment he hated her, and he hated very, very few people on either side of the straits.

Toby didn't say a thing. And there wasn't a graceful thing for him to say.

"I was just talking to Bren," Barb said.

"Why don't you turn in?" Toby asked. "Bren and I have things to discuss."

Barb's glance flicked toward Jago, and the ice crackled. Barb shook her head emphatically at that suggestion. "I'll walk back when you do," she said. "Toby, honestly, we were just talking. I wanted to ask Bren something. His guard *understands* us."

"It was talk," Bren said. The Mospheiran thing to do was to

explode. Among atevi, involving atevi, it cost too much. So did having it out now, on the very first night of their stay. "What is this surprise of yours?"

A wrapped present. Gilt paper. Ribbons. Toby resolutely held it out to him, a box about the size of a small book, and Bren got up and took it. Shook it, whimsically. Toby gave him a suspicious look.

"We're too old for that, are we?" Bren said. "Well." He looked at the paper. It said Happy Birthday. "God, how long have you saved this one?"

"Since the first year you went away," Toby said. And shrugged. "It can't live up to expectations. But I was dead set you were coming back. So I got it, for luck."

"Superstitious idiot," Bren said, and, it being Jago and Banichi alone, he took the chance to hug Toby, hug him close and mutter into his ear. "Barb's mad at me. She made that damned clear. Don't react. It'll blow over."

Toby shoved him back and looked at him at close range. Didn't say a word.

"Truth," he said, steady on with the gaze, and Toby scowled back.

"Truth?" Toby asked him, when that wasn't exactly what Toby was asking, and he grabbed Toby and pulled him close for a second word.

"*My* lady's standing over there armed to the teeth, and she doesn't take jokes. Neither does Banichi. For God's sake, Toby, nothing's at issue. Barb's acting out; she's mad about dinner. I embarrassed her. *You* know Barb by now."

He took a big chance with that, a really big chance. But this time when Toby shoved him back at arm's length to look at him, Toby had a sober, unhappy look on his face.

"Damn it," Toby said.

"Look, you two," Barb said. She stood, arms folded, over to the side. "What's going on between you two?"

"Turn about," Bren said darkly, and held up the present. "Shall I open it?"

"Open it," Toby said. "It's not much."

"Oh, we'll see," he said, and carefully edged the ribbon off, and unstuck the paper.

"He's one of *those*," Barb said. "He never will tear the paper."

"Waste not, want not," he said.

"He reuses it, too," Toby said. "Come on, Brcn. Just rip it."

He reached the box, carefully, ever so carefully folded the paper and laid it on the mantel with the ribbon. Then he opened the box.

A pin, of all things, an atcvi-style stickpin. Gold, with three what-might-be diamonds.

He was astonished.

"Where on earth?" he asked.

"Well," Toby said, "I had it made. Is it proper? Kabiu? I asked the linguistics department at the University."

"The paidhi's color," he said. "It counts as white. Kabiu, right down to the numbers. Now what am I going to do to get back at you on *your* birthday?"

"I got my present," Toby said. "I got my brother back."

"You did," he said, and gavc Toby another hug, and offered—not without the hindbrain in action—his other arm to Barb, and hugged them both. "Fortunate three. Two's unlucky. Has to be three."

He didn't know how Barb liked that remark, but it was fair enough, and Toby duly hugged him back, and Barb did, and he hoped Jago didn't throw him out of bed that night.

"All right," he said, disengaging, "that's a thorough quota of family hugs for the next couple of weeks. I'll see you off to sea in good style, but we've got to be proper in the staff's eyes in the meanwhile. Banichi and Jago understand us, but the staff, I assure you, would be aghast, and trying to parse it all in very strange ways. I'm going to wear this pin tomorrow. I'll wear it in court. I could still get you a lace shirt, brother."

"No. If Barb can't, I won't," Toby said, his arm around Barb at the moment.

"Probably best," he said. He felt better as he went back to his chair, sat down, and took up his brandy. They did the same, chairs near each other. Peace was restored, despite Barb's best efforts to the contrary.

And maybe—maybe he'd actually won a lasting truce and settled something.

"So where did you come in from?" he asked Toby conversationally, and listened comfortably and sipped his brandy—pleasant to hear someone else's adventures instead of having them, the thought came to him. They'd been worried sick about Toby at one point, after Tabini's return to the Bujavid, but he'd turned up, out at sea, doing clandestine things for the human government over on Mospheira, part of a communications network, for one thing, and probably that boat out there still had some of that gear aboard.

His own had a few nonregulation things aboard, too—or had had, before he'd left for space. That was the world they lived in, occasionally dangerous. He hoped for it to stay calm for a few years.

He was abed before Jago came in. Abed, but not asleep: he kept rehearsing the dinner, the business with Barb. He lay in his own comfortable bed, between his own fine sheets, and stared at the ceiling, until Jago was there to improve the view. She stripped out of the last of her uniform and stood there, dark against the faint night light. Rain spattered the windows, rain with a vengeance, hitting the glass in sharp gusts of wind.

"One greatly regrets," he said to that silhouette, unable to read her, but reading the hesitation. "One ever so greatly regrets that unpleasantness this evening, Jago-ji. Barb is, unfortunately, Barb."

"Her man'chi is to you," Jago said, her voice carefully without inflection. "One understands. She places you in a difficult situation. Am I mistaken in this?"

Oddly enough, the atevi view of things said it fairly well. "You are not mistaken," he said. "Very like man'chi. She gravitates to me every time she gets the least chance. But there is anger in it, deep anger. I offended her pride."

"Would it mend matters to sleep with her?" Jago asked.

"Far from it. It would encourage her and make my brother angry. And I feel nothing but anger toward her. Come to bed, Jago-ji."

Jago did settle in, to his relief. Her skin, ordinarily fever warm, was slightly cool, and he rubbed her arm and her shoulder to warm it.

"I might speak to her," Jago said. "Reasonably."

"I shall hold that in reserve," he said. "I think I may have to speak to my brother if this goes on. If she causes him grief . . ."

"It seems likely she will," Jago said.

"Very likely," he said, and sighed. "Barb has good qualities— at best advantage when I appear nowhere on her horizon. Her man'chi, given, is very solid . . ."

"Except to your brother," Jago said.

"Except when I appear," he said.

"Conflicted man'chi," Jago said. "The essence of every machimi."

The dramatic heritage of atevi culture. Plays noted for the quantity of bloodshed.

"Let us try not to have any last act," he said with a sigh. "Not on this vacation."

Jago laughed, soft movement under his hand.

And slid her arm under his ribs, around him, a sinuous, fluid embrace that proved the chill had not gotten inside—a force and slight recklessness that advised him Jago was in a mood to chase Barb right out of the bedroom, in no uncertain terms.

Reckless to a fine edge of what was pleasure, but never over it—and deserving of a man with his mind on her, nowhere else in the universe.

He committed himself, with that sense of danger they hadn't had in bed in, oh, the better part of a year. The storm outside rumbled and cracked with thunder, making the walls shake, and they came together with absolute knowledge of each other—not quietly, nor discreetly, nor even quite safely . . . but very, very satisfyingly.

5

He slept. Really slept.

And in the morning he had a leisurely breakfast—Toby and Barb slept in, but he and Jago were up with the sun, and being joined in the dining room by Banichi, and Tano and Algini, they all five had a very ample country breakfast, absolutely devouring everything on the plates.

"You should consider this your vacation, too, nadiin-ji," he said to his staff over tea. "Arrange to fish, to walk in the garden, to do whatever you like as long as we are here. No place could be safer. I have my office work to do. My brother and his lady will be engaged with me when they finally do wake. I promise not to let them free to harass the staff."

There was quiet laughter, even from Jago, who frowned whenever Barb's name came into question. But Banichi proposed they should go down to the shore and inspect the boat, and see how it was, and Bren said they should do it by turns, because he very well knew that his bodyguard wouldn't consider all going at once.

"Manage to take a fishing pole or two," he said to them. "Catch us our supper, why don't you?"

"And shall you be in your office all day?"

"Oh, I foresee walking in the garden with our guests, or maybe down to the shore, or sharing tea in the sitting room. Nothing too strenuous." In fact, he had some sore spots from last night, and regretted not a one of them. "Just amuse yourselves. I shall assign two servants to the hall, to forestall you having to escort either of them. Just relax. Trust even me to find my way, nadiin-ji. I shall just be going between bedroom, dining hall, and my study."

He sent them off with a gentle laugh . . . sure that, since Banichi and Jago were going to the shore, Tano and Algini were going to be close about, probably finding a place to sit and work on things that interested them . . . and still within call, supposing there should be some sort of emergency. They never quite relaxed. But he tried to encourage it.

He had, first on the agenda, a meeting with the major domo, Ramaso, who brought the household accounts, all balanced and impeccably written . . . the old man never had taken to the computer, but the accounts were simple. The village and the household both sold fish, they bought food and medicines and items for repair, clothing and rope and tackle, they had shipped a boy with a broken arm and a pregnant woman down the coast to medical care, which the estate had paid for, as it bore all such expenses for the village.

All the history of the past months was written in that arithmetic, and told him that the place had prospered, and made do, even during Murini's regime. They sold to neighboring districts, they shipped an increasing amount to Shejidan, recovering the trade they had once enjoyed before the coup, and they maintained a good balance in the accounts.

"Very well done," he said to Ramaso. "Come, nadi-ji, call for tea, sit with me, and tell me all the gossip of the district."

The old man was pleased, and a man brought the tea in an antique and very familiar service with a mountain scene on the teapot . . . there was no end to the things his enterprising staff had smuggled out of Shejidan during the collapse.

"Extraordinary," Bren said. "I greatly enjoy that tea set."

"The staff is pleased, nandi." A sip of tea. "Please visit the storeroom. The moment the irregularities are worked out in the capital, you will have the great majority of your furnishings returned. The Farai got very little of historic value."

He had not been inside that apartment since his return. He had understood the staff had gotten a great deal of his property away, but now that he had reached Najida, there were surprises at every turn, items forgotten and rediscovered. "One is very pleased, very pleased, nadi-ji. Not least to see the faces of staff. One has not forgotten."

"I shall relay that, nandi."

"Thank them, too, for their understanding regarding my brother's companion last night. Her customs are informally Mospheiran. She has no education in the manners of an atevi house. Such actions would rouse no great stir on the island— they are not entirely appropriate to formal occasions, to be quite frank, but they are not, there, scandalous, nor did she understand the nature of the dinner."

Atevi didn't blush, outstandingly, but it was possible that the old man did. At very least he found momentary contemplative interest in a sip of tea. "Indeed, nandi, one will so advise the staff."

"One earnestly hopes to forestall another such event," Bren said. "And one apologizes to the staff. My brother and the lady will guest here—perhaps two weeks, certainly no longer. Kindly station staff in the main hall to see to their comings and goings. During part of that time, I hardly dare wonder if I might leave them here unattended for a day. One is urgently obliged to pay a visit to the neighbors."

That was to say, Lord Geigi's estate, their nearest neighbor— whose regional influence had likely saved the paidhi-aiji's residence during the Troubles, or he might not be sitting sipping tea in this sitting room now.

"You do know, nandi, that Lady Tejo has died."

Geigi's sister Tejo had been in charge, in Geigi's long absence, a fairly young woman, too, though not the most robust in health. "Yes, one did hear that. A loss, especially to that clan. Illness, was it?"

"One is given to understand so."

"Her son is in charge. Beiji? Baiji, is it?"

"Baiji, indeed, nandi. A young man. New in his post, new to responsibility," Ramaso said. And added: "Samiusi clan, on his father's side, nandi, and of a little flightiness that has become a concern to us. One is sure your influence will be as good as his uncle's presence to remind him of responsibilities."

The Samiusi were inland, containing most of the remaining identifiable elements of the Maschi clan, some distance east— no need to jog his memory on that score. All the nuances were important. Alliances outside the coast and somewhat south- ward were uneasy alliances, these days, and the Samiusi had provided Geigi's last wife, who had politicked with the Marid. "Is there some question of Baiji's man'chi?"

"None to speak of," Ramaso said.

"None of his associations?"

"He is young," Ramaso said. "Just a very young man, not in years, but Tejo-daja coddled him extremely. He spends a great deal of his time on his boat, he neglects his purchase debts . . . he simply does not pay his suppliers until the second and third request." Ramaso broke off in some uneasiness. But Najida was one of those suppliers, at least in fish. "One hesitates to speak ill, nandi, but this is a boy who definitely needs a more atten- tive accountant. He was not expected to succeed Tejo for years yet. He was unprepared for this."

"Time I did pay a visit, perhaps." It wouldn't be easy to tell Geigi his nephew was a fool and a dilettante, but his own stron- gest memory of the boy in question was ten years ago, when his mother had had to go upstairs in person to bring a recalcitrant adolescent down to dinner. "Geigi will want to know, nadi-ji, if he delays any further payments. Perhaps one can bring a little fear of clan authority under that roof."

"He seems not a villain, nandi, but one suspects his management is lax. He owes the village some three thousand five hundred fifty-three, in sum."

He blinked. It was a large sum. And it was entirely unpleasant, to go bring the law down on a young fool, the relative of a trusted associate. But he was lord of this district, and the young fool had not well served Lord Geigi, and had brought financial hardship on *his* people, who had their own bills to pay. So there it was, one thing he had to do, and at the earliest.

"Send to Baiji," he said. "I shall write the message myself, and visit him in five days. The letter alone may jar the late payments out of him. Then we can have a much happier visit, and he may be more careful of our accounts. The lord of *this* estate has been absent. Perhaps that has encouraged him to believe our people can wait for payment. One expects we can change his priorities."

They had their tea. He turned aside at the last to pen, with fair calligraphy, salutations from a neighbor and the intent to visit five days hence . . . with absolutely no mention of the debt. He delivered that to Ramaso for delivery by courier. "One has not mentioned the money, but if it does not arrive before the day, advise me, nadi-ji, and it will assuredly arrive, if Lord Geigi has to be the source of the instruction."

"Nandi," the old man said in some satisfaction, and took the message, to properly encase it in a cylinder and send it.

Five days was notice enough.

And five days from now he might be ready for a day's vacation from Barb . . . but he tried not to borrow trouble. He found his briefcase, his reading, and his notepad, and called for a second, contemplative pot of tea—to cool mostly untouched, as he read up on cell phone and wireless technology, and tried to frame a persuasive arguement for the legislators.

All the while he had a Guild pocket com on his person. But that was a security matter—that connected him to his long-suffering bodyguard, who, with that connection, could let him out of their sight for at least half an hour at a time, and know he could still reach them instantly.

There was one legitimate use for the technology—if it saved the life of a lord on whom the aishidi'tat relied.

It would not be a legitimate use, however, to shortcut the process of informing, for instance, young Baiji. One could, in hot blood, call up, call the young man a fool, demand immediate payment, and, due to startling the young man and embarrassing him, have a nasty quarrel on one's hands that might force even a reasonable Lord Geigi to take his own estate's side.

A beautifully written note, in a courtly hand, in a message cylinder that bore the identification of the paidhi-aiji and the Lord of the Heavens—reminding said young fool who he was dealing with, and all the associations involved—gave the young fool time to panic as to the content of the message, to cool down, figure out that owing money was not the best frame of mind in which to meet one of his uncle's closest allies. So with any sensitivity at all, he would pay up, and create the best possible mood in which to meet his visitor . . .

He could hardly use that example in his speech to the legislature. But it was the heart of the problem. There were ways of doing things. Old ways, graceful ways. And not every ateva born was gifted with verbal restraint—to say the least. Things went through channels for a reason.

On the other hand . . . atevi had wisely concluded that phones, however convenient for summoning an airport bus, reaching the space station or the Island, or notifying a receptive associate of an imminent Situation, were *not* for social calls, and ought *not* to replace the appropriate hand delivery of a written, courteous message in its identifying case.

Which was precisely the argument proponents were going to throw back at him. Atevi had coped with regular, nonportable phones.

Portable, into any inappropriate situation—there was the problem.

The speed of wireless messages could accelerate a security

situation out of safe limits, or enable the involvement of non-Guild in Assassins' Guild operations. That was one great fear.

That the young would take to the wireless as a way to save effort, as they had on Mospheira, thus undermining the traditional, conflict-reducing forms of messaging . . . that was a worry. That it would accelerate the exchange of information into an exchange of misinformation or half information—the evening news managed that. On a national scale, at times.

People could get killed over bad information. Information and the misconstruction of information was, history told him, exactly the sort of thing that had led humans and atevi to war—bad information coming too fast, too easy interaction, too many people who *thought* they understood each other.

People communicating without going through channels, obviating the office of the clan lords, making independent contact . . . because humans had no reciprocal institution and didn't want one.

Fracture, of the atevi way of life. Fracture of the associations . . . fracture of the social structure.

Chaos. And reacting on micro-information, only *part* of the information . . . and the other side reacting, and this side reacting . . .

Disaster. *There* was his argument. It was . . .

A slight rap at the door, a servant signaling entry, possibly to see if he wanted more tea.

It was Ramaso himself.

"A phone call has arrived, nandi," Ramaso said, his aged face much in earnest. "The aiji's staff requests you to speak to the aiji."

God. *That* couldn't be good news. He got up and went immediately to the phone on the study desk.

"This is the paidhi-aiji," he said, and on the other end:

"One moment, nandi."

Then, deeply and distinctly: *"Bren-paidhi?"*

"Aiji-ma," he said. His pulse was up. He controlled his breathing with a mindful effort.

"*My son,*" the aiji began, "*is on a train headed for the coast.*"

Breath stopped. He wasn't sure what to say, or what change of the aiji's plans this represented. But he knew Cajeiri, and five would get you ten—

"Have you sent him, aiji-ma?"

"*We have not,*" Tabini said, understandably hot. "*He left in the night, on a freight train, changed at the north Shejidan station for a westbound freight, he and his two associates, and they are quite clearly on their way to visit* you, *nandi. The aiji-dowager has ordered her plane to turn around in mid-flight. Our staffs are in an uproar—justifiably.*"

He was aghast. The danger, the chance just of accident, let alone the boy's exposure to the aiji's enemies—

"One will meet the train, aiji-ma, and personally escort him back."

A pause. A lengthy pause. "*You have guests under your roof. We shall send an escort.*" A sigh. "*If you can intercept him, likely we can persuade his great-grandmother to resume her trip to Malguri. Can you bear with my son for five days?*"

Tabini could get people there far faster than that—could fly them out to meet that train, if need be. Could stop that train with a phone call and have the local constabulary pick up his son. Tabini was giving the young rascal a little extra rein—and likely his plan to get Ilisidi safely settled back in Malguri before the legislative session drew her attention would be easier if he could tell the dowager that the boy was going to be absent. But that five days . . .

Conflicted directly with his scheduled visit to Lord Baiji. That could be adjusted. But it was socially difficult.

"One would certainly do so, aiji-ma," he said. "But shall I treat this as a proper visit?"

"*Yes,*" came the exasperated answer. "*If the paidhi is pleased to have one more guest.*"

"Then may one ask, with trepidation under the circumstances, aiji-ma, that he remain with us seven days. There are local commitments I have already made for the fifth day, a visit to a neighbor that I cannot gracefully break, but within a seven days' stay, I can entertain your son in good style, take him on the fishing trip I promised him, as well as honor my other guests, and make my appointment with my neighbor."

"If the paidhi is so patient as to accommodate my son, yes, do so. Seven days. But speak to him, paidhi-ji, speak to him very strongly. Perhaps you can make him understand the hazards he runs in such reckless ventures."

"One absolutely understands, aiji-ma." He added, on an afterthought: "Aiji-ma, one hopes nothing I personally said to him can possibly be construed as—"

"Encouragement? Paidhi-ji, the presence of Guild at the doors did not dissuade him! The presence of the aiji-dowager did not dissuade him! Gods less fortunate! My certain displeasure did not dissuade him! We have no doubt this thought sprang full-formed from his own mind, and he used his great-grandmother's activities for a screen to his operations. What can anyone do? Seven days, restraining my son! You have my condolences, paidhi-ji!"

"Aiji-ma, I will at least keep him safe until the escort arrives to take him home."

"Do so, paidhi-ji! Perhaps a little country exercise will purge the energy from him. Faultless for a whole month and now this! He is far too clever for his own good."

"I shall do my utmost, aiji-ma."

"Brave paidhi," Tabini said. *"The train is the noon freight from Tolabi. Fortune attend you."* Which said, Tabini hung up.

Bren set the receiver carefully back in the cradle and looked at his anxious major domo.

"We shall be meeting the noon freight," he said, "since the aiji's son has decided to visit us, in company with his young escort. He will be here seven days. The two escorts are youths in their teens, brother and sister, both in Guild training."

"Nandi." A bow, a deep bow, with not a word of question. He had as well announced the young gentleman was landing by spacecraft.

A freight train. There was no possible claim, within the staff, that it was a visit originally sanctioned and arranged by the aiji.

"The young gentleman is resourceful and determined," Bren said, "and we shall do our utmost to keep him entertained and out of trouble. One promised him a fishing trip, once. One believes he has come to ask us to fulfill that promise. See that the boat is ready."

Keeping the young rascal out at sea could guarantee at least things on land were safe for a day or so. Toby and Barb were at their best, in their own element. He could deal with both problems.

Then he remembered . . .

"Have you already dispatched the message to nand' Baiji?"

Comprehension dawned in the old man's eyes. "Regretfully, yes, nandi, one has done so."

"By all means, and no fault at all. Well, we shall manage both things. We have time enough for me to keep my commitment to Lord Baiji, if you can keep the young gentleman and his companions safely contained. And—"

The door opened without ceremony. Toby and Barb walked in together.

"I guess we're way too late for breakfast," Toby said.

"Certainly in time for lunch," he said, attempting brisk good cheer, "in a very little while." Work was clearly impossible this morning. He addressed Ramaso, in Ragi, "I shall be meeting the noon freight personally, nadi-ji. Is there possibly time for Saba to manage lunch for us?"

Ramaso looked at the clock on the wall, and gave a little bow. "Easily. Easily, nandi. Shall I inform your bodyguard regarding the other matter?"

"Do so, nadi-ji," he said, and mustered a bright smile for Toby and Barb. "Well, lunch fairly quickly, as seems. I have to make a run to the train station at noon. Would you care for a cup of tea? I'd intended to take you out to the grounds for a tour today, but it's not that long 'til lunch, I'll imagine, and things are not running on schedule today."

"Tea's welcome," Toby said, and he and Barb found adjacent chairs. Bren gave a last instruction to Ramaso to send in hot tea and folded up his work before he sat down.

"What's the project you're on?" Toby asked.

"Upcoming legislature," he said. "A little speechmaking. Did you sleep well?"

"Having the floor quiet is odd," Barb said. "It rained last night. And thundered. We've spent so long on the boat. I keep thinking—it's thundering: we have to wake up and check the weather."

Bren gave a little laugh and sat down. "Well, please don't develop bad habits! I can at least assure you this place won't sink. And we may be taking a little fishing trip, likely an overnight, out into the strait. Cajeiri is arriving."

"*He's* coming?" Toby asked. "I don't recall you said that you had a state visitor. Maybe we shouldn't be here."

"No, no," he said, "it's rather unexpected, and you're perfectly welcome here. You're a useful distraction, in fact: he'll be delighted to practice his command of Mosphei' on you, and he'll be full of questions. I hope you don't mind."

"No, not at all. He's a nice kid."

"He's a nice kid," Bren agreed. As if that adequately summed up the heir to the aishidi'tat. "I'll pick him up at the train station after lunch, get him settled in—he'll be in the bedroom next to mine. I'll manage the noise level."

"Is the dowager coming, too?"

"No. *She's* supposed to be on her way to the East. Which is good, because we're running out of bedrooms." He didn't intend to tell Toby or Barb all the details—though probably Cajeiri would manage to—the whole tale of his adventure. "I hope you don't mind the extra guests. Cajeiri, his two attendants—teenagers, those two. You haven't met them. They're good kids, too."

"I don't mind," Toby said with a curiously fervent tone. "Not at all."

Toby had kids. Or he had had kids, before the divorce, Bren thought. Damn, he hadn't at all meant to hit that nerve: he hadn't sensed, in fact, that it was quite that live a nerve with Toby. But he had certainly hit it, Barb wasn't looking happy, either, and it was just time to change the subject.

"Well, I'll do my local business, we'll let the youngsters explore the grounds and maybe go down to the village that day if you don't mind being escort. I'm having the staff go over my boat today, be sure it's in good order for a fishing run."

"Our boat is certainly available," Toby said.

"Thank you for that. It can certainly be our fallback if they find anything amiss with mine. So we'll have an early lunch and you can do whatever you like and wait for us to get back from the train station—not a long trip at all, if the train's running on time. We'll probably be doing another small snack for the youngsters. They'll most likely arrive hungry." Since they were traveling by freight, illegally, it was a good bet they would be hungry. "We can just sit here and wait for lunch, meanwhile. My bodyguard is off and about on a little relaxation. They don't get to do that very often—but I promised them I'd stay to my study and give them a little chance to go where they like. I can't break that promise: they almost never get a holiday."

"Oh, well," Barb said, "just sitting still is good."

"So what *is* the news from the Island?" Bren asked, for a complete change of subject. "Gossip is welcome."

"Oh, not so much," Toby said, and then proceded to fill him in on two complex legislative scandals and the failure of a large corporation that had profited and ballooned mostly on the anticipation of the Crescent Island settlement actually working: it hadn't. Buildings stood vacant down there.

And the Human Heritage Party wasn't dead, it seemed, and had gotten all stirred up about the action of the station in dropping surveillance packets all over the map—what amounted to robotic surveillance, and communications outposts. They'd been sure that was an atevi plot, engineered by atevi on the station—that would have been Lord Geigi.

In point of fact, Lord Geigi had helped target the drops on the mainland, but the plan had been to provide surveillance and communication *for* forces loyal to Tabini duing the uprising—a plan that hadn't turned out to be needed, but it had created controversy on both sides of the straits.

And meanwhile, indeed, as Toby had told him, cell phones had become the rage on Mospheira. Communications had improved. Privacy . . . well, in Toby's view, he liked being out of range of phone calls.

"About forty miles off the coast is good," Toby said.

"The wireless phone issue has become a problem here," Bren said, "and certain concerns think it might be a good idea. I don't. I'm preparing an opposition to it. Which is what I'm doing in my spare time on this vacation. Stopping cell phones."

"I don't mind them," Barb ventured to say, "if we're out shopping."

"Finding one another is a convenience," Toby said.

"And the ordinary ateva doesn't have a bodyguard," Bren said, "but he doesn't go about alone, either—people are just not inclined to split up on an outing. It's just the way of things."

"So what *are* Banichi and Jago up to?" Toby asked.

"*Fishing*, I hope. They so rarely get the chance to relax and enjoy themselves. Tano and Algini, too. They might even go shopping in the village—it's one thing I *don't* do. And if they have done that—I may have to violate my own position on cell phones and use the com to track them down. They won't forgive me if I go off cross-country without them."

"Shopping?" Barb asked. But a light rap came at the door. Ramaso entered, announcing lunch.

So that was their morning. They actually had an enjoyable lunch. Barb did nothing outrageous, he and Toby and Barb talked about good fishing grounds just off the peninsula, and Toby and Barb proposed to go down to their boat and do some housekeeping in the case the young lord wanted to see their boat again, too—a good bet, that was.

Anything that took them out of the way of staff, Bren thought unworthily, but he was relieved to be relatively sure they'd be busy for a few hours.

But he had to phone down the hill to tell Banichi and Jago the news—and interrupt their small moment of leisure.

"By freight!" was Banichi's only, somewhat exasperated remark when they all four arrived in the study. Jago said nothing. Nor did Tano and Algini. The four of them went outside the door, probably to consult staff, while Bren, with the servants' help, dressed for an informal reception.

Not a reception at the station platform, on Banichi's advice on the event, but just a little short of it . . . assuming the enterprising youngsters had made their connection and actually gotten off the train at the proper stop.

6

They waited in the estate bus, the three of them, on the grassy side of the dirt road just out of sight of the station, which was on the other side of the hill. It was a pleasant place to wait: sea grass, dune-like little hills, a view of the bay . . . the bus afforded them a pleasant place to sit, given the afternoon air was a bit nippy. Last night's storm had long since swept on eastward, and the sky was sparkling blue with a few straggling clouds. Looking out the back window of the bus, Bren watched those clouds float eastward, chasing their larger, angrier brothers. Another, larger front was due in. He hoped it wouldn't scotch their plans. He was keeping an eye to the weather reports—kept an eye to the west, from this vantage, and still saw no cloud.

They'd dropped Tano and Algini *at* the station. But Tano and Algini wouldn't intercept the young scoundrels there, just tail them and be sure nobody else met the train . . . and also ensure that the train didn't get out of the station without dropping said young scoundrels.

Sure enough, Banichi reported a confirming signal from Tano, and in due time the youngsters crested the hilltop, marching right along as if they owned the countryside. Their jaunty step slowed a bit as they faced the unexpected bus.

Good. They were thinking self-defensively. But they were a little obvious, in mid-road, and stopping like that, as if they *didn't* belong here.

Bren got up, walked forward in the bus, slightly downhill; Jago got up ahead of him and went down the steps first, stepping down to the outside. Bren took hold of the rail and himself descended the tall steps, jumping down to Jago's steadying hand. Banichi meanwhile took over the driver's seat, just a precaution, always, in case of a quick getaway.

No need of that, however. Bren walked along the pebbled dirt as far as the tail of the bus, Jago staying with him. He waited there so their three visitors now could plainly see who was waiting for them—and add up for themselves the fact that their coming had been announced . . . they could well guess by whom, and they could judge for themselves that now they might be in a spot of trouble. They might indeed have been in for a U-turn back to the train station or, more likely, a fast trip to the local airport . . . if Cajeiri's father had been in a bad mood.

Two more walkers appeared on the hill behind the three youngsters—adult, in Assassins' black. That was Tano and Algini, proceeding at a sedate pace, following the road from the train station.

Bren hadn't wanted to make a scene of the meeting, or widely advertise their young visitors. They simply waited for the youngsters to show up—there was one road in the district that led to Najida from the train station, and this was, indeed, it, the single way any visitor to Najida or to Najidami Bay had to come.

So Bren waited for them, arms folded as they started walking again, deciding not to wait for Tano and Algini, and in due time the youngsters arrived at the bus. They all three bowed politely, and he bowed—Jago did not, in the icy chill of her professional manner—and then he looked Cajeiri straight in the eye.

"Young gentleman?" he said grimly.

An apprehensive look. "My father surely called you, nandi."

"He did, young lord. Surely you don't think the Guild in his service couldn't trace a railroad train."

Deep breath. The young miscreant had had a long train ride

in which to put together a story. One was interested to hear what it would be.

"Great-grandmother is going away to Malguri. Great-uncle is in your apartment by now."

"*His* apartment, young lord. This seems a natural enough situation."

"So it is, but it was rude of him all the same, and we support *you,* nandi!"

God, the boy was going to be a politician, no question about it. "And by coming to me in this fashion to say so, you risked your life, the lives and reputations of your associates, and bring me into disrepute as abetting this mischief, not to mention the instability to the aishidi'tat should some enemy find you and call your father seeking an exchange of favors."

"My father cannot possibly blame you, nandi! One will strongly protest any such injustice! And we were very discreet. No enemy would expect us on a freight train. They would be watching the red car."

"Your father called this morning," he said dryly, in the face of this cheeky assurance. "He did *not* blame me, nor my influence, and gave you five days here, young gentleman—"

"Ha!" Cajeiri cried, turning to his unwilling accomplices, beaming with delight. "Five days! *Thank you,* nandi!"

"The young gentleman should thank his father on his return . . ."

"We shall, oh, we shall, nand' paidhi!"

"*Not* in words, but by renewed application to lessons! Is this agreed? Is this solemnly agreed, young lord? One cannot countenance supporting this notion otherwise!"

He caught Cajeiri with his mouth open. It shut, and Cajeiri looked at him and evidently saw, indeed, that there were two ways to go from here, only one of which would offer him the whole hospitality of the estate. Evidently he saw this choice before him, since his expression evolved into due caution, and he bowed in sober acceptance.

"One agrees, nand' paidhi."

"And will one remember, when one returns and the lessons are particularly boring?"

"One will remember, nand' paidhi."

"Then you are very welcome, young lord. We have asked, and been granted, two extra days of your company . . . fortunate seven, in all."

"Oh, *excellent, most excellent*, nandi! You are the best, the cleverest—"

"We seem to have promised you a day or two on the boat, among other things."

"You see, nadiin-ji?" Cajeiri addressed Antaro and Jegari, who had looked throughout as if they wanted to sink into the damp earth of the roadway. And by now Tano and Algini had arrived, so that the young lord's security-in-training had to have it stamped very clearly in their minds that they had been observed by Guild as they got off the train, and they had been observed all the while taking the road toward Najida, walking down the plain middle of it as they had been. They had had time to reflect that had Tano and Algini not been the paidhi's own security, they might have been very, very sorry, and completely unable to defend their young lord. It was very, very likely that his bodyguard would impress that observation on the two in a private conversation yet to come.

The two certainly bowed, bowed deeply and respectfully when those two joined the party.

"Let us go," Bren said, and led them back to the front of the bus.

Everyone piled onto the bus. Jago, resuming her seat, drove, and they made a bumpy descent toward the shore road, a brisk clip which delighted the youngsters. Cajeiri asked questions all the way: whether there might be wi'itikin in the sea cliffs— there were not: the flying creatures were more common in the East, and would not prosper where a gliding dive ended in the water. And were there fish in the bay? There were, abundantly so. And was that to the left Lord Geigi's land, or his?

"It is mine, young lord, and you may even see the adjacent estate during your stay—one is, as a neighbor and associate of Lord Geigi, obliged to pay a visit there in a few days. You hardly had a chance to meet Lord Geigi on the station; but it may be useful, in coming years, for his nephew to have met you."

"Is he my age?"

"One regrets, no, much older. But still a useful association, to you and to him." The visit of the heir to the aishidi'tat would make a deep impression, even on a dim-witted newly-made lord, besides enhancing the nephew's reputation locally. It would give Cajeiri a sense of the man—for good or for ill.

"But, nandi, you promised we could go fishing."

"And that we shall, young lord. We shall spend this night at the estate, and tomorrow early we shall go on the boat, spend all day fishing and spend the night at sea, weather permitting. That is the plan. How will you like that?"

"Very much, nandi!" He turned to his young cohorts. "See? We shall have our fishing trip!"

He had the young rascal's thorough cooperation now, he was sure . . . a little carrot, when the boy had, perhaps, had too much stick over the last few months.

The boy's presence would give his household a focus, too, other than Barb's latest misdeeds.

And Cajeiri, having lived two years among the ship-humans, was far easier in the face of human habits, far harder to shock. One only hoped he didn't learn anything new.

It was an excellent plan, over all, an excellent solution: they all wanted something to do—to keep him and Barb from unpleasant conversation. They could be doing something besides sipping tea and staring at each other. There would be bait to have ready, lines and poles and fishing-chairs to set up, all manner of things that would keep them busy . . . there would be the work to talk about. And Cajeiri's questions to answer. Cajeiri's endless questions.

So. That would all work out splendidly . . . a happy visit, after all.

They wended their way past the first view of the harbor. Cajeiri, of course, had to bounce out of his seat to that set of windows and ask which was his boat and which was Toby's.

"Toby's is the one farthest out," he answered the question.

That started a spate of reminiscences from Cajeiri—who had to tell his companions how he had caught a poisonous fish and scared everyone—understandably, since the lad had swung it all about the deck, including into the vicinity of the dowager. Guild training included many implements of assassination: live fish were, perhaps, a first.

Toby's boat was where this adventure had happened, and there were bedrooms under the deck and the galley was just under the bridge, and you could sleep under the waterline, and they might do that, since they were going to spend the night on nand' Bren's boat . . . all this flowed out of Cajeiri in about one breath.

"And shall we sleep underwater, nandi?" Cajeiri asked.

Bren nodded agreement. "You may, if you choose, young lord." His own boat had sleeping only for nine, and that was going to be room enough to put the youngsters below: but somebody was going to have to sleep on deck, if Barb and Toby came along, as he expected them to do. Problems, and possibly they should use Toby's boat, which accommodated a larger number. But the problems were small ones, and he had promised Cajeiri *his* boat, now that Cajeiri had made the crossing of the straits on Toby's boat—one learned, with the heir, that such details in a promise were a gate through which a whole mecheita could be ridden, sooner or later.

They came down the hill toward the drive, and swept up to the front door, which was a paved stretch. Barb and Toby came out with the staff to meet them, and as Bren got off the bus with Jago and Banichi right in front of him, the young rascal clattered down the steps after him, waved an arm and shouted out, "Hi, Toby! Hi, Barb!"

It was not Toby and Barb that Cajeiri shocked. Ramaso looked completely set aback, others of the staff looked from one side to the other, as Toby called out, in Mosphei', "Hello there! How was your trip?"

"Pretty good," Cajeiri said in a ship-speak accent and let Toby clap hands on his arms. "This time we rode in a car with *canned* food."

Last time had been iced fish. That was true. Bren laughed. Toby and Barb looked puzzled.

And there was the important matter of manners to account for. Bren said, under his breath: "Courtesies to the staff, if you please, young lord."

Cajeiri immediately refocused himself, disengaged, and spotted the important-looking staff quite accurately. Having been properly noticed, they bowed. Cajeiri bowed in return, that slight degree high rank dictated, and Bren said,

"This is Tabini-aiji's son and heir, Cajeiri. Nandi, this is Ramaso, the major domo of my estate, who bids you welcome."

"Indeed. One is very pleased to be here." A second slight bow from the young rascal. "One has heard so much, nadi. Nand' Bren has told me all about Najida. And he has promised me fishing tomorrow, on his boat."

"Then that there will be, young lord," Ramaso said. "The boat is fueled and being made ready, stocked with everything you could wish. And Cook offers a light snack ready, on the chance that young folk may have arrived hungry from such a long trip. Or there is a bath drawn, and a suite made ready should you wish a little rest."

"Food, nadi! Food, indeed, and one is most grateful!"

"Perhaps the bath should come first," Bren said, in his capacity as the adult in charge. All three were grimy, and their luggage, which Jegari had carried aboard the bus and off again, consisted of a single duffle, which was hardly enough for the three for seven days. "And staff may sort out your wardrobe." God only knew what condition the clothes were in by now, in a soft duffle, and packed by these three. "Surely the food may wait an hour more."

"But we're *starved!*" Cajeiri protested in ship-speak, and Bren said, in courtly Ragi:

"A snack, perhaps, delivered bathside. But *baths*, young gentleman, are definitely in order." The visible dirt, and the slight air about the three youngsters was *not* going into Ramaso's tidy dining room. "I am quite firm on this matter, young lord."

"Well, we shall eat in the tub. Shall Antaro bathe with us? Shall she not have as good as Jegari and I?"

"There is the backstairs bath ready," Ramaso said. "It is quite a fine bath, nandi."

"Perfectly adequate," Bren said firmly, "and Antaro will have a maid's attendance, and everything sent from the kitchen just as quickly as you. Trust my good staff, young lord, to offer no slight to yours."

Cajeiri looked at him, and if said young imp had ever observed that Jago shared a bath and a bed with him, and should now mention it, the fishing trip would be in decided jeopardy. Bren made the limits clear in the eye-to-eye glance he returned—Cajeiri being, at eight years of age, about on eye level with him.

The momentary imp faded and left a perfectly agreeable and sensible boy standing there. That boy bowed quite courteously. "We shall be extremely sensible of the honor of your house, nand' Bren. And we shall not behave badly. We are grateful you were willing to receive us and especially—especially that you felicitously improved the number of our days."

The imperial we, the language of a century ago, courtly language: that was the dowager's two years of intense schooling. And the rest of that courtly extravagance? Who knew?

"One is gratified, young lord. You should understand that

your esteemed father gave me no chance to ask for the first five days. Your *father* suggested them himself."

That honestly surprised the boy. "Why did he? Do you know, nandi?"

"Perhaps because he was once your age, and understands the weight of the Bujavid on young shoulders. Perhaps because the world is now somewhat safer than it was, and he wishes you to have a healthy respite from schooling—before the legislature goes into session and the Bujavid exerts itself in even tighter security. He is not ignorant of your considerable accomplishments and your personal efforts over recent months. One believes, in short, it may be a reward in earnest of good behavior."

Several thoughts flitted through those amber eyes, one of them being, surely, My father is not that tolerant of my misdeeds, and another being, Adults in the world are surely all up to something.

"You doubt my truthfulness, young lord?"

"One certainly would not call the paidhi a liar!"

This from a lad who had grown up where a strong word could bring bloodfeud.

"One would never expect so. One offers one's personal assessment of the situation. And one hopes for you and yours to be very happy in this visit. We *shall* have our fishing trip. And if there had been any advance warning, I should never have scheduled the visit to the neighbors. But perhaps it will not be too boring for you. They will certainly be very excited to meet *you*. In the meanwhile, we shall have a reasonably early supper tonight, then board the boat in the morning and put out to the head of the bay for some fishing, then out into the wide ocean—well, the straits, which is as large a piece of it as we need—and a little wide-open sailing for the evening. There should be a fair wind beyond the harbor mouth and we shall use the sails."

"Has it an engine?"

"It does, as does Toby's, but the sails are the best going."

Cajeiri's eyes fairly danced. "One wishes we might stay out for days and days!"

"I shall show you how to steer the boat."

Truly danced. "We shall be extraordinarily careful, doing so, nand' Bren!"

"Off with you. Wash! Thoroughly!"

"Yes!" Cajeiri said, and was off like a shot, cheerful and eager.

Bren looked at Jago, and at Banichi, who had just come in. Both looked amused.

"It seems very likely the young gentleman and his companions will wish to see the grounds and tour the building before dark. An escort would minimize trouble . . . and keep them off the boat during preparations."

Banichi laughed outright. "Gladly," Banichi said.

Banichi had more than once shepherded the boy on the starship, but he had had very little time to spend time with Cajeiri since their return, and it was a fortunate solution on all sides. Jago said she would happily rest for a few hours, Tano and Algini were due a chance to go down to the shore, and take in what staff was doing with the boat. So all in all, it was a relatively well-arranged day.

The little hiatus for the youngsters to have their bath and take a tour provided him—granted there was no chance of resuming his speech-writing—time with Toby alone, possibly the chance to have a cautioning word or two with Toby, in fact, and to find out how things stood between them, granted he'd been back on the planet for months and hadn't had a chance to have a conversation that wasn't witnessed, managed, or otherwise inconvenient. There was so much they'd never had a chance to discuss: their mother's last days, when he'd been absent; Toby's divorce, when he'd been absent; Toby's meeting up with Barb, when he'd been absent. . . .

And in his imagining this meeting during the long years of the voyage, there'd been all sorts of time for them to sit and talk and reestablish contact. Now—

Now he was down to a few hours before dinner on *this* day, before two days or so on the boat with Cajeiri and a day he'd be at the neighboring estate . . . all of which was adding up to most of a week, when Toby wasn't going to be here that long. His chances to see Toby for the next number of months would be scant and the chance of something else intervening beyond that was high.

And the longer some things went unsaid, the worse. He didn't particularly look forward to doing it—but if they let one more meeting go by without ever reforging the links they'd once had—

Well, it just got harder and harder to bring up the topic of his two-year absence, harder for him to find out what had gone on, harder for him and Toby to discuss family business. Harder to be anything but old friends who'd somewhere lost the "brother" part of it all.

They could become more distant than that, if events intervened and made their contacts rarer still. If Toby married Barb, and finally settled. It was a good thing in that sense that Toby had taken to the boat, and lived from port to port. He didn't know what in hell income his brother was living off of—whether the government runs kept him in fuel and dockage and repairs. And he didn't ask. Maybe Barb brought in resources. He hoped she did something constructive.

And he really, really wanted not to have Barb in the conversation.

Sure enough, Barb was there when he gave a single rap on the door and walked in on her and Toby in the sitting room of their suite. She was in the act of getting up, perhaps to answer the door—not the atevi way of things. Lacking the formality of a servant's attendance, and he had absently signaled the maid on duty in the hall that he would not require that—the caller would open the door himself, if it was not locked; and he had done that. He bowed—not their way of things: the bow was as reflexive as the lift of the hand instructing the servant.

"Having a good morning?" he asked.

"A relaxing morning." Barb went back to sit on the arm of Toby's chair, a detriment to fine furniture. Absolute anathema to the staff.

He decided not to say anything. It just led to unpleasantness. And he might not, unless he had Barb dropped in the bay, *get* a chance at Toby alone.

So he did the only thing he could do, decided on intervention, and pulled the cord before he sat down, calling staff to serve a pot of tea.

"I really don't like tea that well," Barb said after the door had shut again.

"Well, it's a bit early for brandy," he said.

"Your *rules*," Barb said with a little laugh, and finally got off the hand-embroidered chair arm, Toby's hand following her, and trailing off the ends of her fingers. "Rules, rules, rules."

He smiled, not in the least amused. "They're everywhere, I'm afraid." And got down to basic business. "The staff is still prepping the boat. Tano and Algini will be down there supervising. I hope you'll go along on this trip. I've rather assumed you both would."

"Sure," Toby said. "Of course we will."

"The two youngsters with Cajeiri haven't likely seen water larger than ponds. I hope they won't be seasick. Probably they won't be: they're athletic youngsters. I promised the boy specifically my boat, or we might all of us fit without sleeping bags. But at least one person's going to end up sleeping on the deck . . . probably one of my staff."

"I don't mind the deck," Toby said, "but Barb would want a cabin."

Notably, Barb did not chime in with, oh, no, the deck would be fine.

"No question," Bren said. "And my staff won't let me do it, I'm afraid. The kids may want to. It's an adventure to them. I wouldn't turn them down. My staff deserves soft beds. But they assuredly won't let you do it, Toby. Kids are one thing—it's play for them. But you're nand' Toby. Won't do at all. Dignity and all. Although they did talk about sleeping below the waterline. I think the notion intrigues them."

"Just the security people are going?" Barb asked.

"Just the four. House staff will be busy here."

"Not too much for them to do without us," Toby said.

"Oh, they're busy: they have the village to look after, too. Not to mention setting things up for the upcoming visit to Kajiminda—that's Geigi's estate. They'll be seeing the bus is in order, that the road over there is decent, all of that. There may be some potholes to fix. Given the recent rain, that's likely. They arrange things like that . . . and that road only gets used maybe once a week, if that." The tea arrived, and service went around, to Barb as well.

"All right," Toby said. "Once a week. Why once a week?"

"Market day in the village. The Kajiminda staff will come over and buy supplies. We have the only fish market on the peninsula."

"Here?" Barb asked.

"The village." Inspiration struck him. "You asked about shopping. I suppose you might like to do that."

"Can we?"

"Well, it's fairly basic shops. There's a fish market, a pottery, a cordmaker's, a weaver's, a woodcrafts shop and a beadmaker . . . I should send you with one of the maids. They'll take you to places they know and I don't."

Barb's eyes had gotten considerably brighter. He got up and pulled the cord again, and when the maidservant outside appeared: "Barb-daja would like to go shopping. Kindly take Barb-daja to the market. Just let her buy what she wants on the estate account. Walk with her, speak for her, and keep her safe and out of difficulty, Ika-ji. Take two of the men with you."

The maid—Ikaro was her name—looked both diffident and

cheerful at the prospect—bowed to Barb, and stood immediately waiting.

"Get a wrap," Bren said. "It's nippy. People will be curious about you. Just smile, buy what you like or what you might need for the boat. Provisions. I'd meant to send those with you, as was. Pick up some of the local jellies—Ikaro will make sure you get the right ones. —Ika-ji, she may buy foods: no alkaloids."

"Yes, nandi."

"Toby?" Barb asked.

"Is it safe?" Toby asked. "You always say—"

"The village is only over the hill and very safe. The men are just to carry packages, in case," he added with a grin at Barb, "you decide to bring back sacks of flour. Just enjoy yourself. Buy something nice for yourself. You're on the estate budget. Get something for Toby, too, if you spot something." He went near and said, into Barb's ear: "There's a very good little tackle shop."

Barb was honestly delighted. She disappeared into the bedroom, with the disconcerted maid in pursuit, and came back with a padded jacket and gloves—and Ikaro.

"You're sure you'll be all right?" Toby said, getting to his feet.

"I'll be perfectly fine," she said, and proceeded to mortally embarrass the maid by kissing Toby on the mouth, not briefly either, and with a lingering touch on Toby's cheek. "You be good while I'm gone."

"I have no choice," Toby said with a laugh, and the little party got out the door—which shut, and left a small silence behind.

"You're sure she'll be all right," Toby said.

"My staff would die before they let harm come to her," he said, and sat down and poured a little warmup into his teacup. He had a sip, as Toby settled. "I haven't had a chance to talk to you, not really. We've been in rapid motion—certainly were, the last time we met. It's been a little chaotic, this time."

Toby wasn't stupid. Far from it. He gave an assessing kind of look, beyond a doubt knowing that he'd just maneuvered Barb out the door. "Something serious?"

"Just family business. Not much of it. Nothing I could have done but what I did, but I am lastingly sorry, Toby, for leaving you when I did. I don't know what more to say. But I am sorry. I had two years out and back to think about that."

"Hey, you have your job."

"I am what I am. I don't regret much, except I know what you went through. I say I know. I intellectually know. I wasn't there, that's the point, isn't it?"

"I read the journal you gave me," Toby said. "I read every word of it."

Bren gave an uneasy laugh. "The five-hundred page epic?" It was, in fact, hundreds of pages, uncondensed, but deeply edited—compared to what Tabini had gotten: the whole account of his two years in deep space, hauling back unwilling human colonists from where they had run into serious trouble, trying to prevent a culture clash—the one that might eventually land on their doorstep.

The kyo would arrive as promised, he had every anticipation—a species that had come scarily close to war with a colony that hadn't asked before it had established itself too near. A colony their own station had had to swallow—a large and unruly item to try to assimilate, given the attitudes in that bundle of humanity.

But that had nothing to do with the situation he'd left Toby in—their mother's last illness and Toby's wife walking out, with the kids. Two years. Two years, and no more house with the white picket fence, no more wife, no more kids. Barb and the boat, the *Brighter Days* . . .

"It's no excuse," Bren said. "Not from your vantage. Go ahead and say it. I have it coming.

"Say what?" Toby shot back. "Don't put words in my mouth, brother. Don't tell me what I think."

"Maybe you'd tell *me*."

"Which is why you maneuvered Barb out of here? She *is* my life, Bren. Not just your old girlfriend. She's my life."

He didn't like hearing it. But he nodded, accepting it. All of it. "Good for both of you. If she makes you happy—that's all that matters."

"You're not still in love with her."

God. He composed himself and said quietly, "No. Definitely I'm not." And then on to a gentle half-truth. "I hurt her feelings when I broke it off. I was rough about it. She's still mad at me. And she probably doesn't want to admit it." It *didn't* account for Barb making a ridiculous marriage on the rebound, divorcing that man and attaching herself to his and Toby's mother, and then to Toby. And lying to his brother regarding the evident tension between them wasn't a good idea. Toby knew him too well, even if Toby didn't *want* to read Barb, in that regard. The hell of it was, Toby *wasn't* blind, or stupid, and Toby *could* read Barb, which was exactly the problem. "I have every confidence in Barb, when I'm not there provoking her to her worst behavior. Is that honest enough?"

Toby didn't look happy with the assessment. "It's probably accurate."

"Doesn't mean she loves me. You want my opinion?"

"I have a feeling I'm going to get it."

"Not if you don't want it."

"Damn it, Bren. Fire away."

"Barb doesn't turn loose of emotions. She doesn't always identify them accurately. That's always been a problem. She's still charged up about me, but it doesn't add up to love. There was a time we were really close. I've tried to figure what I felt about it, but I'm not sure we ever did get to the love part. Just need-you. A lot of need-you. That was all there ever was. Not healthy for either of us. Now it's done. Over. Completely. Where you take it from there—I have no control over. I don't want any."

Toby nodded. Just nodded. How *much*, Bren asked himself, how much did Toby add up for himself? How far did he see— when he wanted to?

"I don't want to lose my brother," Bren said, as honest as he'd been hedging on the last. "Bottom line. I want you around. As much as can be. I don't make conditions."

Second nod.

"You're mad at me," Bren said. "You don't want to be, but you are. Do you want to talk about it?"

Toby shook his head.

"Is it going to go away?" Bren asked. "I'm not so sure it will, until we do talk about it. Is it Mum?"

Toby didn't look at him on that question.

"It is," Bren said. "I wasn't there. Not only at the last. I wasn't there for years and years before that. Flitting in for a crisis. But you were there every time she needed something. You want my opinion again? You shouldn't have done it."

Toby stopped looking at him. Didn't want to hear it. Never had wanted to hear it.

"Toby, I know it makes you mad. But you were there too often. I'm saying this because I love you. I'm saying this because I was sitting safe and collected on this side of the strait and you were getting the midnight phone calls. I shouldn't say it, maybe. But I think it and I'm being honest."

"Think what you like. How was I going to say no?"

"I wish you had. I wish you had, Toby."

"Shut up. You don't know a thing about it."

He nodded. "All right. I've said enough."

"I deserve a woman who was there when I needed her. Barb was there, at the hospital. She was always there. She wasn't throwing a tantrum every time I had to go and see about Mum. She wasn't pitching a fit in front of the kids. She wasn't talking to them about me while I was in Jackson at the hospital. You want the bloody truth, Bren, it was better there than with Jill."

There was a revelation. The happy home on the beach, the white picket fence, the tidy house and the two kids . . .

Toby went home to mother. No matter how rough "home" got, home wasn't with Jill, not the way Toby remembered things now.

It was also true their mother had had a knack for finding the right psychological moment and ratcheting up the emotional pressure . . . I need you. Oh, I'll get along. I had palpitations, is all. Well, go to the doctor, Mother. Oh, no, I don't need the doctor. Smiles and sunbeams. I'm feeling better. You know I always feel better when you're here . . .

After he'd flown home from the continent in the middle of some crisis, because she had one of her own; and she'd hover right over the breakfast table and praise him to the skies and tell Toby what a good son his brother was—salt in the wounds. Absolute salt in the wounds. She'd had Toby rushing to her side because he never loved her enough, never could equal the sacrifices brother Bren made for her, oh, it was so good when Bren was there. She just sparkled.

Hell.

"I love you," he said to Toby, outright. "I love you even when you're mad at me—which I don't blame you for being. You can take a swing at me, if you like."

"Don't be ridiculous."

"It might clear the air."

"Clear the air, hell! Your bodyguard would blow me to confetti."

"Well, they're actually not here, but if you want to, let's move away from the antique tea service."

"Now you *are* being ridiculous. Don't."

"Well, but I'll specifically instruct my bodyguard that if you ever do take a swing at me, they're to let you. You've got one on account."

"Damn it, Bren."

"Yeah. Honestly, I know more than I look like I do. I know

the things Mum did, playing one of us against the other—she did; you know she did. I winced. I didn't know how to stop it. I honestly didn't know. I mediate between nations. I couldn't figure how to tell Mum not to play one of us against the other. She taught me a lot about politics. I never got the better of her."

"Me either," Toby said after a moment.

"Did she ever talk about me, you know, that awful Bren? That son that deserted me?"

"No," Toby said. "You were always the saint."

"Worse. A lot worse than I thought. I wish she'd damned me now and again. You deserved to hear her say that."

"Never did."

"If you'd been the one absent on the continent, you know you'd have been the saint and I'd have been in your spot."

That was, maybe, a thought Toby hadn't entertained before now. Toby gave him an odd look.

"So, well, you and Barb can talk about me. Blame me to hell and back. It's therapeutic."

"I don't. She doesn't. Honestly. She's not bitter toward you. You want the truth—she's mad at you. But it's hurt feelings. Like you say. Hurt feelings."

"Barb's probably scared to death we're getting together to talk about her. She knew damned well I was manuevering her out the door. But the moment dawned, she got her courage together and went shopping. She let us get together and now she doesn't even know if we'll make common cause and if she'll have a boat to get home on. That's Barb. She's upset, so she'll buy something expensive for herself. But she's brave. At a certain point she *can* turn loose and take care of herself. That's the Barb I loved. Back when I did love her, that is."

Toby managed a dry laugh. "She'll want to know what we said. And she won't believe it wasn't really about her."

"Better make up something."

"Hell, Bren!"

"Funny. When I think about *that* Barb that just went shopping, I know I probably did love her. But I don't get that side of Barb anymore. That Barb's all yours now. I don't know how long that'll be so, but I do know she won't come my way again. It's guaranteed Jago would shoot both of us."

"Hell, Bren!"

"Well, Jago would shoot her. That, in Jago's way of thinking, would solve all the problem."

"Are you joking or not?"

"I actually don't know," he said, and added, dryly, "but I'm certainly not going to ask Jago."

Toby actually laughed, however briefly, and shook his head, resigning the argument.

"So—are you and Barb going fishing with us after this? Can we share a boat? Or is there too much freight aboard?"

"Sure," Toby said. "Sure. I honestly look forward to it."

"Good," he said, and because the atmosphere in the study was too heavy, too charged: "Want to have a look at the garden? Not much out there, but I can give you the idea. I actually know what's usually planted there."

"Sure," Toby said, so they went out and talked about vegetables.

He went in after a while, and left Toby in the garden, where Toby said he preferred to sit. Barb was still shopping—that was rarely a quick event. The youngsters were settling in. He had—at least an hour to attend his notes. He went to his study then, and wrote an actual three paragraphs of his argument against wireless phones.

Crack.

Possibly the staff doing some maintenance in the formal garden, he thought, and wrote another paragraph.

No, it was *not* good for the social fabric for wireless phones to be in every pocket, the ordinary tenor of formal visitation should not be supplanted—

Crack!

Skip and rattle.

That was a peculiar sound. A disturbing question began to nag at him—exactly where the aiji's son and his companions might be at the moment.

He put away his computer, got up and went out to the hall.

There was no staff. That was unusual. He went down the hall to the youngsters' room, and found no one there.

That was downright disturbing.

So was the scarcity of staff.

He went to the inner garden door, and walked out into the sunlight . . . where, indeed, there were staff.

All the staff.

And Banichi. And Toby, and the Taibeni youngsters, all facing the same direction, into the garden.

Crack. Pottery broke.

A smaller figure, one on Toby's scale, took a step backward, dismayed, with a very human: "Oops."

Oops, indeed. Bren walked through the melting crowd of servants, saw Ramaso, saw Cajeiri and Toby, saw Banichi on the left. Then he looked right, at the bottom of the garden, and saw a shattered clay pot, with dirt scattered atop the wall and onto the flagstones.

"One will fetch a broom, nandi," a servant said in a low voice.

"Nandi," Ramaso said, turning.

Cajeiri looked at him and hid something, hands behind his back, while Toby just shrugged.

"Sorry about that." Toby gave a little atevi-style bow, showing proper respect for the master of the house.

Bren was a little puzzled. Just a little. He looked at the broken pot, looked at Cajeiri.

"One did aim away from the great window, nandi!" Cajeiri said with a little bow. And added, diffidently, "It was the ricochet that hit it."

"The ricochet?" he asked, and Cajeiri brought forth to view a curiously familiar object—if they had been on the Island: a forked branch, a length of tubing, probably from the garden shed, and a little patch of leather.

"A slingshota!" Cajeiri announced. "And we are *very* good, with almost the first try!"

There had been several tries, one bouncing, probably off the arbor support pillar, into the stained glass window.

"Well," he said, looking at his brother. "Well, *there's* a little cultural transfer for you."

Toby looked a little doubtful then. "I—just—figured the boy could have missed things, with two formative years up in space."

Bren pursed his lips. As cultural items went, it was innocuous. Mostly. "You made it."

"Showed the kids how," Toby said in a quiet voice. "Mistake?"

"Slingshota," Bren said, and gave a sigh. "New word for the dictionary. Just never happened to develop on this side of the water, that I know of. Banichi, have you ever seen one?"

"Not in that form," Banichi said with an amused look. "Not with the stick. Which is quite clever. And the young gentleman has a powerful grip . . . for his age."

Witness the demolished pot . . . a rather stout pot at that.

"Well, well," he said, "use a cheaper target than that, young gentleman, if you please. Set a rock atop the garden wall."

"I am *sorry*," Toby said, coming near him, so seriously contrite that Bren had to laugh and clap him on the shoulder, never mind the witnesses present.

"If the young gentleman takes out the historic ceramics in the Bujavid," he said, "I may be looking for a home on the island. But no, no damage is done. Just a common pot. I'm sure some entrepreneur will make an industry of this import." Or the Guild will find use for them, he thought, but didn't say it. Banichi clearly was taking notes. "Just supervise, will you?"

"No problem," Toby said, and Bren laughed and patted his shoulder and walked away, Banichi in attendance, to have a word with Ramaso. "Let them have a few empty cans from the kitchen, nadi-ji. That will be a much preferable target."

"Yes, nandi," the old man said, and went to shoo the servants back inside.

"Interesting device," Banichi said. "Not nand' Toby's invention."

"No. Old. Quite old."

"We have used the spun shot," Banichi said, "an ancient weapon."

"Very similar principle," Bren said. "Except the stick."

"One does apologize for the pot," Banichi said.

"Just so it isn't the dowager's porcelains, once he gets home."

"One will have a sobering word with him, Bren-ji."

"Quietly, 'Nichi-ji. The boy has had a great deal of school and very little amusement since the ship. Perhaps one may put in a word with his father, to find him space in the garden to use his toy."

The boy had used to have racing cars—almost the last real toy he had ever owned, except what his human companions brought for his amusement. The last of the cars had come to a violent end—blown up, with explosives, in very fact. Banichi had done that—in a moment of need and improvisation. Toys since—no, there just had been very few.

"He will learn weapons," Banichi said. "And hunting."

Guns. And the other items of mayhem in the Guild's repertoire. The boy already knew about detonators and wires. Knew about bombs and had seen things no eight-year-old ought to have seen.

"Not too soon," he said sadly. "Not too soon, Banichi. His aishid is going to have to go off to train. That will be a hard time for him, when Antaro and Jegari go to the Guild."

As they were already beginning to do, to become security for a boy who would be aiji—with very serious threats to deal with.

"Will those two do all right in that, do you think?" he asked, on the opportunity. "Do you think them apt, after this escapade with the train?"

"They have excellent background," Banichi said, and, as they reached the study door: "We have had a serious talk," Banichi said. "If you will, we can take them in hand—and not neglect the paidhi's security. They are trustworthy, to let within the perimeter. Jago concurs. So do Tano and Algini. We think there are possibilities in these two."

Of very, very few individuals would his security say that, he was sure.

"Would working with them take you away?" he asked, when he had opened the door and brought them into his study.

"No, Bren-ji. It would let the youngsters stay closer to the Bujavid, closer to the paidhi-aiji, as it happens. With the boy. We may be able to persuade his father."

He'd missed Cajeiri. Broken pots and all, he enjoyed the company.

"Tabini-aiji said," said Banichi, "that he came very close to death, this last year. He said that you and the heir might need the closeness of mind you gained with him on the ship, that it might serve you well. The boy has needed time to be atevi: he has needed to develop the instincts—the proper sense of being what he is. But, Tabini-aiji has said, this was never intended to sever you from the heir . . . should anything befall himself."

He was a little shocked. Greatly sobered. Grim thought, and profoundly affecting, that the aiji had expressed that intention to his aishid.

"One has regretted the heir's absence," Bren said earnestly. "One has regretted it extremely."

"Your staff knows that," Banichi said, with an uncommon intensity.

"What do *you* think, 'Nichi-ji?" Man'chi, that instinct to group together, that bond that held a household together in crisis, was as profound to atevi as love was to humans. Say that atevi didn't love. Didn't feel friendship. That was true. What they did feel was as powerful, as intense. And emotionally-based. "Do you agree with this notion? Does it disrupt us? Does it affect man'chi?"

Banichi had shepherded the young rascal aboard ship. Banichi had built the cars with him. Banichi had guarded the aiji's son; and Banichi had been in Tabini's own aishid, once. So had Jago. Now they were in the paidhi's man'chi, together with Tano and Algini, who had come to them from a slightly more esoteric attachment—the Assassins' Guild itself.

And *did* potentially having the boy and his household tangled in theirs—somehow disturb the equation?

"We would not accept it," Banichi said, the four-fold-plus-one *we* of the aishid itself. "We would never accept it, Bren-ji, if there was any possibility it would affect our man'chi to you."

Bren bowed his head, deep appreciation, with a little tightness in his throat. "One is quite emotionally affected by that declaration, Banichi. You should know that."

"One is still not a salad," Banichi said wickedly, and made him laugh—old joke. Old, old joke, between them, from their first try at straightening out that particular question. He'd nailed it down a little better since. They both felt keenly what they did feel. The gulf was still there. One didn't ask the other to be what he wasn't, or, to a certain extent, to do what he couldn't. Banichi and Jago had been ever so frustrated with him on one notable occasion, when their charge had risked his neck trying to protect his bodyguard.

He still would, if it came to that. It frustrated all of them that he had that contrary instinct; but they knew, if push came to shove and he panicked, he'd behave in a very crazy way. They just planned on it; and he tried not to.

Idiot, Banichi might as well have said; and he'd say, That's what you have to work with, 'Nichi-ji.

It turned out to have been a good thing he'd sent two men with Barb and Ikaro. Barb had restocked the *Brighter Days'* galley with about a hundred kilos worth of foodstuffs, bought a very, very fine knife for Toby, and a complete atevi child's dinner gown and coat for herself. She came back down the main hall in a froth of high spirits, while Ikaro privately came to Bren in the study doorway and presented the bills with deep and mortified bows.

"She is the associate of the aikaso'aikasi-najawii of my house," he assured the young woman: that mouthful was to say, the companion of my sib of the same mother and the same father. "And by no means will the estate bear this expense on its books. I shall, as a gift to my brother. Tell Ramaso I wish to speak with him, and by no means be in the least distressed, nadi-ji. I am not, in the least."

That was somewhat of an untruth. Ikaro was upset, and on no few levels—distressed that she had not been given the power to restrain Barb, distressed that she had had to worry all afternoon about his reaction, distressed now that the paidhi had possibly been put into a financial position and been finagled into restocking his brother's boat, distressed that the paidhi was now going to have to talk to Ramaso to straighten things out, and distressed that she might not be kindly dealt with in that discussion. He tried to reassure her. He hoped that Ikaro might confide in him anything she felt she needed to confide regarding the event, if there was, say, more than a hundred kilos of goods, a knife, and a dinner gown involved.

Yes. There was.

When he said, "One hopes that my brother's lady was circumspect, nadi-ji," and Ikaro did not look at him eye to eye, but bowed very low indeed, that was a warning.

"She was not circumspect," he surmised.

Intense embarrassment. Another deep bow, still without looking at him. "It was surely a misunderstanding, nandi. One failed to convey."

"What happened?"

Hesitation. "She wished to purchase a ninth-year gown."

He didn't know what to say for a moment. A child's coming-to-notice. Officially. And they were hand-made, a costly center-piece of a family celebration. "One is certain she had no notion that it was a festival gown," he said.

"Indeed," Ikaro said, not looking at him.

"Surely—she did not succeed in this purchase."

"No, nandi. One believes she understood there was a problem." A bow. "One could not adequately interpret."

"Possibly the paidhi-aiji could not have adequately interpreted." He constructed the scene in his mind, the maids, the men, the townsfolk, and Barb, unable to communicate. The gown in question—the gown would have been made for a specific young lady who would have been, yes, Barb's size. But the special-made gown now had been the subject of an argument—exceeding bad luck for the impending birthday—and Barb had offered more money, a suggestion which Ikaro had not dared translate.

"One understands," he said. "You did your best, Ikaro. One will manage the matter. Please call Ramaso. And thank you. You have done everything you could have done."

Besides flinging herself bodily on Barb and pulling her out of the shop.

God!

"One believes it might be best to replace the gown," he said when Ramaso had come in and heard the matter. "May the paidhi do so, at his expense?"

"That would be extremely gracious of the paidhi," the old man said. "The event is for spring. There is time."

"The paidhi might favor the young girl with a festivity in the estate on the auspicious day—might we not?"

"Indeed," the old man said. "Indeed. That would be most generous."

"Do I know the girl?"

"She is the sailmaker's daughter."

"Egien? Then the paidhi will be extremely delighted to offer the event the hospitality of his house if they will take it."

"One will send that message immediately, if the paidhi will write."

Before the ill omen of the criticism of the little girl's gown reached the couple. It had already distressed the tailor, who must be wondering what he could do.

So he wrote two letters, one to the tailor: *The paidhi has learned of a misunderstanding in the village this morning in your establishment. Please accept the apologies of the paidhi-aiji for the difficulty. The paidhi wishes to gift the child with a new gown of the best materials in your stock, and has every confidence in your skill to accomplish this in a timely way. Please bill the paidhi directly, courtesy of the estate, and please add the cost of the discarded gown to the bill. It is my gift to the family.*

Then he wrote to Egien-nadi: *This morning, the paidhi has learned with great joy of the impending felicity: the paidhi has been extremely distressed to understand that a misunderstanding in the shop has compromised the tailor's work for this happy event. This accident must not compromise the omens of the occasion. It is the paidhi's wish to have the happiest of events for this child, the daughter of a skilled craftsman who is an asset to the village.*

Accordingly he wishes, as Lord of Najida, and in gratitude for the work of your house, to offer an ensemble of the finest work. He offers his estate's hospitality with a dinner and celebration for all the guests on the festive day . . .

That would be the whole village.

. . . Please accept this gesture with the paidhi's personal wishes for felicity and prosperity.

Barb's tab for the morning had run to, oh, a considerable figure. The ensemble Barb had admired would have to be burned, and a new gown made, to purge the taint of envy and criticism from the child. For the rest, he'd meant to offer Toby fuel and resupply, he wasn't sorry to have Toby have the knife, and if Barb's new atevi clothes, the clothes she'd actually bought in that shop, pleased the pair of them . . . well, good, he thought. Worse could have happened. The girl would have the birthday of her dreams, the village would be happy: over all it added up to felicity, and that, on the most superstitious of occasions, the entry of a child onto the fringe of adult society, was the important thing.

So when it came to supper, he even fell into the spirit of the occasion by kitting Toby up in one of his less formal coats—the trousers were impossible—and the shirt and coat were a close call: Toby was a little stouter below, and his seafaring life had given him a greater breadth of shoulder than one gained sitting at a desk, never mind the exercise the paidhi attempted to take.

"I swear I'm going to have it in the soup," Toby said, apprehensive of the lace cuffs. "Bren, God knows what Barb's outfit cost this morning. I don't want to ruin a shirt for you."

"I've spilled a little soup in my career," Bren said. The two of them were in his bedroom, with Koharu and Supani standing by to adjust the coat. "You use the wrist, turn the hand and lift when you reach for your wineglass—drop the fingers, pick up the glass. Keeps the lace right out of the soup bowl. I'm not kidding."

"Turn and lift, huh?" Toby gave it a try. The lace wrapped onto his wrist in a decently elegant gesture. "Hmn."

"Works as a gesture, too, just the half-reach. If you really want the water goblet and can't safely cross the territory, wait till the servant takes the soup bowl out of the path: he'll notice your signal. Nobility has some sacrifices."

"It's an incredible life."

"Honestly, I don't even think about it. I just keep my cuffs out of the soup."

Toby laughed. "Never that successfully . . . figuratively speaking. You're always in it."

He laughed, at the same joke, for once. "Still, I try. Shall we see if the maids have gotten Barb into that outfit?"

"I'll check," Toby said. "You go find the royal youngster, why don't you?"

"No smoke has risen," he said. "And there's been no further sound of breakage. I'm fairly sure my bodyguard has been able to keep up with him."

He sent a manservant to advise Banichi and the youngsters, wherever found, that supper was in the offing, and dropped by to consult Jago and Tano and Algini, who had been resting in quarters, playing dice, and actually enjoying themselves.

Deep breath. Calm. Everything was handled. He didn't tell Jago about the ninth-year ensemble. Not on so pleasant an evening. He just met Banichi and the youngsters near the door, advised the youngsters to wash up, and looked forward to what the major domo informed him was a very extravagant effort from the kitchen.

Well, so, they would have all five courses, and helpings on an atevi scale. Time to pace oneself, or be sorry. And the lord of the place was obliged to be last to table—but he paced that, too, and contrived, with Jago and Banichi, to get himself into the dining room and settled into the conversation before Cajeiri and Toby had gotten much beyond, "You look great, nand' Toby, Barb-daja!"

Barb got to preen in her new clothes. She had gotten herself a sea-green dinner ensemble with gold beading. It was, to be sure, styled for a slightly built child, with a high neck—and the sea-green outfit was really quite becoming to her slight figure, with its wide belt, gold embellishment, and a long scarf trailing just a little onto the floor—adjustment would still have been indicated. But there it was. He'd lent Toby a beige informal coat with velvet same-shade collar and, of course, the shirt and lace. Toby had on his best brown corduroys and a pair of boots in good polish, and actually looked quite the figure in it, as long as he didn't reach and split a seam. The youngsters were duly impressed, and consequently put on their party manners—though for this household meal, Antaro and Jegari ate at table, in their best.

So did Banichi and Jago and Tano and Algini, with no visible weaponry. It was relaxed, Cajeiri's youth and rank kept the conversation moderately modest. Everybody smiled, everybody appreciated the cook's efforts and praised the meal properly, Barb *didn't* lean on Toby's shoulder at table, Toby managed not to drag his cuffs through the soup—actually managed the cuffs with a bit of flair, and the youngsters didn't drop anything on the tablecloth.

It was splendid, all in all . . . given the start to the day.

"It could have been worse," he said, finally relating the whole ninth-year ensemble problem to Jago, after hours, in bed.

A moment of silence ensued, Jago with her head on the other pillow, facing him in the darkness. Then:

"Bren-ji, this woman is a scandal."

"She will be gone in a few days."

"And then a birthday party! When are you to get any work done?"

He sighed, heaving upward on one elbow with Jago's hand on his ribs. "I shall manage, Jago-ji. And by the day of the event, we shall be back in the capital, one is quite sure. There are far worse things. *Far* worse things. Toby and I spoke quietly and one believes we have settled some matters between us that were far more troublesome for the future."

Jago rose up on an elbow. "Should your staff know these things?"

"Old matters. Things you do know, Jago-ji. I left on our voyage at a very unfortunate time for Toby and his household, with my mother ill. This was a potential cause of great resentment. We spoke. That was why I sent Barb to the village—to have the chance to speak to him privately. The feeling is very much better between us now. The situation with Barb—well, Barb is Barb."

Jago said not a thing. He moved his hand on Jago's bare shoulder.

"The tension will be better in the morning," he said, "on the boat. Everybody will be busy, and there will be ample distraction. You may even see Toby happy. And if he is happy, one believes Barb will behave better."

Barb and the youngsters alike would be surrounded by uncrossable water, he was thinking. Both Barb and the youngsters would be in a very good mood—the latter all bright-eyed and earnestly well-behaved. And confined to the deck.

"Come here," he said, gathering her close. "Forget about it, Jago-ji. Tomorrow we sail out of reach of shops."

Morning came at a leisurely pace. Jago got up, he did, Jago dressed herself and Koharu and Supani came to dress him after Jago had gone wherever Jago intended to go. None of the rest of the household was awake, except staff. And it was safe here, safe as the Bujavid never was, so he asked for his coat and walked out into the brown, dead garden to take a turn out there, watching the sun come up. The maidservant trailed him: he sent her for tea, and enjoyed a cup. Steam from it curled up into the light of dawn.

Then the rest of the house began to stir—so the servant advised him, and he came back in, invigorated and ready for breakfast—which he shared with Toby and Barb alone until the youngsters came racketing into the dining room, all bright-eyed and anxious.

They settled rapidly and were served their breakfasts. Cajeiri was being so, so good, not asking when they would go to the boat, not asking a thing, and being very elegant with his table manners: Cajeiri and the two Taibeni youngsters wore clearly second-best coats, their roughest clothes probably cleaned by now, for the trip, after their riding the whole way here on boxes of canned goods.

"What *will* be our schedule?" Toby asked him finally, prompting Cajeiri's immediate attention. "Shall we be out and away directly after breakfast?"

"I think so," Bren was in the process of saying when a servant slipped up to him and said, quietly. "There is a call from Mospheira, nandi. Your staff cannot make out the name, but it seems to regard nand' Toby. And the caller is a woman who seems distressed and who asks for you."

"A woman." He was a little bemused . . . until Barb threw down her napkin and left the table without an excuse, and Toby leapt up and went after her.

That narrowed the field of possible guesses.

He got up, bowed to the distressed staffer, and to the youngsters, who had also risen in some degree of concern. "Please finish your breakfast, young lord, you and your household, and please excuse me for a moment. One suspects this is a social matter."

Nothing to do with politics, Cajeiri's father, or armed disaster, at least. He left the dining room at a sedate pace, heard from the servant that the phone call might be received in the study, and walked there, also at a sedate pace.

There a servant waited to offer him the phone, which he took.

"This is Bren Cameron."

"Bren!" He knew that voice. "Bren, I'm so sorry to interrupt your morning. Is my husband there?"

Jill.

"Yes, Toby's here." He was quite careful not to refer to Toby as her husband, which, to his recollection, Toby was not. At least—Toby had said it was final. "But he's not in the room with me. Is there something wrong?"

"Julie's been in an accident." Tears broke through. "She's in the hospital."

Toby's daughter. Bren's pulse rate ticked up. "Serious?"

Sobs. "Bren, she's hurt. She's really hurt, broken arm, broken leg . . ."

"My God, what was she doing?"

"It's not my fault!" Jill cried. "It's not my fault! She was cycling down Velroski and it was raining and she had an accident."

"Her head?"

"She had a helmet. But she hit a pothole and the cycle's a wreck and they don't know how badly she's hurt, Bren. Bren, I can't deal with this by myself. I've *got* to talk to Toby."

How in hell had Jill known Toby was here? Had Toby been in contact? Had she gotten it out of State, via Sonja Podesta's office?

"I'll go tell him. Can you stay on the line?"

"Yes!" Jill said, so he laid the phone down, told a servant not to hang it up, and headed down the hall to Barb and Toby's suite.

He knocked once. Pushed the door open. Toby was standing in front of a closed bedroom door, and looked toward him in some distress.

"Toby," he began.

"I don't know how she tracked me. Dammit, Bren. It's Jill, isn't it?"

"Toby, Julie's had a cycle wreck."

The anger drained from Toby's face. So did the color. "Oh, my God. How bad?"

"Broken arm, broken leg, hit a pothole in the rain. Jill's still on the line. She wants to talk to you."

"Damn it!" Toby said. "Damn it! Where's the phone?"

"My study," Bren said, and stood aside as Toby left out the door, at a near run.

He was still standing there a heartbeat or two later, wondering whether he ought to go to the study and risk interrupting what those two had to say to each other, and delaying what Toby needed to learn about little Julia—hell, little Julia was a young woman now. It had just been that long since . . .

The bedroom doors flew open. Barb stood there, red-eyed. "Where's Toby?"

"Barb," he began to say.

"Where's Toby?"

"He'll be on the phone. His daughter's been in a wreck, Barb. Ease up."

"Oh, in a wreck! How bad is it?"

"Broken leg, broken arm."

"Then she'll live," Barb said shortly. "How in hell did Jill call here?"

That was a real question. "Probably she phoned State . . . Toby works for them, doesn't he? Or is it Defense?"

Barb scowled at him and started for the door.

"Damn it, Barb, calm down. The kid's in the hospital. Jill wants advice."

"Oh, sure, she's in the hospital. That's the magic word. And he'll come running."

He was appalled. The hell of it was—it echoed Jill herself, when Toby would drop everything for their mother's every minor crisis. And the last, that hadn't been minor. It echoed the whole situation that had driven Jill to leave Toby. His warnings to Toby hadn't mattered then. Wouldn't matter now. This time he tried logic with Barb. He snapped, "Well, where did *you* meet him?"

At the hospital, that was to say, when they'd *both*, she and Toby, sat up with Mum and started an affair that had led here.

But maybe it wasn't the smartest thing to have said, after all. Barb's eyes widened and she looked at him as if she'd like to hit him.

So he added, "It's also where you'll lose him if you don't use your head about this."

She did hit him, right across the face. Fortunately for her, Jago wasn't there, nor were any of his aishid. He simply absorbed it and looked at her quite, quite coldly.

"You only wish I would break up with him," she shot back.

"If you think I have any shred of feeling left for you—you're quite mistaken. It's what I told you before: hurt him and you've got a lasting enemy in me. Other than that, I don't give a damn what you do in your life, if you make him happy. It *won't* make him happy if you come running to me. Figure it out, Barb."

Barb stared at him, then renewed her start for the door.

He snagged her arm. "If you don't want to lose Toby for good and all, don't *ever* get between him and those kids. He'll make a choice, believe me, if you put him to it. If he wants to leave here and go to the hospital over in Jackson, you smile and you go with him and you speak nicely and sympathetically to Jill and to Julie, if you have a brain in your head."

"Let go of me!"

He did. She massaged her arm in high theatrics and stalked out the door, with sharp, measured strides.

He delayed a moment, asking himself whether he had played that round correctly, but he thought he had. At least he'd told her the plain facts, if Barb had absorbed a single word he'd said. That was always the problem with Barb: somewhere in her head, between her eyes, her ears and her brain, there was some filter that only let through what supported her beliefs.

And right now he was probably the villain. He gave that phase about ten minutes, about as long as it took Toby to tell her something she didn't want to hear, either. And she was here with no way but Toby's boat for transport back to the island, so those two would have to work through it . . . though he wondered for a heartbeat or two if he couldn't get her on a flight to Mogari, where she could pick up a routine air freight flight or a boat to Jackson, with the canned fish and the sacks of flour that went back and forth in trade.

No. If the relationship really, truly blew up today, somebody would have to escort her—namely him; and he wouldn't get in the middle of Toby's problem with her—no way in hell. They'd just have to patch it up and ship back together, speaking to each other or not.

So he composed himself and walked out into the hall, receiving a concerned look from Ramaso, who had watched the drama and had very little information.

"There's been an accident on the Island, nadi-ji. One of Toby's children-by-prior-contract is injured and the mother called with information. Nand' Toby is greatly concerned. Barb-daja—" He hesitated just a heartbeat on a polite lie, and then decided the household needed pertinent facts. "—is disturbed by the notion he may take some sort of escape to void their contract."

The old man was properly dismayed, and bowed. "One comprehends the distress, then, nandi. Are the injuries life-threatening?"

"No, which is to the relief of us all. You may pass the word on to staff," he said, amazing himself, he was so completely cold-hearted about his brother's distress and Barb's outburst. "They should not accept any blame for the lady's distress or her discord with nand' Toby. Likely the decision will play itself out in his decision to stay for the rest of his visit or go to the bed-side of his child, which will either please or distress Barb-daja, or him. In either case, it is not your fault, nor can I intervene with a solution. This one is theirs to work out."

"And repercussions, nandi?"

"None are even possible, regarding this house, nadi-ji, Mospheira having no Guild and neither lady having connections with anyone who would take exception. But if Barb-daja disrespects the staff or other guests in any particular, cease service to her and immediately advise me of the situation. You are not obliged to bear with bad behavior or to carry out any unseemly order. This also extends to nand' Toby, though from him one hardly expects a problem."

"Yes, nandi," the old man said with a deep bow. What the old man thought he very courteously didn't express in words . . . but if there was one situation atevi did understand it was a marital conflict—to a degree that occasionally resorted to the Assassins' Guild.

"Where is my aishid at the moment, Rama-ji?"

"Somewhere about the house—one believes, in their rooms. They are not unaware of the disturbance."

"Inform them, nadi-ji. I wish to have a word with them." He had the pocket com, but there were times when the deliberation of staff talking to staff and forewarnings being passed—served to calm a situation. Time for things to settle. Calm amid the storm. "And the young gentleman?"

"In his suite, too, nandi."

Waiting for them. They must have heard about the delay and the family fight, and were just doing the sensible thing and staying out of it. Screaming in the halls in an atevi house—it didn't happen. Nerves were on edge. His aishid was holding an emergency consultation. The kids had taken cover. Barb's little scene wasn't a situation he wanted to explain in detail, not until they had some outcome and he himself could say the dust had settled.

So he walked on down the hall to the study, didn't knock, and walked in, quietly shutting the door again. Toby was still on the phone, Barb was standing, arms folded, head down, and not looking at either of them, beyond her darting glance to see who had come in. If looks could do meticulous murder, he thought, he'd be on the floor.

He wasn't. And she couldn't. So he waited, master of an offended atevi house and brother to one side of this phone conversation, which ran to, "Yes," "No." And "That's good." "Yes. That's fine with me." And: "Tell her I love her."

Then: "Thanks so much, Jill. Thank you. I owe you."

Jill said something at length that had Toby looking very sober, somewhat distressed.

"Do you think I need to come there?" Then another long answer. "Well, she'd stay on the boat."

Barb broke her attitude, moved into Toby's field of vision and signed a vigorous negative.

Toby made a sign for patience. Wait, that was.

Jill, meanwhile, was saying something he was listening to . . . something Toby wasn't altogether happy with, but he wasn't mad. He was upset. Emotionally upset.

Then: "Jill, I really appreciate you taking that attitude. I do. I know I wasn't the best husband."

And Barb threw up her hands and went for the door, banging it open to the dismay of two servants outside.

Bren didn't stop her. He folded his arms and stood there. The servants quietly shut the door, restoring some dignity to the house.

Toby finished his conversation. "Thanks. Thanks, Jill. I do appreciate it. If you need me, call. You know how. I appreciate your attitude. And tell Julia, if she wants me, I will come. We'll be here probably another five days if Bren doesn't throw us out. So we'll be in reach of a phone call."

Bren was ready to shake his head no, he wouldn't throw them out, but Toby didn't look at him as he hung up. Toby just looked at the phone and looked at the floor and that went on for a full minute, Toby running whatever emotional math he had to run to get his nerves settled.

Bren didn't move, having decided he didn't need to ask questions of things Toby didn't elect to say, and that he could amply read from one side of the conversation. He just waited.

Deep breath from Toby. Then: "She's taking care of things there. Julie's all in casts, going to be in the hospital another few days, no head trauma, thank God, nothing lasting."

"That's good. Very good. I'm glad. We'd fly you back there if you wanted to go."

"Where's Barb?"

"I think she went back to your rooms."

Toby didn't say a thing. Toby left, and not a moment after Toby had left the study and before the door had quite shut, Banichi and Jago came in, followed by Tano and Algini, all of them frowning . . . that was to say, allowing him to see that they were considerably disturbed.

He returned the forthrightness. "Toby's daughter has had a fairly serious accident and lies in the hospital—a broken arm and leg. Toby's former wife called. Barb-daja has taken this contact as a threat and behaved badly."

"Need we take precautions?" Algini asked.

"Against Barb-daja? Unlikely we need do anything, unless she vents her displeasure on the furnishings. Then, yes, advise me. That will not be tolerated."

There were still troubled looks.

"There is no way," he said, "to deal with this. The dispute is between nand' Toby and her, and one has no way to intervene. One would like to know, discreetly, what is said." He thought he ought to be ashamed of himself for that last, but he was protective of Toby, and if it was a replay of Barb's old arguments with him—"How can you be that way, Bren?" And, "Well, I know where I come in your priorities, don't I?"—he wasn't entirely sure what he'd do with that information, but he'd know the scene, at least, if he needed to talk to Toby.

"One can secure a recording," Jago said. "Algini is set up to do so, quite easily, nandi."

"Probably without the microphone," he muttered, knowing the decibel level Barb's temper could reach. "But do so, yes, nadiin-ji. One needs to know. This is my brother's welfare at issue."

They could be discreet. He intended to be.

But damned if she was going to put his brother through the same set of crises.

"The young gentleman," Banichi reminded him.

They'd promised the boy two days of fishing. Now this. "Advise him we will be some little delayed in setting out," he said. And then thought, no, the boy deserved to hear from his host. "No, Banichi-ji. I shall do it myself, in all courtesy to our guests."

Banichi gave a little nod.

"Go," Bren said, "see what you can find out."

His bodyguard left, on a direct mission of espionage. He, meanwhile, had to explain to Cajeiri why the latest promise Cajeiri had looked forward to was going to go amiss.

He didn't look forward to that.

And he didn't get that far, or need Algini's electronics to know what was happening in his brother's suite. One of the maidservants came hurrying out into the hall, distraught, saying that Barb-daja was flinging clothes from the closet and demanding her suitcases. "Should the staff provide them, nandi?"

Well, *that* was a good question.

7

Nand' Bren hadn't gotten down to the boats yet, and it had been a long wait. But Cajeiri had, right after breakfast, and not by the front doors, where he would have to account for himself to the servants. He'd taken his companions down to the boats while all the adult confusion went on in the house. He knew, of course, he was permitted to be here by the ultimate authority in the house, namely nand' Bren, so he and his companions just quietly used the garden door, and the garden gate.

That had proved a disappointment. It turned out to be just a little nook where the gardener stored pots and such, but there was a great tumble of basalt for a backdrop, and it had turned out easy to climb up and over the basalt and evergreen and down again right onto the regular walkway, this not being a very secure sort of house. So it was just convenient to go this way, once they were started.

So he and Antaro and Jegari, in their warmest coats, taking a change of clothes, and all ready for their trip, had only minor difficulty getting down to the harbor. Nand' Bren would send his staff to the dock fairly soon to bring food and such, and so they would be down at the waterside and all ready to go aboard when they brought the yacht, which was moored off-shore, up to the dock. Meanwhile he could show Antaro and Jegari nand' Toby's yacht, which was moored right up at the dock, and they might not be able to get into the inside, but it was a wide deck and they could walk about on their own. They would give nand' Bren a little bit of a turn when he discovered they were not in their rooms: but nand' Bren would know right where they were, and nand' Bren and even his bodyguard were not dull sticks like Uncle's guards. They could surprise nand' Bren and have a laugh about it. Banichi would laugh and forgive him under the circumstances, and be just as sure where they had gone.

And it was certainly better than sitting up in the house while Barb-daja and nand' Toby had a fight, which was just not pleasant at all—embarrassing, to have Antaro and Jegari hearing such an unpleasant thing in nand' Bren's family, and maybe even dangerous: one had no idea about that, but he was sure nand' Bren would take care of it and get it settled.

The situation was, however, changed, down at the harbor: they saw that when they rounded the first turn of the walkway: nand' Toby's boat, like nand' Bren's, was riding tantalizingly out of reach, both at anchor—Cajeiri knew about anchors, and sailing, and even how the sails worked, all of which he was ready to tell his companions in great detail.

But the staff had moved nand' Toby's boat out from the dock, and had not moved nand' Bren's boat in. That was extremely disappointing.

So when they reached the wooden dock, they stood there looking at the water, and watching the boats, and the few fishermen far, far across the bay, where the shore grew hazy with distance. There was no activity about the immediate area, just the thin strip of sand somewhat behind the jut of the dock, the rocks, higher up than that, but one long band of rock disappearing right near the water's edge, and reappearing just off in the water, a rounded knob of rock where the water danced, covering and uncovering it.

Nand' Toby's boat was somewhat bigger than nand' Bren's boat, but not fancier, Cajeiri thought. Nand' Bren's boat, nearest, was very, very fine, with its shining white hull and a line like a breaking wave painted along its side.

The boats rocked to the light movement of the water, which sucked and slapped noisily against the pilings—pilings was a word Cajeiri knew, from reading. Pilings held up the dock, and went down under the water, and when he got down on his knees and looked down, Antaro and Jegari beside him, he saw streamers of weed there, and they wondered together whether one could see any fish. He thought he had, but the others failed to see it, so he was not sure.

There was a little short ladder down from the dock. He and Antaro and Jegari took turns climbing a little down it to look under the dock, risking getting their feet wet, he was sure—the boards of the ladder were a little wetter higher up than the rung they could stand on, showing how high the water could reach. There were, they all concluded, no fish in view.

But all around them were interesting smells that made Cajeiri remember their trip across the straits on nand' Toby's boat, and when they all sat on the edge of the dock—it must be an hour by now—and looked at the boats, he told them about his trip, and how Toby's boat was on the inside, and about the sails.

And they amused themselves seeing how far they could shoot a stone across the harbor, and then they tried trying to hit a particular rock on the curve of the shore, with the abundance of pebbles the shore provided.

But after all this time there was still nobody down from the house to get them closer to the boat.

And one was tired of shooting stones.

There was, however, back along the strip of sand, a small boat dragged up on shore, and it probably belonged to the estate—which meant it was nand' Bren's.

And then he had an idea. They probably could sail it out to Toby's boat and he could show Antaro and Jegari the boat, and when the staff did come down, they could just sail the little boat back to the shore and surprise everybody. They would look very grand and very accomplished on the water, and nand' Bren would be surprised and relieved they were so competent . . .

which might mean they could get repeated permission to use the boat.

"Come with me," he said, and ran back along the straight-back part of the dock and back onto the rock, then scampered down the rocks, surefooted as Antaro and Jegari themselves, who had grown up in the forests and the hills. This was all new territory, this sandy stretch—sand was harder to run in, much harder, so he strode along, looking very confident, leading, as a young lord should. He reached the boat, assessed the situation with the sail at a glance, and pulled the rope to raise it to the top of the little mast as if he had done it every day of his life. It blew lazily sideways in the light breeze, sending the boom out over the side, but he took the little rope and tied it to the open place in the trim near the tiller. Then it was safe.

"Is this nand' Bren's boat?" Jegari asked. "Nandi, perhaps we should wait."

"Oh, we shall just sail out a little way." The tiller was up. The boat was secured by a knot that was easy to pull loose. "Push it out."

"Are you sure, nandi?" Antaro asked. "Do you know how to manage it? We have never been in a boat."

"I have," he said, and went to the stern and moved the tiller the little it would move. "See. This steers it. See the rope there—that pulls on the sail so you can catch the wind. The oars in the bottom are for emergency, to move the boat if there is no wind. The board that sticks up in the bottom of the boat—that goes down into the water when we push off."

"Nandi, surely we should wait!"

"We shall go out to nand' Toby's boat, and when nand' Bren's staff comes down, we shall come right back to shore. They will need this boat to get aboard. Come. Push!"

They looked doubtful, but they heaved and pushed until the stern was in the water, and then he got in, and they all got in.

They weighed the boat down, and it only rocked, but they could not rock it off the shore.

"Shove with the oars," Cajeiri said, picking up one himself, and put it over the side and pushed and shoved until they were out of breath. "No good," he said. "One of us has to get out and push and then jump in."

"I will," Jegari said, and got up to the bow and stepped out and shoved.

Then it went very fast, the board went down, the boom came around, bang! and the boat, tilting a little, began to move off, but Jegari ran and grabbed it, and got aboard, wet to the waist and nearly spilling water into the boat.

That was bad. But Jegari did get aboard. They had dry clothes, but the servants were bringing those down. Meanwhile nobody was steering and Antaro had gotten her oar overside to row, and because of it, they were going around. A stronger breeze caught the sail, and it popped and snapped against the mast, tugging at the rope.

"Take the oar out," Cajeiri said, settling and tugging at the rope to bring the sail around. Increasingly the tiller was taking hold. "Just sit still, one on a side, and watch out for the boom. It will go back and forth as we go—you have to let it: just duck; and I shall steer with the tiller."

It was all going much better, except Jegari being wet. He steered, but there was something wrong with the tiller, Cajeiri thought in a little dismay, since he was steering for nand' Toby's boat, but they kept going sideways nearly as much as they were going forward.

He steered sharply, and they made it right up alongside nand' Toby's boat, and he tried to come in behind it, where there was a ladder, but he ran into a problem, then, and the wind blew them up against Toby's boat, scraping the hull.

"Get the oars," he said, "and push off before we scratch the hull."

They did, and just then they came around the side of the hull to the end and the boom came over, catching Antaro hard in the back, and nearly threw her in. He hauled on the little rope to try to control the boom, but then the wind was in their faces and the boat was coming around.

That was a problem.

Meanwhile Antaro was leaning overside, trying to reach something in the water.

"Keep in the boat, nadi!" Cajeiri cried, making a reach for her, just as Jegari did, all on the same side of the boat, and for a moment he was sure they were going over, but he leaned the other way, and Jegari did, but now they were entirely past nand' Toby's boat, so he turned the bow to face it, and the wind blew and they just kept getting farther and farther from the boat.

"You must be doing it wrong, nandi-ji," Jegari said.

"There is a way to go upwind," he said. "One is just having a little difficulty."

"Nandi," Antaro said, "I have lost an oar off the side."

"We do still have the other, however," Jegari said.

"I am going to try going fast, and then turning," he said. "Maybe we need more speed."

"Shall I row?" Jegari asked.

"The wind will take us," Cajeiri said, and turned the bow. The tiller took hold again as the boat gathered speed. More and more speed, as the wind gusted and strained the sail.

"Surely this is fast enough," Jegari said.

He thought it was, too: the ropes were singing, the way Toby's big boat could sing when the wind was behind it. He turned, keeping tight control of the boom. But the wind hit the sail, and all that speed faded, so that they were no longer going forward. They had turned, in fact, halfway too far, and the water was even going backward relative to the boat.

Or they were going backward.

"Damn!" he said, one of Bren's words.

"Are we in trouble, nandi?" Antaro asked.

"I think we are in trouble," he said. "Jegari, one greatly regrets it, but we need to row: you need to get into the bow and row one side and the other so we do not go in a circle. I shall steer."

"I shall try, nandi."

By now nand' Toby's boat was much farther away. Worse, nand' Bren's boat and the dock looked quite small now.

"The water is all moving," Jegari said from the stern. "Nandi, one is rowing hard, but the water is taking us with it."

"Row!" he said to Antaro. "Help Jegari!"

He held to the tiller and tried it this way and that, but it made very little difference—more, when they went sideways in respect to nand' Toby's boat; and he began to think that things were getting worse and that if they could steer in any direction at all, they should go that way, so he did, or tried to, but mostly they were going crooked, because of there being only one oar.

They were in serious trouble.

"I am going to try to gather speed again!" he cried. "Give up rowing! I cannot take it straight into the wind! I am going to try to gather speed and angle it to reach the Najida shore. At this point one hardly cares where!"

"Do so, nandi!" Jegari cried, and the two of them settled themselves again, tipping the boat this way and that, and then he brought the bow around and hauled hard on the rope, so that the wind caught them.

At some point, when he had the most speed, they had to turn; and they did. They were closer, now, to the opening of the bay, and in front of them, there was no land.

He turned. He did his best. But it was like magic. Even though the wind was pushing them straight ahead, something else was going on with the boat, and they were moving sideways, too.

Ahead was all blue sky and gray water and it just went on and on, out where the shoreline quit.

That was the sea out there. And they were moving toward it.

Something was very wrong with everything he had read about boats. Something was very, very wrong.

Barb was crying again, and the door had the security lock thrown, which meant Toby was locked out in the suite's sitting room, and not happy about it. He'd gotten mad enough to hit the door—so Algini said—and Barb had shouted back at him that, Jago's report, accurately rendered in Mosphei', he should go to hell.

That was just tolerably lovely, was it not?

But it was useless sorting it out at this point. There was weather moving in, so the report was . . . it was going to shorten their fishing trip as was, they were missing the tide; and Bren sighed and asked himself whether he should not just leave the situation, take all his staff with him, and go keep his promise to the youngsters, leaving Toby and Barb to scream at each other in front of the servants.

Damn it all, they still might have to get Toby to the plane. Or Barb, if things went on as they were going, and that relationship foundered. He'd happily buy the one-way ticket.

And hell, Bren said to himself, and when he had that last report from Jago, that was enough. They'd wasted enough time. He knocked on Toby's door—Toby had the outer door locked, and, with Toby not answering, he hailed him aloud, then indecorously, and in front of at least one embarrassed servant, declared his business from *outside* the door.

"Toby? It's Bren. Do you hear me?"

Silence.

"Look, Toby. I have the aiji's son, who is in my care, to whom I have made certain promises and I have responsibility for his welfare. Let her stew. Just let it go. Weather's turning. We've already lost time. If we need to get you to the mainland we can do that. We can get you to the airport, if we need to."

Silence.

"At least answer me, Toby, dammit. I don't like to conduct business through the door."

He heard steps, finally, approaching the door.

"Sorry," Toby said icily, from the other side.

"Look. Just let her blow. I know this mode, forgive me. She'll have her temper. It'll run its course."

"Don't tell *me* what she's like! I know her better than you ever did."

"Fine. I'm sure you do. And *if* you do, get your coat and come on and let's go fishing for a few hours until the weather turns. My staff can manage. We can put back in tonight and pick her up and she'll be fine, whole thing forgotten."

"No."

"Toby."

"Don't tell me how to handle this! I've got a kid in the hospital and Barb's throwing a fit. You've got the aiji's son in your care. I understand. Just go ahead, take the boat out, I'll get Barb back on this planet, we'll talk it out, and we'll all be fine. See you when you get back."

"Got it," he said, unhappy—deeply unhappy. He moved away from the door, addressed one of the staff, who had stood by worriedly during that exchange. "Kindly advise the aiji's son that we are finally ready to leave, nadi-ji. Just that."

"Yes, nandi."

He went to his own quarters, back to his bodyguard, to advise them they were finally going, without Toby and Barb. He asked himself whether he ought to trust Toby to keep Barb out of trouble or whether he ought to deprive Tano and Algini yet again of what ought to be a pleasurable outing, to stay behind and keep track of his houseguests.

Hell, no, he said to himself as he passed the door. His staff deserved a little relaxation, and Barb's vicinity . . .

He didn't quite close the door. He heard running in the hall. Servants didn't run in the halls.

This one did. And bowed, distressedly, out of breath. "Nandi. No one is there."

"The young lord, and his companions?"

"We have no idea where they are, nandi. But no one remembers seeing them out and about since breakfast."

"Go down to the dock, nadi-ji. Immediately. Find them and tell them stay where they are. We shall be right down." He didn't panic; he calmed himself with the expectation that, yes, bored youngsters had found a way out of the house, had escaped adult notice, and simply gone down to the dock to wait for the promised trip. All that was safe to do, perfectly safe.

The question was how long they had been waiting. Cajeiri's capacity for tedium was very, very small.

He went immediately to his bodyguard's room—they were set up with sound equipment over by the wall—"Nadiin-ji, the young gentleman has gotten bored and gone to the dock."

Banichi, Jago, and Tano immediately stood up, and Banichi headed for the door without a word said. Algini removed his earpiece and laid it down, then got up.

"Nand' Toby and his lady are still arguing," Algini said.

"Let them," he said. Algini wasn't fluent in Mosphei', that Algini had ever let on. Jago was the one who could interpret. Or deliver an emergency message to his brother. Hell with it, he thought. Toby was no help at the moment, having his mind on his fight with Barb. Let Toby worry about *him* this round. "We shall just go down to the boat, and if the young gentleman is ready, we shall leave on the last of the tide."

Algini picked up his sidearm as he moved, and they all five went out together. Ramaso was waiting anxiously at the door.

"The young gentleman has eluded us," he said equably to Ramaso, "but is probably at the boat. This is nothing new. Are we provisioned?"

"Yes, nandi, provisioned last night, and ready to sail. Only the boat is not at the dock."

"We shall manage. We shall go straight down, bring the boat in, and likely shall sail out immediately. If nand' Toby asks questions or seems upset, say the name of my boat, and that should advise him where we are. He knows a very little Ragi. Barb-daja likely knows none but the word yes, and the word no. Use either, as you wish with her. Address yourself to nand' Toby, who is much more reasonable, and should he wish to go to the airport and fly to the mainland, assist him. I will pay the ticket."

"Nandi." The servant who had slipped in behind Ramaso had gotten Bren's outdoor coat from the closet and offered it. Bren exchanged coats, then with a parting courtesy to the old man, took Algini and left, calmly, in good order, and leaving the troubles of the day behind him.

Left them, that was, until he saw Tano sprinting back up the terraced walk toward them, out of breath by the time he reached them, and needing to bend to breathe.

"Nandi," Tano said. "There is no sign of the youngsters and the boat is gone."

"*My* boat?"

"The tender, nandi, that the staff uses. The boat was dragged out—marks are clear in the sand."

His thoughts leapt all over the place—the youngsters had gotten to his boat, or Toby's, let the little sailboat drift away, which could happen—an inconvenience. They might lose it, or it could be battered against rocks along some segment of the shore in the coming weather.

But there were much, much worse ideas.

"Is there another boat, nadi-ji? Can we signal my boat?"

"Jago has swum out to your boat, nandi, to bring it in to dock."

God, the water would be cold as ice. He started down, taking the atevi-sized terraces with bone-jarring steps, and ran, as Algini and Tano ran behind him. He was almost in as bad shape on the downhill as Tano had been on the uphill by the time he reached the dock at the last, and had a view of Banichi standing out on the sand, looking out toward the water.

He ran down the steps from the dock, ran across the shingle out to where Banichi stood, Tano and Algini right with him.

Banichi looked in his direction.

"Is she aboard, Banichi-ji?" *Jeishan* had a stern ladder, so it was possible for Jago to get aboard. He was relieved when Banichi said, "Yes, nandi." And a moment later he saw the slight puff of smoke above the water as the engine started. The bow power winch went into action, hauling one anchor cable up. Then the other started up, and hauled away.

It was bad news. If the youngsters had been aboard, Jago would just have gone to the rail and signaled. Taking in cable took forever. He stood in the chill wind, waiting, watching as *Jeishan* began slowly to move, her anchors still dripping . . . not back to the dock—but over within hail of the *Brighter Days*.

He waited, shivering in the wind, and waited. He heard the loudspeaker clear to the dockside, as Jago queried whether anybody was aboard.

No answer. Nobody came to the rail of that boat. And the last of the tide was moving, rocks standing bare that at high tide were well-submerged along the margin, with far more beach than showed at high tide. Bren's gaze drifted to the mouth of the bay, all that vast wooded shoreline, where, one could still hope, three youngsters, having realized they were no match for the tide, might have turned back to shore and gotten stranded. Not a one of them had ever handled a sailboat. But all they had to do was let the wind blow them straight across. There were fishing docks across the bay. There were boats out. They could get help.

They might be, even now, hiking to some phone where they could call.

Please God they were safe ashore, just stranded by a contrary wind.

"Nadiin-ji," he said to the three with him, "can one of you call the house and tell them to ask the village constable to go along the shore on the far side?" They were skittish and wary youngsters, not prone to trust strangers whose man'chi might be in doubt. They would rather try to walk home, but that was a day's rough hike, just to get to the curve of the bay, let alone clear to Najida.

That was the good supposition. If, on the other hand, they had gotten beyond the mouth of the bay, if they had gotten swept well out, the current off the point bent southerly.

"And phone Kajiminda: tell our neighbor what has happened, and ask Lord Baiji to put out boats to search, in case they have been swept out to sea. Say we have a boat with children swept out into the bay. Tell them we need help."

He had to call Shejidan. He had to admit to Tabini that he had allowed a catastrophe. They had a radio on the boat, and Jago had it underway again, using the engine to bring it back to the dock. He had his coat, his aishid was equipped, the boat was outfitted for their fishing trip, and that meant entirely—food, blankets, everything they needed for a search.

He stood watching as the boat came closer, and listening as Banichi, on com, spoke to Ramaso up at the house, advising him what had happened, passing orders in rapid succession. He said to Banichi: "Tell Ramaso to tell my brother we have an emergency. Tell him get his boat out. Fast. Meanwhile can you find out if there were any life vests in that tender?"

Banichi nodded, while talking and listening. On the life vests, it was thought, up at the house, that there were two.

Two. Marvelous.

Meanwhile Jago was nosing *Jeishan* in to dock, running out to toss a line to Tano and Algini. *Jeishan* hit the buffers, slid along them—Jago had judged the speed tolerably, and there was no great shock as it came in. She ran back up to the bridge to finesse the docking and at that point Tano and Algini had pulled it in, with the engine idling.

Bren jumped for the deck and headed for the bridge, heard thumps behind him as Tano and Algini came aboard, then Banichi. He didn't even look back, except to take a glance out forward and find his course clear. He didn't want to take the time for Jago to get the *Brighter Days* into dock, but none of his aishid were experienced seamen, and it was worth it, if Toby's expertise gave them an expertly-captained second boat to travel line-of-sight and try to figure the currents and where, at the moment, that little sailboat might have gone.

"Jago-ji," he said as he joined her on the bridge, Jago in nothing but her underwear and a sopping wet tee. "Go aboard Toby's boat and get it to the dock—wait for him. You can communicate with him. Call the house and have them send down spare dry clothes." Banichi had come in, meanwhile, carrying Jago's jacket and other clothes, and she declined to put it around her shoulders.

"Yes," she said plainly, to his order, and grabbed her clothes and gear up and went outside in the cold wind, wet and half-naked. They were free of the dock, the lines taken in almost as soon as they had pulled into shore, and Bren throttled up, heading for the *Brighter Days* and maneuvering to avoid her anchor cables. Jago went around to the starboard bow, ready to move across.

He came in close, very close, backed the engine, and gave Jago as steady a platform as he could—no need. Jago made an easy jump, was on, her clothes and gear tucked under one arm, and on her way to the bridge, where, presumably, Toby had left the ignition key . . .

But messages would get Toby down there, and if Toby had the key with him, somebody would have to swim it—likely Jago—one more time. He couldn't wait. He'd given Toby someone who could communicate on radio, somebody with Guild authority. He throttled up and took out toward the southern shore of the bay, confident that Jago would do what was logical and *get* Toby out on the search.

"Fishermen will help us, Bren-ji," Banichi said calmly.

"Put out a general call. Say: Children from the village. Compensation from the estate."

Cover story with the right and useful details: Banichi knew exactly why, and got on the radio and put it out that way—village children swept out in a sailboat from the estate dock, the estate to compensate any fishermen who diverted their boats to the search. There were no better searchers, to know the tide, the currents and the coast, but none of them were going to keep up with the yacht on its way out . . . *Jeishan's* was a potent engine, for security reasons, the paidhi's security, in point of fact.

But it wasn't helping them. Tano and Algini were out along the rail, braving a bitter wind to scan the wooded shoreline unobstructed by fogged glass and spatter from the spray. They were moving under power, moving fast, with the last of the tide.

There was no guarantee if the youngsters had gotten to shore that they would have had the skill or the strength to get the boat in: it might well have gotten away from them, granted only all of them had gotten off if it did float away. It was not guaranteed that there'd been any signal flare aboard or that the youngsters would know what it was for. It was a simple tender-boat, dock to boat and back again, for carrying supplies, and most everyone that handled it was expert, not tending to get into difficulty that needed such things.

The kids had no idea what they were into. He sincerely hoped they hadn't tried to swim the current. Cajeiri had never swum in water over his head, though, bet on it, he'd read a book about it; while the other two, Taibeni, inlanders, were probably worse off than Cajeiri. The possibilities were beyond frightening.

"There are rocks above water," he said, veering off from the coastline and driving close to where he knew such rocks were, right near the mouth of the bay—a miserable perch for anybody, but a lifesaver of more than one fisherman in the history of the estate, as well as the ruin of a couple of boats who hadn't known they were there at high tide. Tano and Algini came into the cabin for a moment to warm up—Banichi turned the heater on, to the relief of all of them; and even started up a pot of hot tea.

They ran by the first rock, with no sign of the youngsters, and on the way to the second, Bren took a cup of tea, as much for the warmth of the cup as the contents. They reached the second half-submerged reef, with still no sign of the kids—the third rock there was no likelihood the kids could reach with the tide running, and he opted to put about back to the shore,

to take up that search again, and to run by a fourth rock dangerously close in.

Banichi meanwhile was on the radio, talking to Jago.
"Nandi," Banichi said, "nand' Toby is on his way. His lady is
coming with him."

"Good," he said. It *was* good. Barb was many things, but she
was an experienced hand with the boat, she had common sense
in a crisis she understood, and she knew the sea. "Advise them
of our status. Then one regrets to say we must concern the aiji
and discreetly advise him of the situation. I would do so personally, and shall, if you will hand me the microphone."

"Yes," Banichi said. It wasn't a call he wanted to make, and
there was a certain hazard in announcing to the world in any
recognizable way that the aiji's son and heir was out in a sailboat on a given stretch of water. Bren listened as Banichi made
the short call to Jago, speaking in a personal code that, apart
from the code the Guild used, was something she and Tano and
Algini understood.

Then Banichi used ship-to-shore to call the Bujavid operator, and the aiji's guard—the best route, Bren thought, gazing
out over a vast tract of eye-tricking water and rough coastline,
and still not a sign of a boat or the youngsters. Banichi used
code there, too, and evidently was able to convey what had to
be conveyed, because Banichi didn't hand him the microphone,
just talked in short, coded bursts to whoever received the call.
At last Banichi closed off the contact, and said:

"The aiji has been informed, nandi. The aiji-dowager is
airborne from Shejidan and intends to come in at Dalaigi. It
seemed more discreet for me to make the call."

"The dowager was back in Shejidan?"

"One apprehends that she had stayed there the night, Bren-
ji, after the last incident, had resumed her flight to Malguri
today and is now turning the plane around a second time, and
coming here. They did not give an estimated time, doubtless a
security concern."

"One is by no means sorry to have her assistance," Bren said. He could only imagine the dowager's state of mind after *two* aborted flights. And he could only imagine Tabini's state of mind dealing with the dowager and his son's second disappearance, this time into real danger. But Tabini's guard were all new men, since the failed coup; the dowager's were not, and they had worked with Banichi and Jago extensively. Bren was himself very glad to know Ilisidi was bringing in her resources . . . upset as he was to be the cause of the problem. He only hoped they could find the young rascals before she got here and end the day with a phone call to Tabini and the dowager presiding over a family dinner party up at the house.

The light, meanwhile, hurt the eyes, glancing off the water. The sun was headed down the sky, now, into afternoon, and the far distance was obscured in white haze.

Banichi surrendered the radio to Tano, and went out with Algini to watch the shoreline . . . but by now certain other boats showed on the northern expanse of water. None of them were the sailboat. They were fishermen from the village and the neighboring district, all spreading themselves out in the bay and sweeping the area they had already crossed, a precaution for which Bren was very grateful.

Tano listened to something on the radio, then said, "Nand' Baiji is launching his boats and Lord Geigi's personal yacht, nandi. They are going out to meet the coastal current. Nand' Baiji is going out personally."

"Good," Bren said. That was the most important thing, to get boats into position to catch the youngsters if they had been swept out into that southerly flow—a current strong enough in some seasons that even larger boats had to take notice of it. It was very, very easy to assume one was making progress northerly, unless one had a shoreline for reference.

More than one fishing boat had been lost when that treacherous current met a contrary wind and the waves turned chaotic. And that was not a situation he wanted to contemplate.

The peninsula that divided Najidami Bay from Kajidami Bay, where Kajiminda sat in much the same position as Najida, had a hellish set of rocks at low tide.

"What does the weather report predict?" he asked Tano, and Tano checked and reported.

"A front will arrive by morning, nandi, with southerly winds and overcast, rain in the afternoon."

Not as bad as could be: winds blowing with the current, not cross-grained, but it would speed the little boat along. And rain and rising wind could swamp a little sailboat, not even mentioning hypothermia.

He wished that the tender had been equipped with a locator. Or a radio. Or—he had to admit it—the detested wireless phone. Any sort of communication. If the youngsters had the presence of mind to use the sun, and a shiny object. Anything.

But there was so much light out there, and his eyes burned with the effort. No sunglasses, no protection, nothing of the like turned up in the bin by the wheel. Damn it all. He wasn't sure he wanted to come back if he couldn't find the kids . . . didn't want to face Tabini and Damiri, or the Taibeni kids' parents. Or the dowager. God knew he'd tried to keep up with the kids. He'd gotten distracted. He'd failed for one miserable hour to post a guard on the kids, even his aishid had been distracted for that hour, under his orders, and they'd just—been kids. The eight-year-old steered the group, the other two didn't have the fortitude to tell Cajeiri no, or didn't think they had the authority to fling themselves on him bodily and stop him. Adults had fallen into the same trap with the boy. A long string of adults.

"Nothing," he said to Tano, beside him. "Has Toby's boat left yet, nadi-ji?"

"They are away and coming up the opposite side of the bay, nandi, in case they went straight across."

"One fears they have been swept out to sea." He didn't trust himself to find the current. They were out far enough now to avoid the rocks. He throttled way back as they nosed into the offshore current and let the current take the boat, just reading that and the shifting wind as best he could. If the wind had kept up as it had been off the point, the youngsters would have been swept northerly. But after a brief lull as they had been outbound, it was shifting to carry them southerly, increasingly so. The change in wind direction meant smoother water for the little craft—but a far, far faster passage, and it was continuing to shift. Tacking against the wind—that wasn't something they likely knew how to manage; and that rocky coast was not their friend. "Get up atop and look out as best you can, Tano-ji. Trade with Banichi and Algini when the cold gets too much."

"Yes," Tano said, and went out, admitting a gust of cold air. His footfalls resounded on the ladder as he went up with the various antennae and the dish—he wouldn't improve reception, but it was the best vantage they had, and that, at the moment, was everything.

The current had them now, and Bren throttled up just a little, hoping desperately that a boat moving under power would not just run past the kids.

Hoping for a sight of a very, very small object, in all the sheet of white light that was the Mospheiran Strait.

The sun was warm, at least, though the wind was biting cold, and they had wrung out Jegari's pants and coat, as hard as they could, even putting the oar handle into the loop of cloth and twisting with all their strength to wring out the last drops of moisture: that was Antaro's idea, which Cajeiri thought was outstandingly clever. They had found two floatation vests, and putting one of those on Jegari offered him some protection from the wind. Cajeiri thought Antaro should wear the other, since she could not swim at all, but both of them insisted he put it on, so he did that, and made them happier, uncomfortable though it was: he and Jegari agreed they would keep Antaro afloat should they have an accident.

The situation they were in, however, was worse and worse,

and the water that splashed aboard was cold as ice. They tried again to row in toward shore, and worked at it, but got nowhere: they let the sail down and just tried not to go too far. Then Cajeiri remembered he had read about swimming that if you were caught in a current you should swim hard with it and get speed enough to swim across it.

So they put the sail up again and tried to do that. They rowed with their single oar in the bow—Antaro doing much of the rowing, since she was the only one not encumbered by a vest; but that was no good, and then Cajeiri tried to turn the boat in toward the rocks, but that was a worse mistake: the tiller went over, but when Jegari put in the oar hard, straight down, and tried to pull on it, it twisted in his hands and then broke right in two. The end went floating right away from them.

Jegari was terribly embarrassed at that, but not half as embarrassed as Cajeiri felt for the whole situation.

Still, mani had taught him not to make excuses when it was really bad, and it was. It was very, very bad. He was so sorry his gut hurt. But that meant his companions were really, truly owed an apology for his bad leadership. And it hurt his conscience that Jegari was doing all the apologizing.

"One accepts all blame for this unfortunate situation," he said to his two companions, "and you should forget the oars."

"We are equally to blame, nandi," Antaro cried.

"We are older," Jegari said. "We saw danger in it. We should not have agreed."

"You are not to say no to me!" Cajeiri snapped. He was determined on that. "Or we *will* disagree." But his associates on the ship, Gene and Artur, had argued with him. They had also agreed with more than these two would ever agree to. "This time perhaps would have been a good time to say no and argue," he acknowledged unhappily, as the waves tossed their little boat in a little space of calm, and the wide, sunlit ocean sparkled fiercely around them. "We have no water to drink. Sea water would kill us. I know that. And we have no food."

"Nand' Bren will come after us once he misses us," Antaro said.

"He will," Jegari said. "And his big boat can go faster than this, surely."

"His boat and nand' Toby's certainly can. They can cross the whole ocean in a day, almost. Well, from the Island to the north coast. And you are right. They will be looking for us. We must surely be easy to see. The big boats have a much better view." He sat and thought, and thought, and the wind puffed at their sail, and the sail filled, and took them further south.

He thought it was south, at least.

And he had learned one thing about boats, or, to tell the truth, remembered something that nand' Toby had once told him, which was that the tiller could not turn the boat if the boat was not going faster than the water was, and they had had ample proof of that fact. So he turned the boat as much toward where he thought land was, as much as he could get without losing the wind, and with his two companions gazing hopefully at him, he tried to remember everything else he had learned from nand' Bren and from nand' Toby and from Barb-daja about boats. He thought he at least *looked* confident, with the boat moving again, and his hand on the tiller.

He did not feel that confident at all, and he was trying to remember his maps, which he had studied, whether they had already passed Kajidami Bay, too, and whether Kajiminda Peninsula jutted out far enough they could run into it. There was Dalaigi Township, beyond that, but Kajiminda Peninsula was a huge hooked jut of land with yet another deep bay that he thought inset into the continent, so they could completely miss it, and end up in the Southern Ocean where the seas got really rough.

It was just a mess, was all. A very unfortunate mess.

Antaro had had the best idea, hoping for Bren to turn up. So did he. Bren would surely be looking for him about the time he failed to appear for lunch. Bren would search the whole house, and know right where to look—and somebody would surely miss the sailboat. The only foreseeable problem was that the sailboat they had taken was the boat that would help nand' Bren get out to the big boat to come after them . . . but Bren would find a way. He believed that.

Bren would be out looking, by now. They would have to search the shore first, and now that he thought about it, he was sure he would have been a lot smarter to use the wind to carry them straight across Najidami Bay to land on the northern shore.

But he had not been that smart. So it would take nand' Bren time to search where he should have been, and only after searching the shores would nand' Bren figure they had gotten out of sight of land, and start looking for them out in open water.

Nand' Bren would search where the wind blew. Nand' Bren would waste no time in the other direction—and if the wind had only changed *before* they had gotten out of the bay, they could have gotten back to Najiminda and had no problems at all.

Wishes are no substitute for planning, mani had told him once, severely.

He had hoped, for instance, that nand' Bren had not called his father to send airplanes, which would just make a terrible fuss.

But as the sun went lower and lower in the sky he began earnestly to wish he would see an airplane . . .

Because the white glare of the water faded to a colder, less fortunate shade, and the sun began to go down not below the horizon, but behind a bank of clouds in the west.

He had learned something about weather from nand' Toby. Weather came out of the west and blew to the east, and clouds in the west always meant rain on its way.

He had thought their situation could not get worse. But the clouds were getting taller as the sun sank lower, and their wind was sinking as it became a reddish sky with purple clouds.

Sunset dyed the water orange where it was not gray. The sky looked thoroughly ill-omened.

They were not moving much, now: the sail flapped. And when he began to wish for a wind, he could only think how storms did come in, swept in on a lot of wind.

With that cloud building to the west, there would be a storm wind coming down on them, pushing them toward land, for certain. But rain was coming, almost certainly, and more water inside the boat meant less difference between the water outside and the water inside.

Which could mean, besides them being very wet and cold and exposed to lightning, that their boat could just fill up and sink. They could throw water out: they had a little metal cup that rolled around under the tiller seat, but if the waves got rough, their boat was very low to the water.

That was a scary thought.

It was very scary.

8

The *Brighter Days* rode off to starboard of *Jeishan,* at the limit of vision, while the sun came down into rising clouds. The Najiminda headland showed as a dark rim on the lee side—a situation which afforded a little hope: that if the wind got up, the lee shore might receive a drifting boat.

Calls to the estate had turned up the information that, yes, the sailboat had oars aboard, as well as the two life preservers: the major domo was very sure of that. But whether the youngsters could row with any skill, or enough strength, was a question.

Fisherfolk had come out past the end of the bay, a fair-sized little fleet, and used their knowledge of the currents to scour the coastline and likely rocks. The wind, which had backed around once, had been fickle, but that cloud on the horizon would bring a driving wind as well as strong waves—two other forces that might push the little boat, this time shoreward and across the current. But waves could easily swamp the boat, in a moment if the youngsters let the boat go broadside to the waves. The boat could survive in the hands of an expert: but one mistake, one miscalculation, and they would just roll under and come ashore like those mysterious splinters of driftwood—from some boat, a long, long time ago.

They had to find them, was all—before the gust front got here.

The dowager's plane should be landing soon—and now they had one search plane aloft, scanning the shore. The young lord of Dur had gotten a call from Najida, and that young man, a pilot himself, discreetly contacted a few southern fliers he knew as trustworthy, so they were coming, but that took time, and involved the airport down at Dalaigi. Right now, only that one plane was aloft, quartering the sky, running out to sea and back, and thus far turning up nothing.

Lord Baiji was out from Kajiminda in Geigi's yacht, searching that outer coast, and all their people who had boats, no few, made a net as tight across Kajidami Bay as they had people to make. *There* was their greatest hope, because the main current ran as it ran, generally southward, and it swept inward right there, give or take what the storm did to the waves. Lord Baiji and the Edi folk were a vast catch-net, to prevent the strayed boat from getting out of their search area.

And if the young gentleman and his companions turned out, after all this, to be asleep under some hedgerow along the estate road—having lost the boat on launch—

Or if the tide had taken the boat, and the youngsters were out on some lark—

He would be outstandingly reasonable if that proved ultimately the case. If it was all a mistake, a missed communication— he would be so everlastingly grateful.

But as evening came on, as time elapsed with no word from the estate, the more likely their almost-worst fears became, that the youngsters were out here in the path of the storm— their worst fears being that the small boat had already capsized out here in rougher water and the youngsters were at the bottom of the bay.

But, he told himself, it was a wooden boat. It wouldn't just sink. It would float along capsized, if the youngsters had sense enough to stay with it and cling to it and its balloon of trapped air—an overturned boat was a far, far easier thing to spot than one boy in all that water. The Taibeni youngsters would insist that Cajeiri should wear that bright yellow life vest. Cajeiri would, of course, insist otherwise.

This time Bren prayed the Taibeni overruled the young gentleman.

"The dowager has landed, nandi," the estate called to report.

"Do as she asks in all particulars," he said, knowing there wasn't much his estate could do more than they had done. They had both boats out, every fisherman was out, Lord Geigi's people were out, and there was nothing Ilisidi could do, except deploy her young men out along the roads where village folk were already searching, and look with whatever high-tech gear her bodyguard had brought with them—that was one hope she brought with her—that, and the fact that the aiji now knew, and would be deploying his own people, a presence that did not announce itself.

But now the light was fading fast, and lightning flickered in the clouds to the west, which loomed up taller and taller. The wind had not changed—yet. But that front was rolling in fast. Radar, they had, but the sailboat had no reflector, and radar thus far picked up nothing—because the boat was so low and so small—

That, or because the boat was not there to be found. But he *refused* to think that.

Out on deck, Banichi and Tano and Algini relied on their night vision, having requested the running lights be cut off. *They* could see in the murk, and Bren cut even the chart light most of the time, relying on the slight glow that lit the compass. He was using the locator; he had told Banichi and the other two that if they saw three rocks ahead or looked to be getting closer to the shore, that they should run and warn him. He had laid a course to miss the Sisters; but they were a hazard, one the sailboat could run right over, but the *Jeishan* couldn't. Even with the locator, it wasn't an area to try to search in the gathering dark.

Ilisidi had not called: that was for security reasons; but he talked to the house, off and on, reporting indirectly about the "lost child." If the aiji's enemies could not put two and two to-gether, with the aiji-dowager having landed at the local airport, they were asleep tonight. But things were as they were.

More lightning, this time with the rumble of thunder, and Bren cast a routine glance at the fuel gauge, thinking that the same wind blew both bad and good—both saved them fuel and made the location of the little boat an even chancier guess.

Big bolt, that split the sky end to end of the windshield, and threw the bow railing of the boat and his bodyguard into stark contrast to the darkening water.

Then a beep from the radio alerted him to a call, and he fumbled the headset up, keeping one hand on the wheel. "This is the paidhi-aiji. Go ahead."

"This is Baiji out of Kajiminda, nand' paidhi. Radar has picked up one brief anomaly."

"Bearing?" he asked, white-knuckled on the wheel, and he absorbed it to memory and signed off abruptly, having no hand to spare to write it down in grease pencil on the chart until he had dropped the headset. He steered blind for a moment, trying to figure that location on the chart relative to *Jeishan*.

Baiji could only be approximate in location: it might have been a piece of flotsam. If he left the search pattern, it left a gap in their net, maybe a critical one.

But it was the first hope they had had.

He snatched up the headset again. Called Toby's boat. Jago answered.

"We shall be moving on the report of a blip in Baiji's search, nadi-ji, as fast as we can. It may be nothing. But we are going there. Keep your pattern."

"Yes," was Jago's terse answer, and he wished Jago's night-sight was out there in the dark . . . but Jago needed to be at *Brighter Days'* radio. Probably Barb was out on deck, at that post.

He didn't want to worry about that. He simply throttled up and veered onto the new heading.

*   *   *

Lightning split the sky, far out from the cloud, and it had gotten darker and darker.

Cloud was much, much taller than it had been. It covered three quarters of the sky and it was still coming.

"Sleep," Cajeiri said to Antaro and Jegari. "Sleep if you can. It will be hard to do once the storm comes. I am pulling us as close to the land as I can without losing the wind. All we can do is what we are doing. When that storm hits, the wind may carry us ashore."

Before it sinks us, he thought, but he did not say it.

They tried to sleep. He sat and thought, and thought, and it seemed to him somewhere in the books he had read there was something about a sea anchor one used in storms on wooden ships.

Well, theirs was a wooden ship. And they had a bit of rope, not much of it, just what one might use for tying up. But he thought about it, and he thought if the wind started pushing them and the waves dashed them around, having something large and soppy trailing them on a string would possibly keep them from rocking so much and maybe keep them aimed better. Truth, he had no clear memory what it was really supposed to do for a ship. But they had their rope, and they had three coats, and if they sacrificed one and just heaved it out, it might help.

They just had to stay upright and not have a wave go over them. Then, maybe since storms went to shore, the wind could drive them there.

His mind raced, trying to think of things they could do.

He thought about ripping up the benches and seeing if they could use those for oars. But they were very solid. He was not sure they could get them free. And it might weaken the boat.

The cloud flashed with lightning, and thunder boomed right over them, rousing his companions.

Cajeiri grabbed up Jegari's coat, which they never had been able to get dry.

"Get the tie rope," he said. It was all the free rope they had. The wind, like a rowdy child, might roll them right over if they kept wallowing about like this. The waves when they hit the boat tended to slosh right into it. And that was getting scary.

They got the rope. He tied Jegari's once very good coat into a bundle and threw it overboard, and tied the other end to the boat.

Lightning showed two worried faces.

"We shall come through," he said to them, and the thunder boomed, and about then a gust of wind hit the boat. He made a desperate try with the tiller, but so far their sea anchor did nothing, and water slapped the boat and rocked it in a moment of following lull.

But slowly, slowly they did slew about a bit—the tiller still not working, but the sail starting to fill. He dared not lose that little boom rope. He took a double and triple tie on its end to be sure that the boom stayed within limits.

"Sit in the bottom together!" he cried. "Link arms and keep out of the way of the boom. It will be rough!" It might be a stupid idea, but it was better than no idea, and the waves were ruffling up and the wind was like a hammer, making the ropes start to sing as the sail strained and the dragging sea anchor lagged behind them. He had no reference point to tell where they were going. But the wind was coming more or less at their backs, and spray came up, mingled with rain as, all of a sudden and with a rush of wind and a crash of lightning, the heavens opened up and let loose on them. Water sloshed in. He kept one hand on the little rope, one on the tiller, and now with that one wave, the bottom of the boat was awash.

"The little bucket!" he shouted out. "Use the bucket!"

Antaro leaned back to get it from behind his feet, and got back again, and they did, one of them and then the other; and meanwhile the rigging screamed, and the rope burned his hand when the boom jerked outward. He hauled as hard as he could, thinking—if the little rope broke, if that little twist of rope let go or something came untied, or he even made a mistake and lost his grip and let the force of the wind hit that knot he had made, they were all going to die.

They bailed and bailed. Jegari was trying to do something in the interval. Lightning flashes showed him trying to link his belt to Antaro's . . . Antaro the one of them with no life preserver.

Antaro suddenly paused bailing, pointed out into the dark ahead and a little to the right. "I see a light!" she cried.

He could not see it. He thought it wishful thinking.

And then he did see it, a faint, faint glow. They had no light to signal back. Water hit him in the face, salt water, that stung. He could no longer feel the tiller under his arm, his face was numb.

But the light reappeared as he blinked clear, a faint glimmer. "The light *is* there!" he cried. It went out again, lost in the murk, and then reappeared. It might be a house on the shore, he thought, and hugged the tiller and feathered the rope as the boat tipped and rocked alarmingly in the gusts. " 'Gari-ji, if we fall in, keep hold of Antaro, hear me? Do *not* both of you try to reach me! I shall float and reach you. That is an order! Hold to each other!"

"We shall come back there, perhaps! I have linked belts with Antaro! She will be all right! We should stay close!"

"You shall not! You will tip the boat over! Stay where you are and hold on to each other! I order you! We have a light! We are going there!"

His voice cracked when he shouted. He hoped they heard. More, he hoped they would do what he told them to do. He had had experience of humans, who did *not* group to their leader as desperately. He understood in his own body—it was hard for them all not to rush together. It was terribly hard; but he had to be here and they had to be there in the middle and balanced to keep the boat afloat in this heaving water, and he was sure of his instruction.

Water hit him in the back. Worse, it crashed past him into the boat, a whole bathtub full.

And when he blinked the stinging flood from his eyes and swiped them with a sodden sleeve, he saw a brilliant light, a blazing white light.

So did his associates, who pointed at it and shouted, and dangerously tried to get up to wave.

"Stay down!" Cajeiri cried, and waved his own hand, hoping to be seen. The light swept away from them, and swept back again, casting the waves into relief against the dark, showing the shapes of his companions ahead of him. "Yell!" he shouted across the wind. "*Help!*"

The light left them, swept back again, glared down on them like a single wide eye, unblinking and turning the water to green glass. "Hold still!" he cried as Jegari started again to try to stand. "Sit *down*, 'Gari-ji!'"

Jegari plumped back down, and that light eclipsed behind a wash of water and then came back again, flaring above them and then on them and then below as the sea heaved. Cajeiri clung fast to the tiller and tried to steer, such as the boat would, toward that light. It was no good. There was no steering.

But the distance between them and that light grew less. Cajeiri heard a steady thumping, that at first sounded like a deep, powerful heartbeat, and then he knew it was an engine, and it was surely nand' Bren or nand' Toby come after them. It was up to them simply not to sink until they could meet up with that boat.

He could see a hull now, a white hull with a blue line, the only color in the world beside the glass-green of the heaving water, The glaring light proved to be a spotlight on a swivel, and some dark-uniformed man worked the light, which the boat kept continually centered on them as it came close.

The boat came right by their bow, towering over them with a loud racket of the engine, and fought to stay there. Their boat bumped into that pristine white hull and turned and grated against it.

Two men then. One flung out a rope with a weight on the end of it, and shouted, "Make that fast!"

Jegari and Antaro scrambled to do that, wrapping it about the middle seat, that being what they could reach. Another weighted line came down to them, and Cajeiri let go the tiller and grabbed it.

Smack! They ran into the side of the big boat. He fell off his seat, and held to the rope, and scrambled in freezing water to tie the rope somewhere, anywhere, which turned out to be the bar across the tiller opening.

"Are you attached?" a big voice shouted. It was Banichi. Surely it was Banichi; and he shouted, "Yes, nadi-ji! Both lines now!"

"Who has no vest?" he heard, above, and then saw, in the wandering and bobbing of the spotlight, another rope come down to them. "Tie that around you!"

"Antaro, go!" Cajeiri yelled out. "Now! Hurry! Get loose and clear the way!"

Antaro unbuckled her belt, then got on her knees and, steadied by her brother, grabbed the line, wrapped it about herself several times. It went taut and hauled her up.

"You next, nandi!" Jegari called out. "Go!"

That was reasonable. He and Jegari both had floatation vests. He lurched upright, grabbed Jegari and the rope came down again, and he wrapped it around and around himself and held onto the rope's end.

Immediately, he was yanked up like a fish on a line, dragged painfully over a small steel rail and dumped onto the deck.

"Rope!" Banichi's voice shouted next, and another man— it must be Algini—raked the rope off him and threw it down again, all the while the boats grated together and thumped and banged. Cajeiri clawed after the railing and clung to it trying to see, with the rain coming down and the spotlight bouncing up and down.

In the next moment a hand seized him unceremoniously by the back of his life vest and jerked him up, hauled him around.

"Banichi-ji!" he protested, but Banichi shoved him against the railing and shouted, "Hang on with both hands, young gentleman!"

Hang on he did. He grabbed the rail and hung on with both arms, this time. He was cold as ice, and beginning to shiver, and sick at his stomach all at the same moment. He was aware of Antaro holding on beside him, and he had a good view as Jegari came over the rail, likewise hauled in like a fish and dumped on the deck.

Last, Tano shouted up at the others and Banichi and Algini together hauled him up to his feet, dripping wet . . . Cajeiri had the reflected light off the superstructure to show him their faces, all desperate, all dripping and drowned in the rain, and immediately Banichi seized him around the ribs and just carried him, so tightly he was close to throwing up, he was so cold and so clenched up.

He saw the doorway from his sideways vantage, the lighted white door. The lighted wooden floor—amazingly real—came up at him and righted itself as Banichi heaved him somewhat upright. The world had been all lightning-shot black, and now it had wonderful things like polished wood, and railings to hold to, and warmth.

He saw nand' Bren at the wheel, very relieved and very worried at once. "Is that all of you?" he asked, "is that everybody with you?"

"Yes, nandi," Cajeiri managed to say, teeth chattering. "We are all aboard."

"We are too close to shore," Bren said. "Cast the tender free, 'Nichi-ji!"

"Yes," Banichi said, and was off, and the door shut again.

Cajeiri saw a bench and got up and sank down on it, dripping wet. The big boat was so much more stable. The air was almost thick, it was so warm, compared to outside.

He saw Bren turn the wheel furiously, and heard the boat's engines labor as the deck pitched.

They could not wreck nand' Bren's boat on the shore. They must not. Between Antaro and Jegari, Cajeiri clamped his teeth on his lip and clenched the edge of the white-painted bench, just holding on as Bren jammed the power on.

Something scraped all down the hull of the boat, and was gone, and then the boat righted itself and the engine sounded different, freer, more powerful: buffets from the waves came at the bow of the boat, and these came faster and faster as the boat took another turn, increasing power.

Then nand' Bren looked easier, too, easing his grip on the wheel, concentrating on the view out the windows, and occasionally down at something Cajeiri could see lighted on the counter.

"One is extremely sorry, nand' Bren," Cajeiri offered. "One is very extremely sorry."

Nand' Bren did not speak to him, not immediately, and that meant nand' Bren was probably framing an educational remark, something he might think adequate to the situation. It was taking a very, very long time to come out, or to organize itself, or possibly a long time for nand' Bren to surmount his temper, and Cajeiri began to agonize about the adequacy of his response, right along with nand' Bren.

"Nand' Bren," Cajeiri said finally, breaking the deathly silence that hovered above the rumble of the boat engine and the noise of the thunder. "Nand' Bren, one understands that our stupidity has exceeded all previous limits, and that we have exposed you to the displeasure of my house, which is entirely unjustified, and we shall tell our father so. We are all three extremely grateful to you and your guard for our rescue, because we could have been killed—though one was making the most earnest efforts to steer the boat and to reach the shore. We are most sorry. We shall obey all instructions from your staff. We shall ask funds from our father to pay your estate for the boat, which we in no way intended to destroy; and we shall pay for the damage to your boat. And we shall forever observe much, much better sense than we did in going out on the water. We shall be much wiser from now on, nand' Bren."

He ran entirely out of breath: his teeth were chattering so he had had trouble getting that much out. But he added, because he had to know: "Have you told my father, nandi?"

"Yes. And the aiji-dowager is aware. You should know, young gentleman, that she had turned back to Shejidan after the incident of your freight train. She started home a second time and has now turned around a second time in mid-flight, hearing you were lost, and come here. She will be arriving at the estate, and one is about to call her to inform her you are safe, now that we are somewhat on even keel."

Great-grandmother. Two flights turned around. He *was* in great difficulty.

He sat absolutely still while Bren took up the handset, punched buttons, and made a call, first to nand' Toby, and to Jago aboard nand' Toby's boat, telling them to come about, that he had them all; and next to a Lord Baiji, which seemed to be another boat, thanking him very much for his assistance in locating them.

And then nand' Bren called the estate, which took several tries before he succeeded.

"Nadi," he said to the person who answered, "inform the grandmother that the lost is found and securely aboard. Request of the grandmother that she inform the relatives. You are breaking up, nadi."

At last he put down the handset and remarked, "One hopes they heard all of that."

"One is very, very sorry, nandi." Cajeiri found himself shivering, and where he and the others sat was now the source of a very large puddle, which was running across the deck, this way and that according to the pitch of the boat. It went here, it went there. It was a large puddle, augmented by what had run off Banichi and Tano and Algini, who were almost as soaked.

"There is weather gear in the locker," nand' Bren said. "Put it on for warmth."

"Yes," Antaro said, and got up and brought back two rain-coats. She wrapped one around him and put the other around her and Jegari despite the boat pitching about. It was warmer, very much warmer, already, and Cajeiri began to shiver.

"I gather," nand' Bren said, "that you attempted to go out to the boat."

"We did, nandi. And one thought one could sail back, but every time we tried, we went further out."

"First, sailing against the wind is not an easy skill. It can be done. But when the moon pulls on the water, young gentleman, it and everything sitting on it move out to sea—in the case of bays along this coast, quite rapidly so."

"Is that what happened?" He was amazed. He knew about tides. But he had gotten caught, all the same, and never realized what was happening to them. "Nandi, we meant only to go out and see the boat."

"No excuses, young gentleman. You should have sailed straight across the harbor when you realized you were in trouble. You would have reached land before the tide pulled you out."

"We were trying to go faster, nandi, and use the speed to go against the wind."

"That will never work. Given time, and if you do not drown yourself, young gentleman, one will be pleased to show you how to sail against the wind. It is a case of patience and sub-tlety. One recommends both."

"One offers no excuses for our behavior, nandi," he said very meekly. "One accepts all responsibility. My companions urged us not to do it."

"Nandi," Jegari said, "you are not obliged to say so. It is our responsibility."

"It *is* my fault," Cajeiri said, angry, and upset. "And we choose to take the responsibility."

"One dares say you will. Antaro."

"Nandi?"

"There is a dry life vest in that bench over against the wall. Go get it and put it on."

"Are we going to sink, nandi?" Cajeiri asked.

"You will notice *we* wear them in these seas."

That was so.

"Put it on," nand' Bren said. "And next time you steal a boat, young gentleman, be sure you have oars and enough life preservers."

"Yes, nandi."

He knew he had to hear very stern rebukes from his father, his mother, Great-grandmother, and eventually Great-uncle Tatiseigi. It made it worse that he had, this time, richly deserved it.

But it was, after all, interesting that they had gotten caught by the tides, which was a mysterious thing, and not something he had ever been specifically warned against . . .

"Hot tea?" Tano suggested, and, indeed, from further back in the cabin, Tano brought a big tray of mugs. Algini was nursing a sore hand—the swelling looked very nasty; and Banichi was soaked and grim, and very gladly took a cup. So did nand' Bren, and they three did.

Hot tea helped. It warmed all the way down. Cajeiri drank half the mug and sat contemplating the scope of the disaster around him. And then curiosity about what Bren kept looking at on the table propelled him to his feet, though everybody else had sat down. He staggered a little on the heaving deck, but he came close, and saw it was a chart on a lighted table.

"Where are we?" he asked nand' Bren, and Bren pointed to a place just off Najida Peninsula.

"We have to go wide into the bay," nand' Bren said, "because those are rocks. They lie beneath the water at high tide, and have taken the bottom out of boats."

It was all more complicated than he had thought. He had known the starship—well, not how to run it, but how to run most everything he met, and to open most any door, and he had always known where things were kept.

The planet was just big and full of surprises. And *tides.* Surprises got you even when you already knew about them, if you failed to use your head. And when you needed something, it might be clear back in Shejidan.

"One is very sorry about the boat," he said. "Nand' Bren, we tried to row back, but we lost the oars."

"It can easily happen, young lord," nand' Bren said. He was less busy now. He managed the wheel with one hand and held his tea mug with the other. "Did you know how to secure them through the oarlocks?"

"No, nandi," he said, since, whatever that was, hc had not secured the oars at all.

"Well, young gentleman, I shall also show you how to row a boat, if the aiji-dowager permits the time."

"One would be most grateful, nandi." He was thoroughly miserable. And he squished when he moved, even if the raincoat made him much warmer. He looked down at his feet, and saw he was still adding to the puddle that was wandering back and forth across the deck. "We shall never, ever take a boat that is not ours again."

"That would be wise, young lord," nand' Bren said calmly. Nand' Bren was always calm, no matter what. He wished he could be as calm. And nand' Bren said: "Not taking *anything* that is not yours, except, of course, should there should be an emergency, would be a very good policy, young gentleman."

"One hopes never to do such a thing again, nandi."

"My household accepts the sentiment," nand' Bren said, and Cajeiri found he hurt in very many places. He would hurt in more places than that once mani laid hands on him, he feared.

This time he was very glad to have only lost a boat, and not his companions. For a while out there it had been very, very serious, and they had all thought about drowning, and that would certainly have been a sorry end to all he wanted to do and to all the questions he wanted to ask.

He was so exhausted he went back to sit down, and Tano poured him another mug of tea. He rested and drank his tea, and found all the energy flowing right out of him.

He had yet to answer to mani, who was going to be very upset with him. He decided not to mention buying nand' Bren a new boat immediately. But it might be easier to ask mani than to ask his father.

He was going to have to think how to explain it all to his father.

It was a far faster trip back than the trip they had made out, searching all the shoreline. The young rascals slept the rest of the way, all of them folded over together, three dark heads bowed, three young bodies making one sodden bundle.

Bren sent his bodyguard below to change to dry clothes, one after another. He was the only one aboard who didn't leave a puddle where he stood, and he managed the wheel easily, downing more than one cup of hot tea. He had turned on the running lights from the time they had begun to use the searchlight, and now through the dark and the rain he saw a red running light, Toby's *Brighter Days* easily keeping pace with *Jeishan* now as they motored down the center of the bay, running fairly fast, in the interests of getting the youngsters safely ashore and into a protective security envelope as soon as possible.

They hadn't heard a word, for instance, from Tabini—but bet that there were forces landed.

And Tabini was likely going to be damned mad—he'd let the elusive young rascal get loose, Bren said to himself. He did *not* deserve credit for a rescue when his caretaking had let the boy steal a boat and go floating off unattended, except by two central district kids who couldn't swim and had never seen a major body of water.

The only harm done, thank God, were scratches to *Jeishan's* hull, and the loss of an aged little sailboat, very minor damage, on the cosmic scale.

The young rascals were still sleeping off their adventure, when he carefully put *Jeishan* into her berth at the dock and turned the controls over to Saidaro, one of his own staff, who waited on the dock in a driving rain, beneath the sole and lonely light, and who caught their mooring line.

"How are we to manage this?" Bren asked him when he had come into the cabin—at the waft of cold stormy air from the door, the youngsters began to stir and blink and realize they were at dock. "There's no room for *Brighter Days* behind us."

"We have help, nandi. One will anchor in harbor, and one of the fishing boats will get me back to dock, after nand' Toby comes in."

Wonderfully managed. He would owe the fishing boat captain, as well as Saidaro. He found himself exhausted, and glad to gather up the youngsters and herd them back onto the deck. He was done in—and the exhaustion of his long-suffering bodyguard was apparent. Estate staff came aboard to see to things— he had been pumping out all the way from the mouth of the bay, considering all the slosh and the rain that had poured into the well, but he left the shutdown to Saidaro, who tended *Jeishan* in ordinary times. He simply joined his bodyguard in getting the young rascals safely off the deck and onto the steady, very welcome dockside.

They waited there, just a little, as Saidaro pulled *Jeishan* out and Toby brought the *Brighter Days* in. The heavens cracked with lightning and water sheeted down as Jago joined them, first off that boat. She also looked exhausted, her ordinarily immaculate hair stringing a bit loosely about the ears.

The rain pelted down, cold, numbing cold, as they trudged up the long terraced climb to the house, and the shelter of the portico and the welcoming light of their own front door was a beautiful sight. Staff was waiting to take coats and whisk them to hot baths the moment they arrived . . . almost.

The aiji-dowager, with her cane, walked out into the entry hall to meet them, to bend a disapproving look on her great-grandson, and lastly to nod slowly at Bren, and at his aishid. "Well," she said, "nand' paidhi, will you take a brandy after your bath?"

"Very gladly," he said, "aiji-ma." It was very courteous of her, all things considered—it was beyond courteous: it was magnanimous, addressed to the author of her second aborted flight, the caretaker of her great-grandson. Physically, he would rather have fallen into bed. Mentally—he would not turn that honor down, even if it came with a stern warning.

He took a quick, almost a scandalously quick dip and scrub in the large marble tub: he came out steaming, and still feeling chill at the core, while menservants wrapped him in towels, and stood ready with a dressing gown. Jago awaited the other bath—Toby and Barb had come up to the house, and were using it, directly after the youngsters, who had taken it in sequence.

"Nand' Toby and Barb-daja—together?" he had asked Supani, and received an affirmative.

At least it would speed Jago's access to hot water, he thought. Banichi and Tano and Algini meanwhile had insisted on waiting their turn for the tub—Algini had been icing his bruised hand; and he insisted now that they go on in and stay there. "Please have your bath and take your time about it, nadiin-ji," he said wryly. "The youngsters have had their bath. My brother and his lady will be out soon, Jago will finally have her turn, and if the aiji-dowager intends a justified assassination, I should have known by now."

"Nandi," Tano protested.

"A joke, Tano-ji, a joke. One promises to tell you every detail of the meeting."

"Yes," Banichi said, the simple weary yes of an order taken, mission accepted. "But if you will hear counsel, Bren-ji, do not accept blame. It was your bodyguard that failed you."

"My bodyguard never failed me, 'Nichi-ji, though one appreciates the motive of the suggestion. Naively assuming the boy was where he should have been, I gave orders that brought you to *me* in the very confusion our young scoundrel used in his escape, and one will report that fact as it stands. Patience in our young guest was not likely, given the promise, and the circumstances. The servant I posted in the hall had naturally run to see to the lady. And I do not wish to express, at the moment, my vexation with the lady. So no more of this. Into the bath with you. Koharu!"

The servant, waiting at the door, held his dressing gown.

"Brandy or whatever else my bodyguard wants," he said. "The best for them. And Banichi, *accept* it."

"Bren-ji." A nod from Banichi. "But you will *not* take all blame, Bren-ji. One will speak to Cenedi."

"No," he said shortly. It was as close as he and Banichi had ever come to an outright argument, and he meant to win it. "This is my personal embarrassment, and I refuse to share it, 'Nichi-ji, I outright refuse."

"Nandi." A bow. Banichi gave in, not that Banichi was *not* reserving the option to talk to Cenedi about the event. Banichi shed the bathrobe to Supani's hands and stepped into the bath ... so with the rest, while Bren belted on his dressing gown and sat down on the bench.

The tub overflowed into its side drains as three replaced one, sinking deep into the warmth and washing the salt off. Bren let Supani braid back his hair in a simple damp knot, even while his bodyguard took to vigorous scrubbing and sloshed warm water over his bare feet. Brandy arrived, with a set of three serving glasses, and none of them turned that down.

"One has requested the same for Jago-nadi," Koharu reported with a little bow. "One hopes this was intended, nandi."

"Indeed," he said. He was exhausted. He was assuming things, leaning on his staff to do his thinking. The distress of an argument with Banichi had rattled him. But his bodyguard was taken care of. The youngsters, his brother, Barb, and now Jago—all were settled.

He was going to ache in the morning. Amazing how fighting the wheel had taken it out of him. Maybe it had been the death grip he had maintained on it throughout, to and from.

Things were better now, much better.

Koharu provided dry slippers, then, clear of the slosh zone, he headed back to his room to dress informally . . . informally, that was, by Bujavid standards: one did *not* visit the aiji-dowager in one's bathrobe, not by a mile.

"One is so glad, nandi," Koharu ventured to say as they entered his rooms.

"How *are* the youngsters?" He had not inspected them for bruises and injuries, but news of such would fly fast among the staff. "Are they well?"

"A few scrapes, nandi," Supani said. "And a few blisters— the young gentleman particularly. But no more than that."

Cajeiri had been at the tiller, managing the boat: likely he had been, the whole time. Brave kid: he'd done all right, past the initial flurry of young, overconfident mistakes. He'd done just all right. And hadn't said a word about the blisters. Probably hadn't felt them until he'd warmed up.

So the young gentleman and his aishid had gotten out with blisters and probably were going to be just as sore; and the aiji-dowager was, meanwhile, waiting, with her bodyguard, in the sitting room. He gathered himself together, put on a proper indoor coat, and went out and down the hall to the study, where the dowager waited, to give his accounting.

He entered, past one of the dowager's young men, who stood guard. Cenedi, Ilisidi's chief of security, rose from his chair as he came in, a warming token of respect to the house, in lieu of

Ilisidi rising, which the aiji-dowager did not. She sat, cane in hand, and Bren came and gave a deeper than usual bow.

"Nand' dowager. One is extremely regretful—"

"Oh, posh. The *Guild* cannot track the boy. How could you?"

"All the same . . ." He had his facts assembled. He was ready to give his account.

"We have heard the entire tale, nand' paidhi, the promised sailing trip, the phone call from the island . . . Barb-daja's distress . . ."

He feared he blushed. He earnestly tried not to, and bowed again. "One is extremely sorry, aiji-ma, that things under my management went so very wrong."

"Oh, sit down," Ilisidi said with a move of the cane. So he sat, which meant Cenedi could sit down, and Ramaso and staff, frozen until now near the doorway, could move in with the dowager's requested brandy. Ramaso gave a bow, the servants served the brandy to the dowager, to him, and to Cenedi, in that order, and Bren caught Ramaso's eye and nodded a dismissal for all staff.

So the first several sips of brandy went down in genteel silence and composure. It was fire on a raw throat, and then comfort, all the way down.

"We have decided we shall stay a few days," Ilisidi said, then, "and escort my great-grandson back to the capital in person. We shall not deprive him of his promised holiday, despite this disgraceful behavior. But we shall not place such a burden on your staff. It is a pleasant venue, what little we have seen of it. We look forward to its garden and its views."

"You honor this house," Bren said, which was pro forma; but it was also true: the household staff would be extremely excited to host the aiji-dowager. "Any hospitality we can offer . . ."

"Oh, just carry on, nand' paidhi, carry on as you would have, with your kinfolk and all."

"Nand' Toby will possibly be here the week," he said, "but he has received word his daughter of another union is injured, and he may opt to sail . . . one has no idea." It was in his head that, under changed circumstances, he ought to ask his brother to leave—one needed to *concentrate* on a guest like Cajeiri, and not have another incident. "One has not had an opportunity to speak to him."

"One believes you were discussing this very matter when my great-grandson chose to go boating."

"The aiji-dowager is, as always, very well-informed."

"One gathers Barb-daja is not pleased at your kinsman's contact with the prior union."

God, the aiji-dowager loved romantic scandal, every morsel of it. Of course she had heard, and she was interested.

"That would be understatement," he said ruefully, and Ilisidi looked pleased. He could only imagine the disaster if the dowager chose to convey her amusement to Barb, and offer advice.

"Pish, pish, your brother should stay. We are acquainted with him and Barb-daja, and shall have no objection to sharing accommodations. No more of this."

"Yes, aiji-ma."

"And Lord Geigi's nephew, this nand' Baiji. We understand he not only aided in the search, but actually provided the first sighting of my great-grandson's boat."

"He did, aiji-ma."

"Inconvenient."

"Aiji-ma?"

"He has *not* presented himself at court."

"His predecessor died during the Troubles, aiji-ma: there may exist some confusion in the house. One understands he is young . . ."

Ilisidi waved a thin hand and took another sip of brandy. "Excuses. But the fact, nand' paidhi, is the fact. Geigi's house, during the Troubles, presented no respects to the assassin of my grandson's staff, true, but has paid none, either, since my grandson's return. There is a list of persons who have not come to court nor contacted my grandson. It is a scandal that the nephew of our trusted associate should be on it, but he is. Geigi has promised that Baiji will attend the coming session—but that is not now."

"One completely understands, aiji-ma." It was not the law that a new lord had to come to court, but it was unusual, and foolish, given the importance of contact with the aiji, for a lord not to take advantage of that opportunity. "Lord Geigi still being lord of Kajiminda, the nephew never having received a face-to-face appointment from his uncle, perhaps, aiji-ma, he feels that his uncle's frequent contacts with the aiji are the valid ones."

The dowager nodded, reached, and began to refill her own glass. Bren started to get up to do so: Cenedi was faster. She had her sip and everyone settled.

"That, certainly, is an unusual circumstance," she said, "and we would overlook his reticence, nand' paidhi, but under other circumstances, notably the situation in the South, we cannot, officially, initiate contact. It would make a very unfortunate precedent that others could use to offer insolent behavior. In point of fact, Lord Geigi does suffice, for my grandson's satisfaction with his house; but in terms of an official thanks to this young lord in Kajiminda, we are distressed to say we cannot pay it."

"The paidhi would willingly do so. One is scheduled to meet with him in a few days. We might change the schedule and call on him tomorrow . . . should the dowager find that useful."

"If you should chance to express our favorable sentiments," Ilisidi said with a slow nod, "that would be appropriate. Baiji. Certainly more enterprising and useful in his performance this night than the reports of him have said. And you will urge him to remove himself from the list of those who have not contacted my grandson: it is very unbecoming company. My great-grandson will go with you tomorrow. He will not express thanks, but being a child, he can at least honor the house that aided in his rescue, and not enter into their debt."

An important technicality: if there was a debt, it could *not* bind a child who would be aiji. It had to be paid in courtesy, but being the visit of a child, would never be at issue *unless* this young lord someday became a true lord and delivered his man'chi to an adult and seated young aiji. *Then* the event might be remembered with some meaning.

So it was an honor the dowager proposed, one with limited current political value, but great potential value, if Baiji had any sense at all and bestirred himself to do what was right.

"I shall make immediate arrangements, aiji-ma. This cannot be allowed to hang fire or become gossip."

"Exactly," Ilisidi said. "The paidhi has an excellent grasp of the delicacy involved." The other brandy vanished, in three sips. "Now we are assured our great-grandson is safe and that the paidhi-aiji has not frozen or drowned, so we shall sleep soundly tonight."

"One greatly regrets, aiji-ma, to have been the source of inconvenience in your trip east."

"Oh, pish, my cousin will still be there a week or two. A little sea air comes welcome. We shall expect to take our own turn on that boat of yours, paidhi-ji, before we fly off again."

"Gladly," he said. "A very pleasant prospect, aiji-ma."

"Then good night to you, paidhi-ji." She set her cane in place, taking just enough time for Cenedi to spring up and reach her side, to provide a more helpful, yet discreet assistance. Bren rose, bowed, and the two of them, Ilisidi and Cenedi, left the room.

Bren downed the other half of his brandy and let go a long, slow breath, then walked on out into the hall himself, and down the little distance to his own door.

Jago, meanwhile, slightly damp from the bath, had made it back to the room. She was waiting for him.

"The dowager is not out of sorts," he said, finding cheer in that—if Ilisidi was still speaking politely to him, Tabini-aiji probably would, also. And he found even more cheer in saying, "One is relatively certain the young gentleman will be in his own bed by now."

"We are assured of it," Jago said. "The dowager's guard is on watch tonight at that door, and will not leave it. The staff reports no more calls from the mainland. One supposes there is no news of nand' Toby's daughter."

"None that I know. The dowager is willing for him to finish his visit here." He sank onto the dressing-bench, and in the discreet absence of Koharu and Supani, began easing off his own boots. "In one way of looking at it, this is a good thing: he has not abandoned his own interests. He was extravagant in his dutiful response, before, which broke his relationship with his first wife: much as I dislike Barb's behavior—I cannot forgive Jill-daja, either, for leaving him when things were at their worst, so I am far from even-handed in the matter."

"And Barb?" Jago omitted all honorifics.

"Has admittedly behaved badly in this visit," he said, "but she has gotten Toby's attention—and gotten him to stay with her despite the crisis on the Island. Given my brother's reactions previously, this is a change in him." He sighed. "But one dreads to imagine tomorrow, when I take the young gentleman to Kajiminda, and the dowager will be under my roof with Barb."

"Is that the plan, Bren-ji?"

"It seems nand' Baiji, in the confusion of his situation, with Lord Geigi in regular contact with the aiji, has not paid due courtesies in court, and the aiji-dowager will not visit him. But the young gentleman will come with me, so one hopes the situation can be regularized. Certainly, we owe the man. And *that* is to the good. And one assumes you will come with me."

"We shall."

"So the dowager and Barb will be under one roof with only the dowager's guards."

"Barb may not survive," Jago said. She was behind him, massaging his shoulders, but there was a smile in the voice.

"Someone who can speak to Toby must be here," he said.

"You would not wish me to do so," Jago said. "I would be honest."

"Tano, then."

"He will not be much more pleased."

"Tano and Algini. They can understand what they hear."

"Some on the dowager's staff can do so. The dowager herself, one suspects, Bren-ji."

"Nevertheless," he said. "Nevertheless, Jago-ji, one makes one's own provisions. I do not want Toby in difficulty. Make Tano and Algini understand this." Algini's hand was painful, and a little light duty would, he thought, be the best thing over the next several days.

"One will explain matters, Bren-ji," Jago said, and a moment later: "I would actually do this duty, if you asked."

"I know you would, but should never have to."

They went to bed. Jago's body was always a few degrees warmer than his. He apologized, on this particular night, but Jago pulled him close and evened out the difference.

It was soon very warm in bed. And he was out in minutes.

9

It ought to have been a leisurely morning. It might have been, had the dowager not been in residence; but Ilisidi took her breakfast at the crack of dawn, and, detecting the stir in the household, Bren got up, which consequently meant more stir in the household, and in the staff.

And that meant the youngsters got up, and once the youngsters were up, nobody was fated to get much sleep.

So in fairly decent time, Toby and Barb arrived at table, too, to meet a truly formal and large atevi breakfast, with staff attending, and bodyguards and attendants properly on duty.

Staff had mightily exerted themselves in the breakfast offering, with the aiji-dowager as their guest—there were eleven items, from grain porridge to fresh fish, eggs, and toast, and the aiji-dowager took to all of them with evident pleasure.

Which was good to see. Ilisidi was in high good humor, which was a great benefit in dealing with Barb and Toby. Cajeiri was on spectacularly good behavior, took particular care of his manners, had his staff standing at formal service, and in short order, actually wrung a good-humored laugh from the aiji-dowager when he nearly overset his water goblet and caught it miraculously before it spilled a drop.

"One tries," Cajeiri said, in great frustration, "one tries, mani-ma, and things fall over."

"One believes you exude a vibration," Ilisidi said, "from the effort of sitting still. Well caught, Great-grandson."

"Mani-ma." A little bow of the head.

"Are you through? You may be excused. You know you have a duty to do today."

"Yes, mani!" Cajeiri got up—thumping the table in his haste to be proper, shaking all the water goblets up and down, and gave a little bow to try to cover that, a bow to his great-grandmother, and to Bren, and to Toby and Barb, last of all to his great-grandmother again, and then he left, back to the halls, drawing his two companions with him.

Toby and Barb hadn't said a thing, a novel and pleasant behavior on Barb's part—who couldn't understand a word of the conversation; and Bren was very grateful. Predictably, Barb's temper had vanished in the excitement, and all seemed smoothed over there.

"So," the aiji-dowager said, in the waning of the meal, during which one might properly discuss light business, "you are off to Kajiminda this afternoon, nand' paidhi?"

"Yes, aiji-ma. The arrangement is made. We may take tea, but no more, as we anticipate: we shall pay our respects and be off. One begs your indulgence for leaving you."

"We shall enjoy the gardens and the coast. Cenedi and I shall walk down to the shore today and no doubt find a shell or two of a sort our Eastern lake does not provide."

"One begs the aiji-dowager to avail herself of whatever diversion or comfort this estate can provide."

"We plan to, we hope without inconvenience to your other guests."

"There can only be felicity in the aiji-dowager's presence."

"Especially since we have recovered my great-grandson from his folly. Tell these persons of your house that we recognize them for their assistance in this latest event as well as the prior, and invite them to take luncheon with us."

A great and appalling honor, one he conveyed with a nod to the dowager and, turning to Toby and Barb: "The dowager has just thanked you for your help finding her great-grandson and for your assistance getting to the mainland in the first place. Understand, her thanks is a very, very high honor in itself, and one an atevi house would memorialize in family records. More than that, she asks you to lunch with her. We are speaking of international relations, treaties, and peace here. There will be limited translation. You should appear in your ordinary clothes and the servants will cue you. Tano and Algini will attend you and supply some translation. I am so sorry to leave you. I have no choice, considering the relations with our neighbor. *Please* be extremely formal. This is beyond any state dinner in the Presidential Palace."

"Understood," Toby said. "Best coat, best manners, and all."

"Best," Barb said.

"Rely on the servants. Rely on the servants to cue you. And Tano and Algini. They will. If they ask you to do something, please don't even question. Just do it."

"I swear we won't embarrass you, Bren."

"I know you won't," Bren said, "or I wouldn't leave you here, because it is that important, Toby, Barb. You both take care, will you?"

"Sure," Toby said. "We're pretty well done eating. Can we excuse ourselves out? Or should we sit a while?"

Bren turned to Ilisidi. "They consider the honor you offer extravagant, are very grateful and will of course be at luncheon. They ask, too, if they may gracefully retire now—atevi portions are somewhat generous for us, aiji-ma, and one believes they have become somewhat over-full."

Ilisidi waved a hand in good humor. "Well enough, well enough. We look forward to the event." Her expression instantly became businesslike, Ilisidi suddenly bent on a point she wished more urgently to carry. "One expects a full report on your return, nand' paidhi, on this nephew of Geigi's. One believes Lord Geigi himself would appreciate a report."

"One will pay greatest attention to details, aiji-ma."

"Then you, also, will wish to proceed, to be back in good season."

"Yes, aiji-ma." That was a dismissal from table, an urging to pursue his day's business without worry, and he meant to do exactly that. He rose, bowed, leaving the table, and the remnant of the excellent breakfast, to the dowager.

He had, first, of course, to gather up Cajeiri and the Taibeni youngsters, pass on their attire—which proved far better than he had hoped. The servants informed him that all three—actually, probably Cajeiri, to do him credit—had had the foresight to pack something decently formal, in case manners were needed. Everything in the duffle had surely been crushed, but the staff, having wasted no time putting things in order, turned them all out quite nicely, given the situation.

"So," he said as they gathered in the hallway, near the front doors, "we shall drive over to the neighbors', pay our respects, have tea, and be back in time for supper. We shall not likely dine there tonight . . . possible, but unlikely." If it had been Lord Geigi, no question he would have expected dinner, but Geigi was just that sort of fellow—nobody escaped his hospitality. Baiji was—so report said—an unenergetic fellow, and given the irregularity of his relations with the aiji, and given the fact he was leaving Toby and Barb in the dowager's care, there seemed no likelihood at all of sufficient reason to overstay their intentions. There might be further exchanges: there might even be a reciprocal visit, if the dowager would agree to receive Geigi's nephew: that would be socially dicey. A phone call from Baiji to the aiji's secretary could straighten some of that out—but it hadn't happened. It was a peculiarly sluggish young man—who just had not stirred out to secure his fortunes, trusting, one supposed, in his famous uncle's relationship with the aiji, and his uncle's ability to do business as needed.

But Baiji had, he chided himself, scrambled right quickly to save Cajeiri's life—so perhaps it was just a reluctance to make moves that might cross Geigi's. He had been fast enough last night. Picking up *any* little boat had been chancy in bad weather, and Baiji had at least ordered Geigi's yacht out. One wondered if it had been Baiji at the helm last night—by what he had heard from the dowager, that seemed less likely; but if it had been, the young man was a very good yachtsman. And it *had* been Baiji who had advised him on the radio where to look for the youngsters. So he had been out there.

So he certainly owed the man. They all did.

Banichi and Jago showed up, and they went out under the portico just as the bus came trundling up the cobbled drive. Iscarti was driving, one of the younger staff, a competent, cheerful fellow who also specialized in mechanical repairs and plumbing, jack of several trades.

That meant Banichi and Jago could settle back to be passengers as they boarded. The youngsters took the third and fourth seats, Antaro sitting up with Cajeiri, right behind the seat Bren claimed, as senior present; and Banichi and Jago across from him, behind the driver. They started out, a little rough over the ancient cobbles, and then more smoothly as they reached the drive.

Bren got up and leaned on the seat railings, with the attention of that young trio, and most especially Cajeiri.

"You know certain things, nandi, nadiin: that Lord Geigi has served the aiji for years as the aiji's representative to the space-faring folk, an inestimably valuable and clever associate. He appointed a lady, his sister of the same father, to be lord of the estate: she died. Now her son, nand' Baiji, has been governing the estate in the lady's stead—and we do not know this man. We have scarcely met—though we are greatly in his debt for his assistance last night. But here is the delicacy in the matter: Baiji has not officially paid respects to your father the aiji, and he held neutral during the Troubles. This does not mean he was ever an enemy to your father. It was a strategy which preserved Kajiminda from attack, giving it a low profile, and probably incidentally preserving *my* estate, on its little peninsula, from any concentrated attack, so it was not badly done. The rebels were quite busy with people who *were* resisting them, we were away in deep space, I presented no threat and had no influence on any large scale . . . in short, because Baiji kept Geigi's estate politically quiet, and because Geigi, up on the station, concentrated on relations with the humans and was not making any great noise about it, either, *my* estate at Najida remained insulated and safe. So I owe him a debt for that. Second point: the people of this coast are largely Edi. Lord Geigi and his relatives are Maschi clan, ruling with Edi consent. The usurper's Southern allies are historic enemies of the Edi. Geigi's absence would easily have been an excuse for them to come up the coast onto this larger peninsula and pay old grudges. But they did not. The reason appears to have been their preoccupation with the capital: they may not have wanted to open a second war, while they were busy with the first. As for where Lord Geigi himself stood during this period, he was laying plans and building a network, should your father have died, young lord, to raise a war against Murini in the north, and his Southerner supporters. Geigi would *not* likely have claimed the aijinate for himself: in my own estimation, he is not a traditional person, nor would he enjoy being aiji. He likely would have backed your great-uncle Tatiseigi, young lord, who would have ruled in the hope of your eventual return. Geigi was responsible for the robot landers. He was responsible for the network of communications along the coast. He was responsible for very many things that made your father's return to power easier. *Therefore*, your great-grandmother is much more tolerant of nand' Baiji's lapses in protocols, so we shall not mention them, agreed?"

Cajeiri listened to this with more apparent attentiveness than he gave most lectures. It involved *him*, and his father, and things Cajeiri did understand far better than most eight-year-olds.

"So," Bren continued, "Baiji. Baiji has been quiet here. He has not visited the neighbors, including my estate. He owes my estate money, which he has not paid, but one does not mention that, either. He seems to be the sort of man who does exactly what he has to do and no more." This with a look directly at Cajeiri, who should understand that this was not an ideal state of being. "But you are not to say I said so nor are you ever to say so outside your own house: this is an opinion taken in council, and should be left there. This man saved your life, and the simple thanks for that is what we are dealing with today."

"Yes, nandi."

"So." Bren brought his hand down on the seat rail. "So we shall hope to meet an excellent if retiring young man, one who, whatever his failings, offered the proper response when you were in trouble. Is that entirely agreed upon?"

"Yes, nandi."

"*Please* stay close to me and my aishid."

"Yes, nandi. We shall be very careful. We shall be absolutely well-behaved. And we shall not touch anything."

"One is grateful. You may justly discharge your debt by visiting him, briefly, and expressing a reserved gratitude . . . in one sentence, young lord! For the rest—you are your father's son and your great-grandmother's great-grandson and you are not obliged to *two* sentences."

A bright grin. A laugh. Cajeiri had one excellent quality, having had the dowager for a teacher: the ability to see when grownups had their reasons, and to sense that complex politics should be left to his elders. "Yes, nandi! One sentence. We promise."

"We will handle other matters."

"Yes, nandi." Eyes flitted to a fair-sized animal bounding along beside the bus. "Is that an ai'wita?"

Hopeless. The kid *was* eight. Bren laughed, and waved his hand. "Go look at it."

A thunder of youngsters leaving their seats, headed for the back windows to have a look, and Bren turned and sank down in his own seat, with a roll of the eyes toward Banichi and Jago, who were amused.

He truly wished he could bring up Baiji's debt, but that was going to have to be finessed, now that Baiji had paid off in other ways. Possibly, too, Baiji had gotten on the wrong side of some of his uncle Geigi's talent—a knack for standing on both sides of an issue—he could still be playing minor politics with old Southern contacts, who knew? It could be useful. Tabini-aiji was working hard from the other side, trying to use the Farai as a wedge into a changed Southern political landscape. Their lay-about lordling Baiji could end up being useful a second time.

Meanwhile, his own day's program involved getting back to the estate before even mild-mannered Tano locked Barb in her room.

The south road, past the intersection for the train station, rose over rolling hills as a slightly muddy track, not well-kept—shockingly not well-kept, one might think. It devolved from a graveled stretch of dirt to a thin pair of wheel marks through tall grass with only the memory of gravel to keep it from mud puddles. It was not overgrown with brush, one could at least say that for the traffic, as the people of Kajiminda had surely come and gone to market in the village, and up to the train station or as various freight might have come from the airport. Surely Najida had sent some small commerce over to Kajiminda's farming village, and conversely. But the upkeep had definitely fallen off since the last time Bren had seen the route, and, Bren supposed, it was not all one-sided. Things must have fallen off during the Troubles.

So *his* estate might make the gesture of improving it, putting down gravel, and cutting the grass, at least to the halfway mark.

He was already seeing certain things he thought he should report to Lord Geigi, once they drove onto Kajiminda: the condition of a low wooden bridge, blocked with brush and ready to become a major problem of local flooding—erosion across the road, a hard bump for a bus or a truck: points against the young caretaker lord. Those inroads of erosion were going to become a gully at that low spot. And he noted loose boards on the second low bridge they crossed. The road definitely should be an issue in their eventual conversation, when they had done their fill of thank you and what a storm that had been.

The outlying signage was yet another matter: it generally needed painting. And the sign that pointed to Kajiminda, where the main market road went on down the coast toward the greater township in the region, and the lesser one went on toward the estate—that was lying on its face in the grass.

Certainly, the factory further down the main road in Lord Geigi's district should be generating traffic clear to Dalaigi, and up to Kajiminda—but it looked no better on the track they did not take. Lack of maintenance up in this direction might have discouraged it, that, or habits and patterns of travel had shifted during the years of the Troubles—granted, this was not a main road, and possibly some change in rail service had encouraged them to use the rails for something that local. But it didn't change the fact that the road needed to be fixed.

He remarked to Banichi and Jago, "We shall want to visit the factory, on some day before we leave the district. There is a certain lack of maintenance. But despite other circumstances, one has no wish to enter upon a neighborly exchange with an excessively critical view. There may be reasons."

"Yes," Banichi said, but Banichi's gaze was otherwise out the window, observing details, marking this, marking that. So was Jago's attention.

The youngsters clearly thought the jolts and ruts were exciting. The road had, to the paidhi's eye, a certain spookiness about it . . . and still he told himself that it was no good going into a negotiation with preconceptions based on road maintenance.

In that view, as they had turned onto the unmarked and overgrown track that led to Lord Geigi's estate, Bren said to himself that he might reasonably extend the gesture at least of mowing, if not patching *all* the road up to Geigi's private road—he should offer that, for an old ally's sake, and for the help Baiji himself had rendered in a desperate situation. If there was any dearth of proper equipment in this estate, there was not in Najida: he had a grader, and a truck, and he could get repairs moving. This young man might have felt somewhat isolated and lacking direction in his situation during the Troubles. Perhaps he had simply not been up to the job he was given—the Maschi line was running thin, down almost to its last. Possible Baiji had come in with no training for the job he had prematurely attained. Possibly he and staff had had their difficulties. . . . Perhaps Najida could help smooth over more than the roads.

Bump! The passage of truck tires—at least more frequent here—had created massive potholes, where the native sandstone, not far beneath the layer of dirt and grass had shattered or eroded into sand.

Well, however, his own two-year departure from the region, almost three years until this visit, had removed the last experienced authority from the district and left everything to Baiji. Could he greatly blame the man, who had at least avoided invasion on this coast? Baiji might be due some credit in areas other than road construction.

And the villa did, when it appeared in the distance, appear much as it had a decade and more ago, red tile roofs above a sprawling structure of the harder, coastside limestone, plastered and painted white.

Well-painted and orderly, still, within its surrounding garden walls, with the little false garden watchtowers, and the villa's general L-shaped roof reflecting the bright sun in a cheerful way. That view entirely lightened his mood. The orchards were still well kept. The stucco wall and towers—built mostly to keep pests out of the orchard—were immaculate. The natural woodland that ran down to the shore was still what it had been. Geigi's dock and yacht were not visible from this vantage: the wooded coast curved somewhat, making a neat little cove where Geigi kept his boats, and from which Geigi's extended household did a little fishing. And when they turned through the gates of the low, white-plastered outer wall, the road became a broad gravel track, leading up to a portico not unlike that at Najida.

The youngsters had moved forward in the bus as they passed within the gates, and now they clustered close behind Bren's seat as the bus pulled into the little courtyard that faced the front doors.

The driver drew to a sedate halt and opened the door. Banichi and Jago exited first, and now the house doors opened and the staff came out to meet them.

In the center of the doors, hindmost, arrived a well-dressed young man, a little plump—could one at all doubt that he was related to Lord Geigi? He looked like every Maschi lord in the lineage. And he seemed quite fond of gold thread—he positively glittered, the whole expanse of him glittered. But that was no great sin, that the young man should have gotten himself up in his absolute best for the meeting. He shone in gold. A shadow attended him, four men in Guild black, his bodyguard, also in their most formal black and silver for the occasion.

Well, discourtesy to the aiji had ruffled some who noticed such things, and true, the young lord hadn't phoned first, seeing a neighbor returning after long absence; but one could not fault the turnout now.

Banichi and Jago got out, and took their position, opposite. Bren quietly descended the steps and gave a little bow, as Cajeiri and his pair came clattering down the steps behind, and landed on the aged cobblestones just behind him with a little crunch of sand.

Lord Baiji was of moderate height, taller than his ample figure immediately suggested; a solid young man, and he had a pleasant expression, a little softness about the mouth, but over all distinctly like Lord Geigi.

"Nandiin," Baiji said, and bowed to him first, and bowed to

Cajeiri. "My house is honored. One hopes you find yourselves well, nand' Bren, after the events of last night."

"Entirely, nandi," Bren said. "Thank you."

"We wish to express our gratitude, nandi," Cajeiri piped up, coming up at Bren's side, and bowing, which occasioned a second bow from Baiji. "We were in great distress last night, and very glad to be found."

That was, Bren said to himself, two sentences. And before he had had a chance properly to introduce the boy.

And simultaneously a peculiarity struck him: *nandiin*, Baiji had said—the plural *my lords*. The presence of young, civilian-dressed attendants with Cajeiri was some indication of higher rank, as was the fairly elegant coat Cajeiri was wearing. The Taibeni youngsters were certainly too young to be attending the paidhi-aiji himself. Village child, they had said. And this morning Baiji met them with *nandiin*.

And came out onto the porch to do it. He had not the manner of a lord in his own hall, rather that of an anxious merchant in his shop doorway.

"The house of Lord Geigi," Baiji said, "is more than pleased to have been of assistance. We beg you come inside, nandiin, and take tea in the solar."

Well, well, the man lacked the manner, but he met them knowing more than he'd been told—that was at least commendable industry. And one so hoped to find some sense of ease with this young man, some good point or two to relay to his uncle Geigi.

So they took the invitation, leaving the driver to park the bus and wait.

Now, in the inner hall, was the proper time and place for the major domo of the house to express his own delight at the visit of close associates of the lord, and to show them to the solarium for tea, never mind that Baiji himself had usurped that office. But in fact a sober, quiet man approached and led the way in silence.

Geigi's major domo had gone with him to space. This man would have been on staff at his last visit—but in some minor post. Other things, however, were much as he remembered. The potted plants in the tiled hall were a bit taller, and when they came into the solar and took their seats, the chairs were a few years more worn . . . the house was not much using this room. There was a trace of dust in the grooves of the chair arm—Ramaso would never tolerate such a thing—but he was not here to criticize.

It was still a pleasant venue. The room had a frieze of sailing ships. Many-paned windows gave a view of a small winter garden. A small rug covered the seating area of the tiled floor, deadening sound.

The solar, Bren thought, had another advantage—being near the front doors. A quick session, and an early out if things turned awkward—if there was, for instance, any business about the debt to Najida merchants, which he truly did *not* want to discuss today, because he would have to say things that would not be auspicious.

So they sat, himself, and Cajeiri, and Baiji, while their respective bodyguards stood in attendance on opposite sides of the room.

Tea was ready with no delay at all: staff must have spotted them coming up the drive, and hastened now to bring forth the service. That provided a decent period of quiet and mental collection.

So they sipped their tea, Cajeiri in very commendable silence, until Baiji asked his young guest how he found the district.

"Very beautiful, nandi. Thank you."

Commendable brevity. And offering the suggestion, on Baiji's side, that Cajeiri was not quite . . . as advertised . . . local.

Hell, Geigi would have asked the facts at the front door. Baiji just insinuated bits and pieces of what he knew.

So it was, Bren decided, on him to explain matters decently. That had been a diffident probe, at least, perhaps the man's attempt at genteel inquiry. He took a sip of tea—his sips were scarcely enough to wet his lips, cautious . . . alkaloids were always a risk, in unknown hospitality. Then he said: "One must apologize, nandi, for the slight deception on the radio last night. You have clearly guessed by now that my young companion is not from Najida village. Let me introduce, nandi, nand' Cajeiri, the son of Tabini-aiji, and his young staff."

"Nandi." Their host immediately set aside his teacup and rose. Cajeiri, a properly schooled youngster, also rose, and there was a brief exchange of bows between Cajeiri and Baiji, then a resumption of seats.

"One is extremely honored, young gentleman, and delighted to have rendered service."

Remarkable. Astonishing. Having already spent his allotted two sentences, Cajeiri merely inclined his head in acknowledgment, and said not a thing, asked not a single question—the perfect model of a young gentleman.

"One should add," Bren said, "that the grandmother referenced last night is the young lord's great-grandmother, who is a guest at my estate."

"One is completely astonished by the honor paid this house." Baiji had broken out in a sudden sweat, and actually reached for a pocket handkerchief to mop his cheek. "One is very gratified at your visit, nandiin."

"Security is tight," Bren said with a calm nod. "We wish no attention to my guests. Nor should it be mentioned beyond staff until my guests have left the region. But as my neighbor, it is useful that you know."

"Indeed, indeed."

"Please," Bren said, accepting another dose of tea into his cup, the servant late to provide it. "Please take my visit as gratitude for your assistance last night. As to your question, nandi, how we find the district . . . it is, of course, as I left it—except the roads."

"Ah! Nandi, one so deeply apologizes—one—"

"If Kajiminda would accept a more substantive token of my gratitude for last night, Najida might mow the road from Najida up to the turnoff, so heavier traffic might be more convenient between our estates." And I would like my people's bills to be paid, he thought, but simply had a sip of tea.

"One would be extremely gratified by that favor, nandi," Baiji said. "We have been short-handed in the estate, and last fall, we let that matter slide far more than we should."

"Short-handed," Bren echoed him.

Another pass of the handkerchief. "During the Troubles, certain staff found the need to be closer to their families. And most regrettably, nandi, they have not yet returned."

"Ah," Bren said. Not returned to their jobs, and it had been months since the restoration of Tabini's regime. Odd. He declined, however, to say so, just letting his bodyguard sum things up.

But he was not as easy now. Something unpleasant in the tea? One could become just a little anxious in their host's continued nervousness, but there was a reason a lord's bodyguard stood while the lords sat at tea—stood armed to the teeth, and did not drink or eat. It was his job not to drink much of the tea, and to find out what he needed to learn.

And he could wish he had not brought the boy on this trip.

"Do you, nandi, hear often from your esteemed uncle?"

"Not often at all, to my regret, nand' Bren. One hopes for his continued good health. One has been concerned."

"One has heard nothing at all distressing regarding his health. We dealt with him briefly on the station, and we have been in contact with him intermittently for months."

"Then one is glad to know so, nandi."

"Indeed. He frequently keeps a hectic schedule. I shall be sure to remember you kindly to him." Banichi meanwhile, in the tail of his vision, had stepped outside the room to have a word, perhaps, with the major domo, maybe to pose his own questions of staff. One of Baiji's men had likewise left the room. That would not be at all unusual, in two staffs establishing contact. And it was the lord's job to smooth things over. But it was approaching time to cut the visit short, the gesture made, and the outcome offering more questions than answers. "One has little time in the schedule today, to let us pay a long visit, nandi, but later, should you wish, one might have that road mowed, and your reciprocal visit to Najida might meet no serious obstacles."

Baiji had looked a little askance at Banichi's departure, his eyes flicking to that doorway.

"So we must," Bren said, "with greatest thanks, be on our way back to Najida, to attend to my other guests. Shall we see you in Najida?" Not while the dowager was there, for certain. But he could deliver her message. "Or perhaps in court, when the session opens?"

"One hopes," Baiji said fervently, "one hopes so. Please convey my earnest good will to the aiji-dowager, and, young gentleman, to your esteemed father."

Profoundly sweating.

Not right, Bren thought. It was time to go. And Banichi had not come back in, but Jago had begun to move toward the door. So, with her, and looking just a little on edge, the Taibeni youngsters moved. Cajeiri might or might not have noticed that action. He was sitting at Bren's right, and his expression was not readable—one hoped he was not fidgeting anxious glances toward the doorway, where Banichi was, perhaps using his old contacts in the house, Geigi's Edi contacts, to ask some pointed questions.

But it was his job to read the signals and get them out of here. He stood up.

"One will be most anxious," Baiji said, rising as Cajeiri rose. "Please convey our most fervent wishes for the aiji-dowager's good will. We had sickness in the house this winter. Please assure the dowager missing the session had nothing to do with political opinion. We feared to bring a contagion to that august assembly . . ."

"Certainly one will convey that information," Bren said, laying a hand on Cajeiri's shoulder, steering him toward the door. He put a little pressure on it, just a brief warning signal, trusting the lad not to flinch. "We shall, shall we not, young lord?"

"Yes, nandi, indeed." Cajeiri properly bowed toward their host, and Bren bowed, and turned the boy toward the door, where he hoped to God that Banichi was waiting. He didn't like what he was getting from Baiji. Not in the least. Jago opened the door, and they exited into the tiled hall with the potted plants.

"Nandi," Baiji said, at their backs, hurrying to overtake them as they headed for the front doors. The servants were at the front doors. Banichi and Lord Baiji's guard were engaged in conversation there, and Banichi had to have realized they were leaving.

But overtake them Baiji did, just short of Banichi and the guards—but Jago turned suddenly and interposed her arm, blocking his path.

"Please!" Baiji protested. "Nandiin, let me escort you to your bus. We are so very pleased that you have come, and we hope to visit while the young gentleman and the aiji-dowager are in residence, if you would be so good, nandi, as to relay my sentiments to her . . ."

"Excuse me, nandi," Jago said, maintaining her arm as a barrier. Her other hand was near her holster—not on it, but near, and she kept it there. Cajeiri's young staff were in danger of getting cut off by Baiji's three remaining guards, who were behind Baiji. "Come," Jago said sharply. "The paidhi has a schedule to keep, nadiin-ji. Come."

The youngsters hurried to catch up—inserted themselves right with Jago.

"Please," Baiji said, actively pursuing as they walked toward the doors. "Please, nand' paidhi. Something has alarmed your staff. In the name of an old alliance, in the name of my uncle, your neighbor, allow me a word. Nandi! Nandi, I *have* met with the Tasaigi. I confess it!"

Tasaigi. The front doors had opened. But at that name out of the hostile South, Bren stopped, cast an astonished look back.

"But one refused them, nandi! Your presence has lent this house strength! Please! Do not desert us!"

He had stopped. Jago had stopped. Banichi held the doors open. And he needed urgently to get the boy out of here.

"Please, nand' paidhi! Nandi, be patient, please be patient and hear me out! They are gone now, they are gone! I sent them off. It is all safe!"

"We cannot wait for this." The door remained open: Jago held Baiji back; and now Jago did have her hand on her pistol, and quietly, deliberately drew it. The two Taibeni youngsters were as helpless as Cajeiri, caught in the middle, trying to figure out where they should be, which turned out to be against the wall. And he hesitated two breaths for a look back. "We can discuss it when you visit Najida."

"Nandi, it may be too late! My uncle—my esteemed uncle— the position he occupies. He protects us. But he draws attention. Oh, favorable gods!" The fellow was sweating, and looked altogether overwhelmed, perhaps about to collapse on the spot: but his bodyguard had frozen in place behind him. "Oh, good and auspicious gods . . ."

"Out with it!" Bren said, with a worse and worse feeling that they were dealing with a fool, and one that might not survive, left alone in this house, having named that name. "I shall hear you, nand' Bajji, for your uncle's sake, and for your service to the aiji's house. I shall hear you at length and reasonably, for your uncle's sake, when you visit us in Najida." Take him with them? Be *sure* that they heard whatever truth he had to tell, before Tasaigi agents caught up to him? "The truth, nandi, only the truth will serve you at this point—only the truth, and do not delay me further! In two words, tell me what I should hear.

Tell me what you know Lord Geigi himself would wish to hear, because I assure you he *will* hear it."

"Nandi, your great patience, your great forbearance—"

"Have limits. What have you *done* regarding the Tasaigi, nandi?"

"Nandi, please hear me! I—dealt with the South during the usurper's rule, that is to say, I dealt with them in trade, I received them under this roof, I encouraged them—I did shameful things, nand' paidhi, because we were, all of us on this peninsula, under threat! It was rumored, nandi, it was greatly rumored at one time that Tabini-aiji might have come to your estate!"

"He did not."

"But it was rumored! And we were all in danger, your estate, most of all."

News. He had not heard anything about a Tasaigi intrusion here. "And?"

"And we—we feared every day that the Tasaigi might be encouraged to make a move against the township, and this whole coast. We expected it. Instead—instead—they wrote to me requesting I visit."

"And you went to them?"

"If I refused them, it would be a matter of time before they sent assassins, nandi, and without me . . . not that I in any way claim the dignity or honors of my uncle—but without me—nandi, I was the only lord in the west, save Adigan up at Dur, to hold his land safe from invasion. The northern peninsula, that went under: the new regime set up new magistrates . . ."

"You are wasting my time, nandi. All this I know. Get to it! What have you done?"

"So I met with them, nand' paidhi, being as good as a dead man otherwise, and hoping—hoping to negotiate some more favorable situation for this district. I reasoned—I reasoned as long as I was still in power here, it would be better than one of their appointed men, would it not?"

"Undoubtedly." Taking him with them to Najida might indeed be the best thing. If there was a problem on staff, it might find Baiji before nightfall.

Or find them, if they didn't get the hell out the door Banichi was holding open.

"So I met with them."

"We have been to this point three times, nandi. Get beyond it!"

"They offered me—being without an heir—they offered me an alliance. They—offered me the daughter of a lord of the South, and I—I said I wished to meet this young woman. I did anything I could think of and objected to this and that detail in the contract—"

"You stalled."

"Nandi, I—ultimately agreed to the marriage. Which I did not carry out. But I know that I have put this young woman—a very young woman—and her family—in a difficult position. Which they urge is the case. So—"

It could go another half hour, round and round and round with Baiji's ifs and buts. "*They* have put this young woman in a difficult position, nandi. You are not morally responsible. And one will discuss this at length in Najida. Order your car, nandi, and join us there, should you wish to discuss it further. I will not stand in the hall to discuss this."

"One shall, one shall, with great gratitude, nandi, but let me go *with* you!"

"This is enough," Jago said in the kyo language, which no Guild could crack—but which all of them who had been in space knew. "Nandi! Go!"

"Good day to you," Bren said, and with his hand firmly on Cajeiri's shoulder, steered him out the door, where to his great relief Banichi closed in behind them all and let the door shut.

It immediately reopened. "Nandi!" Baiji called at their backs, and Jago half-turned, on the move. "I shall go with you. Please." Baiji ran to catch up.

"Stay back!" Jago said, and Bren glanced back in alarm as Jago's gun came up, and Baiji slid to a wide-eyed, stumbling halt just this side of the doors, none of his guard in attendance.

Bren turned, drew Cajeiri with him, and Cajeiri looked back. The Taibeni youngsters were trying to stay close.

Meanwhile their bus, parked out in the sunlight of the circular drive, rolled gently into motion toward the portico.

A sunlit cobblestone exploded like the crack of doom. Bren froze, uncertain which direction to go.

A whole line of cobbles exploded, ending with the moving bus—which suddenly accelerated toward the portico with a squeal of tires. Fire hit it, stitched up the driver's side door, and it braked, skidding sidelong into the right-hand stonework pillar with a horrendous crash.

The whole portico roof tilted and collapsed in a welter of stones and squeal of nails, the collapsing corner knocking the bus forward. In that same split-second Banichi turned and got off three shots up and to the left.

An impact hit Bren from behind—hit him, grabbed him sideways as if he weighed nothing and carried him the half-dozen steps to the bullet-riddled side of the bus—then shoved him right against it. It was Jago who had grabbed him, Jago who yanked the bus door open while the portico resounded with gunfire.

"Get in," Jago yelled at him, and shoved him inside, and he didn't argue, just scrambled to get in past the driver's seat, and down across the floor. Their driver was lying half over the seat in front. Jago had forced her way in, and threw the man onto the floor, as Banichi got in. Bren got a look past his own knee and saw Banichi lying on the steps holding someone in his arms.

Jago jammed on the accelerator and snapped his head back, tumbling him against the seats. The bus lurched forward, ripping part of the bus roof and pieces of the portico ceiling, tires thumping on cobbles as they drove for sunlight and headed down the drive.

Glass broke. Bullets stitched through the back of the bus, blew up bits of the seats and exploded through the right-hand window.

Jago yelled: "Stay down!"

They hit something on the left and scraped along the side of it—the bus rocked, and Bren grabbed the nearest seat stanchion, sure they were going over, but they rocked back to level, on gravel, now, three tires spinning at all the speed the bus could manage and one lumping along with a regular impact of loose rubber.

But they kept going. Kept going, and made it to the gate.

Bren looked back, then forward, trying to figure if it was safe to move yet, trying to find out was everybody all right.

Banichi had edged forward, on his knees, and the person he had was . . . Baiji.

Baiji. Not Cajeiri.

"*Where is Cajeiri?*" Bren cried, over the noise of the tires on gravel, one flat, and past the roar of an overtaxed engine. "*Where is Cajeiri, nadiin-ji?*"

Banichi was on his knees now, trying to staunch the blood flow from their wounded driver, whose body only just cleared the foot well. Jago drove, and as a disheveled Lord Baiji tried to crawl up the steps and get up, Banichi whirled on one knee, grabbed the lord's coat and hauled him down, thump! onto the floor, with no care for his head—which hit the seat rim.

Baiji yelled in pain, grabbed his ear. His pigtail having come loose, its ribbon trailed over one shoulder, strands of hair streaming down beside his ears.

But no view, before or behind, showed the youngsters aboard the bus.

"Banichi!" Bren breathed, struggling to both keep down and get around to face Banichi, while the bus bucked and lurched over potholes on three good tires.

"He ran, Bren-ji." Banichi didn't look at him. Banichi concentrated on the job at hand and pressed a wad of cloth against the driver's ribs, placing the man's hand against the cloth. "Hold that, nadi-ji, can you hold it?"

A moan issued from their driver, but he held it, while Banichi tore more bandage off a roll.

They owed this man, owed him their not being barricaded in Kajiminda with God-knew-what strength of enemy.

But the youngsters were in that situation. All three of them. And Banichi and Jago had left them there.

"Were they hit?" he asked Banichi. It was the worst he could think of.

"The boy will have taken cover. He is not a fool."

And was Baiji their hostage, intended to get Cajeiri back? What the hell were Banichi and Jago thinking?

He didn't know. He couldn't figure. He'd been about to look around for them when Jago had hit him and carried him forward, straight into the bus. He was stunned, as if something had slammed him in the gut. His heart was pounding. And he kept thinking, This can't be real. They can't have left the kids. They can't have left them there.

He sat on the cold, muddy floorboards, with their driver's blood congealing in the grooves in the mat, trying to think, trying to get his breath as the bus slung itself onto the potholed estate road and kept going. Banichi got up for a moment and pulled the first aid kit from the overhead, with the bus lurching violently and what was probably a piece of the tire flapping against the wheel well at the rear. Banichi got down and started to work again, got the man a shot of something, probably painkiller.

They reached the intersection and took a tolerably cautious turn onto that overgrown road, and then gathered speed again.

They'd lost Cajeiri. They'd grabbed Baiji.

And the hell of it—he, who was supposed to understand such things, didn't know why in either case.

10

Firing had been deafening . . . and now it was silence, with people moving about. Cajeiri had no view of the proceedings, nor any inclination to make any noise, not even to rustle a dry winter twig. He was flat under the front shrubbery with his chin in the dirt, and Antaro and Jegari were lying on top of him. The roof had come down on the bus—he had thought it was wrecked. But it had gotten away. He had struggled briefly just to turn his head to see what was going on, but thick evergreen was in the way.

Then he had heard the bus take off again. Either the driver alone had gone for help from Great-grandmother, or Banichi and Jago had gotten nand' Bren into the van and taken off. He should not have dived for the bushes. He had thought the bus was finished.

And now that it had gone, that left him and his companions, as Gene would say, in a bit of a pickle.

A fairly hot pickle, at that. A whole dish of hot pickles.

He rested there, struggling to breathe with the combined weight on his back, trying to think.

Going back into the house, even if things were quiet, and just asking the Edi staff: "Did you get all the assassins?" did not seem the brightest thing to do.

Damn. It was very embarrassing to die of stupidity—or to end up kidnapped by scoundrels. Again.

What would Banichi do? That was his standard for clever answers. Banichi and Jago and Cenedi.

They'd probably moved fast for that bus, that was what they'd likely done. He remembered its motor still running. He hadn't marked that. He'd thought it had been crushed by the roof when it came down. It must have been able to move. They'd have gotten nand' Bren there, fast, and one of them would have been shooting back, which would be why the fire had been going on as long as it had—he was mad at himself. He could think of these things. But he should not take this long to think of them. If he had been thinking fast enough they would be on that bus, and headed for nand' Bren's estate.

So could he not think *ahead* of the next set of events?

It would be really, truly useful if he could. All Jegari and Antaro were thinking of right now was keeping him alive and trying to get him somewhere safe, but they were in a kind of country they had never seen before—neither had he—and he did not think he ought to take advice from them, not if it sounded reckless. There were times to be reckless. There were times to be patient. And this seemed maybe one of those times to be very, very patient.

He was afraid to whisper and ask them anything. The Assassins' Guild used things like electronic ears, and might pick him up. Once that bus got to the estate, there would be a rescue coming back, that was sure; and maybe Banichi and Jago and nand' Bren were still here, hiding somewhere nearby, themselves, just waiting for reinforcements, if the bus had gone and left them.

That meant he and his aishid had to avoid being found and used as hostages, and if they moved at all, they had to do it extremely quietly.

Voices were still intermittently audible: someone was talking unseemly loudly in the hallway, and the doors of the house were still open. It might be staff. But if the lord of the house was giving orders, did it not make sense he would now order the doors shut, for protection of the staff who were in the house?

"Is it safe?" one asked, which indicated to him that they had to be worried about being shot, and *that* might mean staff had not been in on the plot.

It did not mean that nand' Baiji had not been in on it—nand' Bren had told him there might be faults of character in nand' Baiji, and it was very instructive, lying here on the cold dirt, under the weight of two people trying to protect him, and with the smell of gunpowder wafting about. Great-grandmother had held up faults of character—*ukochisami*—as a thing he should never be thought to have. And now that he had a shockingly concrete example of a grown man with faults of character, he began to see how it was a great inconvenience to everyone for a man to have such faults, and to be a little stupid, too, another thing of which Great-grandmother greatly disapproved. To have faults of character *and* to be a little stupid, while trying to be clever—that seemed to describe Lord Baiji.

And he thought that Lord Geigi, his uncle, up on the station, must have been at a great loss for someone better to leave in charge on his estate . . . that, or Lord Baiji, being a young man, had been a little soft . . . Great-grandmother was fond of saying that soft people easily fell into faults of character and that lazy ones stayed ignorant, which was very close to stupid.

Great-grandmother would have thwacked Baiji's ear when he was young, no question, and told him what she had told him: If you intend to deal sharply with people, young man, deal smartly, and think ahead! Do not try to deal sharply with *us*, nor with anyone else smart enough to see to the end of matters! You are outclassed, young man, greatly outclassed, and you will have to work hard ever to get ahead of us!

It was absolutely amazing how Great-grandmother could foresee the messes and the bad examples her great-grandson could meet along the way. *Ukochisama* did describe Baiji, who had described a fairly good plan, a policy of stalling the Southerners and keeping them from attacking, but it would not have gone on forever. He would eventually have had to marry that Southern girl, who would be either extremely clever herself, or extremely stupid—and her relatives would just move right in.

Perhaps they had. One had a fairly good idea that the Southerners were somewhere in this situation. And one began to think—there had been very few servants in sight. They had not said very much. Baiji had let the roads go and he had told nand' Bren it was because people had gone to relatives down in the Township during the Troubles and things had gotten out of hand.

That meant—maybe there were not many Edi folk in the house.

Or maybe there were none. Maybe those had been Southern servants. Southern folk had an accent. But you could learn not to have an accent.

The only thing was—Baiji had saved his life, when they had been about to sink out there in the sea.

Baiji had told nand' Bren where to look for them.

But maybe Baiji had hoped to get to them first, for completely nefarious reasons—nefarious was one of his newest words. Maybe Baiji had had them spotted and was trying to get there ahead of Bren and sweep him up, or maybe just run over the little sailboat . . . while pretending to be rescuing him.

That had not happened, at least. And Baiji *could* have kept the information to himself.

That was confusing.

Baiji had trailed them out the door, pleading with nand' Bren, before the shooting started. It had gotten confused then, and his memory of those few moments was a little fuzzy, but had not Baiji been talking about his engagement to that Southern girl and asking to go with them?

"Should we call the paidhi's estate?" one of the servants asked, standing near their hiding place in the bushes. He had heard the Southern accent. The Farai had it. And that was not it. Maybe it was Edi. And another voice said: "Ask the body-guard." And a third voice, more distant, from what seemed inside the foyer: "No one can find them."

That could mean anything. It could mean Baiji's bodyguard had taken him and run . . . somewhere safe, like clear away and down to the Township, or to some safe room: great houses did tend to have such.

It could also mean Baiji's bodyguard had been in on the attack and were somewhere around the estate hunting for nand' Bren. Or for *him.*

That was a scary thought. He was cold through, in contact with the dirt. He started to shiver, and that was embarrassing.

"Are you all right, nandi?" the whisper came beside his ear.

He reached back blindly, caught Antaro's collar and pulled her head lower, where he could whisper at his faintest. "We must not move until they shut those doors," he said.

"Dark will not be safe," Antaro whispered back. "The Guild has night scopes. We will glow in the dark."

"We need full cover," he whispered. "Did nand' Bren get away, nadi?"

"His guard took him," Antaro said. "They left."

That was good and bad news.

"They will come back," he said. "My father will send Guild. We have to stay out of sight."

"Wait until they all go in. Then I can go along between the bushes and the wall and see how far we are from the edge of this place."

"There might be booby traps," he said. "Banichi taught me. Watch for electrics, watch for wires." He heard the doors shut with great authority and that was a relief. For a few heartbeats after that it was just their own breathing, no sound of anyone any longer outside, just the creak of the wreckage settling: that was what he thought it was.

"I shall go, nandi," Antaro said. She had had *some* Guild training. Far from enough.

"One begs you be careful, nadi."

It took some careful manuvering: she slithered right over him; and it was very, very dangerous. They were behind evergreens, on a mat of fallen needles and neglect. That could mask a trap, and Antaro necessarily made a little noise, and left clear traces for somebody as keen-eyed as Banichi. That was a scary thought, but it was scarier staying here once night fell and nand' Bren came back and bullets started flying . . . not to mention people using night scopes on the bushes.

Antaro reached the end of the building, and Jegari, still on top, pushed at him, insisting it was his turn. So he moved. He saw no threatening wires. There was a wire that went to some landscape lights. But nothing of the bare sort that could take a finger. Or your head. He slithered as Antaro had done, as Banichi had taught him, intermittent with listening, and he was fairly certain Jegari moved behind him. He crawled past the roots of bushes, and along beside the ancient stonework of the statcly house, trying to disturb as little as possible with the passage of his body, trying to smooth down the traces Antaro had left, and hoping Jegari would do the same, on the retreat.

Antaro, having reached the corner, had stopped. A little flagstone path led off the cobbled drive, and passed through an ironwork gate, a gate with no complicated latch.

That gate was in a whitewashed wall as high as the house roof, and it led maybe a stone's easy toss to another whitewashed wall that contained the driveway. Where they intersected, there was a little fake watchtower, with empty windows and a tile roof with upturned corners.

Beyond that wall were the tops of evergreens and other, barren, trees. A woods.

Safety, one might think.

But he had read a lot. And he had talked with Banichi and Jago on the long voyage.

And Banichi had told him once, "The best place to put a trap is where it seems like the way out."

Too attractive, a woods running right up to the house walls.

"The woods is going to be guarded," he whispered. "Look for an alarm on the gate."

"Yes," Antaro said, and rolled half over so she could look up at the gate. She did that for some little time, and then pointed to the base of the gate and made the sign for "alarm."

He looked for one. He could not see it, but when he looked closely, he saw a little square thing.

"Over," she signed to him. And "Come."

He moved closer. Antaro signaled for Jegari to come close, and he crawled close. Antaro stepped onto her brother's back, and he braced himself, and she took hold of the top of the gate and just— it was amazing—lifted herself into something like a handstand. She went over, and lit ever so lightly.

She waited there, and Jegari offered his hands and whispered, "Go, nandi."

He did, as best he could. He climbed up onto Jegari's hands, and Jegari lifted him up to the top of the gate. Antaro stood close, so he could get onto her shoulders, and then she knelt down and let him gently to the ground, turning then to offer her hands to Jegari, who had pulled himself up and climbed atop the gate. Jegari was a heavy weight—but she braced herself and made a sling of her hands and he got down.

They were over. They were clear.

But they were also *inside* an alarmed area. It was a very bare, very exposed corner of a small winter-bare orchard—walled about with the same house-high barrier, with those intermittent little watchtowers. The old trees were just leafing out, not a lot of cover. And the orchard ran clear back out of sight, beyond the house, and evidently the wall went on, too, just a few towers sticking up above the slight hill. Probably it enclosed the whole estate grounds.

But something interesting showed, nearest, at the base of that corner tower: steps. One could go up there. Cajeiri pointed at it, pointed at a second tower, somewhat less conspicuous, beyond the gray-brown haze of winter branches. Pointed at the shuttered great windows in this face of the house.

Jegari nodded grim agreement. That little tower—that might be somewhere they would not look.

Antaro nodded, and moved out. Cajeiri followed, trying to move without scuffing up the leaves; and Jegari came after him. They reached a sort of flagstone patio that probably afforded very pleasant evenings in summer, with the trees in leaf. Tools stood there against the wall, rusting in the winter rains. Mani would never approve.

They trod carefully on that little patio, with its dead potted plants, its pale flagstones, and its upward stairs. And Cajeiri started to take that stairs upward to that whitewashed wall and tower, but Antaro pressed him back and insisted on going up first.

There was a chain up there, blocking off the top. She slipped under it, and slithered up onto the walk and into the tower, then slithered back again, signaling "Come quickly."

Cajeiri climbed the steps as fast as he could, with Jegari behind him, up, likewise slithered under the prohibiting chain, crawled onto a little concrete walkway along the fake, whitewashed battlement. A very undersized door went into the tower from there, slithering was the only way in. Glassless windows lit the inside—and a very modern installation, a kind of box with a turning gear.

Cajeiri's heart went thump. They had come on the very sort of surveillance they were afraid of. But the sensor was aimed out the windows: it shifted from one window to the other, whirr-click, left to right, right to left, watching out in the woods. Towers like this one were all along the wall— there were several in view just from the orchard, and probably every single tower had something similar inside. But the machinery was all dusty and rusty, even if it was working. There were big cracks in the wall, starting from two of the windows, the outermost and the innermost cracks which nobody had fixed. It was not the best maintenance that kept this system.

On their knees, peering through the crack beneath the garden-side window, they had a good view of the house from here, and a lot more of the orchard. They could see where the portico had collapsed in front.

Worse—much worse, there was somebody in Guild black just coming over the house roof.

They all dropped down, and Cajeiri kept his eye to the crack.

"Guild!"he whispered, with a chill going through him. There was an enemy, they were still hunting for them, and in a little while, as he watched through that crack, two more Guildsmen came around the corner of the house. They opened the alarmed gate, and shut it, and started methodically looking through the orchard.

Cajeiri knelt there, watching the search go on, watching that solitary black presence on the roof, out of sight of those below, and he shivered a twitch or two, which embarrassed him greatly.

Not good. Not good at all. Nand' Bren was going to come back, and there was a trap, and they were already in it. These people, however, were standing around and pointing, more than searching. Pointing at the roof, and pointing at the front gate.

One could almost imagine them laying plans for exactly such a thing as an attack from Bren's estate. They were devising traps.

They might come up here to check the security installation.

That would not be good. They might need to be out of here. They might urgently need to do that.

11

The bus was running on the wheel rim on the left rear. Their driver, Iscarti, was not doing well, but they had gotten the blood staunched, and there was local help—the aiji-dowager never traveled without her personal physician: the man was a surgeon, and the best there was likely to be in the district. Banichi continually held pressure against the wound, and Bren had gotten up off the floor at least to look out the window and learn where they were.

Jago drove for all the bus was worth. They all kept as low as possible. Lord Baiji stayed in the well of the steps—under Banichi's advisement that if he said anything whatsoever or moved from where he lay, he would be sorry he had.

Lord Baiji hadn't budged.

But they were onto Najida Peninsula now. It was speed or it was caution, and right now, speed counted. Jago's attention was all for the road—a good thing, at the speed she was driving, considering the condition of the bus—and a sharp jolt and bounce both drew no cry from the driver—in itself, ominous. Bren sat ready to spell Banichi at maintaining that pressure on the wound, but thus far Banichi managed without him.

Objections at this point were futile. They were where they were, headed for help, and that was all they could do. Questions he had aplenty, and knew most of them came down to him. He was the one who had left half his bodyguard in Najida. He was the one who had relied on a neighbor. And the one who'd valued stopping Barb from another embarrassment at a higher priority than Tano and Algini going with them.

Bad choice. Bad decision. And his call, totally. He was the one who was supposed to know the temper of the human side of his household and make the best decision—how in hell could Banichi and Jago figure how serious it was and wasn't, with Barb and Toby's situation? Jago had made her own heated recommendations regarding Barb not being under his roof, and he had dismissed her objections as personal jealousy. What more could she then say?

Wrong, he thought now. Wrong. Wrong. Impossible situation, for his guard. Absolutely impossible.

Second bad move, when he'd delayed them after he'd gotten an indication from Banichi that things weren't right.

And at the doors, almost out of it, he'd turned his head to pay attention to Baiji and slowed them down—at which point everything had gone to hell. Somebody had had to get out of there alive—and his bodyguard had done *exactly* what his bodyguard was supposed to do, and grabbed *him*. He understood that now, intellectually, even if his gut hadn't caught up to the situation. Man'chi drove Banichi and Jago: they'd go through fire to get to *him*. They had to. He understood that part. Intellectually.

What he didn't understand yet was why Banichi had grabbed Baiji instead of Cajeiri.

Baiji was—he still thought—weak, a lord likely to collapse under anybody's threat. He *wasn't* likely behind anything, unless Banichi read something entirely different . . .

And that was always possible. There were times when the paidhi read atevi just very well; and there were occasional times he didn't, and right now his confidence in his reading the situation was entirely shaken. Right now he didn't know *what* Baiji was, except related to a very major ally of theirs, and possibly involved in something very, very dangerous.

Banichi had made the gut-level choice to take Baiji with them. And Banichi didn't make mistakes under fire, never had.

So what in the situation wasn't he seeing?

He didn't know, and he sat still and listened to Jago tell Banichi they were close to the house, and heard Banichi suggest they avoid any communications. That told him Banichi worried about a compromise in the house system, but that was a reasonable precaution, if they'd been caught by surprise. It was just a precaution, wasn't it?

And what in hell was he going to tell the dowager?

Sorry? Sorry I misplaced the boy—again?

They made a turn, scraping brush on the side. "We are on the ridge," Jago said. "We are going down the short way."

"Bren-ji," Banichi said, and indicated he should take over pressure. He did, and Banichi used his com at the last moment for a short, coded exchange, likely a heads-up for Tano and Algini, while Jago took them downhill, hard, and finally onto gravel.

Then he thought: a heads-up, maybe; or maybe checking to be sure everything's all right *at the house* . . . God!

Final stretch. He turned the driver back over to Banichi and got up on his knee, elbows on the seat, to see where they were.

They made the final turn, came down the drive, onto the cobbles, and swerved under the front portico, so similar an arrangement to Kajiminda—but intact. Safe. Bren started to get up. Banichi seized his arm, said, "Hold it, Bren-ji," meaning the compress, and got up, towering there, bloody-handed—he snatched Baiji unceremoniously to his feet as the bus came to a stop.

Jago pulled the brake, and opened the door.

Tano and Algini were there, and received Baiji when Banichi shoved him off the bus. So was the physician, who climbed aboard. Bren gladly surrendered the driver to the doctor, and stood up—his own pale clothes were as bloody as Banichi's.

"Bren-ji," Jago said, taking his arm and urging him up and to the steps.

Cenedi was outside. Bren didn't know what to say to him, about the youngsters; and the ancient rule—one didn't, in a crisis, ever discuss anything delicate with Guild not one's own—seemed to cover the situation. He ducked his head and got down the steps, letting Jago guide him.

As her feet hit the cobbled ground, however, she stopped them both, and said, to Cenedi and Nawari, "One had no choice, nadiin-ji. The young lord is at lord Geigi's estate—in what situation, by now, we are unable to determine."

"Details," Cenedi said shortly, and they stood stock still, facing the gray-haired senior of Ilisidi's bodyguard.

What followed was what Bren called, to himself, Guild-speak, a lot of information freighted in a few words and a set of handsigns.

"Positioned at the door, bus coming. Shots from the right, wing of the estate roof, bus exposed. I took my Principal, Banichi took the lord, the young lord's party moved apart, taking cover."

Was *that* it? Man'chi, in crisis, moved emotionally-associated elements together. What moved apart might be allied on a different mission; might be hostile. Man'chi was situated somewhere in the hindbrain, in the gut—Mospheirans would call it the heart. It moved people in certain directions, and Cajeiri's man'chi hadn't been to a human, never mind Cajeiri was a minor child. If he'd followed his aishid, that would have been a topsy-turvy response, a fault in his character; and if he'd led his aishid—he was emotionally in charge; but he'd instinctively *left* the paidhi and his guard . . . going in his own direction, getting under cover. It was crystal clear—if you were wired that way from birth.

He, personally, wasn't wired that way. But his bodyguard was. Right now Tano and Algini were taking a man of his house to somewhere the doctor could work on him, and Jago was making sure Baiji stayed put, and Banichi—Banichi was facing down his old ally Cenedi's justified anger, protecting the paidhi. Cenedi, their old ally in a hundred crises, was absolutely expressionless—not happy—and probably assessing what he and *his* could do about the situation that had developed.

He wished he had an answer. He wished he understood half the undercurrents in the situation he'd let develop.

"We stand ready to go back ourselves, Cenedi-nadi," Bren said. "We shall get the boy back. We do not intend anything less."

"In the meeting with nand' Baiji," Banichi said to Cenedi. "We were dealt half-truths and equivocations. This lord knows something more, and will tell it to us and the dowager's guard."

Cenedi glanced toward Baiji with the first gleam of inner heat in his impassive facade, but said nothing.

"One needs urgently to speak to the dowager," Bren said, "if she will see me."

Cenedi gave a jerk of his head, said: "Nandi," and turned and led the way.

Toby had showed up at the door. Barb, thank God, had not. Toby made a sudden move to grasp his arm that sent hands to pistol butts—a motion restrained as Bren lifted a hand and then laid it on Toby's shoulder, sweeping him along with him. "Toby, this is very serious. Get back to your suite and stay there. *With* Barb. Assassins made a try at us. Cajeiri's missing. Go. Nobody's in the least patient here. Ask house staff if you need anything."

"Any way we can help," Toby began.

"There isn't. Not at the moment. Just go. Stay low."

Toby had that basic sense; and he trusted Toby, at least, to stay put—even to sit on Barb, for her own protection.

One of Cenedi's men, Kasari, had now moved in to take charge of Baiji. Bren headed down the hall as far as the door of the dowager's suite of rooms, and Cenedi and Nawari, in the lead, opened the door.

The dowager was on her feet, waiting, leaning on her cane.

Her eyes flashed sullen gold as they took in the bloody spectacle that confronted her.

Bren bowed his head, met her eye to eye with: "Our driver was shot, aiji-ma."

"Cajeiri separated himself from the paidhi, aiji-ma," Cenedi said in a flat tone, "seeking cover. He was left behind."

"How?" Ilisidi snapped, and the cane hit the floor. "What occasioned this?"

"We were about to board the bus," Bren said, having gathered the atevi-wise salient facts from Jago's initial explanation. "Shots from the roof, the driver fell, Jago grabbed me and took the wheel. Banichi took Lord Baiji into keeping, aiji-ma. He is here. Cajeiri is there."

Ilisidi actually, astonishingly, relaxed a little, hearing that set of facts. "In their hands?"

"Uncertain, nand' dowager," Banichi said. "One saw no such thing. Nand' Baiji was addressing nand' Bren, pleading to go with us to Najida. Shots met us outside. And the young people separated from us in the confusion of motion."

The cane hit the floor much more gently, twice. The dowager was thinking, and her jaw was set.

"You have Baiji," she said.

"The young gentleman moved toward cover," Banichi said. "The young companions were between me and him."

The Taibeni youngsters—an untrained guard—had moved between Banichi and their young lord: Banichi would have had to flatten them to reach Cajeiri. That might have taken one precious second, and two more to bring Cajeiri back to the bus—a time in which Jago might have been shot and the whole situation unraveled. Their bus in jeopardy, unknown man'chi around them, and Cajeiri *and* him to protect . . . Banichi had saved what he could, and picked *him.*

The dowager nodded slowly, grimly. "The paidhi is the more valuable," she muttered.

He understood it all right down to the point Ilisidi said that, regarding her precious great-grandson. He was appalled. Didn't know what to say.

And Ilisidi turned and walked away into the inner hallway of her suite.

"Cenedi-ji," he said. He thought maybe, under the circumstances, Cenedi might not favor the familiar address, but he knew the man, and did it anyway. "I will personally move the heavens and the earth to get Cajeiri back safely. One begs you let me and my staff assist you in what we do next."

Cenedi nodded shortly in the affirmative. "We shall begin," Cenedi said, "by asking nand' Baiji what he knows about this. Will the paidhi wish to question him? The paidhi heard his prior responses."

"Yes," he said, and looked at Banichi and Jago, who gave him no sign to the contrary. "Nadiin-ji, I shall have to call the aiji."

"One believes 'Sidi-ji is doing so at this moment," Cenedi said. "There will be reinforcements within a few hours, asked or unasked."

"Baiji's household is suspect," Banichi said grimly. "We did not recognize the men with him. Not a one. And we did not see all of them. Nor do we know about the servants."

"Number?" Cenedi asked.

"Four uniformed, downstairs. The shots came from the roof."

Crack. Tap. Ilisidi came back *out* of her room down the hall and said, with perfect and terrible calm, "We shall have a personal word with Baiji. I will spare half an hour. Come dark, we shall go get my great-grandson."

Diplomacy might be his job. But security was wholly Guild business, and Guild was going to be in charge when they moved tonight. Dangerous enough, that they'd apparently just called Tabini to respond to the situation. Communications were a leaky business ever since the new technology had taken hold; and the Messengers' Guild, in charge of the phones, had never been wholly reliable. The matter had gotten noisier and noisier, and if the lines were compromised, there might be more moving than a handful of Assassins over in Kajiminda.

Jago left quickly and quietly, and a very short time later came back in with two of the dowager's security and Lord Baiji between them.

Baiji immediately bowed, a deep, deep bow, an apology, with: "I am innocent, aiji-ma."

Thump! went the cane on the carpet. "I care nothing for your innocence or guilt or competency, man! I care for the whereabouts of my great-grandson! Where is he?"

"I—do not know, aiji-ma."

Ilisidi flung up a dismissive hand. "Then you are *useless!* Why are you breathing?"

"I know who is behind this, aiji-ma! I am sure—I am certain—I am relatively sure I know—"

"Gods less fortunate! Make up your mind, man!"

"His guard," Banichi said ominously, "left him under fire. They were new men attending him, not born to the house. And one is not certain we met a single Edi on the premises."

"There were," Baiji protested. "There were. My staff served you! And those Assassins on the roof—my guard—my guard was as stunned as all of us."

"Splendid!" Ilisidi's voice was like the damning crack of the cane. "Splendid. His guard was stunned into retreat, and there may or may not have been Edi! Give us your wisdom, lord of Kajiminda, while we have any patience left!"

"They might have known Lord Bren would visit . . ."

"They might have known," Ilisidi said, and now her voice had sunk, silken soft. "Are you a total fool, boy?"

"I—"

"—you have no idea how they would know this? And you are not sure? Do you know to whom you are currently speaking? Do you imagine we will be taken in by lies and maybes, considering the offense against our house and the breach of man'chi with your own uncle?"

"My guard—"

"Your guard is dead, incompetent, or in collusion! *Where are the Edi?*"

"My staff is there, aiji-ma, they have always been there."

"But some have gone to Dalaigi Township," Bren muttered. "Tell her."

"They are there! Some left—long ago. But the faithful ones, the ones that know I am a good lord . . ."

"And your bodyguard?" Banichi asked. "Why did they desert you?"

"They—they were confused . . ."

"They have no man'chi!" Ilisidi's dreadful cane extended, upward, and rested on Baiji's shoulder. "They are not yours, or they would not have retreated."

"They—they—are mine. They just—"

"The truth, man! Out with it!"

Baiji bowed, hands on knees, and came upright again, waving his hands desperately. "Aiji-ma, the Tasaigi of the Marid came to me, Lord Bren knows, during the Troubles. I temporized with them regarding a marriage—a marriage, a marriage which kept this peninsula safe, nand' dowager! I—"

"So. The Marid. The *Marid.*"

"You assisted the search for nand' Cajieri yesterday," Bren said. "With what motive? To find him yourself? To kill him?"

"No! No. One had no idea—no idea of who the boy was. No idea. One only wished to be neighborly."

"Kill this man," Ilisidi said.

"No!" Baiji wailed, lifting his hands, then bowing. "No, aiji-ma. I can tell you—I can tell you everything!"

"Why did you search for my great-grandson?"

"It was the paidhi, it was the paidhi-aiji, aiji-ma, one knew—one knew he was here, one wished to warn him . . ."

"We were in radio contact, nandi," Bren said. "Why did you not?"

"You left," Baiji stammered. "You left. One—one thought of sailing into Najidama Bay, but—they might have come here. They might have come here and we all would die."

"Tell us," the dowager said quietly, "tell us the details of this, tell us once, and be accurate, as you hope for my patience. My great-grandson is in danger. Is he not?"

"He is in great danger, aiji-ma. The Tasaigi came a few days ago. They came with new proposals—regarding—regarding the wedding. One has—one has not wanted to trouble those waters. One had hoped—they would simply go away and not renew their offer."

"A few days ago," Bren said, "notice came that made them move. Some in the Bujavid knew I was coming here. Some at Tirnamardi knew. My staff here in Najida knew. But one would wager on someone within the Bujavid."

"The Tasaigi flew in, we take it?" Ilisidi snapped, looking at Baiji. "They arrived in the district, you met with them. Where did you acquire your personal guard?"

"They are—they are a—"

"Gift from the proposed in-laws?"

Again the deep bow. The appeal with the hands. "No. No, nand' dowager. My guard vanished—in the Troubles—greatly mourned. The Guild itself sent these two. One has never, never, nand' dowager—one would never be so foolish—they are not Southern! I would know if they were Southern."

"Central district," Ilisidi said sharply. "Let me guess. The traitor Murini himself sent them."

"No, aiji-ma. The Guild in Shejidan."

Ilisidi looked ceilingward and turned away.

Then looked straight at Bren.

"One bears blame for this, aiji-ma," Bren said with a bow. "I divided my staff. I trusted our old relations with Kajiminda."

"*We* trusted Kajiminda," Ilisidi said bitterly, "trusting an old ally, trusting in those two *children* who attend my great-grandson, besides . . ." She spun on her heel and looked straight at Baiji. "Elaborate, man! The nature and extent of this contact. *Now* you may go into detail and meander as much as you like."

"I—"

"And use nouns! They, they, they! No more *they!* Give me names!"

"Aiji-ma—"

"Sit down," Ilisidi said sweetly. "Nand' Bren, send for tea. And no, nephew of our esteemed Lord Geigi, *ambitious* nephew of our Lord Geigi, we do not intend to poison you. Let us sit down and talk reasonably. We lack some time until dark, when we shall take action."

Bren himself went to the door, opened it, and signaled the major domo. "Kindly provide tea, a service for three." He added: "*Not* the historic set, if you please, Rama-ji. I think that would be best."

"Nandi." A bow, and Ramaso was off like a shot, giving orders to two staffers on the way. Four of Ilisidi's young men were out there. Tano and Algini were.

"Come in," Bren said to them, increasing the coverage of black in the room, black uniforms wall to wall. He had assumed a tea service for three. He assumed he would sit with the dowager, and indeed, the dowager had taken a seat, and Baiji had, and, indeed, the dowager gestured to him that he should also take a chair, fortunate three.

"So," the dowager said with sweet-voiced patience, while her great-grandson was at hazard of his life, while, very probably, hostile Southern interests had taken possession of Lord Baiji's estate, while Assassins from the Marid were, very probably, moving against her as well. "How *is* the spring planting shaping up?"

As if they were preparing to take tea with the traditional discussion of small topics, peaceful topics, pending service of the refreshment. Baiji stammered answers, sweat standing on his brow.

"And the dawi festival? How was it this year?"

"One did not attend, aiji-ma."

"Did not attend?" the dowager asked with sudden sharpness. "Or do you *fear* to travel, Lord Baiji? Can it be *fear* that kept you from, for instance, *other* festivities—such as, say, my grandson's resumption of the aijinate? Or were you not *celebrating* that event?"

"Aiji-ma," Baiji began to answer. But Ilisidi had a flawless sense of timing. The tea service arrived, when conversation ceased for a moment and Baiji could not answer.

The service went around, one, two, and three. When Baiji picked up his cup, he had to steady it in both hands.

"Now," the dowager said. "We were speaking of your attendance at court. Collect your thoughts, nand' Baiji, and make your accounting as thorough as possible."

Baiji shut his eyes—thinking, it was likely, possibly thinking harder than Baiji had ever thought in his life.

"Do not," the dowager said sharply, "waste any moment of this contemplative time on a lie, an equivocation, or appeasement. We desire information on a political scale, and a full accounting of your dealings with the Kadagidi, with the Tasaigin Marid, with others that may be pertinent. Do not omit any detail and any person from this accounting. Name names. Cenedi-ji."

"Aiji-ma."

"Record this session."

"Yes," Cenedi said.

"So. Baiji."

"Aiji-ma."

"If we later discover an omission or a gap in your account, you will most profoundly regret it."

Tea went down all in one gulp. The servant, standing by,

moved to fill that cup, and yet again as Baiji swallowed—a certain dryness of the mouth, perhaps.

Bren himself swallowed small sips, as did the dowager. They both emptied their cups, and had another. It was late afternoon, now. His mind raced, trying to find logic in the situation, and one thing occurred to him—that if the Edi in Kajiminda were unconstrained and knew they had the boy in their keeping, they would have sent a courier, or at very least made a phone call.

So either they dared not or could not make such a call. They were constrained. He did not believe they had turned.

And no one had called to ask for ransom.

My God. The airport. The train station. He was asleep.

"Nand' dowager," he asked, ever so quietly, "has anyone been stationed at the airport?"

"Flights are grounded as of your return here, nand' paidhi. Trains are stopped."

The whole district was cut off, then. That left movement by car. The dowager had made that one phone call to Tabini. Of course. He was a fool. He'd been rattled. It was a Guild matter.

"Nand' Baiji," the dowager said, and set down her cup on the little side table. "Speak to us now. Never mind an apology. State the facts."

"The facts, aiji-ma . . ."

"Aiji-ma! Am I *your* aiji? Have you man'chi to us? Or *where*, precisely, does it reside?"

"With my uncle, nand' dowager, one knows that . . . one is so confused . . ."

"*Focus*, man! Where is your man'chi at this moment?"

"To my uncle, aiji-ma, and his is to the Ragi aiji, which has always been . . ."

"You do not have to defend your *uncle*, boy. *Your* man'chi is the one in question, gravely in question. Has it lately wavered?"

"Nand' dowager, it—I—one has—one has been beseiged. One has been alone . . . one has hardly known where to turn. . . ."

"Go on. Now you have your pieces in order. Where did you first question it?"

"When—when the aiji your grandson was rumored dead, when Murini had taken Shejidan and all the midlands."

"Go on."

"Districts were going down one after the other, so fast, so fast, aiji-ma, and the South had made an association with the Kadagidi: the Atageini were threatened; Taiben—Murini had struck there first, and one had no notion any resistance remained there or whether the aiji was alive. All the coast, aiji-ma, all the Marid was Murini's ally, and all the southern islands, and we on the southwestern coast—we knew the Northern Isles had gone to the humans—but the Northern Isles are difficult to take. The southwestern coast, with its deep bays—we were vulnerable. The Marid would roll over us on their way to attack the Isles—it was—it was a matter of time, aiji-ma."

"Keep going."

"Except—except the South knows how serious it is if the Edi should get stirred up. The Edi hate the Marid; and my uncle being up on the station where, if the Edi were attacked, my uncle might have human weapons to use . . . the Southerners had to think of that. They *feared* me."

"Let us proceed at least with that assumption," Ilisidi said dryly. "It was a great inconvenience that they could not reach your uncle; and a great relief that your uncle could not reach them. Nor had your uncle Geigi ordered the Edi to war against them."

"Nor me. He gave me no such order, aiji-ma."

"The dish at Mogari-nai being down, and other communications going only through the north—one wonders what he would have told you if he could have gotten in contact."

"I had no word, aiji-ma, none!"

"Not even a message relayed from Mospheira, where he did have contact?"

"None, aiji-ma! None, ever!"

"I wonder. But no matter, now. Go *on*, nand' Baiji. We are enthralled."

"Please, aiji-ma! Nand' Bren's estate, here, and mine—we made common cause. We—that is—I sent a messenger to Ramaso-nadi here asking advice, and they said they would not surrender to the Usurper; and I agreed I would not."

"Easily confirmed, aye or nay. Let us assume aye. And we omit who sent first to whom. Go on."

"But—one knew it was a matter of time. At first—at first there was a rumor your grandson might have fled to Najida, and we feared the worst would come. And then it was rumored Najida had smuggled out state records and treasures. And we feared that would bring trouble down on us. But it was our strategy to keep quiet. The whole peninsula kept quiet. We knew how they installed certain people in power in Dalaigi Township the way they did elsewhere, but the Edi assassinated them; and we—we stayed quiet."

"And then?"

"Then—one told Lord Bren—then they sent to me proposing a marriage, myself with a daughter of the Marid. One had no better advice, nor any communication with my uncle. One could stall it off—one could make requests: they wanted this badly. They might agree. It would all be meaningless once my uncle came back from the heavens, but in the meanwhile if I agreed to marry this girl, and then I kept asking for things and got the best bargain I could—it seemed the best thing to do."

"A very dangerous bed."

"It would be. One knew it. And then you came back, aiji-ma, and the paidhi-aiji, and Tabini-aiji, may he live long, drove Murini out, and Murini's own clan repudiated him . . . and then—and then the Marid began to make new approaches to your grandson, and they were going to make peace with him.

So I thought—see, even the aiji is hearing them . . . so when they also came to me, and said they were still interested in this marriage—I thought—this might not be a bad thing for the peace . . ."

"And you never presented yourself at court. You never consulted with my grandson about this daring maneuver. Do go on." The dowager had *not* supported Tabini's hearing the South. If not for the aiji's playing Southern politics, Bren thought, he might be in his own apartment in the Bujavid, the Farai would be out, and none of this would have happened at all.

"One had missed court. I was sick, aiji-ma. I was truly sick."

"But you had visitors."

"I had word from them. A message. A letter. And then—then I thought—now I shall be ashamed, aiji-ma, I thought to myself how things are not settled yet, and I should see how stable the aijinate is and how stable the South is before I commit to them or say no. One is profoundly ashamed."

"The brightest thought you had had yet," Ilisidi muttered. "The most honest you have yet expressed. Say on. Be precise, now. When did you acquire these guards?"

"The Guild of my house had gone to the fight in Shejidan, and never came back, so I had had members of my staff pretend to be Guild . . ." Baiji cast a nervous glance about at the Guild in black, grim attendance. "I had no choice but that, nadiin!"

"You were not the only one to do so, nandi," Algini said quietly.

"Then—" Baiji said, looking back at Ilisidi, "then when the Usurper was going down, and it was clear my own guard would not come back, these Guildsmen came saying they had served in the Guild itself, but that there was a new regime coming in, there was a great deal of bloodshed, they had lost relatives, and they wished the peace of serving in a country house, remote from troubles. They had credentials!"

"Did you write to the Guild to confirm them, nandi?" Cenedi asked.

"I *asked* them to write."

"You did not confirm what they said," Banichi said grimly, "by writing to the Guild yourself, and by a Guild representative officially confirming their man'chi."

"I had no idea of the procedure, nadi! Kajiminda has never been without Guild until now. One had no idea what to do— one knows—one knows now this was not the thing to do!"

That, in itself, was possible. There had always been such a closely-woven network—and it was true that Baiji had been isolated from advice, out of society, getting his advisements in protocol mainly from the Tasaigin Marid, to be honest, while the neighbor at Najida, whose security might properly have advised a young neighbor what he should do, was light-years off in space, leaving *no* Guild at all behind on his estate. His apartment in Shejidan—the place was rife with Guild in and out of uniform, active and retired; but in the fall of the regime, indeed, Guild had gathered to the Guild headquarters, and dispersed on this side and that of the action.

And, as Algini had said, certain desperate houses had put up a facade of Guild protection where it did not exist.

"Do you believe him, paidhi-aiji?" the dowager asked.

"Logically, I follow what he says," Bren said. "But myself being human, and this being a question of man'chi, I would not venture to have an opinion about his loyalty."

"Cenedi?"

"Hadjaijid, aiji-ma."

A mental condition. Isolation from the networks of society. Aiji-like, in having no upward or lateral man'chi—no connection to which he emotionally responded; but pathologically isolated, in that he had no real leadership—and no man'chi downward, either. Isolated. Delusional. Disconnected.

Sociopath.

"I am not," Baiji cried, and flung himself out of the chair—a dozen guns flashed out—and onto his knees and onto his face on the carpet.

And there went the teacup, Bren noted, in surreal detachment. It shattered in an unfortunate four pieces.

Bad omen.

Baiji lay on his face on the floor, crying, "Aiji-ma, I am not disconnected. I have man'chi to my uncle, to my people, to this place, to the aiji in Shejidan and to *you*, aiji-ma! I have never broken it!"

"And man'chi to my great-grandson?"

There was a moment of heavy silence.

"And association with your neighbor nand' Bren?" Ilisidi pursued him.

"I have only met nand' Bren once before," Baiji said into the carpet, and lifted his head and sat up and bowed again. "I beg pardon. I beg pardon. I had no idea my security was disconnected!"

And had been a spoiled brat at that one meeting, when his mother had had to beg him to come down to dinner. There was a problem, in establishing man'chi with that person. A serious problem.

"Then why," Bren said, divorcing himself from all mercy, "did you not visit me? Why did you not, knowing I am connected to the regime, come *here* to consult Ramaso, knowing that your estate has had problems in security? Why did you not propose coming here instead, when you knew I proposed to visit you with the young lord?"

"Because—because they would never agree!"

"They," the dowager snapped. "*They* would not agree and you knew it!"

"Aiji-ma!"

"Your aishid would not come here," Bren said sharply. "And you are quite sure they would not have approved the visit. Do you or do you not lead the house?"

"Where are the Edi?" Ilisidi asked from the other side. "Is your staff still alive, or did they leave you?"

"Some—some are there, aiji-ma. Some stayed!"

"While you assure one side and the other of your good intentions," Bren shot at him, "all the while courting the Marid? *Explain* this to a simple human. One fails to understand this complexity. But one very well understands your motives in rushing to find our lost boat!"

"No!" Baiji cried. "Nand' dowager, one had no idea you were here! One had no idea the heir was here at all, or that you were! A village child, he said. He said it was a simple accident—"

"Really?" she asked. "You have no source of gossip, considering we arrived at the public airport in quite a large plane? You have no news from Dalaigi Township? None from the market? We are quite *astounded*, nandi!"

"No, no, no, we had no idea."

"Then your aishid failed to inform you of a critical event, one touching on your welfare. What a remarkable thing!"

"We saved your great-grandson, aiji-ma! We had no advisement of the dowager's presence! We had no warning of any such incident! The Tasaigi had contacted me days ago—one had no idea they were advised—"

"By your own staff. You *are* not the aiji on this peninsula," Ilisidi said. "You are not even aiji over your estate. You are the major domo for your uncle, who does not make mistakes like this. You will *not* remain lord of Kajiminda, let alone of Sarini province!"

"Aiji-ma!"

"We will choose one of the Edi, with adequate guard of our choosing, to manage the estate in your uncle's name, granted we can correct these matters short of regional war. And thank me that you are not awaiting your funeral, boy, nandi no longer! Nand' Bren."

"Aiji-ma."

"This person will lodge here until we have exhausted the information we may draw from him. Keep him comfortably situated, for the sake of his uncle. But do *not* give him freedom of the grounds."

"Yes, aiji-ma." Bren caught the eye of the servant, who had cautiously rescued the fragments of the teacup. "Advise Ramaso-nadi."

A silent bow, a quiet departure. Baiji, having gathered himself onto his knees, continued to rock to and fro in distress.

"We are appalled," Ilisidi said, and, leaning on her cane, and with Cenedi's hand, rose. "Cenedi. *Get my great-grandson back.*"

"Banichi," Bren said. "With the dowager's permission, my bodyguard will assist. And I shall. Personally."

"Nandi," Banichi said, with a small nod.

Ilisidi's men gathered up Baiji, who made no protest to being taken away from Ilisidi's vicinity, and escorted him out.

"We shall *both* be involved, nand' paidhi," Ilisidi said. "Is the bus damaged?"

"Not significantly," he said, "granted a hole in the back roof and the resources we have to replace a rear tire—if not a wheel."

"Be ready," Ilisidi said.

That was a dismissal. Bren bowed, gathered his aishid, and went out into the hall, where Ramaso waited.

"We have disposed nand' Baiji in staff quarters downstairs," Ramaso said, and with a distressed look. "It is the only place we can secure."

It had no windows. His brother and Barb, Cajeiri, the aiji-dowager, Cenedi, her physician and her young men—guests had collectively taken the last suites left in the house. He could draw his own aishid into his suite and gain that room, but better Baiji have just a little less lordly accommodation. No windows was a good idea, not only considering Baiji trying to go out a window—he could not imagine it—but considering someone trying to come in.

"Are the storm shutters in order?" he asked. "I want them ready, if you get the word."

"They are, nandi."

"And Iscarti," he said. "Is there news regarding Iscarti?"

"Awake, nandi. Very weak, but the dowager's physician is encouraging."

"I will see him as soon as I possibly can," he said. "He saved us, Rama-ji. If he had not gotten the bus to us despite being shot, we might all be dead. He deserves the best we can do. The very best. One will never forget it."

"One will convey that to him," Ramaso said, "nandi."

His bodyguard had gathered around him. "Nadiin-ji," he said to them as Ramaso left, "the paidhi-aiji owes you the greatest of apologies. My foolishness divided the aishid, sending you to Barb and Toby. It was even numerically infelicitous." None of them believed in the superstitions, not in the least, but there were reasons, with the Guild, that they worked in odd numbers—counting the one they protected. He had slipped that far from ordinary, and basic, considerations. "One cannot say enough—this was very much my fault."

"We were taken by surprise," Banichi said ruefully. "Not by the Guildsmen. We would not *let* them position themselves. We would have shot them had they had made a move—we would have taken them down when shots were fired."

"But?"

"But the young lord moved to disadvantage relative to his guards. Return fire would have come at him."

"He moved apart," Jago said, as if that summed up everything. To a certain extent, it did.

"Everyone has worked hard to waken the proper sensibilities in the young gentleman," Banichi said. "And he moved in his own direction." A rueful shrug. "Aiji."

"*Where* did he go, 'Nichi-ji?"

"Into the bushes, the nearest cover. They may not have found him. If his companions have learned anything in their training, he will not stir until dark. Then he may attempt to come here. *That* is our greatest concern. The Southerners may not have the equipment in place to find him—yet; and they may not have clearly seen that we did not get the youngsters aboard the bus. But there will be action, tonight. They will be expecting *us*. They may come *here* in the thought we may throw all our resources into attacking Kajiminda."

"One fears we may have to. To what extent do you think they have taken over nand' Geigi's estate?"

"If the nephew is truthful," Tano said, "and some Edi staff have stayed on—possibly out of man'chi to Lord Geigi—we must use caution. Certainly all armed staff are likely to be infiltrators."

Any of the Edi that had tried to leave—would be lucky to survive the attempt. It was a terrible thought. These were decent people, all of them, staff of a good lord, who had appointed a reasonably decent woman to stand in his stead.

"One wonders how Baiji's mother died," Bren said. "She was sickly, but not that old."

"She was not," Jago agreed. "And one is suspicious."

"One would not accuse the man of matricide," Tano said. "Of weakness, of stupidity, both these things. The Tasaigi may have well known who they wanted in such a key position, and taken action to put him there."

"They well may have," Algini said. "And hoped, perhaps, eventually to get Lord Geigi himself in their sights. They may not have been that anxious to attack us. They may have been most worried that Baiji might talk to us. They had to put pressure on him."

"Baiji rushed out to rescue a village child gone adrift," Banichi said, "and says he considered running here for refuge."

"If that was so," Jago said, "he lost his best chance when he went back to Kajiminda."

"*Guild* may have known very well who was lost out there," Banichi said. "Guild back at Kajiminda would surely have found out the aiji-dowager had landed at the airport. At least late in the operation, they had to have an idea."

"And have time to call in reinforcements of their own," Tano said.

"We cannot leave Najida undefended," Banichi said. "If they have the young gentleman or know he failed to leave with us, they will come here. If they have assets arriving in Dalaigi Township, they may bring those in. It can only get worse."

"Granted they are ready for a confrontation with Tabini-aiji," Bren said. "Which may give them some hesitation. Are they here yet?"

His guards' faces were uncharacteristically blank of expression for a second. Forbidden topic. Highest security. Some were here, and had been ever since Cajeiri had taken the train in: he took that on faith.

"One does not need to ask," he said. "But, nadiin-ji, the dowager herself has it in mind to go out there tonight. Can we intercede with Cenedi to argue against this?"

"We are fortunate she does not call in mecheiti for the venture," Banichi said. The dowager, not that many years ago, had ridden under fire with *no* protection. Hell—she'd done a stretch of it this winter, for all practical purposes. The dowager's great-grandson was in danger, and the dowager was going after him—no argument about it.

"Then I shall be with her," Bren said. "At the rear, one assumes. Have we a plan?"

"Jago and I will go in," Banichi said, "having had a chance to see the current layout of house and grounds. Cenedi and Nawari will be with the dowager and with you. Tano and Algini will be assigned to you. Five of the dowager's men will stay at Najida, and the village will be on alert."

He didn't like it. Banichi and Jago proposed to go inside, and he didn't like it at all. He couldn't pick and choose among his bodyguard, who took the risks, and who didn't: it wasn't, for one thing, his choice: it was Banichi's.

But God, he didn't like it. *None* of their choices were palatable.

"I have to go talk to my brother," Bren said, "very briefly. All of you have things to do: I shall be safe to do this much alone. Call me immediately when we need to leave."

"Yes," Banichi said. "But do not go outside without us, Bren-ji. Do not stir from this hall without us."

"I shall not," he said. And headed off down the hall to talk to Toby.

12

Dusk was coming, and Cajeiri was bored. He sat, jammed in the little tower as he'd learned to sit in a worse situation—very, very still, the way the Taibeni sibs had also learned to sit from very early, being hunterfolk, and used to waiting—all in silence. They knew voices carried and small movements caught attention, and they were sitting right at the feet of the security system that swept the forest beyond.

Occasionally they made handsigns. People had eventually come out and searched the orchard, which was a situation worse than being bored, and to Cajeiri's great relief, they had finally gone back in.

The figures on the roof had gone away for a while, too, giving them some hope everybody would just go inside; but after a while the man reappeared near the chimney, and sat there on the red tiles, holding a large rifle with a sight.

That probably meant, in Cajeiri's best guess, one of two things: the people who had tried to kill them were watching the road for nand' Bren coming back with help.

But maybe some of these people were actually Edi, and maybe they would be on their side. There was the remote chance, if the way to Najida was watched, that they could go over the wall, keep close to it, below the angle at which the surveillance worked, and hike to Dalaigi Township to get help.

But that was a long way, as best Cajeiri recalled his maps.

They could steal a car from the estate. But there was none in sight.

They could sneak down to the harbor and steal a boat—but that had not worked so well last night. The wind was blowing fairly steadily to the east, and the tide might be moving and the wind would just carry them right back to the Kajiminda dock, while the tide could get them into the same trouble they had been in yesterday.

He bet that the Edi staff was probably not happy with Lord Baiji, who, by his embarrassing performance with Lord Bren, had not managed well at all and who had been incredibly suspicious-acting on a lot of accounts, even *before* the Guild with Lord Baiji had started trying to assassinate nand' Bren and kidnap him. He personally had had his fill of being kidnapped, and he was not going to let that happen again. He supposed the Edi might be considerably put out with Lord Baiji.

And if *he* were an Edi major domo and he had a phone that was working, he would call the local magistrates down in Dalaigi Township, or he would call nand' Bren at Najida and ask for help or at least apologize, and if he had time he would call Shejidan and tell them the situation here . . . if the Guild was not running things.

But probably the major domo, if he was Edi, had not had a chance to do that. He was very much afraid the Edi who had served Lord Geigi were not in charge at all, if it was Southerners who had moved in. Probably the Southerners had killed people. They had certainly done that in the Bujavid. So the Edi might all be dead. And that would make Lord Geigi very unhappy, and it would probably make Lord Bren very, very mad, all things considered, not to mention Great-grandmother, who, with nand' Bren, was very certainly going to be laying plans to get him back before morning—one did not have to think hard at all to know that.

He did not, however, want mani to be where people were going to be shooting each other. Mani did not move as fast as she used to, and just getting up and down stairs was sometimes hard for her, and if these people hurt mani—

That worried him. That worried him most of all. Because mani had a temper. Nand' Bren did not, not the way mani did, and he really, really hoped nand' Bren would call his father and get some people here he did not care about as much, who would not get mad and take chances the way mani would.

Not to mention Cenedi was getting a little old to be climbing walls, too. He wished he had not gotten into this. People important to him and important to everyone were getting too old to be coming after him in places like this.

And it had all gone wrong when the shooting started.

He had tried to figure out how. He had tried to figure out what he had done wrong, and he had built in his head how the portico had been and how the driver had been shot and still got under the portico where they could reach the bus.

But when the bus had hit the pillar and the roof had come down he had started—he thought—to the side, just a step.

But that was not all of it. He had moved. And Jegari and Antaro were studying to be Guild; and among the very first lessons they had come home with was how to take cover, and how to position themselves to be sure to know where their Principal was—that being him.

And the disturbing fact was, they were still bumping into each other in practices—which happened. They were still learning how to watch out for him, and watch everything else, too, and he'd moved that one step sideways when the crash happened. It had not been the gunfire that had scared him: it had been the pillar. And he moved *sideways.*

That was just scary. He'd left nand' Bren. He had just lost all common sense and shied off *away* from the bus; and *that* was when everything had gone crazy.

What had he thought he was doing?

He had confused Jegari and Antaro, who had probably bumped into each other, what he had done was so crazy. And a half a second later Banichi had been going without them and after that he had no idea. He was worried that either Jegari or Antaro had consequently gotten in Banichi's way, all because of *him*, which was so embarrassing he could not even think about it right now. It was just humiliating; and he hoped with all he had that Banichi and Jago had gotten nand' Bren out all right.

Everything depended on that bus getting back to the house, one hoped with nand' Bren and Banichi and Jago both—or everything was going to be running very late, and people at the house might not *know* what had happened here.

Mani herself was hard to fool. He was very sure of that.

So somebody *would* come. Eventually.

And they sat. Silent. It was very uncomfortable where they were, in a little space that looked like a grand fortress tower, but which inside was dusty and crowded with canisters of fertilizer and rusty old tools and hose, besides. Some of the garden claws could be nasty weapons. But trying to use something like that to threaten real Guild—that was outright suicide. He had no illusions. Hand-to-hand with those would get Jegari and Antaro killed in short order. So those were no good.

He had his *slingshota*. He had taken that along as a very precious thing: he had no wish to have some overzealous maid, cleaning, decide it was a dirty old stick and toss it out.

It was their only good weapon. But it needed rocks.

The plan had been to wait until dark and then climb down from the wall. If they hung by their hands, or maybe by a loop of that brittle hose, it was not too far a drop to the outside, to run through the small woods and then open land, trusting to speed and luck to get away.

But the closer dusk came, the more he began to think that that was going to be a very chancy thing to do, because that man on the roof might spot them. That outward window of the tower made it a scary bit further drop than it was from the landing outside the tower, from this one window where there was cover.

And the closer they got to dusk, the darker and scarier the woods got, and they *knew* these towers held this perimeter equipment that would spot somebody moving in the woods.

Not, however, if they kept right up close to the wall—unless there was a system they had not spotted.

Still—if they left, and mani came in looking for them—

It was getting scary as it got closer to dark, was what.

It was going to be real scary, either way, trying to go cross-country in the open, or waiting.

They could head for the train station instead of Najida. That might surprise the hunters. But the train station was farther, and might be watched, too, if there were Guild hunters out.

And, again, if nand' Bren came hunting them here, being *there* would be a problem.

The enemy had not searched the patio and tower. He had no idea why, except Antaro had been very clever, spotting that trap and getting them over the garden gate.

Or maybe these big Guildsmen were thinking of only hiding places on an adult scale. It was a very, very small tower, so small they sat all tucked up together inside it, with knees and elbows so cramped up together, they had occasionally to apologize to each other and shift around to relieve really painful cramps.

Small places had worked on the starship. Sometimes searchers would go right by them and never think to look where they had hidden, because it was too small to be useful.

He tried to think of other things they could do, being here, which was sneak down to the house after dark and see if they could talk to the Edi servants, and see if the servants, given direction and a plan, could lock the Guildsmen into a room. Or poison them. That would be a plan, too. Mani would do that. But trying and missing could get the Edi killed. And he was not sure how he would tell who was Edi and who was not.

He was thinking about that.

And then they saw one of the Assassins come out the back

door, and down into the orchard, and start looking around. He came close to the patio. And instead of looking up at the tower— Cajeiri watched him through the crack below the window—he kept looking back at the house and up at the roof.

They were starting to do another search, though: he doubted this would be the last. It was getting dark, and they would probably get out the night scopes, which could actually spot them better by dark.

Cajeiri wriggled a little to see better. The slingshota poked him in the ribs.

It was what they had.

If they had rocks. Which had made it useless.

Antaro and Jegari had no idea what was going on. But he could hear that man moving around on the patio pavings.

That was that. The men inside the house were getting curious. They had to get out of here.

"Toby," Bren said, entering the suite. He was still in bloody clothes. There was going to be no time to change, he feared. Toby stood there by the table; Barb came in, both of them quite sober. "Toby, I'm sorry. This would probably be a good time for you to go back to the boat and just get out of the bay while you can, way clear of the coast."

"What are you going to do?" Toby asked, worried-looking, slipping an arm around Barb.

"I'm going after the boy," Bren said, "in about ten minutes, if that long. We want to get into position, get in there around dark—and take the place."

Barb put her arms around Toby. They looked like two figures in a cold wind. She looked at Toby, looked at him, and Toby patted her shoulder.

"Bren," Toby said, "can we help? Is there any way we can help?"

"Not in this," he said. "This is going to get wider. It's a Guild operation. This wasn't the neighbor's idea. This was the South behind what happened. An attack on this house isn't impossible, and it may already be underway. They'd like to lay hands on my relatives. They wouldn't as likely take after the staff as hostages—at least I hope not. But it's definitely going to be a lot safer for you two to get out of the bay."

"Look," Toby said, "Bren, we can't just cut and run. You're in trouble. The boy's in trouble."

"You can get yourself out of harm's way and relieve me of one worry."

"We can manage," Toby said. "If you're worried about the house—"

"Don't argue with me, brother. This is no time or place. You don't know the rules. Tabini-aiji's involved, no question in my mind. His men will be here. The dowager's men are going in. So is she. This isn't going to be small-scale, much as we're trying to finesse getting Cajeiri out in one piece. We're hoping he hid. But we don't know that. I'm frankly real upset right now."

"We can help," Barb said. "Bren, don't be stubborn. We can take care of ourselves. We can help here."

"Not a thing you can do," he said. He didn't even say, to Toby, Go back to Jackson and take care of that kid of yours. He didn't want another Barb incident. "Just get out of here."

"We've got a radio," Toby said. "We've got communications with the mainland, hell, we can radio Shejidan if you have phone troubles. We can radio Jackson and get you air support if it's that bad."

The *Brighter Days*, with its radio, was, in fact, an asset. "You'd be a target. There are those that would want to shut you down."

"We dodged them for months on end while you were gone," Toby said. "Trust me. This is an old game for us."

"Get out of the bay. Get out at sea. The bay is a trap made to order. I'll accept your running communications if you just get out into open water."

"Got that picture," Toby said.

"Then you go ahead, get down to the boat," Bren said, "as fast as you can while you still have some safety doing it. We have no guarantee Guild Assassins aren't moving on this estate, or moving to close off the harbor. Don't take safety for granted. Just pack up the essentials and get out of here, well out, as fast as you can. Contact Mogari-nai." There were Mosphei'-speakers manning that post, in the Messengers' Guild. "Figure we'll contact you if we need any help from the Island. And I hope we don't."

"Done," Toby said, and disengaged from Barb to come and embrace him. Hard. "Bren, I know you take care of yourself. I know they take care of you. But for God's sake, don't take chances. My regards to the kid. Deepest. I'm so sorry this happened."

"You be careful." Barb put her arms around him and for once he didn't flinch. Even hugged her back, even took a kiss on the cheek and hugged her tight. "Take care of yourself, Bren. Toby and I will be all right."

"See to it," he said, and slipped free and left, out into the hall, where one of Ilisidi's young men was carrying a heavy bag toward the outer doors. The doors stood open, with Ramaso and several of the staff waiting there.

He made a brief trip to his room, delved into his top dresser drawer and drew out the gun staff always packed. He had not had it with him this morning. Now he did.

He went out into the hall and picked up Tano and Algini as he passed the dining room hallway. Banichi and Jago were already outside, loading gear on, and the tire had been replaced—the bus, battered as it was, was sitting more or less level. He was about to get on board when Ilisidi, Cenedi, and Nawari came out of the house.

He stopped, bowed, gave Ilisidi precedence in boarding, and delayed for an anxious look at Banichi.

"Jago and I shall ride with you to the village, first, Bren-ji," Banichi said, "and from there, we shall take the village truck overland, along with Nawari and Kasari. The estate here is secure: two of the dowager's men are on the roof, one inside, two standing guard over Baiji-nadi in the basement."

He didn't like it. He never liked knowing Banichi and Jago were going into action, but they were the hand-to-hand experts. Send Tano and Algini into a situation and things exploded—no asking what was in *their* gear at the moment, and God knew he didn't want things blowing up with the youngsters unaccounted for. So Banichi and Jago were the ones for getting into the estate on a surgical strike, taking out just the enemy, and getting the kids to safety. . . .

But—

"You take care, 'Nichi-ji," he said. One didn't touch, ever, especially not here. His human instincts were raw-edged at the moment, but Banichi's and Jago's minds had to be utterly on business. No distractions. Suggest they take Tano and Algini for backup? Twice divide their forces?

Neither half of that set would leave him without assurance the other would be protecting him. Wouldn't. Banichi and Jago were free to do what they proposed to do *because* Tano and Algini were with him; and Bren just shut up and climbed onto the bus, taking his seat near Tano and Algini. He caught a glance from Tano that said "all business" and ready for anything.

The sun was touching the horizon—they'd have well and enough time to get to Kajiminda around dark, even with the detour to drop Banichi and Jago down at the village, but he had a notion, as the bus started to move, that they would hardly slow down at the village, that Banichi and Jago and Cenedi's two were going to go out that door before the bus had quite stopped rolling, start up that waiting market truck, and they wouldn't see anything from that team until this business was done.

Baiji, taking on marriages with the Marid, for God's sake. If Ramaso had ever heard that tidbit of information and once, just once hinted of that dealing, he'd *never* have taken the boy over there, nor would the dowager have let her great-grandson come near a man even on the outskirts of such a bargain.

But nobody at Najida had been in regular contact with Baiji. Not even indirect contact . . . since the Troubles. He knew about the unpaid bills. He'd seen the unmown grass. He'd had a bad feeling about Baiji and let his relationship with Geigi rule his thinking.

The disappearance of the regular staff . . . God, that was thirty, forty people. At least. All missing, and no word of warning reached outside Kajiminda to alert his staff at Najida?

He had confidence in Ramaso. If information had been floating outside, village gossip, rumors from the train station, the airport, even clear to Dalaigi Township, they'd have picked it up. Ramaso would have warned him. But no, they had walked into a situation at the neighbor's, a completely unwarned situation—but all ordinary methods of information-gathering had failed. The Southerners had been secretive—nothing new—and Baiji had been cooperating in that secrecy, keeping it even from his neighbors, with far more skill and thoroughness than Baiji radiated at other enterprises.

How long had the Tasaigi been setting up for a move against Najida? And what *had* they been aiming at?

And how the hell had Baiji kept the Edi he claimed were still on his staff from telling their relatives, who would have told relatives in Najida district? Would they not? Had threats kept them silent? The Edi tended to keep their own counsel, but not to have gotten *any* word out—

Oh, there were a dozen questions he had yet to ask Baiji when he got back.

And God, when Geigi did find out—good-natured, easygoing Geigi was not all sweetness and affability. No knowing what Geigi would do when he learned what had happened in his house, but coming down like a hammer on his nephew was head of the list.

And Geigi's sister: another bad bit of business, and murder

was a high likelihood: it was too convenient for the Marid. Geigi's sister taken out, and her son, a fool, set in her place, last of a waning line and without relatives at hand to advise him. The Maschi remaining in Kajiminda—the last of the clan besides Baiji and Geigi's niece—were two young men who'd gone to space to work with Geigi. Beyond that—

Beyond that—there were a few Maschi relatives in the Samiusi district, who, be it admitted, had been a problem in their dealings: Geigi's former wife had gone to the Marid and married there: that was an old bit of business; and Geigi—

They relied on Geigi. They weren't in the habit of questioning Geigi's connections, because, up in space, Geigi had absolute control of his associates, and he was never exposed to problems. A security lapse up there just didn't happen.

If he were down here, however . . .

There would be problems. Clearly there *were* problems, and the staunch loyalty Geigi felt to the aiji in Shejidan, that they treated as dependable as the sunshine—the lines of man'chi that ought to have made the nephew cling tightly to his uncle's commitments—were not reliable at all.

The Marid, Tabini's old enemies, didn't do things without a purpose. The Farai had gotten into the Bujavid. Others had gotten into Baiji's house, in the heart of Sarini province. His coming here—the Farai were clearly in a position to find that out, and he had a strong suspicion there had been a phone call or a courier. Dalaigi Township was a sprawling hub of transport, boats going in and out, rail, air—all kinds of things could go in Dalaigi. All sorts of people could be in Dalaigi—the missing Edi. Their relatives. Or a small cabal of Marid folk trying to look like locals. It was not a comforting prospect, not for the peace of this district—not for the Edi—not for his own estate, or Geigi's.

Or for the Western Association, for that matter. Tabini was newly restored to power: the usurper Murini was dead. But the issues that had driven the attack on Tabini's power were still there, old as the aishidi'tat itself. The matter of local rule. The ambitions of the Marid for power. The old issues of the displacement of whole populations from Mospheira, when it became a human island. All those things were still rattling loose, and nothing that had ever happened had settled them.

An impromptu move against the paidhi?

Oh, far from a single move. It was a movement he had stumbled into. The Farai might be bitterly regretting now that they had taken the paidhi's apartment—that a chain of events had moved the paidhi to the *other* old Maladesi estate, the one the Farai hadn't dared claim.

He had come out here, the Marid had made a fast move to be sure Baiji didn't pay a visit to Najida, Toby's daughter broke her leg—three bored kids had decided to take to the water in a sailboat. And when he'd come over to do the socially correct thing, a handful of local trouble trying to contain Baiji had decided they had a chance at taking out the paidhi-aiji.

Maybe they'd been misinformed as to the identity of the youngsters, or just—as the dowager seemed to think—counted the aiji's son inconsequential, if they could take out the aiji's advisor.

He thought about that. And his heart rate got up. He was, he decided, mad. Damned mad about that.

Count on it—if low-level agents had blown their secrecy, the Marid was probably moving assets from wherever it had situated them, maybe *in* Dalaigi, maybe in Separti—because an operation intending to spread Marid influence onto the coast wasn't going to rely on a handful of agents holding Baiji silent. There was more out there. There could be a lot more out there.

God, he hoped Tabini had read between the lines. Ilisidi had made the call; protocol had dissuaded him from following up with a call of his own, and now, on a bus headed into the thick of it, he had second thoughts. Not about getting the kids out— that was increasingly imperative. But about what they were dealing with.

They needed help out here. They might need a lot of help, very soon, and if they didn't move quietly, they could see events blow up in a major way—a little action spiraling out of control, into major armament, movement of forces—

It could get very, very nasty. He needed to talk plainly to Ilisidi—who wasn't talking, at the moment. Nobody was, among her group. All he could do was put Tano and Algini into the current of his thinking, and trust if there was information flowing down Guild channels, they could be sure at least that Cenedi was thinking about it.

Dark was coming fast. It was just light enough for the white-washed wall to glow a little in the twilight. For the windows of the house to show light.

And Cajeiri's legs were asleep, a fierce kink getting worse in his back. Jegari and Antaro did not complain, but one was sure they were in more discomfort, being larger.

There was still no sign of nand' Bren or Banichi or a rescue. That was getting scary.

Pain.

Excuse me, he signed, and had to wriggle about to his knees on the concrete floor, just for relief.

"Are we going to go, nandi?" Antaro signed back. And that was getting to be another trouble. They signed, to stay quiet. But it would reach a point soon when that would hardly work.

"If we go over the wall," Jegari whispered, right against his ear, "we are bound to make some noise. Those are Guild, nandi, they are real Guild! We cannot take a chance."

Noise.

Noise.

He had had an idea which had been simmering a long while, considering present resources, and with the lights in the house more or less indicating where people actually were—except the man on the roof, who must be getting very tired up there, and probably bored. . . .

There was printing on the side of the fertilizer canister.

It said: fertilizer *stakes.*

It was just worth curiosity. He wriggled around where he could get into the canister, pried up the lid, and found curious hard sticks of smelly stuff. He tried breaking it.

It broke. It broke into nice pieces. It belonged in a garden, did it not?

So if they missed a few shots and somebody looked down, that somebody would only see fertilizer bits. Right? He thought he might just lob a few pellets into the trees. Hitting the windows . . . that would bring another search of the garden, and maybe their patio, which he did not at all want . . . but if he could get enough range, if he could get a clear shot . . . And nobody would see anything but fertilizer for the plants.

There was that gap in that very white garden wall. There was that black gap, which was the potentially noisy metal gate.

That was a fair-sized target. He could risk it. And that would get a lot of attention, and maybe show them how many enemies were out there.

He had Jegari's and Antaro's curiosity. He stuffed the pieces in his pocket, kept one, handed them a stake apiece to break up, and took the slingshota out of the other.

Then they understood him.

"Nandi," Jegari whispered, not against his ear, but very, very softly. "Please be careful."

"Pardon," he said, took his piece of a stick and the slingshota, and worked his way out, very low, behind the little stucco wall beside the downward steps, putting his head up very, very slowly. His dark face and hair were going to show against the white stucco, no question, if he got up above the level of the wall. But from the far angle the steps offered, he had a good view of the iron gate.

He put his missle in the slingshota, having the other two ready. He had just one perfect alley, right between two trees that would block the shot.

He let fly.

Damn. Hit the branches. Rustled them. He didn't stop to see whether the man on the roof had noticed. He fished more pieces out of his pocket, laid them down in front of him and fired the first. Muted clang, where it hit the gate. Third. Clang.

He ducked down immediately. Then scrambled back on the miniature landing, behind the little wall.

"The man has gone from the roof," Jegari hissed.

The best outcome. He had planned to peg whoever came to investigate the noise. But that was the best.

"Now, now, now," Cajeiri hissed, giving a shove of his knee to Jegari. "Over! We are going!"

They had prearranged, that when they did go, Jegari would go first, to test the distance, then Antaro, then himself, with them to help break his fall. He saw Jegari go over the wall, saw that Antaro had picked up the rusty garden claw. She was supposed to be counting: thirty-two the sweep of the sensor to the left, thirty-two to the right. But she solved it. She jammed the garden claw into the track. Hard. And slithered out along the walkway and went over the wall.

The man had reappeared. He came out onto the tiles. He was looking their way just as Antaro went over the edge.

Cajeiri snatched up the last missile and shot it straight across the gap. Hit. The man fell back, hit the tiles, tiles came loose, and slid, and Cajeiri did not watch a heartbeat longer: he stuffed the slingshota into his shirt, then he flung himself astride the battlement and spotted Antaro and Jegari with upheld hands below.

He got half a handhold and slid around and off: the handhold failed on the rounded surface. He scraped his cheek on the rough stucco, raked coat buttons on the way down. His companions' hands broke his fall, snatched him around, and all of a sudden they were running for the woods, exactly what they had agreed not to do. They were supposed to run along the wall, sheltered from the sensor-units.

But Antaro had jammed this one. There was a hole in the net. And they were going straight through it, into the trees, Jegari and Antaro half-carrying him in their breakneck haste to get to deeper cover.

They had made a lot of noise when he hit the man on the roof—tiles sliding, what sounded like a lot of tiles sliding and hitting the ground, and whether the man had gotten clear—whether he was in shape to report them—he had no guarantee they had not been spotted. He had not planned to shoot anyone; Antaro had been supposed to count the sweep. They were supposed to have followed the wall back away from the road to stay out of the sensors and then get into the woods, and now the plan had unraveled, and they were just running as fast and as far as they could, dodging among the trees, avoiding branches, no matter the noise they made.

There was no knowing where the Guild might have laid traps or put sensors.

But there was no time for looking. No more time for plans. They just had to get out of reach.

Fast.

The bus reached the intersection with Lord Geigi's estate road . . . and there the dowager's man stopped and cut the motor off, and Cenedi got out and walked a little up the road. There was a woods some distance down the road, a finger of the peninsula's woodlands that ran up beside the house.

They had packed the bus with the dowager's men, and with equipment. When Banichi and Jago and the dowager's two men had left and picked up the village truck, that had given them a little breathing room, but no more seating; and Bren had no view of the dowager, or anything else: Tano sat by him, next to the window—between him and the unarmored side of the bus: Bren knew exactly why Tano had insisted on that seat. Algini stood in the aisle, holding to the overhead rail, and it was shoulder to shoulder. They talked. Tano and Algini listened to what he had to say, but offered no suggestion of their own.

Their bus had stopped. And the door opened, in the middle of grassy nowhere, the bus in plain view, if not of the house, at least of somebody watching for trouble to come down the road.

Algini shifted into a now-vacant seat behind him as the dowager's men piled off, taking gear with them, pulling gear down off the roof rack. Most dispersed into the tall grass and the brush, so far as Bren could see. Tano and Algini sat near him, now, both with rifles and sidearms. The dowager was across the aisle, and two of her young man were right behind her with a massive lot of firepower.

Cenedi climbed back aboard the bus and came back to her to report: "We have a perimeter set up."

"We shall wait," the dowager said. Cenedi left. And Bren drew a deep breath.

"Aiji-ma," he said, and got up to speak quietly. "Thoughts occur—that these people will be moving assets in. If they have your great-grandson—they will not hold him here. There may be a base in Dalaigi."

Ilisidi looked at him in the diminishing daylight, a side-long and upward glance. "The paidhi-aiji now gives military counsel."

"The paidhi-aiji is concerned, aiji-ma. Desperately con-cerned. This was not Baiji's idea."

"We have advised my grandson," Ilisidi said with a dismis-sive move of her fingers. "What happens in Dalaigi is outside our reach. What happens *here* is within our concern."

"Aiji-ma," he said quietly, took the hint and went back to his seat.

She had advised Tabini. Tabini was taking care of Dalaigi— one hoped—if there was anything he could lay hands on. They were on the same wavelength, at least.

From here on until disaster, Bren thought, here was their

only job. They were going to prick what was here, and see what came out.

He wanted Banichi and Jago back unscathed. He wanted the boy back and both the Taibeni kids unharmed.

He just hoped to hell the boy, in his dive into the bushes by the front door, had found a hole and stayed there, waiting for exactly this development—they were canny kids.

But asking an eight-year-old with the power to give orders to a couple of sixteen-year-olds to stay put and not move at all for hours and hours and hours—that was asking more than most eight-year-olds or even sixteen-year-olds could bear. It was worse, even, that Antaro and Jegari had had a *little* Guild training. They'd tried to protect Cajeiri and gotten in Banichi's way, or they might not be out here now. They had training— and might think they were called on to use it, and that could be disastrous. Guild that the Tasaigin Marid had sent to keep Baiji under control was one thing. Guild that they might move into a higher-stakes and messed-up operation weren't going to be house guards. They would bring in serious, serious opposition, and the time that would take might be measured in days—or, if they *had* something down in Dalaigi Township—it might be here by now.

It was totally dark now, at least to human vision. It was deep twilight for everyone else. A kid, even one who'd eluded capture, might now think it approaching time to do something. And one hoped the Taibeni youngsters' Guild training had included night scopes, listening devices, and wires.

Banichi had tried to hammer basic principles of self-defense into Cajeiri himself. Cenedi had had a go at it. They all had tried—Remember you are not adult, young gentleman. You cannot take on Guild. Nor should your companions ever try it.

Young aiji. Born leader. Literally. Whether it was genetic or subtly trained or God knew what, he'd gone his own way.

And *he*, if he were ateva, might have felt an atevi urge and followed the kid into the bushes, which at least would have kept them together. If not for their man'chi to *him*, Banichi and Jago would have followed the boy, and everything would have been all right.

Machimi plays had an expression for it. Katiena ba'aijiin notai'i. A situation with two leaders. A real screwed-up mess. And this one was that.

It also meant, right now, that if the enemy had expected the boy to do what the average atevi boy would do, they'd been taken by surprise, too, when Cajeiri headed sideways. If only, if only they'd assumed he'd gotten on the bus. The portico might have shielded them from view. The attackers had been on the roof. The rest of the staff had been in the hall. They hadn't been in a position to see, either.

Maybe they weren't even looking for the youngsters. Most unlikely of all—maybe the people running the operation—not the ones in the immediate area, who had heard everything— were already planning their next move.

Maybe Tabini-aiji, who was very certainly involved, could take out their communications.

But they were moving closer and closer to widespread action, and civil war.

And he wished he could have persuaded Ilisidi to stay put and let the Guild sort it out—before they had worse trouble.

If the youngsters were now hostages, they would stay alive: the enemy would be outright idiots to waste that advantage. But damned sure the enemy would want to get them to some more secure place than a flat and open villa. Considering who the enemy likely was, that would mean getting any hostages southward as fast as they could—

For their part, he supposed they would leave any possible escape routes to the aiji's men.

But getting in there . . .

That boiled down to four people. Banichi and Jago, backed by Nawari and Kasari.

Sorrowfully, Lord Geigi's yacht might go to the bottom of the harbor. Banichi and Jago would not leave the sea as an escape route, and that boat had to be taken care of, among first targets.

God, he should have told Toby to get down the coast, block any boat coming out if he had to call in the whole Mospheiran navy to help him.

Thinking too much.

Banichi and Jago knew what they were doing. They knew their list of priorities, and they were very much the same as his . . . except . . .

Except they themselves were his priority, and they wouldn't see things that way. Not when it came to a mission of this importance.

God, he wanted them back in one piece.

13

It wasn't, unfortunately, a large or deep woods . . . except in the scaward direction.

And that, Cajeiri thought, might still have been the best way to go, staying under cover the whole way to reach Edi fishermen or farmers.

But associations among the neighbors, given the goings-on here at nand' Geigi's estate were not clear to him; and Antaro had done what she had done, and Jegari had led off in this direction . . . which could be smarter. Nand' Bren himself had gotten surprised, so that was a big indication that ordinarily reliable people in this place were lying.

Especially nand' Baiji had been somewhere involved and guilty of something, whatever it was. And that meant there was no knowing which of the neighbors down toward the coast or *anywhere*, for that matter, was reliable. He knew that; but his side hurt from running, and it was a long, long way to Najida, and they were going to run out of trees before long.

"Maybe we should stop running," he gasped, the faintest of whispers, far softer than their running through the woods. "Very likely nand' Bren will have gotten to his estate, and mani and all her people are going to be out, and so will nand' Bren and before long my father will have people here, so all we need to do is get out of the way, find a hole and get in it until they settle this."

"You should, nandi," Jegari whispered back, likewise bending, hands on knees. "And Antaro and I can go find help."

"We all should!"

"Then Antaro can stay with you, nandi, and I shall go."

He shut his eyes. Opened them again, trying to imagine the maps he had studied, among the many things he had studied. "No," he said. "No. We shall just walk a while. We shall walk. If we find a good place, we can hide. But if we can get to nand' Bren's estate first—that would be safest."

"They may attack there, nandi. This whole coast may be in rebellion."

"Lord Geigi is Maschi. Baiji is Maschi. The coast is Edi. The Tasaigi are in this." He was out of breath. He bent over again and gasped for air. "Southerners. They do not belong here. There cannot be that many of them. We shall go—we shall go until we reach nand' Bren's estate, and then—then we shall just sit there and watch. And, by morning, people will be out and about and if it looks all right—we can go in. It is far better than sitting here hiding on Kajiminda land."

"We have to be careful, nandi," Jegari said. "We have to be very careful if we go out in the open."

"When shall we do it? By sunlight?" He held his side, where it ached. "Now is the time, nadiin-ji. Let us just walk a while. Let us walk quietly."

They began, then, to do that. And he thought they were going in the right direction: he hoped they were. The sea, he thought, all the peninsulas and the woods that did not grow up and down, but tilted, made him unsure of direction. This whole coastline tilted, in his estimation. It wandered: at ground level it was nothing like it was on the big map in the library, and the coast was very irregular.

And that was *stupid*. It was an entirely infelicitous and careless approximation. The librarian should be thoroughly ashamed of such records.

Jegari stopped, frozen. Antaro seized Cajeiri's arm, and pulled him to the side, signaling he should be quiet.

She backed him into a shelter of thorny undergrowth, crouching there as Jegari likewise edged into that cover. He heard nothing. Nothing, as they made themselves as inconspicuous as possible.

He shivered, and tried not to. It seemed a long time.

Then his ears told him someone was out there, somebody not as shining bright as he knew he was in his pale coat. Somebody maybe in Assassins' black.

But in stalking and being stalked he told himself he was in very good company. In a forest, if not a sailboat, his Taibeni companions were very much at home.

He held his breath while something like the wind moved through the woods. For a scary moment he saw their shadowy shapes, and there were two or more of them.

The enemy was going toward nand' Bren's estate. Where mani was.

The night grew chill. Bren rubbed knees gone half-numb and watched out the bus window in the only directions he could watch, westward and south. Cenedi had gone outside a little time ago, and delayed about matters, whatever he was doing, likely talking to men posted outside. The dowager simply waited, with the rest of her guard. Those who did speak, spoke together quietly—a whisper too low for Bren's ears to pick up.

Then Cenedi came back, and Tano and Algini, who had been busy with some sort of electronic equipment to the rear of the bus, got up and conferred with Cenedi, also very quietly, in the front of the bus.

Bren folded his arms for comfort and waited, Ilisidi not saying a thing, but then the formidable cane reached across the aisle and thumped his seat. He looked. Her face was utterly lost in the darkness, just a glimmer of silver about her hair.

"Aiji-ma," he said in the lowest of voices.

"You are very quiet and contemplative tonight, Bren-paidhi."

"One apologizes, aiji-ma. One is extremely concerned for the situation."

Silence. Lengthy silence in the dark.Then the cane went softly thump! on the bus deck.

"If they harm him," Ilisidi said, "they are dead. And there will be retaliation."

"Aiji-ma," he said. That was all. He was the peacemaker, the bridge, and in all his career, he had never been able to make headway with the South.

He had damned sure not read the boy accurately. God, where had an eight-year-old suddenly got the notion to grow up on them and take his own way?

Even atevi hadn't seen this coming—maybe because they'd attributed the unorthodox behavior to a human influence they were trying to diminish in the boy. Aiji-born: Cajeiri was apt to do any damned thing, was what, and neither species was going to predict him. A brilliant, if erratic prospect.

If he lived to grow up.

The conference forward broke up. Cenedi came back solo, a looming shadow in the dark, and said, to Ilisidi, "We consider that Banichi and Jago have likely moved all the way to the house by now, nandi. There has been no sound of fire. We have gotten the regular signal from them."

They would use a simple blip on a given frequency, nothing that could be easily read by the opposition, who probably were using their own signals . . . which their security would be simultaneously trying to pick up. Tano and Algini had broken out gear of their own, and he would about lay a bet it was involved in trying to do exactly that.

Himself, he took Cenedi's information for comfort, and kept his own observations quiet: it was Ilisidi's call, if orders were to follow. Guild operations were not the paidhi's domain.

"If we were to move closer to the house," Ilisidi said, "we might more likely draw out persons of interest."

"No, 'Sidi-ji," Cenedi said with no doubt at all, and added: "Besides, we cannot leave this road open. This is our task: we have simply to sit here."

Thump! went the dowager's cane, a quiet and very dissatis-
fied thump. But she did not countermand her bodyguard.

So they sat some more.

Two, and now four shadows moved silently through the
woods. Cajeiri hunkered down with his companions and held
his breath. They had been lucky so far, having made as much
noise as they had, and having rushed through the woods head-
long getting away. When the Guild had investigated why that
sensor-thing had jammed in the orchard tower, the rusty claw
was as good as a written note to say, "Someone was here."

But then, the people occupying the house had just had a man
slide down the roof, whether or not the man had actually gone
off the edge, and if that man was able to say he had been hit by
something before he lost his balance, that was a reasonable and
very noisy indication in itself that someone had been spying on
the house, someone who did not much mind a man falling off
the roof. It was possible that man would not talk, and would
never talk, and one had the luxury to somewhat hope he had
not killed the man; but he had shot someone before this, so it
would not be the first, and if this was the man who had tried
to assassinate them he was not going to have bad dreams about
this one. He was determined on that. He would not be sorry in
the least, if this was the man who had tried to kill nand' Bren.
He had been desperate. And he had had to do something fast . . .
had he not? He had *had* to.

They moved now, the three of them, without saying a thing
to each other. They did their best to sound only like the wind
moving, and to avoid breaking branches—a very un-windlike
sound.

Here was where the Taibeni were expert, and he tried to
learn from them, never letting a branch snap back, bending
every opposing twig gently and passing it to the next behind,
to release very, very softly. He copied their way of setting the
feet down very surely, and with as little disturbance as pos-

sible; and sometimes stopping—just suddenly stopping cold, frozen, so they could hear, Jegari informed him, touching his own ear—clearly meaning he should listen, too. They had seen four men pass them. They had no way of knowing if there were more coming behind them.

And the shadows were moving in the direction *they* needed to go, which said to him that they were going toward nand' Bren's estate. Nand' Bren was meanwhile almost certainly coming *here*, to find him; and these people were going *there*, or maybe to the train station, which was also in that direction, up to no good at all. If all these men wanted to do was just to get away after they had been exposed for what they were, they could go the other way, south to the Township and the big airport, completely away from nand' Bren's estate. Or right where they could lay hands on it, there was Lord Geigi's yacht, which, supposing *they* knew how to run it, could carry them out of the bay and down the coast or most anywhere. So it was clear these skulkers were on their way to work mischief, and he could warn nand' Bren's people and they could send somebody and call nand' Bren home, fast, and protect Great-grandmother.

They could phone his father, too. His father had probably sent people here as fast as planes could land them. And *they* would be moving in . . . maybe from the little airport near Najida, maybe from the much larger one near Dalaigi, to come in and cut off these scoundrels from one escape.

That was what *he* would do, if he were aiji in Shejidan. He would cut them off in one direction and have nand' Bren and mani cut them off from this side—with a little help from the local airport.

And he and his companions meanwhile had to stay out of the hands of these people. So they had gathered ammunition more serious than fertilizer stakes. At one place where they had crouched down, which had happened to be at a rocky little streamside, there had been a nice supply of little water-smoothed stones, just the right size. He took a nice lot of them, never minding the gravel they brought into the pocket of an already hard-used coat. And Jegari had gotten himself a sturdy stick, while Antaro had just pocketed a fair number of rocks.

And meanwhile they just kept moving and moving toward nand' Bren's estate.

The scary thing now was that the woods were playing out on them: they reached the edge, and the woods gave way to brush, and the brush to tall grass, where the trail the men had made going through the grass was perfectly plain to see. Jegari bent some grass down himself and stood watching it a moment. It recovered a bit, but not much; and Jegari looked at Antaro, who looked as if she were absorbing things, too.

So were they reading it, somehow? Could they tell things? How fast they were going? How long?

Jegari started walking exactly in one of the tracks the men had left . . . so, Cajeiri thought, following, there would be only one track, if anybody was behind them. That was clever. He began to think they were doing everything right.

It was getting harder, however. He had been tired and sore all day from their adventure on the boat, and now hiding all day and creeping through the woods, and he had no idea where to go or what to do. Nand' Bren and mani were in terrible danger, and he did not know how to reach them.

They were out there somewhere, moving on the estate, now that it was dark.

Maybe they had been fools to have left.

But it still seemed safer to be out here. Out here they had some choices, and they had not gotten caught in the crossfire. Still—

Jegari slowed to a stop, leaning on his hands, catching his breath, and then folded down into the tall grass. They all did, squatting low. "They seem to be avoiding the road, nandi. If we get onto the road and go beside it, we can move faster: we can run."

Run. He was hardly sure he could walk at the speed they were using.

But they had to do better, not to get caught out here.

"Yes," he said. "Let us try it."

They got up. His stomach hurt. But it was going to get worse.

They were going into the open. It was dangerous. But there was a reason these men were going the way they were—because it was safer for the enemy.

"Nandi," Jegari whispered. "Nandi, if they spot us, one begs you, duck, and stay with Antaro. I run fastest. I always beat her. I shall keep going."

And get shot, he thought, appalled. But it was what a bodyguard was supposed to do. He nodded. "Yes," he said.

"We are going to be leaving a trail," Jegari said. "We should at least make speed, nandi."

With which, Jegari struck off at a run.

He ran behind Jegari, and it hurt. His boots were not sturdy for out of doors. Rocks hurt his feet. His ankles faltered, and his knees hurt. His ribs began to ache. He stumbled, and Antaro caught his arm and kept him going.

But they both were lagging back now, both were running to accommodate him, and he tried as hard as he could, harder than he thought he could, grass whipping at his shins and his breath coming like a locomotive.

"Halt!" a man said out of the dark behind them, just right behind them.

He ran harder, expecting to be shot at. But Antaro had stopped, and Jegari did, ahead of him, facing back toward him.

He stopped where Jegari stood, and looked back past Antaro.

A man rose out of the grass. He had what could be a rifle. He could have shot them, so things were not as bad as they could be—just stay alive, just keep himself and his companions alive. Mani was going to have to get them out of this one.

It was over. At least this round.

He stood still, panting hard. He could hear Jegari breathing.

He saw Antaro tamely fall in beside that man as he walked toward them, and he figured that man had threatened to shoot him and Jegari.

The man came right up to them. "Young lord," he said, in an Eastern accent, and gave a sketchy, wary nod, and Cajeiri's breath gusted out and didn't come back for a moment.

The young man's name was Heien. He was one of mani's youngest, from Malguri.

"Come," the young man said, "quickly."

"There are men, nadi," Cajeiri said, pointing, "further that way, moving northwest, toward nand' Bren's estate. Four men."

"Hurry, then, young lord," Heien said, and gathered him by the arm and dragged him into motion. "Quickly!"

Cajeiri ran, gasping as he did so; and Jegari and Antaro kept pace, but it was not far, just over a slight elevation, and there was the double track of the road through the grass, and of all things, the battered estate bus sitting in the middle of the road, where another road branched off and this one just kept going.

Had they even gotten beyond the estate road, with all their effort and their running?

Even before they got to the bus, more men were getting out—Cenedi was in charge of them. His pale hair showed, when little else did but shadows.

Cajeiri really ran, then, with all he had left.

The dowager had gotten up into the aisle and Bren deferred to her intention. "Ha!" was all she had said, when Cenedi told her that Heien had just swept up the youngsters. She had gotten up, painful as that process might be, and showed every inclination to go to the door and descend the steps. Bren, behind her, with Tano and Algini, waited in the aisle.

Some signal had passed, one of those prearranged sets of blips that the dowager's guard used among themselves. And Bren ducked his head and asked, "Can you tell Banichi and Jago that we have them?"

"We have done so, nandi," Tano said.

So Banichi and Jago did know the field was clear—the young-sters turning up was one of the eventualities for which they had arranged a code. *How* the youngsters had done it was some-thing he was sure they were about to hear, in exquisite detail, once Ilisidi had given the princely ear a smart swat . . .

Or maybe she wouldn't, for this one. Precocious lad. And the Taibeni kids—were Taibeni: out of their element in a state din-ner, but not in moving across the country, thank God.

"Will Banichi and Jago come back now, nadiin-ji?" he asked Tano and Algini.

"They likely will not, nandi," Tano said, and Algini:

"They are likely committed, now."

"To *what?*" he asked.

"To removing these people from Lord Geigi's estate, nandi," Tano said. "The aiji's men have likely moved up from the Township. The field is clear now. One doubts they will give up that advantage."

Two of Cenedi's men had gone with them—*not* their accus-tomed team—so both sets were working at personal disadvan-tage, and four of them were going to probe into the estate and attempt—

God. Bren bit his lip, knew he should not interfere in Guild operations, but, dammit—

"I did not approve this, nadiin-ji, this—extension of the mission."

Algini said: "When the aiji requests it, nandi . . . we are not his; but he can request it."

Damn, he thought. He *wanted* them back. He couldn't bear it if he lost them. Couldn't—couldn't even think of it.

Cajeiri had come onto the bus to be shaken and thwacked by his great-grandmother on the bottom step—she was astonish-ingly mild in both. And then:

"Mani-ma, nand' Bren, Guild is going toward the estate—nand' Bren's estate. They passed us."

"On foot?" Ilisidi asked sharply, while Bren immediately thought of staff, of Ilisidi's men—of the fact he had only half his bodyguard in a position to do anything about it . . .

"Yes, mani-ma," Cajeiri said on a gasp for breath. "One is sorry. We were running. We were going there . . . and they were going . . . ahead of us. East of the road."

"Cenedi, did you hear?"

"Shall we move, aiji-ma?"

"Yes," Ilisidi said sharply. "We shall." She gave a shove to Cajeiri. "Get back there and keep quiet, boy. You and your companions are to stay low and stay quiet."

Bren started to move. The knob of the dreaded cane came gently against his chest. "Paidhi-ji, we have resources, but this may entail damage to your estate."

"The staff and villagers are my concern, aiji-ma. I told my brother to leave. One trusts he has done so."

"Good," Ilisidi said, and the cane dropped. Bren headed back to his seat, Tano and Algini preceding him, and he knelt with one knee in that seat as he reached it, facing them.

"How much can you advise them?"

"Nandi," Algini said, "we can signal 'base compromised' and 'base open.' That is the best we can do."

"They need to know that much," he said. The bus engine started, the bus started to back and turn around, and he dropped to the seat and sat down. Tano moved up with him; another of Ilisidi's men, in the scarcity of seats, sat down with Algini.

"Bren-ji," Tano said, "one begs you will get down to the floor. We may take fire."

It was an eggshell of a bus. There were already bullet holes perforating the door and sniper fire was a distinct possibility. That was true; and doubtless Cenedi, who still on his feet in the aisle, leaning over the seat behind the dowager and Cajeiri, was intensively debriefing the youngsters regarding what they had seen—how far back, how long ago.

Meaning what were their chances of the bus outracing a group of attackers moving in on foot?

Quite good, if the attackers hadn't *been* moving for several hours. He thought about his assessment of more and higher-level Guild coming into the situation.

Bren dutifully got down on his knees, elbows on the seat, not a comfortable way to ride, but safer, considerably. Algini and the man behind, meanwhile, passed a heavy blanketlike affair forward, which Tano stood up to hook into the window frame. Small *wonder* the baggage they had brought had weighed considerable. Another blanket was going into place on the far side. Not bulletproof, but certainly bullet-resistant, and protecting several rows of seats, notably the dowager and the youngsters, and him.

That secured, Tano sat down again.

"It is not entirely effective, nandi. One asks you stay as you are."

It was uncomfortable. It was oppressive. It deprived him of all information about where they were. "Perhaps if we cut cross-country toward the village and came up to the estate from there," Bren said, and then told himself just to be quiet and let people who knew what they were doing do their jobs.

"We may well do so, Bren-ji." Tano was the gentlest of souls, given his profession; his voice relayed calm, even while the bus was bouncing along over unkept road and apt to come under automatic arms fire at any moment. "When we do exit the bus at the estate, kindly stay between us."

"I have my gun, Tano-ji."

"Rely on us, nandi."

They had enough to worry about. He laid a hand on Tano's knee. "Tano-ji. One relies on you both with absolute confidence."

"One hopes so, nandi," Tano said, and then there was an added energy to his voice. "We shall defend the house. Or take it back, if we come late."

"One has every confidence," he repeated. He didn't want, either, to think of that historic residence occupied by persons bent on mayhem, its staff threatened and put in the line of fire. These were not fighters, the staff he had dispersed to this estate. They were brave; they had stayed by him during the worst of things, and taken personal chances rescuing his belongings; they were every commendable thing—but they were not fighters. They had nothing to do with the Guild.

Bounce and crash, potholes be damned. The speed their driver got from the overloaded bus was the very most it could do. It roared along with no care for the racket it made, bouncing over rocks and splashing through the remnant of rain puddles in the low spots, scraping over brush at the next rise, and rumbling over an ill-maintained bridge at the next low spot.

But at a certain point, after Bren's knees had gone beyond pain from being bounced on the hard decking, and after the chill of that decking had migrated upward into his bones, they began to encounter brush that raked the side of the bus. One did not remember the brush being that close, and Bren twisted about, trying to see out the windshield, wondering whether they were still on the road at all.

Horrid jolt, and crash, and then the bus ran over something, multiple somethings that hit the undercarriage.

They were *not* on the road, and Cajeiri had flung himself over to assist the dowager.

"What did we hit, nandiin?" Cajeiri asked in distress.

"A stone wall, by the racket," the dowager said. God knew—there was a hill out in the fallow land. There was the old road, where now only hunters ranged—but the wall had been timber railing.

"We have dropped out of contact with the house, nandi," Cenedi said. "We are not going to the por—"

The nose of the bus suddenly tilted downward. No one of this company cried out, but Bren swallowed a gasp and grabbed the seat as they took the hard way down, through more brush.

He lost his grip: his head and back hit the seat in front, and Tano grabbed his coat and hauled him close to the seat.

"What are we doing?" he had time to ask.

"The estate road is a risk," Cenedi said, holding himself braced in the aisle. "Get to your seat, young lord. And *get down!*"

"Yes," Cajeiri said, and went there, handing himself across the aisle, and obediently ducking, with his companions.

They took another neck-snapping bounce, crashing through brush in the dark, scraping the underside of the bus, and when Bren looked around at the windshield, they had lost the headlights, or the driver had shut them down, never checking their speed.

My God, Bren thought, holding on, telling himself that atevi vision in the dark was better than his.

Another plunge, a hole, a fierce bounce and then a skid. He cast another look to the windshield.

The road. Even his eyes could pick up the smooth slash through the dark. They had swerved onto it—were ripping along it at fair speed. But where the hell were they?

Suddenly they turned. The bus slung everything that was unsecured toward the other side—Cenedi intervened, standing in the aisle, and supporting the dowager.

They hit a wooden wall, scraped through brush or vines or structure, and came to a sliding halt. There were lights—outdoor lights, from somewhere. They had stopped. The engine died into shocking silence, leaving only the fall of a board somewhere.

And then he realized they had just crashed through the garden gate of his estate, the service access at the back.

The bus door opened. Two shadows—Ilisidi's men—immediately left the front seat and bailed out to take position.

Then people came running out of the house . . . *not* armed, people in house dress, people he recognized . . .

"They are ours, nadiin!" he shouted out, getting to his feet, as staff all innocent and alarmed, came to a halt facing leveled rifles.

"Quickly," Cenedi said. "Disembark!"

"Go, paidhi," Ilisidi said—practicality, perhaps, it being his estate, his staff: he steadied himself on Tano's shoulder, and Algini's arm as they sorted themselves out and headed for the bus steps.

"Nadiin-ji," he said, descending.

"Nandi!" Ramaso's voice. "Are you all right?"

"Everything is all right," he said . . . as boards went on creaking and settling. The stout pillars and vines of the arbor had withstood the impact. The garden wall and shed were not so sturdy. He found himself a little shaky getting down the steps and into the midst of dismayed staff.

"Rama-ji" he said. "We are a little ahead of possible attack on the house. Has anything happened here?"

"No, nandi. Nothing!"

"Get men down to the harbor, phone the village, and if you have not yet thrown the shutters, nadi-ji, do it now, as quickly as you can. We have the young gentleman safe, with his companions. Did nand' Toby and Barb-daja get away?"

"Yes, nandi," Ramaso said. "They have sailed."

"Excellent," he said. *That* problem was solved. "Go. Quickly!"

"Nandi," Ramaso said, and as Cenedi helped the dowager down from the bus, gave the requisite orders on the spot, distributing jobs, ordering guns out of locked storage, and telling three young men to get down to the dock, take the remaining yacht out to deep anchor and stay with it.

"Nadi." Algini intercepted Ramaso as they walked, to give him specific orders for the securing of the house, the emergency bar on the kitchen door, Ilisidi's men to have absolute access; and Tano said, urgently, seizing Bren's arm.

"Stay under the arbor, Bren-ji."

"We left men in charge here," he protested.

"They are still there," Tano said. "But take nothing for granted, Bren-ji."

"Cenedi-ji," Algini said. "If you will take the northern perimeter of the house, we shall take the main southern and center."

"Yes," Cenedi said, and hastened the dowager and Cajeiri along toward the house. Jegari and Antaro had caught up, and hurried. Bren lost no time, himself, with Ramaso keeping pace with him, along the main part of the arbor, into the house, the doors of which stood open.

They had not thrown the storm shutters. Those were going into place, one slam after another.

"Is there any dinner?" Cajeiri's voice, plaintively. "One is very sorry, but we missed dinner."

"We *all* missed dinner, boy," Ilisidi said peevishly.

"One can provide it," Ramaso suggested, at Bren's elbow, "in very little time."

"For the guards stationed on the roof as well," Bren said to him.

"So," Ilisidi said with a weary sigh, as they reached the indoors, the safe confines of the inmost hall. "So. We shall meet at dinner, nand' paidhi."

"Aiji-ma." He gave a little bow, half distracted, home, but not home: Banichi and Jago were still out there, at risk, and he wanted to know more than non-Guild was going to be allowed to know about what was going on out there.

Footsteps overhead.

"They are ours," Cenedi said. "We are in contact."

"Good," he said. He worked a hand made sore by gripping the seat. "Good, Cenedi-ji. Aiji-ma, if you need anything—"

"We have all we need," Ilisidi said, with her hand on Cajeiri's shoulder. "We shall be in communication with my grandson once we dare pass that message, nandi."

That was dismissal. Bren left them, headed for his own suite, as Ramaso turned up at his elbow. Tano turned up on the other side, staying with him.

"See to the dinner, nadi-ji," Bren said to Ramaso. "If the enemy is moving out there, they will probably try us before morning. Four were spotted. There may be others. Let us take advantage of what leisure we have."

"Yes, nandi," Ramaso said. They reached the door of his suite, and even before the door had closed, Supani and Koharu turned up, solemn and worried-looking

He still had the blood from the early event sweated onto his hands and under his nails, the mud from the bus floor on his trousers—he was, Bren thought, a mess, the clothes were irrecoverable, and he was, despite the rapid movement getting in, cold to the core. A bath would be the thing, he thought; but he was not about to be caught in the bath by an enemy attack.

"Tano," he said, "I shall be all right here. Go see to yourself. Help Algini. Be ready if Banichi and Jago need you. And have staff bring you something to eat. I shall be all right: I shall stay faithfully to this area of the house, excepting supper."

"Yes," Tano said. "But, Bren-ji, in event of trouble, take cover. Do not attempt to fire. Rely on us."

"Always," he said with a grateful look, a little instinctively friendly touch at Tano's arm: he was that tired. "One has no idea how long this night may be. One promises to be entirely circumspect."

"Bren-ji," Tano said, and made a little bow before leaving.

Bren peeled off the coat. The lace cuffs of his shirt were brown and bloodstained.

"Hot, wet towels, here, to wash with in the bath," he instructed the two domestics. "For Tano and Algini, too, if they can find time. Moderate coat and trousers." He walked on to his bedroom and took the gun from his pocket, laying it on the dresser. "This I shall need."

"Yes," they said, and Supani went on toward the bath while Koharu helped him shed his boots and peel out of his hard-used clothes.

Appearances mattered. The staff was possibly going to be at

risk of their lives, and *their* lord was obliged to look calm and serene, no matter what was going on.

He bathed not in the tub, which would have taken time to fill, but within it, with running water and a succession of sopping towels, had a fast shave—he did that himself, with the electric—and flung on a dressing gown, trusting the pace Koharu and Supani had set to get him to the dining room in good order.

Somewhere out in the rocks and bushes, somewhere near the intersection of roads they had dodged, coming overland, or maybe up toward the train station, and on Lord Geigi's estate, action was probably already going on—action was too little a word. The first moves of something far, far larger, if he read it right.

Banichi and Jago—

He hoped they weren't taking chances out there. Lord Geigi's Edi staff was on their side: they well knew that; but that was another question. They had seen no one they recognized from Lord Geigi's tenure. If there were Edi about, where were they? What had become of them?

Banichi and Jago were still obliged to be careful about collateral damage. So were Tabini's forces. If there was one solitary thing he could think to comfort himself, it was that there would not be random fire incoming in that situation . . . but it made it doubly dangerous, necessitating getting inside. Finesse, Banichi called it.

God, he didn't want even to think about it.

He left a soaked pile of dirt-smeared towels in the tub and headed out to his rooms to dress, with staff help. It was surreal. Attack was likely coming, and so far, everything stayed quiet, quiet as any night in the house.

But he tucked the gun into his coat pocket when he had finished dressing, dismissed Supani and Koharu to go get their own supper, and, going out into the hall, suggested to the few younger members of staff who stood about looking confused and alarmed, that they might usefully occupy themselves by removing porcelains and breakables to the inner rooms. "Just put them in the cellar, nadiin-ji. One cannot say there will be disturbance inside the house at all, nadiin, but one hardly knows. And at the first alarm, go immediately to the cellar and stay there with the door shut, one entreats you. I would sacrifice any goods in this house to preserve your lives."

"Nandi," they said, and bowed. He headed for the dining room.

In fact, he and the dowager arrived at the same moment, himself alone, the dowager accompanied only by two of her youngest bodyguards; and Cajeiri and the two Taibeni youngsters, who had almost matched the paidhi in dirt, immaculately scrubbed and dressed, likely having used the servants' bath.

"Aiji-ma," Bren said, bowing to the dowager. Staff had laid the table for three, the two Taibeni to stand guard with the two senior guards. Only the paidhi was solo—absolute trust for the security that was on duty; and a lonely feeling. Tano and Algini were in quarters, likely trying to monitor what was going on while the dowager's men, under Cenedi's direction, took defensive precautions.

And still no word from Banichi and Jago. He wished he could haul them out of wherever they were, whatever they were into, and let the aiji's guard handle the mess at Lord Geigi's estate. He was too worried for appetite. Given his preferences, he would have paced the floor. Sitting down to dinner was hard—but at this point necessary—besides being a demonstration of confidence for the staff.

The before-dinner drink, a vodka with fruit juice—that came welcome.

Supper consisted of a good fish chowder and a wafer or two, warm, filling, and quick. He took his time, somewhat, in general silence, in pace with the dowager, while Cajeiri wolfed his down with a speed that drew disapproving glances.

"Such concentration on one's dinner," Ilisidi remarked.

Cajeiri looked at her, large-eyed. "One was very hungry, mani-ma. One sat in that tower forever."

"Tower," Bren said.

"In the garden, nandi. We went over the wall and through the woods. We hid in a tower on the wall."

"You have gotten quite pert," Ilisidi said. "Have we heard an apology, boy?"

Cajeiri swallowed a hasty mouthful and made a little bow in place. "One is very sorry for being a problem, mani-ma, nand' Bren."

"How did you separate yourself?" Ilisidi asked. "*Why* did you separate yourself."

"One—hardly knows, mani-ma. May I answer?"

At the table, there was properly no discussion of business. And the dowager's table was rigidly proper.

"Curiosity overwhelms us," Ilisidi said dryly. "You may inform us. We shall not discuss."

"There was the bus, and Jago, and nand' Bren, and Banichi; and the shooting started, and the bus was hit, and one just—we just—we just—the bushes were closer. We thought they would fight."

It was a fair account. And contained the missing piece. We thought they would fight. He'd assumed Banichi would go for Cajeiri; and the kid had equally assumed Banichi wouldn't. And the kid had assumed they were going to stand and fight, so he'd taken care of himself.

Ilisidi simply nodded, thoughts flickering quickly through those gold eyes.

"Indeed," she said. "Indeed. One expected a sensible boy would then find his way down the road."

It was more than the paidhi had expected of a boy. A lot more.

"One did, mani-ma. As soon as it was dark." Cajeiri's brows knit. There was something more to say, something unpleasant, but he didn't say it.

"May one ask, young gentleman," Bren said, "what you have just decided not to say?"

A flash of the dowager's eyes, which quickly settled on Cajeiri.

"One fears one may have caused a serious accident to a man on the roof. One hopes they were the enemy."

"What time was this?"

"Right at dusk, nandi. He was on the roof. He probably fell off."

"Good," the dowager said, taking a drink. And added: "Hereafter, you will have your own security."

"Antaro and Jegari, mani-ma—"

"You are beginning to think independently. These young people will benefit from senior Guild constantly attached to you, young man. This should have been done before now."

"Not Great-uncle's! One asks, not Great-uncle's!"

"No," Ilisidi said, "*not* Atageini. Nor Ragi. *Malguri.*"

Oh, that was going to be an explosion, once Tatiseigi heard *his* great-nephew was dismissing his Atageini guards; and once Tabini *and* the Taibeni heard that the senior pair in his son's bodyguard was not going to be Ragi atevi, from the center of the aishidi'tat, but Easterners—that explosion would be heard end to end of the Bujavid, and Ilisidi's opinion might not, for once, prevail.

The paidhi was going to stay well and truly *out* of that argu—

Quick footsteps sounded in the halls. One of the serving staff came in, breathless, bowed once to the dowager and once to him. "Nandiin. Movement is reported across the road."

He cast a worried look at Ilisidi, whose face remained impassive. He swallowed the bite he had and with a little bow, got up from table.

The dowager likewise rose, Cajeiri offering his hand beneath her elbow as she gathered up her cane.

"Aiji-ma," Bren said, "one would suggest the office, which

has no windows: there is a comfortable chair, and the staff might provide an after-dinner brandy."

"An excellent notion, paidhi-ji." One earnestly hoped the dowager would provide sufficient psychological anchor for her great-grandson to keep his burgeoning personality from flaring off down the halls to help them out. Clearly, the paidhi had not been adequate to keep him from picking his own course. Cajeiri had been looking for cover when the shooting started, not looking for direction from the paidhi-aiji. So write the paidhi off as a governance. Write off the boy's most earnest promises: one suspected he was hitting an instinct-driven phase.

"Go," Ilisidi said as he lingered, ready to assist her. "Go, nand' paidhi. We are just moving a little slower this evening."

"Aiji-ma." He bowed, then left with the anxious servant, asking,

"Where are Tano and Algini at the moment, Husa-ji?"

"In the security office, nandi, one believes."

In most houses, that was near the front door. In this one, by revision, it was a comfortable nook in the suite his bodyguard used, a left turn at the intersection of halls.

"Carry on, nadi," he said to the servant, "with thanks. Check the garden hall locks. Put the bar down."

"Nandi," the servant murmured, and diverged from his path.

That beautiful glass window offered a serious compromise to house security. That was why there was a very stout mid-hallway set of doors to close the garden hall, with deep pin-bolts above and below and a sturdy cross bar that resided upright in the back of the right-hand door. The two doors that led off that hall, one to the kitchens and the other to the staff rooms, had equally stout single doors, as solid as if they were opposing the outside world . . . which, being next to more fragile sections, they were counted as doing.

The last of staff was on their way to defensive stations or to cover. Those last doors were about to shut. Kitchen would not be gathering up the dishes. They would be sealing themselves in from both sides.

He turned his own way, his bodyguards' door being wide open. He entered without knocking, into the little security office where Tano and Algini had set up their electronics, black boxes of all sorts, and a low-light monitor screen.

No need to tell them what was going on. And if they had wanted that door shut yet, they would have shut it.

They acknowledged his presence with nods of the head, that was all, eyes fixed on their equipment, and he slipped into the nearer vacant chair and watched the monitor. He didn't see anything but shrubbery and a small tree. The view changed to the front door. The garden, and the damaged arbor.

"Have you contact, nadiin-ji, with the aiji's forces?" he asked.

"Cenedi has," Tano said, and added, after a moment, "Banichi has now missed a report, Bren-ji. We are not greatly alarmed, but we are obliged to say so.

He didn't want to hear that. He bit his lip in silence for a moment, and forbore questions. Their eyes never left the equipment, with its readouts and its telltales.

"The roof still reports all quiet, but movement on the perimeter," Algini said. "We remain wary of diversionary action. Two of Cenedi's men are interrogating Lord Baiji. And names are named."

"Report as you find leisure," Bren murmured, meaning he would not ask for a coherent report, busy as they were. He was in the nerve center of their defenses. Some of those lights represented certain points of their defense. The monitor showed a view of the stone walkway that led down to the harbor and the boat dock.

Movement somewhere, though it didn't show at the moment.

"Where is the dowager, Bren-ji?" Tano asked.

"The office," he said, "with Cajeiri. Staff hall doors, garden doors, front doors, all shut and secured."

"Tano-ji," Algini said sharply, calling for attention. Both brows furrowed, and the pair exchanged looks, a shake of the head. Bren sat very still. Didn't ask. They were busy, both of them, at their specialty, and Cenedi's men were out and about, including on the roof, including down toward the dock, and some likely in the village. Right now, having been left in charge of his safety as well as their regular duties, they needed no divided attention: needed to know where he was, and that he wasn't in need of their help. That door to the hall was open, but it, like the other secure doors, was steel-cored, capable of being shut and security-bolted.

What they had in that console, whether it was officially cleared, he had no personal knowledge, didn't technically understand, and frankly hadn't asked—deliberately hadn't asked. Tano and Algini had spent the last couple of years on the space station. While the planet below them had broken out in chaos, they'd spent their time becoming familiar with equipment the paidhi, who was responsible for clearing new tech to be generally deployed on the planet, had never cleared . . . and under the circumstances of their return from space, he hadn't asked.

Hypocritical? He had no question it was. But maybe he should have—considering that Captain Jules Ogun, in charge of the space station, had decided to drop relay stations on the planet. Maybe he should have asked what part Tano and Algini had played in that decision, whether they *had* advised Lord Geigi, governing the atevi side of the station, that this communications system was a potential problem.

Mogari-nai, the big dish, had been their sole contact when they'd left for deep space: now, with the proliferation of satellites—God knew what was going to be loose in the world.

Things that threatened the operation of the Asassins' Guild, which hadn't had to worry about locators. Or cell phones. There was a time they hadn't had night-vision, or a hundred other items he suspected his own security staff and Geigi's now had—and he hoped no one else did.

But *he* had been out in space for two years, leaving the job of determining what technology ought to go to the planet largely to Yolanda Mercheson, essentially an emissary of Captain Jules Ogun. More, once the coup had happened, she'd interfaced—not even between Mospheira and the atevi—but mostly between the humans of her own ship and Lord Geigi, whose eagerness to snatch whatever tech he could lay hands on was only surpassed by that of Tabini-aiji himself.

The paidhi had *not* been doing his job for two critical years. The paidhi had come back to find the world girded by satellites, a grid laid out, and relay stations—armed and mobile relay stations—dropped into strategic areas, satellite phones, cell towers on the Island, and all the preparation to loose, even worse, either cell phones or far less restricted wireless on the continent. The Assassins' Guild was the worst, the very worst affected. Keeping the aishidi'tat, the Western Association, together—meant keeping each member of the Association sure that his advantage was exactly the same as everybody else's; or at least sure that if somebody else cheated and got an advantage, the aiji in Shejidan was going to come down on them fast and hard. Guild members didn't talk about Guild business, but the Assassins' Guild itself had had one internal power struggle, only last year.

The aiji's side had won, but what was going on tonight out in the bushes around the estate contested that conclusion.

He'd been coasting along since his return trying to catch up on what had happened, what technology had come in, what atevi had invented themselves, or modified. He'd been writing letters, answering queries, trying to find out what was a fait accompli and what he could still get a grip on, and possibly stop—

He'd *been* coasting . . . in the technology questions since his return . . . and now he had a growing, sinking feeling that he might utterly have lost the war.

They had aliens out there that were promising to come calling, atevi wanted their share of the situation . . . and that meant technological advance.

They had one hell of a problem in the world, was what they had. *He* had a problem. The Guild certainly had—and wouldn't be happy about it. The aishidi'tat had a problem—manifested in a coup, a counter-coup, and God help them if things went wrong tonight—possibly a civil war . . . in which the technology he'd delayed banning was likely to turn up, full-blown, possibly inciting certain factions, possibly giving advantage where it hadn't been and meaning all bets were off on the outcome.

It was the paidhi's fault—at least in the sense he hadn't been able to prevent it.

And Cajeiri was going to have it all in his lap, if he survived his childhood.

The dowager was right. Time they did get the boy full-time, technologically sophisticated security to keep him alive, considering the world he'd been born into, and not Great-uncle's socially impeccable but less than adaptable old men. They needed two very young Guild, somebody who'd keep *ahead* of the boy, and train the two Taibeni practically in *situ*. Thank God, he thought, the Taibeni youngsters had come in with some natural advantages of their upbringing. But it wasn't enough.

Something had to change. Soon. It wasn't a safe world. And the boy's tendency to go off on his own wasn't going to get handled if Tabini, Uncle Tatiseigi, and the dowager started quarreling about the ethnicity of the guard.

God. His brain was wandering. The upcoming cell phone speech seemed suddenly so little, so small an issue. He was trying to stop a flood with a teacup. It couldn't be another regulation. It had to be an attitudinal accommodation in the society. They'd accommodated tech on ship. Why couldn't they adjust—?

They'd handled phones. They'd handled trains crossing provincial and associational boundaries. They'd *adjusted*. They'd taken computers, and done things *their* way, that the paidhi couldn't even have conceived of. That had been a dicey step. And they'd survived it.

If he could just explain to them—

Something happened. Tano gave that sign that meant trouble, and then said the code word for intruder, getting up from his chair and reaching for his pistol as he did so.

Bren got up out of the way immediately and reached for his own gun, while Algini kept his attention fixed on the equipment.

Tano got into the doorway, angled to the left, fired up at an angle, and fired again as a shot came back; then dived out across the hall. Bren stayed where he was, in the vantage Tano had had, safety off the gun and the gun at the ready, eyes scanning not only Tano's position, but things up and down the hall. It wasn't just Tano's life at risk. He was Algini's protection, and Algini was busy relaying their situation to other units of their team.

Maybe, he thought, he should shut the door—barricade himself and Algini inside. Don't rely on the gun: his security had told him that more than once.

But Banichi had given him the damned thing. What was it for, but for backup?

Tano, meanwhile, moved out and down the hall toward the servants' wing and the dining room corridor, moved, and moved again, not without looking at ground level for traps. He reached that nook, tucked in against the slight archway, and held position.

The dowager, with Cajeiri, with her immediate guard, was just beyond that intersection, in the office. Bren personally hoped that door stayed shut. They were all right. Nobody was in sight.

Scurrying movement from right over his head, beyond the ceiling.

"Tano!" Bren cried. "Above!"

Shots broke out, up above the ceiling, breaking through the

paneling. Tano suddenly eeled around the corner he was holding. Fire came back from the direction of the dining room.

"Hold!" Tano shouted out to someone down the dining room corridor. "Hold place! Call off your partner! Truce! We offer truce!"

Bren held his breath, flexed his fingers on the gun grip.

Suddenly a shot sounded overhead, running footsteps headed down the hallway ceiling where there was no room.

"Tano!" Bren shouted, and about that time Algini knocked him aside and fired into the paneled ceiling.

Splinters exploded near Tano from overhead and chips ricocheted off the floor tiles.

A volley came out of the dining room hallway and hit the intersecting wall. Tano had dropped into a sideways crouch right into the open and fired back. More fire came from overhead, splintering a ceiling panel, Algini moved and fired back, and Bren darted across the hall, his back against the same wall Tano had used.

A volley of fire went overhead, above the panels, and one came back.

Algini stood mid-hall and fired nearly straight up. Something up there thumped, and then there was quiet, except that Tano got to his feet. A dark dot appeared on the stone floor near where Algini was standing. A second spatted down in exactly the same spot. It took a second before Bren realized what was dripping.

"Clear!" Tano called back to his partner, holstering his gun, and cast a look down the hall. Bren leaned against the decorative paneling and far from automatically, working a little, put the safety back on his gun.

Curious. His hands had used to shake considerably. Now he was thinking they'd kept the hall safe, he was thinking they'd kept the dowager safe, that it had been a better-than-average lot that had actually gotten through their perimeter—someone damned *good*, in fact; and thinking, with a small shudder, that, thank God, some on *his* side were better. But he was worried about Ilisidi's men on the roof. And just too cold-blooded about it. He didn't recognize himself.

And then he did give a shiver, thinking how Banichi and Jago were out there somewhere trying to pull exactly what they'd just killed two people trying to do, here.

That didn't make him feel better. Not at all.

Algini gave him a solemn look and nodded, then listened to something for a second, frozen quite still.

Down the hall, the library door opened slightly, and one of Ilisidi's young men glanced out, and came all the way out to exchange a handsign with Tano up at that end of the hallway.

The stain on the stones was widening.

But they had no all-clear yet. They might not have one for some time. Standard procedure would send a search all through the area.

And in fact, while they stood there, shots sounded outside, maybe out on the road.

More came from their roof.

"Not safe yet," he said under his breath. "I hope they're alive up there."

"That may have been an all-clear signal, Bren-ji," Algini said. "But we should not rely on it. Best go back to the station and wait."

Strong hint. There was mop-up yet to do. And Cenedi's men would bear the brunt of it, if there was more to come. They had someone dead, likely, in their attic, bleeding a puddle onto the hallway floor. Someone down that hall was likely dead, right in front of the dining room, having shot a piece out of the paneling near the office. Bren found himself angry, a sense of outrage for the broken peace, for an attack his domestic staff hadn't deserved, except for their service to him.

"Yes," he said, to Algini's strong suggestion, and began to walk in that direction, Algini walking with him.

Algini had to let them in: the door had shut and the lock

had tripped. And Algini went right back to his console. In a very little time Tano came back and joined him, and took his former seat.

"Two of them," Tano said.

Algini nodded. "Yes. That seems to have solved the immediate alarm."

Bren took his former seat, trying to find in himself what he had used to feel, some sense of sympathy for a dead enemy, regret for the waste. It was there, but it was scant at the moment. Far stronger was his concern for Banichi and Jago, for the dowager's pair with them; concern for the village, which had little protection but the general Guild policy of not involving such places—and the Marid had broken no few pieces of Guild policy. Hell, the Marid had tried to subvert the Guild itself, charging it was overly Ragi in leadership.

That hadn't held. The Guild had solved its problem when Murini went down.

Murini was dead. His own clan had repudiated him. The Guild was the Guild again.

But that didn't mean the Marid Association had reformed. And the quiet behavior of the Marid since the Troubles didn't guarantee anything.

Worse, since the Troubles, with new weapons, new techniques—the old rules about keeping Guild business out of civilian venues were weakening. It was more than the traditional weapons and equipment at issue. Traditional limits of warfare were in serious jeopardy. Atevi hadn't, historically, tended to have wars, just local skirmishes. Guild work. Professionals against professionals. Only a handful of times had it escalated to involve non-Guild. That was more than custom. It was a foundation of society. When somebody crossed that line, as Murini had—

"Tano-ji," he asked. "How *is* the village? Have you any word?"

"We have no reports of difficulty there," Tano answered him. "We have observers able to report."

Good for that, he thought, but decided not to accord the Marid any points for civilized behavior: not yet.

Things could get much, much worse than the attempt of just two Assassins to get inside.

Maybe, on the other hand, they were lucky: maybe that *was* what they had to deal with tonight, and the Marid didn't have reinforcements ready to move in.

Failure of intelligence on the Marid's part, perhaps. Failure of the local crew keeping tabs on Baiji to seek new instructions in time—either not having been told that the aiji-dowager had moved in with her guard; or being unprepared with higher-level Guild where they most needed them: inside Baiji's household. They'd missed killing him. This was the second try—a better one than the first, for damned certain, but again—not with massive force.

Dared one think—they hadn't been ready to deal with him yet?

Maybe Baiji had in fact made a try at warning him when he'd showed up at Baiji's door . . . give Baiji credit, he'd been sending signals. Or fear had been getting the better of him, once he was faced with the reality of the paidhi and the aiji's son walking into a trap. Baiji had started sweating, and known he wasn't lying with any skill, which had made him more and more nervous—which had blown everything.

If he'd never come calling on Baiji, if Geigi ever did pay his long-threatened visit home, Geigi might not have survived the first day on the ground. And everything would have been tolerably quiet, if the Assassins had managed it with some finesse.

Baiji would have inherited—married that Marid girl. The whole thing could have played out over five or ten years in which things on the coast just went from bad to worse. Like sitting in the stewpot with the water heating slowly—at what point would the aiji have made a countermove?

Sooner than they'd hoped, maybe. But all that was moot, since the kids and the sailboat. Baiji had taken his boat out—

Maybe Baiji really had wanted to make a break for it.

Maybe . . . Baiji or his handlers had had other plans.

He'd never seen Baiji's yacht—seen its lights in the distance, or thought he had; but he hadn't stayed for conversation. He'd picked up the kids, turned around, rather rudely, but necessarily, and gotten them back to safety—to call on Baiji this morning. Contact made. Bait set. They'd have taken him out last night if they'd gotten a chance. But maybe they'd kept the operation to low-level Guild, who might not be traced to the Marid.

Mistake, if that was the case. *His* bodyguard had gotten him out, and the whole thing had blown up when Banichi had grabbed Baiji . . . with all Baiji knew. All the key pieces. All the agreements.

Damned sure somebody had to be sweating now, and not just Baiji. Maybe the Marid had just called in higher-level operatives, and *that* makeshift fix had just failed.

He sat there listening to operations he couldn't wholly hear and watching what he had only the most general means to understand, watched until a little of the recent affair had drained out of his veins. The report came in—Tano told him, that two of Cenedi's men, on the roof, had been killed—by darts. Ancient Guild weapon, silent and lethal without the necessity of foreign technology. The perpetrators had gotten through the roof, into the attic of the house itself. They had likely been assigned to penetrate the inner defenses, but the attic, a defensive measure, was partitioned into strongly fortified rooms. The intruders had broken out of the area they had gotten into, and then used what amounted to a central walkway agreeing with the main hall of the house itself. It was a centuries-old, traditional building pattern—not that different from other houses of the period. So they hadn't had much trouble figuring where they were, once they had hit that central hall. They had been trying to get to their target, in his suite of rooms . . . him, specifically; only he hadn't been there. He'd been with Tano and

Algini, listening to that hurrying step in the overhead. One of them had gotten into the servant's wing and broken through down there . . . Tano had attempted to gain that man's surrender. But that movement had been a diversion.

The other one had gone for the main hall, and *hadn't* found an access panel. It was, Tano said, tricky up there. There was such a panel, to get down into the building on the east side of the house. But one had to be *in* his suite to get to it. Comforting thought. He'd never even *thought* to take a personal tour of the attic.

"It was used once," Tano said, idly, "to enable the Maladesi lord to get Guild to the dining room to poison his wife. It is in Guild records. They used a string, let down from the ceiling, in the preparation area, and dripped poison into the dish. A servant spotted what she thought was a flaw in the preparation, tasted it with a finger—quite imprudent. She scarcely recovered."

"One takes it that that marriage ended in divorce."

"Actually in the assassination of the Maladesi by the wife's relatives," Tano said. "This left a younger daughter. She married into the Farai. Another imprudent move."

Business outside had slacked off considerably, or Tano would not have indulged in conversation. He still spoke without taking his eyes off his console.

"The current owner should know such things," Bren muttered.

"The current lord of Najida has been somewhat busy," Tano said, "while Algini and I spent a great deal of our time on the station in the company of Lord Geigi and his staff."

"It was useful information," Algini said quietly. Rare that Algini turned conversational, when there was business afoot. Like Tano, he never looked away for a heartbeat. "Lord Geigi knows all the houses in the district. We have communicated certain things to the staff. *Banichi* has made his scheduled signal."

Bren let go a long, slow breath, and now a shiver ran through him, totally out of control. "Is he all right? Are they both, can you tell?"

"The signal is not that specific, Bren-ji," Algini said. What it was, how interpreted, fell under the heading of Guild business, and Algini was not one to break the rules, but he went that far. And further. "Banichi would have signaled trouble, one surmises, if there were trouble."

They had two dead among their staff, two more from among the enemy. They had the aiji-dowager and the heir sealed in the office. They had the junior lord of the province locked in the servants' quarters. He was incredibly glad to have gotten word from Banichi. He kept shivering, and finally got it stopped.

It was still bound to be a long night.

14

Morning arrived with gray light slitting through the storm shutters, and various outlying watchers reporting clear.

It also arrived in a communication from the aiji's forces that they had secured the factory and the town hall of the adjacent township.

And in the relatively matter-of-fact squeal of brakes under the portico.

Bren heard it from his office—the dowager and the heir both having gone back to their respective suites. He came into the hallway, and a young maid looked out the spyhole and came flying back to him at all speed.

"Banichi and Jago, nandi, Banichi and Jago are here, and the dowager's men!"

For once he was ahead of Tano and Algini—who came briskly down the hall and said that they had gotten word and Banichi and Jago were arriving.

"Get Ramaso, Matru-ji," Bren bade the maid, and added: "You may run, nadi."

She did that, at all speed. He fell in with Tano and Algini, and pulled the floor bolts as Tano and Algini first lifted the heavy bar and slid it into the slot, then pulled down the four top bolts, which were entirely out of his reach.

Then they pulled back the heavy doors and indeed, Banichi and Jago stood there under the portico, along with Nawari and Kasari—all dirty, dusty, a bit scuffed, hair flying a little loose—

rare in itself: they hadn't taken time for neatness. Kasari had his left arm in a sling.

"Nadiin-ji," Bren said, the most undemanding, unchallenging salutation he could come up with. "One hopes to hear the details at your leisure. We came through it. Are you well?"

"Well enough," Banichi said, hauling out a heavy bag of gear from the truck bed. "One can report, Bren-ji, that the aiji's forces are now in charge of the estate, and are taking an accounting of such staff as they can find."

"Good," he said. "One is extremely relieved, nadiin-ji." There were unresolved issues. There were many of them. But the middle of the hall with the four of them only just returned was no place for them. "You should go off duty a few hours at least."

"A mutual sentiment, Bren-ji," Jago said. She was holding her side somewhat, or favoring a shoulder: he could not determine. And Nawari and Kasari, lugging their own gear, paid the courtesy of a small bow, which Bren returned, which Jago and Banichi returned with a nod, and then Nawari and Kasari went off toward the servants' wing, where Ilisidi's more numerous guard had set up a makeshift barracks.

"Are you all right?" Bren asked. Clearly they were not. But they were here.

"The Marid has made its attempt on Lord Geigi's estate." That was the definitive past she used. Over and done. Put "paid" to. "There are other things to concern us, but not, at least, apt to show up here within the next few hours."

And about that moment Cajeiri put his head out of his own doors, exclaimed, "Banichi-ji! Jago-ji!" and came hurrying up, belatedly attended by his coatless and embarrassed companions. "One is very glad you are safe, nadiin-ji." A second, deeper bow, as he walked, a feat of agility. "One apologizes, one very profoundly apologizes for the difficulty."

"The sentiment is greatly appreciated, young gentleman," Banichi said quietly.

"There will be breakfast very soon," Cajeiri reported.

"That, actually," Jago said, "will come *very* welcome." She hitched the bag higher on her shoulder as she moved. "We shall, however, wash."

"Use both baths, nadiin-ji," Bren said. "You have complete priority, there and in the dining hall. Please use it."

"We shall manage," Banichi said. "I shall go down with Cenedi's men." He evaded Cajeiri's attempt to help with his heavy bag, and winced a bit. "One is grateful, but this is heavy, and the Guild handles its own baggage. One is very glad to know you are safe, young gentleman."

"One is ever so sorry, Banichi-ji! One is ever so sorry to have mixed things up!"

"You survived. Your companions survived."

"We are all safe, Banichi-ji."

"Good."

"Shall one alert nand' Siegi, nadiin-ji?" Bren asked. Siegi was the dowager's personal physician.

"Not if he prevents us from breakfast," Banichi said, never stopping. "Or our bath."

"We shall call him!" Cajeiri exclaimed, and was off at a run, Antaro and Jegari lingering for an embarrassed bow.

"Nand' Siegi is not to come upstairs until he has tended Kasari," Jago said.

"Nadi," they said, bowing, then ran after Cajeiri.

Bren walked with Banichi and Jago down the remainder of the hall; so did Tano and Algini, as far as their suite and inside.

"The dowager's company," Algini said grimly at that point, "lost Pejan and Rasano."

Jago stopped, and let the baggage she carried thump to the floor, unhappy punctuation.

"They were experienced," she said. "How?"

"It was Nochidi and Keigan that got past them," Algini said. "Those two got inside, through the roof, likely in the distraction of our arrival."

"Are they still a matter of concern?" Jago asked.

"Dead, both," Tano said.

"Settled, then," Banichi said. "So is Lord Baiji's guard." He shed his coat with a sigh, then helped Jago pull hers off. Jago's left shoulder was bleeding, or had bled, into thick bandages.

"Jago-ji," Bren said.

"Minor, Bren-ji," Jago said. "Quite minor. Bath, stitches, breakfast, in that order. The driver is taking the truck back to the village to refuel. But it will be available at need."

"One fears the estate bus is not capable of being driven, nadiin-ji," Bren said.

"One noticed the condition of the south gate," Banichi said, "from the road."

"The driver opted not to ask the front door be unbolted," Bren said. "Please. See to yourselves, at greatest priority. Shall I send breakfast here—if you would be more comfortable?"

Jago said, with a little wince, "That would be welcome, Bren-ji."

"Very welcome," Banichi said, and pulled off his shirt. "We would be most obliged."

"I shall then," he said, and left the room—left it to Guild debriefing to Guild, as they urgently needed to do. The first encounter with a maid in the hall sent that message to the kitchens: service for his guard and the dowager's, in quarters.

They had the aiji's men next door, at Kajiminda. That was an improvement. That he wouldn't have to send his bodyguard back in to settle that business, that was an improvement.

But they had two dead, a loss that the dowager would not forget. Nor could he.

Settled, Banichi had said. But he was very, very dubious that it was at all settled. Geigi's estate had taken damage—in several senses. The Korisul Coastal Association might have had an attack come into its midst: but the Marid Association, the four-clan aggregation that lay at the heart of the Southern Coastal Association, had both flexed its muscle and committed a critical error of timing.

That was good, in the sense that the situation had gone no further.

But where were Geigi's people? All quiet, the Edi, while outsiders had prepared to assassinate the paidhi-aiji and while Baiji had made extraordinary gestures—extraordinary effort from such an unenterprising man; but on which side he had exerted such effort, and with what intent was not in the least clear.

Likely nobody they could trust for information yet knew all the things he wanted to know . . . but pieces of that information might be had, here and there, and he meant to have them.

He had a unique responsibility now as a regional lord, in Geigi's absence, in the situation with Kajiminda. He'd never had to exercise it. Still, he knew what that responsibility was, and that was to defend his people and assert their rights; and to extend a stabilizing influence throughout the Korisul Association. He had to represent his people with the aiji, had to secure what was good for the district, and the occupation by Tabini, a Ragi lord, was not, ultimately, going to be acceptable with the Edi . . . who, for one thing, had to be approached, and asked what the hell had happened here. They were not likely to talk to Tabini, on general principles.

They might talk to him. He couldn't swear to that. They might not, given the situation, even talk to Lord Geigi himself.

That had to be dealt with.

They had the Farai in his apartment; they had the Marid trying to disrupt the aishidi'tat; they had the Edi coast in disarray, for starters, and they had the aiji having had to move Guild into action in the Korisul, where Ragi-directed Guild historically had never been welcome.

He was, when he added it all up, mad. He had been mad last night. He was damned mad this morning.

And no little worried about the future.

Not least of which was a matter that had been nagging the back of his mind since last night on the bus.

The Edi. Edi—who constituted part of the population of Najida village. Who were partially the *reason* Kajiminda estate and Najida estate had enjoyed such a steady, reliable flow of information.

Ramaso hadn't warned him. Ramaso hadn't said a damned thing about the mowing, just about the debt. Had said there was a lapse in contact. But absent the critical information about Edi leaving Kajiminda—it hadn't conveyed the real situation there.

And Ramaso hadn't known that fact?

He wasn't mad at Ramaso—yet. But that question was forming in his mind.

Edi. And total silence. Not unlike them. They pursued their own business. They were not a government, officially, within the aishidi'tat . . . but they settled their own affairs, handled their own disputes, and generally didn't make outsiders aware of their business. A silent, self-directing lot—they frowned on their secrets being discovered. They'd run illicit trade. There was a tacit sort of agreement with the aishidi'tat: the aiji's law didn't investigate things in the Edi community and the Edi didn't do things to annoy outsiders.

So there was at least a situation behind the silence about the neighboring estate—and he understood Ramaso had one foot in the village community and one foot in the estate, so to speak.

But not warning him? Worse, letting him take the aiji's son over there with him?

There were questions.

There were a lot of questions—some of which he was prepared to ask, and some of which he was prepared to investigate.

But theirs was an old relationship. And Edi reticence and the Edi reputation for piracy and assassination had managed to keep the coup from touching Najida in his absence.

So it was worth a little second thought—his frustration with Ramaso's silence.

It was worth a careful approach, and a due respect for what services the man had given him. Maybe, he thought, he ought to talk to Banichi about the matter—doubtless Banichi had also added up certain missing pieces of information; but Banichi was not from the district; Banichi and Jago came from further inland, part of the aiji's household, once upon a time, and that—

That could be an issue that might complicate any investigation his bodyguard tried to make.

Diplomacy, besides, was *his* expertise.

He found Ramaso in the servants' hall, supervising a temporary repair on the ceiling paneling—one of the young men was on a ladder taking measurements—and approached him quietly. "Rama-ji," he said, and before all other business, inquired about their driver. "How is Iscarti this morning? One is distressed not yet to have gotten down to see him—my guard does not want to be parted from me—or from their monitoring equipment."

"He certainly will understand. He is much improved, nandi. Awake and talking, with diminishing doses of painkiller. His mother has come up from the village."

A piece of good news. "Brave woman. One is very glad. Tell him not to worry in the least about his family. Tell him we will see his salary paid, and his family protected, not even a question about the medical bills. And we will get down there, among first things when my guard lets me leave this hall."

"One will do so, nandi. Though he asks us what did happen. He says he cannot remember."

"Then I shall personally tell him what he did. With all gratitude."

"That will so greatly please him, nandi."

"One thing more you can do for me, Rama-ji."

"What would this be, nandi?"

The question.

And the wider question.

"We have had a dearth of information, Rama-ji—information coming to us, and information coming from us. It seems perhaps the village has felt abandoned in my absence."

"No such thing, nandi. They have known you were about important business."

"Nevertheless—it seems I should be more concerned with Najida's business. One hopes to speak to the village councillors about the general situation—about Kajiminda. About what has gone on in my absence, and during the Troubles. One wishes to address the council courteously and ask its advice."

The young man on the ladder had had his head up above the ceiling. He had looked down, and now descended the ladder, casting a look at Ramaso and giving a little bow.

"This is Osi, nandi," Ramaso said. "He is from the village, the council senior's grandson."

A bow to Bren. "One would be glad to carry a message, nandi."

Council senior was a woman. That was generally the case in the countryside, in any village. Council senior was *everybody's* grandmother; but this was a blood relationship.

"Tell your honored grandmother, tell all the council, Osi-nadi, that Najida will not accept Kajiminda falling into the hands of the Marid; it will not accept Marid presence on this coast. The lord of Najida estate wishes to meet with the council, in the council's premises, and asks to be invited to speak, at a time not to interfere with their session."

"Nandi!" A deep bow from the dusty young man. "Certainly they will be honored."

"Nevertheless," Bren said, "Osi-nadi, make the request for me. One wishes to listen to advice as much as to give it. One *requests*, Osi-nadi. And *advice*. Please say that, exactly."

"Nandi." Another bow.

"Go, Osi-ji," Ramaso said. "The lord's commission outweighs mine."

"I have my measurements," the young man said, tapping his head, and made a third bow. "Ramaso-nadi. Bren-nandi. I shall, one shall, as fast as I can."

The young man was off like a shot, back toward the main

doors, not the nearest, which were probably still secured. His footsteps echoed on the retreat.

"It is a great risk to go down to the village, nandi," Ramaso said, "a risk for you to leave these premises."

"Not from them."

"No, nandi! Of course not!"

Honest distress. They let him run into danger. They didn't know how to stop him without unraveling everything. He began to see that. No danger *from* the village. But the village couldn't feel safe. Nobody could, as things stood.

"My guard will keep me safe, I have no doubt. My worry is my attracting attack into the village, Rama-ji, and I know what I ask. Guide me in this. If one asks protection from the aiji in Shejidan, it will be counter to all I hope to achieve. One does not wish to see Najida village dragged into politics with the South."

"With the South, nandi?"

"The Marid will seek to divide Maschi from Edi, Edi from Korali—wherever they can find a weakness. One believes— one sincerely believes, Rama-ji, that in the aishidi'tat is the best association for all the Western clans. But this needs to be proved—to the Western clans. And it cannot be proved by bringing central clan Guild in here to settle things by force. It was never the power of the aiji in Shejidan that protected this coast. It was the people."

Ramaso himself was Korali. And Ramaso nodded solemnly and slowly. "The absence of both the paidhi-aiji and the Lord Geigi has been a weakness on this coast. Our isolation from politics protected us. But Najida *welcomes* your return, nandi. I am, at least by birth, an outsider, though my wife is from Na-jida. But I believe the village will heartily welcome your close involvement."

"One regrets extremely the necessity of my service in space. Najida has deserved better."

"Najida could not find better than you, nandi. That is your

staff's sentiment. You are—if the paidhi will forgive a political opinion—outside the regional rivalries. You are not Edi. But you are not Ragi. There was a reason your Bujavid staff fled here; there was a reason Najida welcomed them and hoped for your return; there was a reason the Marid found it inconvenient to attempt to take this coast, and the reason was exactly as you say. The resistance in Dalaigi relied on this house to reach Dur; and so we did; and Dur reached the Island, and from Dur we acquired direction and advice at need; and we gave each other assurances that there *would* be a rising against the new regime. We were not idle in your absence, nandi, even though we counted on no help from Kajiminda—and less from the center of the continent. One must ask the paidhi's forgiveness—his great forgiveness—for *not* warning the paidhi about the situation with Kajiminda, which we did *not* know. We did not know Guild had come from the South. We were unwarned."

"The grass was not mown on the road, Rama-ji. There were so many signs. One laid them all to a decline in trade."

Ramaso bowed his head, shaking it slowly. "We thought it irresponsibility. We thought it—perhaps—that the house *could* not pay its debts. We thought perhaps the presence of the Lord of the Heavens would bring Lord Geigi's nephew to a better frame of mind. One feels personally at fault, nandi. Should you wish it—one is prepared to be dismissed from this post of responsibility."

"Do not consider it. The aiji's own information failed."

Ramaso's face showed rare emotion, a soul greatly disturbed. "This I can say, nandi. I have been in touch with—with the activities of the village council, in matters here and—those things I spoke of—the contacts with the North. And if my knowledge will serve *you*, nandi, I shall answer to you. Not to the aiji, nor even the paidhi's distinguished guests. I answer to *you*."

He was stunned. He had corresponded with Ramaso before and after his return. He had exchanged observations with Ramaso, and trusted this man, in happier days, to bear with his family, at a close range that would have worried him—were it not level-headed Ramaso. He had not had the least inkling what this man had been, or done, during the Troubles.

"Rama-ji. What can one say?"

The impassive mask resumed, and, with a little quirk of the lips: "Say little, to the aiji, nandi. And little to any of your staff who might report to him. But our records—will be open to you."

His bodyguard. Who were extremely closely tied to the aiji's house.

And it *was* Najidama Bay he was dealing with, which had had a local tradition of smuggling, and even of wrecking; and there had historically been business enterprises Najida village might not want to have told to the aiji, and there was a time a light up by the Sisters had lured the aiji's shipping to ruin—

But . . . not to tell his bodyguard . . .

"One even asks, nandi, *did* the aiji send his son here, so conveniently?"

"No, Rama-ji. On that point, one is relatively certain, there was no planning in that."

"No desire, nandi, forgive me, for an *excuse* to send Guild to the coast?"

"No, Rama-ji. The young gentleman is entirely what he seems. Fluent—in Mosphei', at least as the ship-folk speak it. He is many things, but not—not orthodox Ragi, nor ever will be. He has associates among human folk. He has a great attachment to the aiji-dowager."

"One detected that attachment," Ramaso said, and nodded slowly. "One has readily detected that." And then Ramaso added: "This coast, up and down, has always respected the grandmothers."

The same little chill ran through that statement, a chill of antiquity, ancient belief, ancient connections. The people of the coast had owned Mospheira once—the Edi, and the Gan, up in the Northern Isles, were the aboriginal peoples of the island.

The treaty that separated humans onto the island enclave, and atevi to the mainland, where the Ragi ruled . . . had made those two peoples homeless, refugees on this coast. It had been expedient. It had saved thousands of lives—assured the survival of the human species on the planet.

But it had left the former Mospheirans separated from their sacred sites. Their monuments had gone to museums. Their traditions had been swallowed up.

There had been two particular reasons that Tabini-aiji had appointed the paidhi as lord of Najida, when the clan that had had it went extinct. One reason: that a Marid clan, the Farai, had claimed to succeed the Maladesi, and Tabini didn't want a Marid clan to get its fingers on Najida—and the other . . .

The other reason had been that no central lord could have been accepted on this coast, no more than this coast would accept anyone from the Marid.

"Ramaso-nadi," he said, "I will *not* discuss inappropriate things with the aiji; you have my word on that. My aishid may be Ragi—but they are in my man'chi, Rama-ji, and as they will not betray me, I will not betray them. I find myself connected here. I had no notion of the indebtedness I would come to feel toward this place. I am far more foreign. I do not feel in the same way, but I feel deeply. I shall become, at whatever time I speak for you, partisan *for* this region . . . and I shall keep its secrets, whatever of them I learn. And so, if you will forgive me, will that young man under this roof. He is not one who forgets a kindness. And he learns. Enlist him by means of your good qualities; enlist the aiji-dowager, who remembers favors done her great-grandson. These are not inconsequential allies, Ramaso. Tell *that* to the village, if you will speak for me. I shall always be a foreigner. But not so much so here, one hopes. One earnestly hopes so."

"You are *also* an exile from Mospheira, nandi. In that sense, you are one of us."

True—if not in the same bitter sense as the Old Ones.

"Nadi-ji," he said to Ramaso, with a little bow. Ramaso bowed. And he walked away, disturbed to the core.

Homeless on this earth. Except—here. Except one warm spot that—of all cold things it could possibly do to him—questioned Banichi's man'chi, of all people.

He didn't question it. True that Banichi still reported to Tabini, and came and went more easily with Tabini-aiji than some of Tabini's own new bodyguard. But it never meant that Banichi or Jago would betray him.

It occurred to him to ask himself—if he took a stance for the people of the coast—did he, in fact, betray *Banichi's* man'chi, in a way that would put Banichi in an untenable position?

He didn't feel that. He had no such intention. If he found a limit he could not cross in that regard—he thought—he would stop at it. Banichi would never betray him; he would never betray Banichi, nor Jago, nor Tano, nor Algini.

He was what he was. Maybe Tabini had understood enough about him when he'd given him Najida, and maybe Tabini hadn't.

He hoped Tabini had.

But he couldn't turn his back on these people. Couldn't go back to Shejidan, in the legislature, and sell out these people's lands, or be in Tabini's inner councils, and have the consideration of peace or war come down to the edge, and sell out these people's interests. Last week—he might not have felt it that personally.

Since dodging bullets under his neighbor's portico, it had become just a little—

The front door opened, making the dowager's guards, who were stationed there, react. But it was just one of the youngest staff, out of breath and windblown.

Whose eyes darted to the leveled guns in alarm, and then went to him, large and desperate.

"Nandi! Nand' Toby is coming in!"

"Sailing into dock?"

A bow, and the young man caught his breath, hands on knees. "Forgive me, nandi. Yes. Sailing in. The boat—nand' Toby's boat—is damaged, low in the water, and pumping hard . . ."

Damn, he thought, in a cold chill. "Come," he said, and led the way into the study.

There he sat down while the servant waited, and wrote a quick note.

"*Toby—I'm delighted you're all right but concerned you're back here, which is not safe. We came under attack last night, we lost two on the dowager's staff and have one man shot. We got what we went in after, all of them, and I hope you and Barb are both all right and will forgive me for not coming down there. My staff is getting medical treatment and we're shorthanded. The way up and down the hill is exposed and snipers are a possibility, so be extremely quick and careful if you decide to make the run up here. Leave the baggage. You may be safer just to stay on the boat offshore. If you do come up here, you will have the safety of the house, but we're in fortress mode at the moment and we can't say this will be the last shooting that goes on. Staff will give you every possible assistance and get you up here if you choose to come. Stay well.*

"*Love to you,*

"*Bren.*"

He folded the note, didn't even use the wax seal, just handed it to the boy.

"Forgive my asking this of you, nadi, but go back down; and if there should be gunfire, fall down, get under the bushes and stay there. Someone will come to rescue you. The letter inquires into nand' Toby's situation and says he is welcome under this roof, but the situation up here is still hazardous and I personally cannot come down to the dock. He may be safer to remain in the harbor, possibly offshore. There may still be snipers. If he chooses to come up here, he will have the safety of the house. Advise persons guarding the dock exactly what I have said, and wait for a written reply from nand' Toby if he chooses."

"Yes, nandi!"

"Samandi is your name, is it not?"

"Yes, nandi!" A second bow, a bright, so-innocent look. "Thank you, nandi."

"Please. Please be careful."

"Yes, nandi."

The boy was off like a shot.

And twice damn!

No calling the law in the district. He *was* the law in the district.

The two that attacked had been high-level Guild, no question, and on the highest levels, the Guild all knew one another. Algini in particular, who had served the last Guildmaster, likely knew their affiliations, and probably there was a host of other questions about the attack that his bodyguard would be discussing in detail. It was a discussion in which no non-Guild was welcome, not even the aiji.

Meanwhile his brother might be on his way up, most likely, with Barb; and God knew what "damage" meant. Or how incurred. Toby was a good sailor. A very good sailor.

He went out to the hall, down into the dining room, and went to the kitchens himself, or nearly so . . . he had reached midway in the serving hall before he met a servant, and he had only reached midway to the turn to the kitchen before the cook came hurrying out.

"Nandi! We are nearly ready to serve. One has your message, your staff and the dowager's men—"

"There is more, Suba-ji. My brother and his lady have just put into dock. He may or may not come up to the house—be warned that there could be two more. At very least we shall need to send supper down to them."

A bow. Suba carried a towel, and wiped his floury hands with that, looking somewhat satisfied. "Nandi, we have cooked enough for a seige. Every dish can be reheated, saved, served, or added to—nothing grand, but nothing to disgrace the house."

"Every credit to the house, in your forethought, Suba-ji. One should never have been concerned. Excellent."

"We shall be serving momentarily. We have rung the bells."

Up and down the servants' halls, that was: staff was advised of breakfast in the offing.

"Thank you. Thank you, Suba-ji," he said, and walked out into the dining room, down the hall. He got no further than the intersection when the dowager emerged from her quarters with a grim-faced Cenedi in attendance, and the young gentleman and his two attendants . . . the dowager disconcertingly resplendent in morning-dress, and from some source—possibly clothes the dowager had picked up in Shejidan when she refueled—the heir was himself kitted out in an impeccable blue coat. The paidhi was far less elegant.

"Aiji-ma," Bren said, encountering them, and gave a little bow.

The dowager said, with a little inclination of her head: "The paidhi's house is set in disarray this morning. One hears the lost are found. How are your people?"

"Well enough, aiji-ma, with thanks for the attendance of the physician."

"One regrets the situation, nand' paidhi."

"On the other hand, aiji-ma, the stir did thoroughly beat the bushes. We know now things we had not known. One only deeply regrets the cost of it."

"Indeed," Ilisidi said grimly. "And my grandson has work to do, a great deal of work to do."

"Our staffs should consult, aiji-ma."

"Our staffs will consult," she said. "Meanwhile my grandson will be making inquiries in Dalaigi. But enough business. We are here. We are alive this morning. Things might have gone differently."

They had reached the door of the dining room. Bren stood just to the side to let the dowager and her escort, and Cajeiri and his, enter.

In that moment he caught a motion from the tail of his eye, Koharu and Supani coming fast.

He could not forbear a smile. Staff would not let him be caught at disadvantage. Supani whisked his day-coat off, Koharu helped him on with the jacket, just that fast, and he entered the dining room with the honor of the household assuaged, before his guests had more than reached their chairs.

He had noted a tableful of place settings. It turned out to be sufficient for all present, Cook's sense of protocols, including their guests' personal staffs. Suba thoughtfully stood in the service doorway to receive initial compliments, thus signaling he expected no further formal notice for this informal breakfast: only serving staff would interrupt them.

So Cenedi sat by the dowager. Therefore the Taibeni might sit with Cajeiri, Bren sat to himself, and there was hardly a word exchanged, while the initial serving—eggs—diminished.

"A bit of news. My brother has returned to dock," Bren informed the dowager. "The report is that his boat has suffered damage. He may elect to come up the hill. One has advised him of hazard up here."

"Damage," the dowager said.

"One has no idea, aiji-ma, of extent or nature. One is concerned. But there is no word as yet."

"The paidhi should remain here," Ilisidi said firmly, "and let staff ascertain this."

"One has sent a note down. We may hear during breakfast, aiji-ma."

Tano and Algini might agree to go down: they could communicate. Most of the staff could not. But they might elect not to leave him. And Ilisidi was right: he had become a target.

Trust staff. Believe that his staff would not leave Toby and Barb unattended or their needs unguessed.

"Well, well, one hopes the damage is slight. No injuries?"

"Not that I have heard, aiji-ma."

"Good, good."

After that, and properly so, not a word of business else. The dowager put away a healthy breakfast, drank three cups of tea—Bren managed one helping and a half.

"We need not wait for removal of the dishes," Ilisidi said. "We have business to undertake. Young gentleman, you may retire."

Cajeiri's mouth opened in dismay.

And silently shut. The head bowed. The young lord rose. His companions rose, and they all bowed in near-unison. "Yes, mani," Cajeiri said.

That, perhaps, won redemptive points for the young gentleman. Bren sat still as the youngest left the table together. He did suffer a second's concern, that it meant Cajeiri and his companions were now loose and unwatched, but there was a sort of rhythm to the young gentleman's bursts of energy, and the youngsters this morning looked to be at a low ebb.

"One has heard from the dockside, nandiin," Cenedi said, with a little tap at his ear and a glance toward Bren. "Nand' Toby's boat has suffered some hull damage. He and his companion are uninjured, but he and his companion are pumping some volume of water and continue to do so, while seeking a way to pull the boat up on skids. Local fishermen are assisting. Nand' Toby has asked regarding your safety and the young gentleman's, and has been reassured. Meanwhile Jago-nadi has been in contact with them by radio. They have indicated they came under attack, meeting hostile presence further down the peninsula, but that boat sank. The village has been alerted. So have other Guild."

Other Guild. That would be the aiji's forces. And a boat sunk. He was appalled.

"Did he say how it sank, nadi?" Bren asked.

"Apparently there are submerged rocks. The other ship hit the rocks."

The old cottage industry of the area. The wreckers' point. Fake lights, and natural currents that ran ships into trouble."The

Sisters. A little off the point of the peninsula, on this side. They turned short." His heart had picked up a beat. He *wanted* to go down the hill and help—but there was too much going on. He wanted even more to haul Toby and Barb up to the house for safety, but if Toby's boat had taken a scrape from the Sisters, it was lucky to be afloat, and the fight to save it could be desperate.

Most of all, he wanted to hear what had happened out there. Toby had charts. "Toby knows these waters, nadi. He would have known about the rocks."

"Evidently the other boat did not," Cenedi said. "It pursued, firing. And ran aground. Nand' Toby came on in, as soon as he had made emergency repairs."

God. What a mess! "One is grateful for the report," he said. "My bodyguard is in debriefing and breakfast. One is sure you have heard from Nawari and Kasari, but mine will surely want to consult with you, Cenedi-ji, before all else."

"Indeed," Cenedi said. "As I understand it, nand' Geigi's yacht was still at its mooring when Banichi turned the situation at the estate over to the aiji's men . . . so we are relatively certain that Lord Geigi's is not the boat at the bottom of the bay. We suspect the boat may have been acting in concert with the incursion here, and launched much earlier—perhaps up from Dalaigi. We are attempting to learn. We are attempting to find any survivors."

One got the picture: a two-pronged assault, one on the house, one to mop up if they had attempted to get out to sea. Toby had run right into the ambush.

"It was more than luck," the dowager said, beginning to take a sip of tea. She did, then asked: "Do you, nand' paidhi . . . ?"

But then she set the cup down. It missed the table edge, fell onto the carpet, a soft thump. "Cenedi," the dowager said quietly.

"The physician," Cenedi said, dropping to one knee by Ilisidi's chair. "Nand' paidhi, may one beg you—"

"I can find him," Bren said, and sprang up and went to the door, hailing a passing servant. "Mata-ji! Run to my aishid's suite and if the physician is still there, bring him here, immediately!" He went looking for other servants, and sent them below, to find Siegi wherever he was and advise him to hurry.

But by the time he had gotten back to the dining room, Siegi was there, indeed, having come from down the hall. The physician was in the process of taking the dowager's pulse—the cup, unbroken, had been set back on the table.

Bren stopped at the door and bowed, standing there quietly.

"Nand' paidhi?" Ilisidi asked. "Come in. Come in."

He did so. "Aiji-ma."

"You were speaking of the Edi, paidhi. What did you intend to say?"

"It can wait, aiji-ma. May one suggest, a little rest . . ."

"Pish! What observation, paidhi-aiji?"

Bren cast a desperate look at Cenedi, who gave him a distressed look back again, then bowed slightly. "One hopes," Cenedi said, "that the paidhi having stated his opinion will lead to nand' 'Sidi retiring for a few hours, since she did not sleep last night."

Thump! went the cane on the carpet. "One hopes this report will lead to truth, 'Nedi-ji! And do not carry on conversation above our head! Paidhi, report!"

"One has had a thought, aiji-ma," Bren said, "that Lord Geigi could get truth from the Edi staff, which the aiji's men may not as easily come by. One proposes a phone call to the station, which I am prepared to make at a convenient hour. Geigi may well be abed."

"Geigi can drag his bones out of bed at whatever hour things are afoot," Ilisidi said. Her color was not, one observed, good. But her eyes flashed. "So can we! High time we did rattle our old associate out of his complacency. He relied upon this worthless nephew, and we are entirely out of sorts with him!"

Bren paid a second and apologetic glance toward Cenedi.

"At least," Cenedi said unhappily, "it does not entail a trip overland."

"One will make the call," Bren said, "But—" He took such liberties with Tabini. He hesitated, with the dowager, but as the physician had stood up, he dropped to one knee by her chair, at intimate range. "Aiji-ma. A request. Once we speak to Geigi, you will retire for a few hours and get some rest. The dowager has been halfway across the continent and back, and camped out in a cold and unreasonably uncomfortable bus for hours and then suffered a ride which has all her young men and the paidhi nursing bruises. One by no means even mentions crashing through the garden shed. One begs the dowager, most earnestly, to take the opportunity to rest today while subordinates sort out the situation. We all may need the dowager's very sage—"

"Paidhi-ji, you risk annoying us!"

"—*advice*, aiji-ma, and those of us who serve you would gladly risk your extreme displeasure to urge you to *go to bed*."

"I concur," Cenedi muttered. "Listen to the paidhi. You take his advice at other times. Take it now."

A lengthy sigh, and a glittering sidelong pass of gold eyes beneath weary, slitted lids. "You are both a great annoyance."

"But I am right," Bren said. "And the dowager, being wise, knows it. Be angry with me. But one begs you rest while doing it."

"Shameless," Ilisidi muttered, and scowled at nothing in particular. "Well, well, let us call Geigi. And while we are about it, let us rouse out that scoundrel Baiji to the phone, and see what Geigi will say to his nephew. If that fails to enliven the hour, perhaps we *shall* go to bed for a few hours."

"Immediately, aiji-ma," Bren said, and got up and headed out to his study, alone, scattering a trio of young male servants who had gathered in the main hall. "Bring Baiji to the study," he said, "nadiin-ji, and you are instructed to use force should he object. *Sit* on him, should he attempt to escape."

"Nandi," they said, astonished, and hurried off on their mission.

He entered the study, sat down, and immediately took up the phone.

Getting through to Mogari-nai offices took authorizations. Ramaso couldn't do it without going through Shejidan; but he could. And when he had:

"This is the paidhi-aiji. Put me through to the space station."

"*Nandi,*" the answer came, a little delayed. "*Yes.*"

And a few moments after that:

"*This is Station Central. Mogari-nai, transmit your message.*"

"Live message, Station Central. Give me the atevi operator. This is Bren Cameron, key code under my file, BC27arq."

A pause.

"*Confirmed, sir.*"

The next voice spoke Ragi, and his request to that station roused out, if not Geigi himself, one of his personal guard, probably out of a sound sleep.

"*Is there an emergency?*" the deep atevi voice asked in Mosphei', and he answered in Ragi.

"This is the paidhi-aiji. This call is with the concurrence and imminent presence of the aiji-dowager. With apologies for the hour, we request Lord Geigi's immediate response. The matter is of dire importance."

"*We shall hurry, nandi,*" the answer came, just that, and the speaker left the phone.

There was, now, a small stir at the door. It opened, and Bren punched the call onto speaker phone as the stir outside proved to be a scowling and unhappy Baiji, in the company of the three young servants.

"Nandi, we have had no breakfast, we have been subjected to—"

"Take a seat, nadi. That one will do."

"Nandi!" Baiji protested. "We are by no means your enemy! We protest this treatment!"

"What you are, nadi, will be for others to judge," Bren said, and noted a further presence in the hall, past the still-open door. "On the other hand, you may as well remain standing. The aiji-dowager is here."

"Aiji-ma!" Baiji turned in evident dismay, and bowed, however briefly, as Ilisidi, not relying on Cenedi's arm, appeared at Cenedi's side in the doorway, walked to the nearest hard chair and sat down unaided, leaning on her cane. Cenedi took his usual post behind her.

"Aiji-ma, one protests . . ."

"Silence!" Bang! went the cane. "Fool."

"Aiji-ma!"

"Nand' Geigi is present," a voice said on speaker, and a moment later: *"Nand' Bren. This is Geigi."*

"One rejoices at the sound of your voice, nandi," Bren said. "The aiji-dowager is here with me. One regrets, however, to inform you of a very unfortunate situation: my life was attempted under the portico of your house, which is now, intact, except the portico, in the hands of Guild in the aiji's employ. Among other distressing matters, I saw none of the Edi that I knew when I was there. More, your nephew has had certain communications with the Marid—"

"I am innocent!" Baiji cried. *"I am unjustly accused!"*

"He is at my estate, under close guard, nandi, considering a negotiation regarding a Southern marriage, and the suspected importation of Guild of the Marid man'chi, and the ominous disappearance of staff loyal to you, nandi. One cannot adequately express the personal regret one feels at bearing such news."

"I rescued the aiji's son at sea!" Baiji cried. "If I were of hostile mind, I would have delivered him to these alleged Southerners!"

"One might point out," Bren said, "that I personally, aboard my boat, followed your nephew's indication to locate and pick up the heir, who was at no time actually in your nephew's hands. What he would have done had he been the one to intercept the aiji's son is a matter of dispute."

"Unfair!" Baiji protested. "Unfair, nandi!"

Ilisidi signaled she wanted the handset. Immediately. He picked it up, passed it over, and it reverted to handset mode, silent to the rest of the room.

"Nandi," she said. "Geigi? Your nephew has become a scandal. Your estate reverts to *your* capable hands. Settle whom you wish in charge, *except* this young disgrace! The connivance of the Marid to take this coast has continued and your nephew continues to temporize with the South as he did during Murini's tenure. There was excuse, while Murini sat in charge, but this flirtation has continued into inappropriate folly and a reluctance to go to court. One cannot imagine what this young fool hopes to gain, except to extend the Marid into northern waters and settle himself in luxury funded by my grandson's enemies!"

"I never did such things!" Baiji cried.

"And he is a liar!" Ilisidi snapped. Then she smiled sweetly, and extended the phone toward Baiji. "Your uncle wishes to speak to you, *nadi.*"

The servants who surrounded Baiji still did so, and Cenedi would not let Baiji touch the dowager, even indirectly: Cenedi transferred the phone to a servant, who gave it to Baiji, who put the receiver to his ear with the expression of a man handling something poisonous. His skin had acquired a gray cast, his face had acquired a rigid expression of dismay, and as he answered, "Yes, uncle?" and listened to what Geigi had to say, he seemed to shrink in size, his shoulders rounded, his head inclined, his occasional attempts to speak instantly cut off.

"Yes, uncle," he said, "yes, uncle, yes, one understan—" A bow, a deeper bow, to the absent lord of his small clan. "Yes, uncle. One assures—uncle, one in no way—Yes, uncle." And then: "They just left, uncle. One has no idea why. One did nothing to—" Baiji was sweating. Visibly. And Ilisidi sat there with the smile of a guardian demon, staring straight at him, with Cenedi standing by her side.

Bren—just sat listening, until a movement in the doorway caught his eye.

Cajeiri had shown up, his two companions barely visible in the hall . . . Cajeiri in an oversized bathrobe, hugging it around him and drinking everything in with large eyes and two very good ears. He didn't create a stir, didn't say a thing.

And, silent, like two black ghosts, Banichi and Jago turned up behind Cajeiri, likewise listening.

Bren found he himself had dropped a couple of stitches in the moment of noticing that arrival: Baiji was handing the phone back to one of his servant-guards, who offered it back to Cenedi, who offered it to Ilisidi.

"Yes?" she said . . . and looked fiercely satisfied. "Excellent. We shall see he does, Gcigi-ji. We shall try to learn the whereabouts of staff. And we shall expect you."

"Expect you." So *Lord Geigi* was coming down from the station, on—Bren found he had lost track of the launch schedule and had no idea of the date of the next shuttle flight; but it was weekly. It would not be long, likely, before Baiji found himself accounting to his uncle in meticulous detail.

Ilisidi handed the phone to Bren. "Lord Geigi has signed off, nand' paidhi. But he wishes you well."

"Indeed." He set the handset back in its cradle. "And you, neighbor?" *Lord* Baiji, he did *not* say: Ilisidi had removed that title with that simple, deliberate *nadi*, and he didn't argue.

Baiji clasped his hands between his knees and compressed his lips to a thin line as he bowed to the dowager and to him. "One apologizes," he said. "One so profoundly apologizes, nandiin."

Whack! went the cane.

"About time!" Ilisidi said. "Confess, wretch, or we shall

lose all patience! What began your unfortunate association with these notorious troublemakers? Name their names, each one!"

Baiji stammered something. Bang! went the cane a second time.

"You have this single chance to redeem yourself," Ilisidi snapped. "Your uncle will ask us what your subsequent behavior may have been, and we assure you we *shall* answer him. As things stand, we cannot construe a use for you. As things may become, we *may* consider a quiet settlement that may let you recover some respectability. *Choose, and choose now!*"

"With greatest appreciation, aiji-ma, with greatest appreciation for your intercession—"

"You bore us. Talk! Give us your account!"

The dowager did nothing to steady Baiji's nerves. His mouth opened and closed. He mopped his face with his sleeve, and he said: "Aiji-ma. My fault began with the Troubles, when the whole world was going toward Murini. The Marid supported him in everything. But the lords of the Marid—after supporting Murini in his—in his ill-considered enterprise—"

"Attacking my grandson and murdering his staff. Let us be specific."

"Attacking—attacking the aiji, yes, aiji-ma. Once Murini had done that, once he had taken over the central clans, the Marid would, one is quite sure, have replaced him if they could. One saw them manuevering for power, in the old way."

"A reasonable assessment," Ilisidi said mildly.

"And in their maneuevers, aiji-ma, in the nature of their manuevers, one feared they wished to extend their power up from the South without challenging Murini up in Shejidan. It was no profit to them to go eastward. All the economic profit lay in their going westward and north, along the coast, which is a kind of enterprise—fishing, and all—that they understand. They were sending out emissaries and promising extravagant things in their own name, saying that they were Murini's allies and that favor and economic union with them would gain great profit. The alternative—the alternative—was down in Pura, where they assassinated—assassinated Lord Kaien and his whole household."

"A disgrace."

"It was so tiny a house. It threatened no one, but it suggested independence and no one could protect it. That was the point, aiji-ma. From where we stood it was very clear. And houses capitulated, one after the other, the Udiri, the Wori, the Maisi and the others, right up the coast. Even Dalaigi was . . . was growing quite chancy: Southerners openly walked the streets, and there were assassinations of small people, even shopowners, for refusing to deal with them. The Edi were not able to withstand these assaults. The little villages—these people could by no means pack up and go into the hills, and there was no safety in the inland, nor any aiji to hear their request for help. There was nothing for them to do, aiji-ma. I had no support—I could no longer contact my uncle! I could no longer protect Kajimında!"

"Go on. Omit nothing."

"Aiji-ma, a letter from the South was by no means unexpected. Murini was by then in Shejidan. Receiving this letter—one might have appealed to Shejidan and voiced one's opinion that the Marid was only supporting Murini as a convenience, and that they meant to assassinate him once the center of the aishidi'tat was in any sense stable under his rule. One thought of this act. But from a coastal lord and a relative of Lord Geigi—one had no confidence that Murini-aiji would hear such an opinion with any understanding or gratitude. He would be just as likely to report all I said to the Lord of the Marid, and then where would I stand? I would be dead. I believed I would be dead in short order did I attempt to reason with Murini or divide him from his Southern allies."

"Not badly reckoned," Ilisidi said more mildly. "You begin to interest us . . . even to make some sense. Name names and recall that we have been out of the current of Southern politics for three years."

A soft movement brought Cajeiri to the back of his great-grandmother's chair, beside Cenedi. That space in the doorway having cleared, Banichi and Jago entered the room and stood against the wall, grimly listening.

"The Dojisigi district of the Marid," Baiji said, "the lord of Amarja, Tori . . . he sent to me, offering his granddaughter, Tiajo—promising support for this whole district if I made this alliance."

"Tori," Ilisidi said, "son of Badissuni."

"The one, yes, aiji-ma. The proposal said—that the western coast—that I—had the choice of falling by force and assassination to the Kadigidi aiji and the North—or I could join with the Marid, by a close alliance that would respect the existing Associations of the coast. And one knows—one knows, aiji-ma, and knew then—"

"Out with it!"

"One suspected Lord Tori lied about respecting the coastal Associations. The Edi and the Marid are old enemies. But it has always been the position of the Maschi to protect the Edi of this coast—which we have always done, aiji-ma!"

"Then where are they?"

"Aiji-ma, one asks understanding! This was my thinking—that if one started to form new alliances, if you were lost, if the Marid and Murini of the Kadagidi were going to divide the world between them—at least one could save something. I could not contact my uncle. If one began to negotiate with the Marid at least with a starting agreement that the existing associations should persist, then one at least had a basis on which to negotiate for better things. One was no longer negotiating for things as they were—that was lost. One was trying to save what could be saved. The wars of the Edi with the Marid, the piracy, the raids—all these the Maschi had been able to calm. Could one not do this best in a new age by making an association *with* the Marid, rather than fall to the Kadagidi and become a target when the Marid ultimately moved to assassinate Murini and seize the aijinate? If I had attempted to fight either of them, this whole coast would be under assault—and all the ancient agreements would be trampled down. All the old grudges would be paid off, Contracts would be issued on every hand . . . the very living of the people would become impossible if the coast came under blockade, in a struggle between Murini and the Marid, and the humans would—" Baiji's eyes shifted anxiously to Bren. "One has no idea what the humans might do if the Kadagidi and Marid started fighting in the strait, off their very shores. If humans invaded, and we had no association to protect us—we would become a battlefield."

"Humans would not have invaded on their own behalf," Bren said, hoping he believed it. "One strongly doubts your scenario for an invasion, nadi. Mospheira was aiding the Northern Isles to remain independent. Had you appealed to the Presidenta, you might have joined the Northern Isles and *they* might have interdicted the Marid. Their navy might have saved you."

"But it was an association we have never made, nandi," Baiji protested.

"The Edi have close connections with the Isles," Ilisidi said. "You might have asked them . . . if they had not already seen in you a policy and a future they would not tolerate."

That panicked Baiji for a moment. His eyes shifted from one to the other of them, wildly. "So. But—with a successor, me being a young man, my honored mother having died . . ."

"Another interesting point. *How* did she die?"

"You cannot think, aiji-ma! You cannot, you *cannot* think—"

"She was in ill health, we understand. And *when* did your flirtation with the Marid begin?"

"Aiji-ma, no! That had nothing to do with it! One never— *never* would have tolerated such a thing."

"Back to the Edi. *Why* did you not use their good offices

to reach the north? Was it possibly too great an exertion for a young man? Or did the Edi already question your dealings?"

"They—they were upset by the death of my honored mother. One was in shock, aiji-ma—one hardly knew when—one day there were no servants. There were just no servants."

"Indeed."

"One was overwhelmed, nand' dowager! One had no means to ask Uncle what to do. There was—there was this offer of marriage. This offer of alliance. If I refused it—it might be fatal. There might be no time for such maneuvers. So I thought, I thought—being new to my post, aiji-ma, and without your sage advice—"

Bang! "Do not annoy me, wretch! Your mother was dead, unfortunate *doting* woman, and you, still more unfortunate for the region, were alive. Go on!"

"I was stalling, aiji-ma. I was continually pretending to agree. One hoped—one hoped, aiji-ma, that your ship would any day reappear in the heavens with the true aiji's heir, and that would solve everything. And if one could play for time . . ."

He had looked to Ilisidi a second time, and his voice faltered.

Bang! went the cane. "Go on. We are listening."

"So I protested I had favored a lady of the district, and I lied, aiji-ma, that I had spoken to the daughter of the Hesi. But—" A tremor entered his voice. "This unfortunate girl—this entirely innocent girl, whom I had only met socially—she died within the month. At her own father's table." Baiji's lips trembled. "And I knew—I knew surely it was my fault. It was because I used her name. They removed—removed her from consideration. And now—now I have the gravest doubt whether my mother's death was from her illness . . . I had not thought that. I never had thought that, aiji-ma."

For the first time Bren felt a twinge of sympathy for the man who had harbored assassins . . . not overmuch, since they had shot one of his people, killed two of Ilisidi's, and attempted to kill him and Banichi and Jago. But the young man was a fool. Possibly he *had* tried to match wits with the Marid.

"Go on," Ilisidi said.

"Within two days I received a letter expressing condolence and renewing the offer. I have this letter. I have saved everything, aiji-ma—if you wish to have these things."

"We shall expect it. Say on."

"So—I could not call my uncle; I had the fate of the young lady of the Hesi on my conscience. One had the estate to protect—"

One noted he never said "my people." And that he reverted to the remote formal when speaking of them.

"—so one hoped to temporize, never naming names: one pleaded grief for my mother, grief for the young lady. One asked questions, pretending not to understand clauses in the agreement. One conjured every remote provision of treaties and agreements which I wished specifically to be preserved—I have the list, aiji-ma. I have all those papers."

"On, I say! You were grieving. And you saved the papers, as any reasonably careful accountant might do. What more?"

"Then—they wished me to visit the Marid, aiji-ma, but—but then you came back from the heavens, and Murini was about to fall, and I—one feared to travel in those days in the first place, and then my bodyguard left me, just like the servants. I thought they had gone to fight for you, aiji-ma, but I never saw them again."

"Where did you acquire the ones you had?" Banichi asked from the side of the room.

"They came from the Guild. They gave me regards from my own guard and said they had taken their place."

When the Guild itself had been suspect, in those last days of Murini's administration.

"One fears you may never see your bodyguard again," Bren murmured.

"The replacements," Banichi said, unasked, "are dead."

Baiji looked from one to the other of them, and his jaw trembled. "I was afraid of them, nandiin. I knew—I knew they reported elsewhere."

"My grandson's men," Ilisidi said, "have taken the estate in hand until your uncle's return. *In him* we have confidence, and there will be questions and an accounting, a rendering of the books and records, a task in which he will have your assistance, if you wish to regain anything."

"Aiji-ma." A seated bow. "One longs to be of service."

"We hold this notion for consideration," Ilisidi said, "since we have not heard how you continued this dalliance with the Marid *after* our return from space and *after* my grandson took Shejidan and drove Murini in retreat. *Now* present us your excuse! Was there some unreported difficulty with the phones, that would prevent your calling Shejidan or sending a messenger covertly?"

"I was afraid, aiji-ma! My very guard was sending secret messages! I had no idea whether they were reporting to the aiji or—or to the Marid! How could I move in any regard without them knowing?"

"Ingenuity might have overcome this. A phone call, I say. A visit to your neighbors. A shopping expedition to Dalaigi. Shopkeepers would surely have acted for you at your request."

"They would know."

"They would know. A call to my grandson, man! A note, contained in a basket of produce, sent to your neighbor!"

"But—one thought—aiji-ma—the aiji himself was negotiating with the Marid. Things might yet change. Perhaps—perhaps I could do something favorable by marrying the girl. I could draw her house into association with the coast . . ."

"Marry a Dojisigi girl, part of a scheme the Tasaigi clan no longer had any motive to move forward? Draw the Dojisigi into conflict with the Tasaigi, perhaps? Bring the eastern peninsula of the Marid into conflict with the western, which has had their man'chi for seven hundred years? Gods above and below, what do you think your help is *worth*, man?"

"Aiji-ma—"

"You had *one* value to them: as a foothold on the western coast, within its association, a foothold that would be short-lived, but one from which they could work to alienate the Edi from the aishidi'tat; one from which they could plan an assassination that would shake the entire world. *Not* my great-grandson. *Not* a power for the future of the aishidi'tat. That was not their aim. The paidhi-aiji was their target, the power that connects my grandson with the Mospheirans and with the heavens and all its factions—and you agreed."

"No, aiji-ma, by no means!"

"You *ignored* the chance my great-grandson would perish in your scheme. No, that was of no import to you and your advisors. You were set on the paidhi's life, and have made two attempts on it!"

"Not I, aiji-ma! Not I!"

"Where is your aunt, man?"

"My—aunt."

"Lord Geigi's wife. Lord Geigi's Samiusi clan wife. Did she maintain ties with your mother?"

"Not—not that I know, aiji-ma. She—"

"Once before, the Marid tried to achieve a foothold in Sarini province—attempting to impoverish your uncle, do you recall that event? They made every effort to bring him down, and Lord Geigi's last-contracted wife, your aunt, was in frequent correspondence with her sister, who—ah! I remember—just happened to be married into the Marid! *What* a grand coincidence! And Lord Geigi's sister—"

"I cannot hear you speak ill of my mother, aiji-ma!"

"Your mother was a virtuous woman, certainly, in Lord Geigi's confidence—ah, but how could I forget? She *corresponded* with Geigi's former wife . . ."

"Innocently, aiji-ma!"

"Well, well, she administered Kajiminda well enough in difficult times. I wonder where the change happened. A message from your aunt's end of the continent, perhaps? Communication from your cousins in the Marid? One is *certain* you have cousins in the Marid. . . ."

"They are not in my man'chi, nor am I in theirs, aiji-ma. And my mother very rarely corresponded with that branch!"

"So you say. What would you have done if you had found my great-grandson at sea? Ridden him under? Or held him hostage, pending nand' Bren's walking into a trap?"

"I wished to rescue the boy, and to meet with the paidhi-aiji, on the boat—I would have told him—I would have asked him to rescue *me* from my predicament—I would ask to sail into Najida, and for the boy's safety, I would be safe in his good opinion." Baiji cast a frantic look at *him*, and Bren drew a deep breath. "I would have done it! I would have asked for your help, paidhi-aiji! I did so even under my own roof!"

Lost your nerve twice, Bren thought. Or did you only just think of that explanation?

One could want a bath.

"Or," Ilisidi said, drawing Baiji's attention back to her, "Or shall we tell you what we *really* think, Baiji-nadi? Let us favor you with our opinion! You became fearful of the new changes, yes; and you found *comfort* in your Marid bodyguard, who promised you their man'chi, who made you dangerous to your neighbors, who made you a threat to the whole coast—"

"Aiji-ma!"

"Can you deny you had become so?"

"One wished only peace, only to deal out the pieces as one had to, and keep the peace. My uncle was safe in space. He would not return. One would wait to see how the negotiations went between the aiji and the Marid."

"And if well, you would be important . . . and you have cousins in the Marid, part of their politics. Perhaps you would marry that girl after all."

"One meant to straighten it all out, once the aiji in Shejidan had given some indication how all the dealings with the South might come out."

"When it was all perfectly safe! Does it occur to you, Baiji, that it will never be perfectly safe, so long as you have any power at all? Did you have any notion where you would ever tell these people no?"

"One is uncertain what—"

"One is uncertain what atrocious thing you would stick at, if it crept up on you by degrees, Baiji son of Dumaei. Your failing came on you by degrees. Your involvement with the Marid came on you by degrees. Is there no time you have imagined when you would *ever* call a halt and take a stand?"

"I warned the paidhi-aiji!"

"Not in so many words," Bren said. "No, nadi. Your behavior warned my guard . . . and killed your own."

"Aiji-ma!"

"Fool," Ilisidi said. "If you had acquired any power, if you had brought any independent power to the hands of the Dojisigi, the Tasaigi would have had you for appetitzers, and them after. It was their game, it was their game all along, and now one understands the occupation of the paidhi's apartment in the Bujavid by the Farai . . . who doubtless pass along whatever tidbits of information they scavenge. The Marid, four clans of the mainland, is One, that is how the numbers of four districts work out: the One is centered at Tanaja in the hands of Machigi, who has inherited all the ambition of his predecessors Saigimi and Cosadi—Cosadi, who backed Murini in his adventure—and, ah! indeed, they have your aunt's man'chi."

"Not mine, aiji-ma!"

Machigi. The new aiji in Tanaja. Quiet, hitherto. Bren tried to put a face with the name, and failed.

"You surely," Ilisidi was saying to Baiji, "have met the man."

"We—we have never corresponded."

"*We* have been remote in space, and yet *we* can comprehend the maneuverings around you. The numbers of them are not hard to parse. Why cannot you?"

"One—one begins to see, aiji-ma."

"Oh, one begins to see! Blessed gods, man, need I say so? Machigi backed his cousin Murini of the Kadagidi so long as it profited him. We have wondered whether his latest moves were represented more strongly by the Farai's approach to my grandson, their offering of man'chi—their repudiation of Murini—or exactly what they might be up to. In what more sinister direction it might manifest was *not* apparent, since *you* kept their secrets and conspired with them in actions that threatened the paidhi's life *and* my great-grandson's."

"No, aiji-ma, I never conspired!"

"Fool, I say! You are right in one thing: had Murini survived and my grandson perished, Murini would have lasted a scant year or two before the Tasaigi killed him—one imprudent marriage too many, one cup of tea in the wrong hands, and Murini would have been out of the question altogether, and I have no doubt Machigi of the Tasaigi would by then have positioned himself with the help of your alliance with that Dojisigi child. Machigi would kill you the moment you produced an heir, foolish boy. The Dojisigi relatives would move in with your heir. And they would have the coast, and Machigi would have *them!*"

"One never—never—" Baiji's eyes were wide and astonished. "One never saw such an outcome. Aiji-ma, one begs forgiveness."

"Of me you do not have it. I do not say beg it of the paidhi-aiji: he is too gentle! Obtain your uncle's request for clemency, and I may, *may* broker you a marriage with a nice Eastern woman of good sense and more mature perspective. Live to produce children! That will be your use to the Maschi clan, if Lord Geigi fails to strangle you with his own hands!"

Marry off this fool? Bren thought, somewhat set aback.

But part of the situation was that the Maschi clan had worn

away to near nothing, diminished to a single clan in Sarini province, while its privileges and influence had grown immense, enough to tempt suitors. Geigi, the aishidi'tat's old ally, was growing no younger, had never produced an heir, and *this* was what he had to leave in charge?

It was suddenly much clearer to him what the issues were, and exactly what the dowager was offering, in brief: there was one ability Baiji had left to make himself useful, and the dowager would personally make his choice for him, as a favor to Lord Geigi—thus providing the fading Maschi clan a sure link to a clan on *her* side of the continent, lacing up the aishidi'tat into a safe, tight unity.

"Aiji-ma." It was a very quiet voice, a very shaken one.

"Oh, come now. You like your soft, safe life, do you not, boy? You *enjoy* being called nandi, you *enjoy* good food, good wine, and a dearth of responsibilities. You scarcely have to appeal to the Marid for a marriage. We can arrange that—and a younger daughter of a middling-strong house of the East. You can have all of this and live a long life, so long as you stay out of politics and hire strong-minded tutors we approve for your offspring. This is your chance. Take it!"

"Aiji-ma." Increasingly shaken, but with eyes utterly fixed on Ilisidi. "One would be grateful. One would be very grateful for your speaking to my uncle on this matter."

"Have you any other thing to tell us? Be forward in helping us!"

"Only—only that there are papers in my office. Behind the desk, a panel in the wall, nand' dowager. You would find these of interest. One has kept every incriminating thing."

Covering all possible directions he might ever go, Bren thought with distaste, and whoever he might need to blackmail. He didn't believe this reform. He didn't in the least believe it. And in the way of atevi power marriages, it was very little likely Baiji would have charge of any offspring. An heir. Any heir—and his responsibility was accomplished.

"Then you may retire and have your breakfast," Ilisidi said. "You may have saved your future."

"Aiji-ma." Baiji rose and bowed, and bowed to Bren as well, as the three servants came alert—so, before that, had Cenedi and Banichi and Jago.

"But you do know," Ilisidi added casually, "that you will not survive long, resident in this district, so close to the South. You have no resources to take on Guild of sufficient level to save your life."

"Aiji-ma!"

"We do, in the East. Perhaps that would be a safer haven for you . . . far, far from the lords you have betrayed. You would be a great fool to contemplate going to them. You understand this. Now that you have assured *we* shall not kill you, you have assured that they *will*. Within our shadow is the only safety for you, from henceforward."

Baiji was certainly not the most intelligent soul on the continent, Bren thought. But the facts of the situation did apparently come through to Baiji at that point.

"You will stay to meet your uncle," Ilisidi said, "and then fly east. Far east. Where you may *have* a future."

Snow and ice was the reputation of the East. It was far, far from the sunny harbors of the western coast. But Baiji bowed profoundly, murmured his parting courtesies and left the room with his escort.

"He will turn any way convenient, aiji-ma," Cenedi said.

"A hiltless knife," Ilisidi agreed. "Great-grandson, I daresay you have not met as great a fool as Baiji."

"No, mani. I am only one short of nine and *I* know better than he does."

"And what are you doing here in your bathrobe?"

"Mani, protecting you from that man."

Ilisidi laughed gently, and set her cane so she might use it. Cenedi quietly offered his hand, and she rose. So did Bren, with a bow.

"Aiji-ma."

"We are improved," Ilisidi said. "We are much improved, nand' paidhi. We have a solution to that fool, and we shall have a solution to the South. Cenedi, communicate with my grandson's forces and have these alleged papers at Lord Geigi's estate found and brought. Nand' paidhi, we shall keep our promise and retire for a few hours. Perhaps until dinner. Great-grandson?"

"Mani?"

"Do *not* do anything that requires you to leave this roof."

"Yes, mani."

There was not even any resistance about it. Everyone looked exhausted, and the company departed its separate ways.

All but him. All but Banichi and Jago, who stood to the side.

"My brother and Barb-daja?" he asked of them.

"They have come up to the house, Bren-ji," Banichi said, "for their breakfast. House staff is attending the repair of their boat—which has numerous bullet holes. It was a very narrow escape they had. If not for the pump, the boat would have gone down, so nand' Toby says. It was still running when staff brought them up to the house."

Bren let go a long sigh and came around the chair—he took each by an arm briefly, atevi custom be damned. "One has you back and safe, nadiin-ji," he said. "Forgive me. Words cannot express—how glad, personally, how glad I am." He let them go. "Now that a foolish human has said so, I shall stop being rude."

Banichi made a sound in his throat, half a laugh, and Jago tilted her head and gave him a down-the-nose look that said she had things to say on that rudeness, but wouldn't until later.

"Tano and Algini report," Banichi said, "that they believe the enemy penetrated house defenses here while they were absent with you, nandi. Even past the dowager's protections here—they got through . . . to a grievous mistake on the part of the two who died."

"Algini knew the intruders," Jago said. "They were high in

the Guild under Gegini." That was to say, the Guild leadership during the overthrow. "Nochidi and Keigan, senior Guild, within the Guild itself. They survived the service of both Sarini and Cosadi."

Previous bids to unseat Tabini: Sarini was dead. Cosadi, now deceased, had been another problem out of the Marid, and an elder cousin to the current one. Now they had a new problem. Machigi. Who had come damned close to doing what the others had failed to do.

That the two intruders Algini and Tano had done for had been senior Guild, good enough to get past Ilisidi's guard—that sent a chill down the backbone. They'd gotten far enough, deep enough into house defenses to have taken any of them out . . . except Tano and Algini, except Cenedi and Nawari. Close call. Very. The Marid didn't spend its elite teams lightly.

It was of a par with Ilisidi saying that the paidhi-aiji had become the primary target.

Leave the coast, go back to the Bujavid? That was a *worse* situation, with the Farai right in their midst, with their secretaries, their guards, their staff . . . their access to install anything from listening devices to a bomb in his apartment—or against Tabini's apartment wall.

"Not a comfortable thought," he said. "One surmises this will not be the end of it, nadiin-ji. One *assumes* the aiji will now move against the Marid."

"One does assume the aiji will now dislodge the Farai from the paidhi's apartment," Jago said dryly, "for a start."

It could be downright treasonous, that utterance . . . the implication that Tabini-aiji had been a fool.

Or perhaps Jago had meant something else. Along with the aiji's power came the obligation to be both subtle and clever.

"He did *not* force me out here to draw fire, surely." One entertained that uncomfortable thought, momentarily. "He need only have suggested I visit my estate. One would gladly have gone . . ."

"The aiji at least permitted the Farai to be inconvenient to him," Banichi said with a lift of the brow. "But one surmises he was concentrating on doings in the South when he made the decision to be patient with them, and perhaps he was testing the Farai's intent. One by no means believes he would have allowed his son to remain here a single night, had he had the suspicion of hostile presence."

That was true. The assassination attempt had been opportunistic, he believed that. But it led inevitably right back to the Marid and this new problem. Machigi. He had to study up on the man. Baiji's value to the Marid had plummeted when Tabini-aiji took power back from Murini, but the value Baiji had retained was that of a staging area for a very important operation . . . namely removal of some of Tabini-aiji's key assets. An heir? Grievous as that would be, rumors were that Damiri might produce another before the year was out. The dowager? A very hard target, and one that would *not* thoroughly or immediately disrupt the west coast—which was the arena of Marid ambitions. The East was irrelevant to them.

But the paidhi-aiji held Najida—which was a property on which the Farai had at least some legal claim . . . had the paidhi not come back from space. Najida—which was poised just below the Northern Isles, and right next to Kajiminda and Dalaigi—the largest town on the western coast.

Click, click, click. Things began to drop into little slots.

"Dare one wonder," Bren asked them, "if the paidhi has been a desired target for some time? They have not appeared to relinquish their hope of setting the west coast in disarray."

"Cenedi has requested still more reinforcements," Banichi said. "They should be arriving by morning."

"One is glad to know that," Bren said. And again touched both of them. "You should take as light a duty as possible, nadiin-ji. Let Cenedi's force manage things. Baiji poses no threat. Cenedi has men on the roof. Rest."

Banichi looked at him as if thinking of asking when the

paidhi-aiji had appointed himself to the Guild; but then he nodded. "We both shall," Banichi said.

"Go," he said. "Now."

"And you, Bren-ji," Jago said.

"As soon as I have talked to nand' Toby," he said. "A courtesy. No need of escort. And then I shall go straightway to my
office and do a little work."

They looked not of a mind to agree to that. They were on the
last reserves, and perhaps not at their most reasonable. They just
stared at him, both, in adamant silence that indicated that, orders
or no orders, they would neither one be off duty until he was settled somewhere they approved . . . nor would Tano and Algini.

"Then I shall do my work in your quarters," he said, "where
you all can keep an eye on me."

Banichi looked slightly amused. "We will provide you a
chair in which to work, Bren-ji. No more of this wandering the
halls alone."

"Not when people drop out of the ceiling," Jago said.

So it was out into the slightly damaged hall, down to the
dining room, where Toby and Barb, windblown and in shocking condition for the dining room, were just finishing up their
breakfast.

"Bren!" Toby said, looking up.

A little bow—he'd been in atevi mode: was, still, mentally;
and tried to adjust. Toby looked a little nonplussed, then said,
"Oh, hell, Bren, it's me," and came and embraced him, hard as
Barb got to her feet.

"Glad you made it back," Bren said. "I hear you ran into
trouble out there—I heard about the other boat. There should be
people out now looking for any intruders on the peninsula."

"We managed," Toby said, standing at arm's length. "And
you got the kids back."

"They got themselves out," he said. "The aiji's men are mop-
ping up over there, and the dowager's dealing with the details.
How close is your boat to seaworthy?"

"My own estimate?" Toby said. "With luck, about two days."

"I'd send you off in mine," Bren said, "but you met a good reason not to be out at sea at the moment. This is a major operation. There's a good likelihood the boat that tried to sink you came out of the township to the south, and that means either the opposition stole it or they have allies there with assets. The aiji will be calling in naval forces, probably from up in the Islands, but it's going to be a few days. You're better off here."

"Are we *safe* here?" Barb asked.

"Safe as anybody can be with Guild on the hunt," Bren said. "The whole region is going to be dangerous. There could very easily be another boat out there, trying to make a run in here. The village is on the alert, watchers up and down the coast, so we hope we will get a warning. Figure that any move that's easy to see could be a diversion. The enemy lost a senior Guild team trying to get at me. And they damned near made it—might have, if we hadn't scrambled who was in what room."

"At you," Toby said, "specifically? Twice?"

"Very possibly. Sounds a little egotistical on my part, but my security seems to read it that way. They'll take other targets if they can get them, no question. But the operation probably started when they knew I was coming in. They're making a play to get at their old enemies the Edi, and to own the southwest coast—the Marid is a maritime power; they have no assets in the central regions. But they do have ships. They've got more ships than the aiji's navy does, if it comes to that: they can convert their island traders and become real damned difficult to deal with if they can get a few ports to use unchallenged, up on this coast."

"This is the same bunch that supported Murini."

"And that made the trouble in the aishidi'tat before that," Bren said, "when Cosadi made a try to link up with the Kadagidi. We've got that one troublesome clan up in the Padi Valley. . . ."

"The Kadagidi, you mean."

Bren nodded. "That lot has been conniving with the Marid from the time the Ragi set up the Western Association. They're Ragi—skin deep. But they have Southern ties and they tried to stop the Association getting organized in the first place. They were the holdouts. They were trying to form an association with *themselves* at the center—at the same time the Marid was trying to pull out of the Ragi Association. That's the history of it. But the rest of the Padi Valley Ragi were so relieved to find somebody knocking the Kadagidi in the head, they came right into the new Association and turned on the Kadagidi—then helped the Association organize the west coast. Then the Marid came into the Association—before they got forced in—and immediately demanded special privileges—which they didn't get; demanded to run the Southern trade—which they did get, in return for giving up some of their navy. They'd started to try to form an alliance with the East, when the aiji—Tabini's grandfather—knocked the pins out from under them by bringing Ilisidi in."

"This Ilisidi."

"There's only one," Bren said. "The Marid would like to see her dead . . . for old time's sake, if nothing else. Murini and the Kadagidi made their recent try at overthrowing Tabini—Murini went down. The Kadagidi are in disarray. The Marid has the space station over their heads now, they have Tabini back in power, they have the Western Association more united than they've ever been, and the weakest spot they can reach is their old enemies the Edi, up and down the southwestern coast. The Edi have never had a strong central authority. They're inclined to go their own way, village by village, house by house. They were always on the losing side with the Ragi, until they linked up with the Maschi, who understood the Ragi and understood them—Lord Geigi's house. Tiny clan. Big influence. Lord Geigi's in space, indispensible up there. But he's going to have to come back to deal with the mess in his affairs down here . . .

his nephew's been a fool, playing politics with the Marid during Murini's administration. He thought he was being smart. Now he's got bedfellows, and Geigi's house, the house that holds the Edi together—the house that has the Edi man'chi, if Baiji hasn't lost it—is just damned close to disintegrating. That's what's going on, brother. If the Edi fragment and start fighting among themselves again, the Marid can start gnawing away at them, piece by piece, village by village, right up the coast. The Marid has got the ships; Tabini doesn't. If the Marid can find some handful of Edi willing to make deals, they'll *create* some figurehead to be another Geigi. I'm getting the impression the new aiji in that region was using Murini—and Murini would have been dead the first time he disappointed the Marid. Now this new fellow—remember his name for Shawn—" Toby was not unacquainted with the President of Mospheira. "Machigi."

"Machigi."

"Out of the Tasaigi district, Tanji clan, aiji in Tanaja. Bad news. *Really* bad news, if this whole thing is his planning. Apparently he's got the Senji and the Dojisigi districts and probably the Dausigi district of the Marid working with him. Meanwhile the Farai, out of the Senji district, are sitting in *my* apartment in the Bujavaid, right next to Tabini's—claiming, incidentally, kinship with the Maladesi, who used to hold this peninsula, besides that apartment. The Maladesi no longer exist as a clan. Their last generation married into the Farai's adjunct clan, the Morigi, and the Farai consequently have a claim on the Maladesi prerogatives and territory, because now the Morigi are extinct and the Farai claim all they had. The Farai, of the Senjin Marid, *claimed* my apartment under Murini's occupation; they then turned coat again and opened the doors of the Bujavid to Tabini's forces when he came back. Supposedly they've been trying all winter to broker an agreement between Tabini and the Marid to settle all the old bad politics, which is why I've been living in Tatiseigi's apartment and not bothering the Farai.

The hell they're brokering a peace deal! They're in this Tasaigi move up to their ears, and unless they prove to have secretly informed the aiji and set up Machigi for a fall, they're going down, and *I'm* getting my apartment back."

Toby blinked. Barb looked totally puzzled.

"It's quite simple," Bren said. "I get my apartment. And very bad news for the Marid that I'm still alive and even more that the Edi are going to be massively upset if they aren't already. Geigi *has* to get down here and take the reins in person—kick Baiji out officially and probably stay here, patching up what's been disturbed. That means *he'll* become the main target, and the aiji's going to have to take special measures to protect him. Tell Shawn that, too. This coast's become a powder keg and my coming here lit the fuse just a little prematurely."

"You're not safe here."

"I'm on a peninsula—well, at the head of it—with a loyal village at my back, a harbor where I can see trouble coming, and the aiji's forces occupying the neighboring estate and township, with help from the dowager besides. This is as safe as I could be, for now, granted there isn't a landing party from that wrecked boat working its way in this direction. You're both safer here than trying to run for it until the aiji is in firm control of the sea approach. Trust me in that."

"Trust you," Toby said, "no question. How can we help?"

"Stay in the harbor. Get that boat of yours patched and fit to sail. You may have to take out of here before you get her beautified. There's a guard on my boat: but just keep an eye on things in the harbor, be my eyes on the shoreline, and keep radio contact with the house if you see any movement. If something comes at us overland, protect yourselves and get out when you can. There's no way you can go up against a Guild operation. All right?"

"We'll be out there," Toby said.

"Stay under cover as much as possible. Don't present a target. If you need anything, get one of the staff or the villagers to run up to the house. Don't expose yourselves to snipers—or a kidnapping."

"Got it," Toby said. "We'll be going back down there. You take care."

"I intend to," he said, and hugged Toby—and Barb. "Stay alive. If we can get you a navy escort to calmer waters—"

"Don't distract anybody from necessary business," Toby said. "Just—you be careful, Bren."

"I intend to be," he said, and walked them out of the dining room and on toward the main hall—Banichi and Jago joining them as soon as they exited the dining room.

Another and scandalous public exchange of hugs as he sent them out the door. He did it anyway, while Banichi used his communications to call the escort to the door, to be sure Toby and Barb made it down to the boat safely—and equally to be sure the dowager's men on the roof didn't mistake the movement of someone down the winding walk.

"See you," Toby told him, in leaving.

"See you," he said in turn, and the escort took Barb and Toby in hand.

Then the servants shut the doors between them, shut them, locked them, and threw the substantial bolts above and below.

"Now we rest," he said with a deep breath. "I pick up my computer, and we all go to your room, nadiin-ji."

15

"**B**ren-ji." Tano turned his chair at the security console to face Bren. "A report has come from the dock. Nand' Toby and Barb-daja are back on their boat and safely so. There has been no incident. The boat is under repair. The workmen estimate to have the hole sealed before midnight. The pumps are very adequately keeping up with the situation."

"Thank you, Tano-ji," Bren said fervently. He had his own place, a chair pulled up to make a workspace at the end of the counter, next to an array of equipment, and he'd been writing reports on the situation while it was fresh in memory. Banichi and Jago took a little time in their respective beds in the next room, and they spoke in low voices, so as not to disturb them.

He hadn't realized how tightly his nerves had been wound, how anxiously he'd awaited that word from the dock, but he'd ceased to trust momentary lulls in a situation—which often simply meant the enemy had drawn back to reorganize. Getting Barb and Toby out to sea was of great importance—but not overriding their safety. "Message in reply, Tano-ji: tell nand' Toby wait for a clearance before he sails unless things go very badly here. If you yourself can possibly ask the aiji's forces for an escort to get nand' Toby out to sea . . . one would make that request."

"Indeed," Tano said, and turned back to his console, to busy himself in communications for some time. Bren went back to his report.

He was uneasy about asking a personal favor from Tabini—diversion of a naval vessel from a major action wasn't exactly the sort of thing most people asked to be sure a relative got away safely, but the fact was, Toby wasn't just Toby. He was a potentially valuable hostage. And he wasn't just a Mospheiran citizen in the wrong waters; or even just the paidhi-aiji's close relative: he was occasionally and perhaps currently an agent of the Mospheiran government—a spy, in plain fact; a spy who had served Tabini's interests and hurt those of the Southern conspirators. And that meant he twice over ought to get out of here before he fell into hostile hands. Toby had personal enemies in the South: the South might not know precisely who he was beyond being the paidhi's relative—which was enough. But once they twigged to what he had done during the Troubles, they would very quickly move to get their hands on him for very different reasons. The fact that Toby had a small operational Ragi vocabulary only put him in worse danger, in that regard.

So he wanted Toby the hell out of the bay and out much, much closer to the Mospheiran coast, just as soon as they could be sure that by sending the *Brighter Days* out toward open ocean they wouldn't be sending Toby straight into the jaws of some force coming *into* the bay to launch a sea assault on Najida. A naval escort from Tabini's side of the mess was the only sure answer.

That, and being sure that repair to the hull was going to hold up under whatever conditions Toby ran into out there once he left his naval escort, whether he had to run hard or dodge fire, or just bear up under the usual spring weather on his way to Port Jackson.

It was, however, the solution to one problem on his hands.

Having his old associate Geigi's nephew locked in his basement, however—that was not going to be tidied up in one stroke.

Damn, he did not look forward to—

Ramaso himself came in, very somberly, with an underlying tension, and bowed.

"The village, nandi—the elders of the village—one has presented your sentiments. They have requested you come to speak to them in person, in a session of the council, tonight."

That was a surprise—a disturbing surprise, since he was unprepared: he had no speech, he had no notes, only an untidy situation to report; but an honor—he wasn't sure a lord of Najida had ever been asked to a village meeting.

"Tonight," he echoed.

"At sunset, nandi."

"I shall need to dress," he said. The protocols of the situation were unprecedented. "In whatever would be appropriate, Rama-ji. I leave it to your discretion."

"They have also invited the aiji-dowager and her great-grandson."

For about a heartbeat he was astonished, and could not imagine what the dynamics of that situation were . . . and then he thought. Edi. With ties to Mospheira before the Landing. The Edi, who traced their descent through their mothers, and especially the grandmothers—the foremothers, guardian spirits, deities to the Edi. The aiji dowager. The aiji's grandmother, great-grandmother to an aiji-to-come.

It wasn't just a meeting. It was a precedent-setting Event, this meeting, and it didn't, perhaps, only have to do with Najida.

"Convey the message to the dowager and ask her, from me, if she would decide about the young gentleman. Say that it may have an interesting relevance to the disappearance of the Edi from Lord Geigi's household."

She would go, he judged. Visit Baiji? She'd had conscious reason not to, well-taken, as it turned out. But an Edi village might pique her curiosity, if nothing else. Curiosity was a potent inducement to Ilisidi.

"Yes, nandi," Ramaso said, and went off to do that.

He sat down and took another note—more, he started pulling up data from his computer, historical notes, geography, a list of names, all in the data files. The Edi ancestors had come down from the north coast, up from the south in ancient times, coastward somewhat when the Ragi Association formed: there had been fighting. And notably, the large group of associated clans had come across from Mospheira, having been forced out by the War of the Landing and subsequently dispossessed by the Treaty of the Landing that ceded the whole island of Mospheira to human rule.

The data listed clans, where each was thought to have been, where they were thought to have moved, what names were common in each. Descent through the mother.

Put upon for two centuries and before: the Edi had been at odds with the Ragi Association, and the Southern Association; and when the Ragi Association had become the Western Association, the aishidi'tat, and made it known they were going to knock some Southern heads, the Edi had found a needful buffer in Geigi's clan, the Maschi, who were on good terms with the Ragi—smartest move they'd made in a long while. But then the holder of Najida, the last of the Maladesi, had married into the Farai of the Morigi clan in the South—*that* little piece of business had linked the northern finger of the coast into the Southern Association . . . simultaneously betraying the Maladesi's village, which was mostly Edi, mostly related to the Edi all down the coast.

That was the pleasant little winter home Tabini-aiji had bestowed on him some years back, and he knew Tabini had never meant him to have to cope with a mess like this—Tabini had only intended to signal the Ragi weren't going to tolerate a Southern Association foothold on the Edi coast, which had made the Edi happy, he gathered, as better than the alternative. The paidhi was not Ragi, not Maschi, certainly not Southern— the Southerners would have cheered en masse if he'd been assassinated. And he and the village had gotten along tolerably well during the period in which the Ragi grew stronger—not a plus for the Edi—but also more peaceful. Prosperity had come to the coast, largely thanks to Lord Geigi and the aerospace plant. Everything had just gone swimmingly right for the Edi during that period.

Until the paidhi became a very absentee landlord and conspiracy threw Tabini out of office for a year. During that time the Southerners had been very active, had stuffed their pockets and gotten people in power here and there—not to mention the damned Farai had taken over the paidhi's apartment as if the paidhi would never return. Baiji had started playing courtship games with the South, Geigi hadn't been able to communicate with the world to find out what was going on, and the Edi serving Baiji had—one hoped—just walked out. One hoped there was no worse answer . . . but he might get a clue to it tonight.

He read and made notes.

And Ramaso came back to inform him the dowager *and* the young gentleman would be attending.

Security problem, was his first thought, and he had been hoping halfheartedly that the dowager would decline the invitation. But so was he a security problem, as far as that went. Banichi and Jago were going to need their rest. They'd have a full complement of the dowager's guard. That was considerable. And the dowager and the next Ragi aiji meeting with that assembly might have political reverberations far outweighing—

Another intervention. *Saidaro* came in from the hall, Ramaso's second-in-command, a little ruffled, for that steady, reasonable man. He bowed.

"Couriers from the aiji's forces have come to the door, nandi, with the papers you requested. And more. They bring two persons to be assigned to the young gentleman. Cenedi-nadi has gone to verify their credentials.

That had the attention of both Tano and Algini, for certain. And that could be a problem. Counting the long-running insistance on the part of Uncle Tatiseigi of the Atageini to provide security for *his* grand-nephew and the several times Uncle Tatiseigi's security had failed to keep track of the boy—it had been a problem. Counting the importance of the Atageini in keeping the central region stable—it was an ongoing problem. Counting the dowager, who was an old lover of Uncle Tatiseigi, providing the boy her *own* security when she was at hand—and threatening to provide it permanently—that was a problem. And counting the fact the boy's father, Tabini, had *had* internal security problems that had come within a hair of getting him assassinated on the floor of the legislature—*that* had been a problem.

The latest arrangement with Tabini's security, who were generally Ragi in ethnicity—itself a noisily controversial reliance on his own clan—had seemed at least to be an improvement on the security front.

But now Tabini was going to step in and have the final say in the ongoing battle—that was going to ruffle the Atageini and the boy's mother's Ajuri clan, at minimum.

And to have the boy acquire Ragi-ethnicity Guildsmen just as he accepted the invitation from the Edi to go meet with them—bad timing. It could have been done when the boy got back to the capital.

Except Tabini was understandably a little disturbed to have known his son had taken unauthorized leave on a freight train, stolen a boat, and developed independent notions that had gotten him stranded in the middle of a firefight. He certainly could not blame Tabini for concluding that his son needed specifically-attached adult security. Two Taibeni teenagers were clearly not enough to exert authority. And Tabini *was* the boy's father.

He got up from the console to go meet the aiji's men, and, of the two, it was Algini that got up to go with him, though Tano had started to do so, until the two exchanged a glance. That was unusual: Algini was not the one who dealt with social situations; but Algini had been, until his apparent resignation from the post, very high in the Guild. In a personnel question, Algini knew faces, knew names, knew the current man'chi of individuals in the Guild in a way even Banichi did not.

He didn't question, just headed down the straight central hall to the group at the front door, a cluster of black uniforms like an incoming storm front, contrasted against the lighter colors of staff—Ramaso among the latter group. Among the Guild who had arrived, there was luggage, presumably belonging to the ones who were now assigned here.

Bren approached. The visiting Guildsmen, four of them, were standing with Cenedi and Nawari. They bowed, and the seniormost visitor handed him a folder.

"Nand' paidhi," Cenedi said, "these are close associates of Jaidiri-nadi: Elidari and Nadrasi, of the Guild."

Jaidiri was Tabini's chief of security: these two were the highest level currently in the field, very likely.

"Nadiin," Bren said with a courteous nod, "the house is honored."

"Nand' paidhi—" The one who spoke would be the senior of the elder set, and also the one Cenedi would have named first. Elidari: a man of about middle years, smallish as Taibeni tended to be, quick-eyed and all business. "The aiji sends two persons whose man'chi is in no doubt: Vejico and Lucasi, sister and brother, of the Guild. They will attach to the heir."

No ifs, ands, buts, or "if the dowager pleases." Damned sure the paidhi-aiji wasn't in a position to object, even if Algini should give him some sign in the negative.

The other pair, the younger set, bowed. They looked typical young Guild: athletic, slim, the both of them, bright-eyed, early twenties, Bren judged.

"The young gentleman is resting," Bren said, "but staff will direct you to his quarters, which he shares with two others. Be welcome to this house."

"Nandi." A third bow, in exact unison, somewhat disconcerting. And they picked up their luggage, each bringing two heavy bags.

"Ramaso," Bren said, indicating that the major domo should see to that matter, and that group moved off about their business.

"Nandi." A bow from the senior pair.

The Guild did not expect tea and ceremony. They did what they did and they departed. The door shut.

"This team is," Algini said, "good. One had no idea they had attached to a house."

Cenedi regarded him somberly. "Not Taibeni."

"From the mountains. Their training continued during the Troubles, under Ajien."

Clearly Cenedi knew the name, and was suitably impressed.

He thought of the various hand-picked tutors and several security arrangements that had gone over the horizon already.

It didn't mean the young gentleman would be grateful.

Or polite.

"Let us hope," Bren said, "things go smoothly."

"Let us hope," Cenedi said with a dour expression.

They *all* knew how that might go.

16

"Nandi," Jegari said, or Cajeiri thought he said, and pulled his head off the pillow to find out.

In fact it was Jegari, looking anxious. And Jegari would not waken him on a whim. It was still daylight out, though the room was dark, what staff called the storm shutters were still in place, only admitting slits of daylight. But he could see, all the same.

"We have *not* overslept," he said. He was sure of that. And then anxiety crowded after: "Mani is all right?"

"The dowager is asleep, one believes, nandi," Jegari said, "but your father the aiji has sent two guards to stay with us. One believes they have been assigned."

His *father* had sent guards.

He pulled himself up to a sitting position. "When are they coming?"

"They are *here*, nandi. Nand' Bren sent them in."

He could deal with Uncle Tatiseigi's men. He had been threatened with his Ajuri-clan grandfather's gift of guards, which mani had said were *far* too little skilled. He had mani's guards sometimes, Nawari and Casari and others, and they were all right: he greatly favored Nawari, who let him do things.

But somebody from his *father?*

He got up. "Assist, 'Gari-ji." He could call servants to help him muster a decent appearance, but all that would have to go past whoever was waiting out there, and would indicate that he had been found *without* a decent appearance. He helped Jegari find an unrumpled shirt, and he put that on, and his morning trousers were acceptable. He got into those, and put his boots on, while Jegari took out the rust-brown coat he had been wearing for breakfast, which he had not spilled anything on. It was good. He used that, and sat down and let Jegari braid his queue and tie on a fresh ribbon, the Ragi red and black.

The mirror showed him a fair figure of authority. He trusted in it and walked out to confront the latest offering from adults in charge of his life.

They were young. Not too much older than Jegari and Antaro, and one was a girl, kind of nice-looking in Guild black. But he didn't want appearances to get past his guard. They bowed. He bowed.

"Nandi," the girl said, "my name is Vejico. My brother is Lucasi. You are entitled to know: we are fifth-level Guild."

Impressive. He knew that much; and was not supposed to talk about it.

"Your father the aiji has sent us, expressing the hope that you may find our service acceptable."

No one had ever asked his opinion. That was a definite improvement.

And clearly now, in their silence, his opinion was called for. "Vejico and Lucasi, this is Jegari, and this is Antaro, out of Taiben."

Bows all around, Jegari's and Antaro's that degree deeper that acknowledged authority.

"You may know," Cajeiri said, in his father's tones, and his great-grandmother's, "this house is the house of Lord Bren, the paidhi-aiji, who is our closest associate; and we came under attack last night by Southerners who have taken over the neighboring estate, which belongs to Lord Geigi, who is Lord Bren's and my great-grandmother's close associate. Lord Geigi's nephew Baiji is at fault for his associations, and Lord Bren and my great-grandmother have him locked in the basement, and *we* are supposed to visit Najida village tonight to ask the Edi where the Edi are who used to serve Lord Geigi. Baiji—my great-grandmother says he is not to be given any title—says the Edi just went away, but Baiji has lied even to my great-grandmother, so he is not to be believed."

He left off there, not to be seen to run on with his sentences, which Great-grandmother said was a sign of poor self-control and afterthoughts. But it was a fair account. He thought he had given it well.

And he was gratified to see two deep and solemn bows.

"Nandi," the girl said, evidently the older of the pair, "we would be honored to provide security tonight, respecting the efforts of Jegari-nadi and Antaro-nadi."

Oh, that was nicely phrased, and polite to Jegari and Antaro, who did not have the credentials even to let them wear the Guild uniform.

"We shall see," he said. Ultimately, he knew he was going to have to have more than Jegari and Antaro. But *he* had planned to pick them, and *not* to have spies that would stop him from everything—especially very *good* spies.

"Your father says, nandi," Lucaso said with a little bow, "that a sense of humor is requisite for this post. And we are not to report small irregularities, only to be sure nothing is broken, no one is hurt, and that you are not locked in somebody's basement."

He stared at Lucaso in consternation, astonished that he had just heard anything so outrageous.

"Should you, for instance, nandi," Vejico said, "take out on such an adventure, we shall have to report you have left the capital, but we would stay with you. We will *not*, however, use Guild tactics, except defensively, in abetting your escape. Your father says you should rely on your own ingenuity and do nothing in excess of what you can do successfully on your own."

He became aware his mouth was open—and shut it. He had

suspected his father of many things, but a sense of humor was not one of them.

He supposed he blushed. And then he scowled—became aware he was scowling, and decided it was what mani would do, but then he recalled something else mani had told him: when someone surprises you, rethink what you know about that person until it is not a surprise.

Mani had said his father had been difficult.

"Well," he said as if he had always had it figured out, "one should not be surprised. We may get along. And that will make mani mad, and Great-uncle mad, and Grandfather. Everything I do makes somebody mad. So you should get used to it."

They looked a little surprised, themselves. Antaro and Jegari were standing over against the door and met his glance with a little handsign from Jegari. All right, that meant. *Jegari* was fine. Probably Antaro was.

So.

There had been no explosions from the young gentleman's quarters. The dowager was asleep, beneficially so, Bren hoped, and no one wished to disturb her.

The arrival was, however, worrisome—not least because he wanted the meeting tonight to go well, and wanted no cause of suspicion in the interference of Ragi-directed Guild inside Najida—never mind Banichi and Jago had come from Tabini's household: that was years past, and this was current, while Ragi Guild sat in what had been the key holding on the peninsula, namely Kajiminda. Double-crossed a dozen times in recent history, the Edi had been very specific in their invitations, were probably very upset at the fate of Lord Geigi's estate, and he wanted to calm that situation down, and get the Edi back, not drive them further away.

Banichi and Jago had slept through the mild commotion, or at least declined to stir forth, relying on Algini and Tano to keep him out of trouble. And when they did wake, in late afternoon, their only comment on the business of the two arrivals was, from Banichi, a "Good choice."

Well, he thought. That was encouraging. That there was still total silence from the young gentleman's premises—that was encouraging.

"One hesitates to observe," Tano said mildly, "that the young gentleman may now have Guild assistance in his mischief."

Bren looked his way. Algini remained fixed on his boards, taking some sort of note, and speaking to someone, and Tano did not elaborate. Banichi and Jago had opted for an off-schedule lunch, and had gone out to see to that. So he had no word from them, either. But he gathered that the two newcomers had a certain reputation, and Algini did not bestir himself to deny it, only to say that they were very good.

Interesting, Bren thought.

Word from the dock was, currently, that repairs had a bit to go. The *Brighter Days* might be fit for sea tomorrow, not tonight. They had her hauled over so they could come at an underwater patch, and that was still in progress—besides which the disorder that made inside the boat despite closed lockers and tight storage he could only imagine.

It also meant there was no safe quarters for Toby and Barb aboard the boat.

"Get Toby," he said, and it took a while, but Toby himself came on with:

"Hello, brother. What's up?"

"Nothing, I hope, but I understand you're boatless for the night and we're bedding people in the hallways up here. Can I ask you and Barb to bed aboard my boat for the night and report up to the house for breakfast in the morning?"

"Sounds like a good plan." Toby sounded cheerful: work on the boat did that for him. "If I get any phone calls, you'll tell me."

"Certainly I will. I imagine the kid's fine by now. They bounce, at that age. But I'll call you at whatever hour if there's any emergency."

"You take care up there tonight. You think there's any chance those guys are coming back for another try?"

"Never can tell. But we've gotten everything fixed that has to be and we're fine with that." He didn't mention to Toby about going down to the village. It was a phone, it wasn't that secure, and he didn't want to advertise his movements in any degree. "Things are settling. I just want to be sure you and Barb are comfortable."

"Couldn't be better. We're all over glue and paint. Happy as we can be."

He grinned. "Great. Come up for a sendoff tomorrow, all right?"

"Deal," Toby said, and signed off.

On any other day, he'd figure he'd had a day at that point, and take to his study—which was occupied at the moment—and sip tea and do his correspondence.

On this particular day he hadn't even started his day's work, which entailed kitting up in something suitable and—

"Are we taking the truck to the village, Tano-ji?"

"The bus is beyond repair, nandi."

"One would prefer a healthful walk," he said with a sigh, "but probably the truck is the better idea."

"We shall insist on it," Tano said.

He was quite sure they would. And considering the dowager's state of exhaustion—it was an even better idea.

"Get some rest yourselves," he said. "All of you. I shall take Koharu and Supani and figure out my wardrobe for the evening—we shall have supper as we can, and then we shall be needing the truck, Tano-ji. I leave it to you."

"It will be there," Tano said, not objecting to his leaving in search of Koharu and Supani—no, Tano went *with* him to the hall, and, once he had passed orders for the pair he wanted, to his suite. Tano stood by, pleasant and affable, while he and his dressers took account of the wardrobe; and while those two consulted with Ramaso, and Ramaso himself came to fuss over the problem.

Simple beige coat, little lace, but enough to be respectful: a country gentleman, with the paidhi-aiji's white ribbon for his queue, not the grandiose black with stars.

And when he turned out for dinner, to meet Ilisidi and the young gentleman and his enlarged company, the dowager had chosen simple black with a great deal of lace; and the young gentleman was nicely turned out in a brown coat with his hair done up with a smallish black-and-red ribbon, the colors of his father's house, but not extravagantly displayed. Ramaso had been behind that, he would almost bet. The dowager had her own sense of proprieties.

And she was, Bren was glad to see, energetic and bright-eyed, perfectly herself, plying her cane as she entered the dining room with Cenedi, taking her place at one end of the table, while Bren with Tano and Algini in attendance—Banichi and Jago were taking their ease at the console in quarters, and doubtless doing a little touchup on the evening's arrangements—took the other end of the table, and settled with minimal flourish and fuss.

A small dinner, he had ordered, and a single glass of wine, followed by water. Mental acuity would be a very good idea this evening.

The young gentleman settled in, with his entourage attending, the two newcomers quite stiff and proper.

And: "The paidhi may have noticed the addition to my great-grandson's company," the dowager said. "Do you approve, paidhi-aiji?"

"My approval is neither here nor there, aiji-ma."

"Ha!" Ilisidi said, and picked up her water glass. "My interfering grandson."

"He has, however, assured that your staff will be protecting *you*, aiji-ma, which pleases all of us who—"

"Shameless," the dowager said. "We shall watch this carefully," she added with a sharp look toward the nearer of the pair in question, who affected not to have heard a thing. "And we starve ourselves this evening, one trusts, with the promise of a small offering before we retire."

"If the dowager is in appetite for a sweet and a cup of tea when we return, one is very certain the kitchen will be delighted."

"Oh, give us an argument, nand' paidhi. Everyone is agreeing and dodging. Probably these two are a politic choice and we shall have some of those cream pastries, shall we?"

"Granted a felicitous outcome tonight, aiji-ma, one will be extremely delighted to argue with you over pastries."

Dinner consisted of a good chowder and whole grain crackers, a small glass of wine, and a fruit compote . . . by no means up to the dowager's usual standard, except she had a second bowl of chowder.

And by then it was toward dark, and they had only time to gather up essentials and to go out to the portico, where the village truck had pulled up to take them down to the village.

But not just the village truck. Someone had wired substantial iron sheets to the wooden sides. It was the cab that was the more exposed to fire; and consequently their security proposed to put their principals on a small bench roped in place within the truck bed, and to have Nawari drive, with Cenedi and Banichi up front, and the rest all behind, under cover.

"This is ridiculous!" was the dowager's protest. "We shall be bruised from head to foot."

"We shall sit by you, mani," Cajeiri said. "We shall not let you fall."

"Impudent youngster! We do not fall off a mecheita going cross-country. We hardly plan to fall off a bench on a graded road!"

Cenedi had climbed aboard, and, standing over the small iron ladder that was welded to the back bumper, offered his hands. Ilisidi climbed gamely up, pulled aboard, and, cane in hand, stalked over to take her seat on the wooden bench, while Cajeiri scrambled up, with a shove from Jegari from below.

"Just wait until your bones carry a certain number of years, great-grandson! You will appreciate the discomfort of a bare bench and truck springs!"

"One is certain, mani. But one is certain Nawari will be careful."

Bren climbed up, just behind Jago, who reached down to haul him aboard. He took the end of the bench, where, indeed, he could assist the dowager if they did hit a pothole.

Cenedi climbed back down, and the rest of the dowager's men and Cajeiri's young contingent climbed up. They settled in, most of the company sitting on the truck bed, the engine started up, and they moved fairly sedately around the arc of the cobbled drive and onto the unpaved country road.

It didn't stay a sedate pace. Security concerns, Bren was certain, had them picking up speed. But the road, though winding a bit downhill and alongside a small and ominous woods, was well-maintained, and lacking potholes . . . that, or Nawari was to credit for missing them.

It was with a sigh of relief that they entered the central (and only major) street of Najida village. Twilight showed very few lights at all, the habit of mainland country folk: nobody burned lights to keep away crime, since there was none to speak of . . . just the occasional rowdy youngster. There were no police, just the local constable, who was in charge of talking people out of quarrels, and officiating at the occasional marriage, supervising the village clerk, and the village—Mosphei' had no exact word for it except commissioner, but there was no commission, just a woman and three aides who scheduled the bus and the truck, and oversaw the procurement of some supplies held in common, such as the village nurse's needs, the grading equipment, the school, and public sewers and sanitation.

And all such persons had their offices in the village hall, along with the unelected but empowered council of elders, the heads of families, who met when they decided to meet, and once a month met to review the doings of the regular officials.

. . . or in this case, to receive the Lord of Najida and his guests the aiji-dowager and the heir of the aishidi'tat, to which they belonged mostly in name. The doings of the aishidi'tat rarely touched the doings of the village, or rarely did so in any official way; and no member of the aiji's household, including the paidhi-aiji, had ever darkened the door of the village hall, not in all the time it had stood.

They were here to change that.

People of the village—mostly women, young folk and children—were standing about the entry, and came to watch as they disembarked, an immediate flood of Guild in black leather uniforms, and then, with great solicitude, the dowager, who did not take kindly to being lifted down from the truck bed in the arms of her young men, and wanted to climb down, but that itself was an undignified process, and a very chancy little thin-runged ladder, so down she came, and set her feet on the ground immediately with a solid whack of her cane.

Cajeiri scrambled down on his own, steadied at the last by Jegari and Antaro, his new guards standing by in commendable deference.

And Bren climbed down and met up with Jago at the bottom, Banichi appearing almost immediately and making shift to get them all inside and under at least the cover of a roof.

So in they came, in a surrounding flood of black uniforms and with a distressing lot of firepower, but there was reason for it, and he by no means protested Guild precautions. They walked down a broad hallway, wooden-floored, and into open double doors at the end, where the village dignitaries waited somewhat informally, standing among their orderly tables.

There were bows, not as deep as country folk might ordinarily make in meeting the aiji-dowager or even the paidhi-aiji, but it was not a discourtesy, rather the situation, that they were in the place of their own authority.

"Nand' dowager." The speaker was an old woman, a seam-faced and weathered woman wearing her go-to-meeting best, a black shawl with years of service, but it was an excellent garment, no matter the era, beautifully embroidered with vines. A deep bow, then. "Nand' paidhi. I am Aieso, eldest of Najida village."

"We have come to listen, Aieso-daja. In all courtesy, I shall speak briefly. But in the main, considering the situation, we believe we should be advised before giving advice. We have come to ask."

The old woman nodded, bowed again, all around, including to Cajeiri, then walked to the head table and rapped on the wood with her gnarled knuckles.

A silence gradually fell. People sought chairs, and two young men came offering chairs at the head table to the dowager, Cajeiri, and him.

They took those places. It was no polished historic conference table, but it had its own history, evident in the scratches and digs and occasional wounds in the rough-finished surface. The chairs likewise were age-smoothed, neither stained nor polished.

"Nand' Bren says he and the dowager and the young gentleman have come to listen tonight," Aieso said. "But he has a few words of his own, nadiin. Listen to him."

A little final settling, a last couple of people in place. Guild stood about the walls, bristling with weapons. But the assembly they watched were all old men and women, the business owners and tradesmen of the town, people of local substance and excellent reputation—well, as much as went with long politics in a village.

Bren rose in place and looked over the assembly—no brilliant electrics here, just oil lamps that gave a gentle glow to the place, and not that electricity was not available in the village. It just was not here, in this place of local tradition.

"Esteemed neighbors," he said, with a little bow, "what I have to say is brief, counting that I know less than I should. First, thank you, and the dowager and the young gentleman thank you most earnestly, for the efforts of our neighbors in rescuing the young gentleman from the coast. Had you not helped us, we might have been far slower to take the search out to sea, and the event might have had a very bad outcome. Please make known any damages incurred during the search, and I will gladly bear any expense for repairs. Thank you, personally, for your hospitality toward my brother's lady, and most of all for your understanding. Thank you for your support during the difficulties at Lord Geigi's estate, and the attack on my house. The aiji-dowager has spoken to Lord Geigi directly, advising him of the situation, and Lord Geigi has agreed to return very shortly and take possession of his nephew and of the estate, to attempt to set matters right."

That created a little buzz in the room, words exchanged sotto voce and behind hands, but it seemed to be welcome news.

"Among matters of utmost concern in my own mind," Bren said, "is the fact that when the young gentleman and I visited that house, we saw no familiar faces, none of the people we would have expected to be there. We are greatly concerned for the welfare of that staff."

A sudden thump of Ilisidi's cane. "The nephew neglected business in Shejidan. Evidently he had a situation he wished not to report, and the aishidi'tat has been remiss not to inquire more closely regarding this sudden change in attitude and relations. The aishidi'tat took for granted the favorable association which has long existed in this region and took an attitude of patience with this young nephew. This was a mistake. We hope it has not cost lives, nor will cost them, but we fear to the contrary. The aishidi'tat has no wish for a continuing Guild presence in this region, and forces will withdraw as soon as we are sure Southern influence does not threaten the peace of this district."

With which, and a second thump of the cane, Ilisidi fell back into silence, leaving a ripple of whispering and disturbance in her wake . . . again, not hostility, but hard to read what precisely it was—except honest fishermen and craftsmen trying to read all the way to the bottom of a remark by a master of Shejidan politics. Aieso, her gnarled hands laced before her lips, sat in silence, her eyes, gold dark nearly to bronze, taking in every movement.

"Neighbors," Bren said, with a nod to that lady, "people who have a birthright on this coast should be reassured. The Southern influence which moved into Kajiminda has been dislodged, permanently, and there will be no threat to the region from that quarter. One wishes one could claim that one's own cleverness detected this intrusion and laid all this plan to deal with it, but, baji-naji, there has been more chance on our side and more plan on the Southern side. They thought they had caught me without allies. They were mistaken. I thank the dowager, I thank the aiji, and the brave folk of Najida that we have overturned that scheme . . ." That drew pleased looks. "But we remain concerned for the fate of people harmed by these goings-on. If there is any help the estate can give, we would be very glad to provide it."

A single young man stood up, a thin, shabby-looking young man in the far corner of the room; and every Guildsman around the periphery went on alert. "Nand' paidhi."

"Nadi?"

A bow. "My name is Teigi. I came here as the son of Paigi. This was a lie. I am Edi, from Kajiminda—a youngest, and expendable."

His security would not be happy with this deception. But none of them were surprised by it. He simply bowed in acknowledgement.

"One rejoices to hear from Kajiminda, Teigi-nadi. Say on."

"This is what the Edi say. Throw the Southerners out or let us do it. Let us have our lordships and our law and our land back. I am the youngest. If you arrest me, you have no one."

"There is no question of arresting the spokesman for the Edi," Bren said, and in the tail of his eye, saw the dowager rising to her feet, when she was, being who she was, perfectly entitled to sit to address anyone in the aishidi'tat. It was a courtesy, and it was hard for her.

She stood upright, however, and planted the cane firmly.

"We are an Easterner," she said in that incisive, absolute voice, "and we comprehend the position of the Edi people. *We* of the East have Malguri and those in its man'chi. Where is the house of the Edi lord? There *should* be a house of the Edi, and one of the Gan." Those were the other aboriginal people, the latter, like the Edi, dispossessed from Mospheira. "We think so. We have not expressed this thought to our grandson. But it is our opinion."

My God, Bren thought. She was proposing two new provinces.

The young man stood there, just stood for a moment.

"We would not expect," Ilisidi said, "that representatives of the Edi and of the Gan would bring such proposals to the aiji in Shejidan."

The proposal of an Edi and a Gan estate had thorns all over it. The Edi and the Gan had *never* officially joined the aishidi'tat, because the Edi and the Gan were both inside other provinces.

"You have suffered," Ilisidi said, "as have other peoples of this coast, from the chaff of the quarrel between the South and the Ragi of the central districts. This is a case that should be made. The aishidi'tat is not weaker because it contains the intact East. The aishidi'tat would be stronger if it contained an intact West. Right now you are the majority on this coast. And you have no lordship. Take my encouragement to pursue it, and set up your own defenses."

The young man still stood. The dowager sat down again, and Bren drew a breath, finding the silence beginning to fray into a mutter.

"The dowager's opinion," he said, "will carry weight. You have a potential ally."

The young man finally came alive to give a sketchy bow.

"One is by no means instructed on a reply, nandiin. One will carry the message."

Cajeiri stood up. Bren took in a breath, starting to signal the boy to the contrary, but Cajeiri was unstoppable in the best of circumstances.

"Listen to my great-grandmother, nadi," Cajeiri's young voice rang out. And, God, he could not have done better, with the matrilineal Edi, if he had targeted it. "My father does."

There was a stir in the room. Everybody reacted.

And Cajeiri promptly sat down, leaving Bren alone to deal with the assembly.

"The young gentleman has many virtues," Bren said, "including forthrightness. He says what he thinks, and what he thinks will one day be the policy of the aishidi'tat."

There was a pause, a murmur, and then the stamp of a foot. Which became many feet, until the room thundered.

Bren bowed, and sat down, as the young Edi sat down, and all around the room security stood just a little easier.

It wasn't going to be the safe direction. It was going to kick up one hell of a storm in Shejidan. But the coast had the backing of the East, and it was a natural ally against the South, a back and forth piratical war that had gone on for centuries.

Policy had just shifted. The thing once named had the power to exist, and once it existed, it would change the aishidi'tat.

Policy had just shifted and the wind had begun to blow, a sea wind, into the heart of the continent. The dowager, who had once bid to become aiji herself, had just tilted policy and directed the future course of politics.

And the paidhi hadn't the least clue how he was going to explain it to Tabini.

An Excerpt from
Bren Cameron's notes.

The House of the Maschi

The Maschi clan has declined over centuries to a handful of the name, resident within the Sulesi clan, the inland limit of Sarini Province.

Within the Maschi clan:

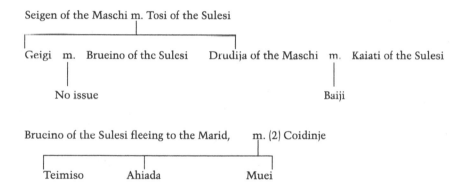

Seigen of the Maschi m. Tosi of the Sulesi

Geigi m. Brueino of the Sulesi   Drudija of the Maschi m. Kaiati of the Sulesi

        No issue   Baiji

Brueino of the Sulesi fleeing to the Marid,   m. (2) Coidinje

Teimiso   Ahiada   Muei

The Marid, subdivided into the Tasaigin Marid, the Senji Marid, and the Dojisigi and Dausigi Marid—the four major districts that, with their clans and septs, rule the South. There are also the Sungeni, the local islands, ruled by the Tasaigi.

The Tasaigin Marid has been the most persistent problem to Tabini, but the other three districts, jealous of the power of the Tasaigi, have been laying their own plots.

One of the first indicators of trouble to come was the stir the Marid tried to make over the space program. They attempted to ruin Lord Geigi, who was a major supporter, and who had an aerospace plant in his district. They had subverted his Samiusi clan wife—who then fled to the Marid, married again, and had three children with Coidinje of the Tasaigi.

Badissuni was a previous problem to Tabini-aiji . . . he appeared in the early accounts of Marid troubles: he was very much against the space program, mostly because it gave him an issue to use against Tabini. He came to consult with Tabini after the assassination of Lord Sagaimi of the Tasaigi, on a notable occasion of a visit from Lord Tatiseigi to the Bujavid, and that didn't go well.

Here's how the Sagaimi of the Tasaigin Marid's descent runs:

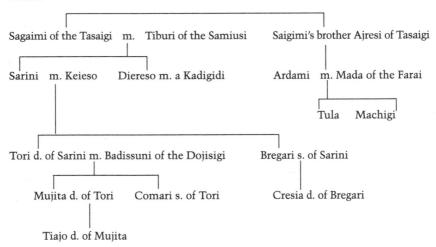

Sagaimi of the Tasaigi m. Tiburi of the Samiusi   Saigimi's brother Ajresi of Tasaigi

Sarini m. Keieso   Diereso m. a Kadigidi   Ardami m. Mada of the Farai

Tula   Machigi

Tori d. of Sarini m. Badissuni of the Dojisigi   Bregari s. of Sarini

Mujita d. of Tori   Comari s. of Tori   Cresia d. of Bregari

Tiajo d. of Mujita

Ardami ruled the Tasaigi after the death of Sagaimi, Sarini, and then Cosadi. His marriage to Mada of the Farai has produced a union between the Senji Marid and the Tasaigin Marid, and he has produced Tula, a daughter, and Machigi. Ardami was assassinated, and Machigi is now aiji of the Tasaigin Marid.

This Machigi, a son, is trouble . . . first as a threat to the independence of the Senjin Marid.

The Senjin Marid is the one that has been courting Baiji . . . through Baiji's ex-aunt, and his cousins, because they have old relations with the Samiusi, part of Sarini province, which is *not* part of the Marid, but part of Geigi's association. They have been helped in this by Badissuni's clan, the Dojisigi.

If the Senjin Marid, through marriage and assassination, could get control of the west coast, Najida and Kajiminda, they would challenge the powerful Machigi of the Tasaigin Marid for control of southern politics. But they are very likely being egged on and encouraged by Machigi himself, who sees advantage in their actions. Machigi is very likely to double-cross them the moment they gain any territory.

And meanwhile the Dojisigin Marid, home of the daughter being offered by the Senjin, is looking for any advantage and feeling itself threatened by the rise of this powerful Tasaigin aiji.

There are two other Marid districts of much less power: the Sungeni Marid (the islands) and the Dausigin Marid, the lower east side of the Marid, which has never been strong enough to contend with the others.

Within the Tasaigin Marid, there is one powerful district: Sarini's district of Tanji.

Within the Dojisigin Marid, there is Badissuni's Amarja.

Within the Senjin Marid, there is Morigi-dar, stronghold of the Farai.

The Dojisigin Marid is sparsely populated, and usually bows to the Dojisigi or the Tasaigi, whichever they fear most at the time.

The Marid as a whole was all once a separate nation from the aishidi'tat, but a succession of skirmishes and assassinations brought it into the fold in Valasi-aiji's time. Tabini has inherited the situation, and has had several times to bring the Marid back into line. But it remains a district in constant turmoil.

History of the Marid

The Marid used to claim the whole west coast of the continent, from the peninsula of Dalaigi down to their modern territory in the central South.

But after the War of the Landing, the north coast territory was given to the displaced Gan, the southwestern coast to the Edi, and the Samiusi and Maschi clans were set in authority over the district, definitively freed of the domination of the Marid.

The Edi, seafarers and fishermen, took up their occupation out of the several bays of the continental west and began to shove the Marid ships out of their area—piracy was what the Marid called it. Certain districts, notably Najida, profited by luring passing Marid ships onto the rocks and looting them.

The Gan, northerly, were more strictly fisherfolk, and mostly peaceful.

The Edi, consisting of several subgroups, mostly fought among themselves, when they were not fighting the Marid, until they agreed to accept a Maschi lord, the father of Lord Geigi of the Maschi, seated at Kajiminda.

Among the clans of the Marid, the loss of the west coast in the Resettlement after the War of the Landing was a serious blow. The Marid still has exclusive rights in the whole southern fishing grounds, but it regards the loss of the west coast, though they had few settlements there, as an ongoing wound to their pride . . . and Edi raids on their shipping and commerce as a grievous wrong.

Affiliations of critical groups

Major Clans that are Ragi or affiliated with the Ragi

Taiben (Tabini's clan: Padi Valley district: historic enemies of the Atageini)

Atageini (Tatiseigi's clan: Padi Valley district: lady Damiri's maternal clan)

Malguri (Ilisidi's clan: Eastern, far side of the continent)

Dur (the north coast Islands)

Ajuri (lady Damiri's paternal clan, northern)

Samiusi/Maschi (Geigi's clan, west coast)

The Edi clans (loosely bound to the Maschi, therefore to Tabini: an aboriginal coastal people akin to the Gan. Both Edi and Gan are matrilineal.)

The Gan clans (loosely bound to Dur, therefore to Tabini: an aboriginal Mospheiran people; matrilineal.)

The various mountain clans

The various northern clans

Clans that are not firmly Tabini's

Kadagidi (Murini's clan, Padi Valley district: historic allies of the Atageini: they have relatives among the Atageini and the Tasaigi)

The clans of the Marid: the Farai sept of Morigi clan; the Tasaigi; the Dojisigi; etc.

Some clans of the East (bound to Tabini through Ilisidi of Malguri clan, who is their aiji)

A Brief history of the Marid Rebellions

Saigimi and his Samiusi-clan wife, produced Sarimi, who produced Cosadi, who launched many attacks on the north, in attempts to unseat the aiji in Shejidan, the aiji of the whole aishidi'tat—currently Tabini. The whole Marid belongs to the aishidi'tat by treaty, but would like to run the association.

When Saigimi was assassinated, Badissuni of the Amarja District of the Tasaigin Marid went to Tabini hoping to gain favor and a foothold and an apartment in the Bujavid. He died, but had previously married and produced two offspring with Tori, Cosadi's sister: a son, Mujito and a daughter, Comari. Mujito's young daughter Tiajo is the one offered in marriage within this account . . . in, just to confuse matters, a scheme led by the Senjin Marid, who have the useful tie to the Maschi (Lord Geigi's house). They are aided by the Dojisigi Marid, where Mujito's former wife is aiji . . . who have the available daughter, Tiajo (who is half Tasaigi)—and they are egged on in this venture by the Tasaigin Marid, where Mujito's blood relative, Machigi, is now aiji, and seeking power on a scale with what Sarimi once had.

This is a situation to watch.

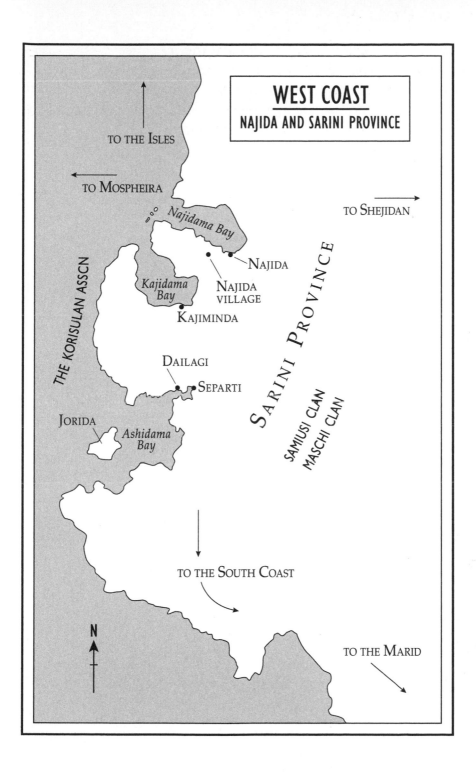

WEST COAST
NAJIDA AND SARINI PROVINCE

TO THE ISLES

TO MOSPHEIRA

TO SHEJIDAN

Najidama Bay

NAJIDA

Kajidama Bay

NAJIDA VILLAGE

KAJIMINDA

THE KORISULAN ASSCN

DAILAGI

SEPARTI

S ARINI P ROVINCE

SAMIUSI CLAN

MASCHI CLAN

JORIDA

Ashidama Bay

TO THE SOUTH COAST

N

TO THE MARID

SOUTH COAST
THE MARID

HOMA
(CARATHO CLAN)

SENJI

MORIGI-DAR
(FARAI CLAN)

DOJISIGI

AMARIA (BADISSUNI)

TAISIGI

TANAJA

TANJI
DISTRICT

SUNGENI ISLES

MORDANI

DAUSIGI

HAPRINJO
(LUSI CLAN)

N

7/14 (15)   10/11 (12) 8/11
2/19 (17) 3/18